Dead Line

Also by Brian McGrory
The Nominee
The Incumbent

Dead Line

A Novel

BRIAN McGRORY

ATRIA BOOKS

NEW YORK LONDON TORONTO SYDNEY

ATRIA BOOKS

1230 Avenue of the Americas
New York, NY 10020

ISBN: 0-7434-6366-8

First Atria Books hardcover edition January 2004

10 9 8 7 6 5 4 3 2 1

ATRIA BOOKS is a trademark of Simon & Schuster, Inc.

Manufactured in the United States of America

For information regarding special discounts for bulk purchases,
please contact Simon & Schuster Special Sales at 1-800-456-6798
or business@simonandschuster.com.

To Carole and to Colleen, for being there, always.

Dead Line

Prologue

Life shouldn't be this complicated. That's what Hilary Kane was thinking as she took another sip of overpriced red wine at the bar at Jur-Ne, a pretentiously slick lounge in the newer Ritz-Carlton Hotel in downtown Boston. Well, she was thinking of that and exactly what had made it so complicated.

On either side of her, two coworkers, Amanda and Erica, prattled on about the energy and emotions that go into raising only mildly maladjusted kids. Men in suits coming from their jobs with mutual fund companies and white-shoe law firms jostled past for much-needed drinks. The too-cool bartenders were taking their time serving $13 Dirty Martinis.

None of it had the slightest effect on Hilary, who continued to sip her wine at a rapid clip and stare out the movie screen–size windows at the fading light of the city streetscape.

She had become a bad cliché, she told herself, queuing up the scene yet again in the videocam of her mind. She had been in Phoenix the week before on a rare business trip, a legal conference that her boss had sent her to. She had called her fiancé, Chuck, at 11:00 P.M., Boston time, eight o'clock her time, to wish him good night. She had said she'd see him when she arrived home the next evening, Saturday, his birthday. They'd have a nice dinner

1

at a restaurant where she had already made a reservation. She didn't tell him that she planned a morning surprise.

And that's what she did. A few hours after her call, she climbed aboard the redeye flight from Sky Harbor International to Logan Airport. She took a cab to their Beacon Hill apartment. As she walked into the building foyer with her luggage in her hand, she had this vision that she'd find him standing before the bathroom mirror, shaving, the stereo playing Clapton or maybe B. B. King. She could picture the wide grin that would break out across his handsome face, the deep, familiar hug, the I-missed-yous and the happy birthdays as the two tumbled into their king-size bed.

She put the key into the hole and turned the lock. She nudged the door open with her shoulder. She walked into a silent apartment, and immediately, she knew something was wrong.

The first thing she smelled was Chinese food, and she looked over to her left at her loft-style apartment and saw open containers sitting on the coffee table next to a pair of used plates and two empty wineglasses. When she moved closer, she saw one of the glasses was smeared with lipstick. One of Chuck's shirts was tossed haphazardly on the floor.

She looked slowly to her right, toward the rear of the apartment, her open bedroom area, her stomach churning so hard she thought she might throw up. She had known him a year and a half. When they first met, he was a high-flying software entrepreneur, about to sell his company to one of the giants for an obscene amount of cash. He was magnetic and charismatic and justifiably confident. It took him about an hour to have her completely charmed.

Then the sale fell through. His company washed out in the receding high-tech tide. He went from expectations of a hundred million dollars to barely having bus fare, so he moved out of his penthouse apartment and came to live with her.

He'd get up every morning, read the papers from front to back, then sit at her computer in the bay window and plot out the next big thing. She went off to her sometimes grinding job as a government lawyer. It wasn't great, but it was a life. They were due to be married in six more months.

As she walked toward the back of the apartment, she heard her cat, Hercules, crying for help. Someone, she saw to her disgust, had shut him inside his tiny airline carrier. She looked at the rumpled bed, at the shoes—men's and women's—that were tossed haphazardly around it, at the clothing that littered the hardwood floor.

Then she focused on the closed bathroom door and listened for a moment to the pale sound of cascading water that came from within. She moved toward it, slowly, quietly, steadily, as if she were sleepwalking. She allowed her hand to rest for a moment on the brass knob. Then she pushed the door open, not forcefully, but decisively.

Instantly, she was met by humidity, the sound of the streaming water, the smell of lathered soap. She stood in the doorway staring through the floor-to-ceiling door of the glass-paneled steam-shower at her boyfriend having sex with a woman she had never previously seen, the shower jets pelting against their hair, the big droplets of water streaming down their respective bodies.

She stood watching them for an awkward, agonizing moment, as if they were an exhibit at a zoo, not out of any curiosity, but because neither of them had noticed her enter the room. Finally, she picked up a tube of toothpaste from the vanity and fired it at the shower door. Chuck whirled around and, in a voice muffled by the glass and water, called out, "Honey, no!"

She heard the woman ask, "Is that her?" At least that's what she thought she heard. Chuck turned off the water. He flung open the door and grabbed two towels that were hanging on a nearby hook. He handed one to the blonde woman, who began unapologetically drying herself off as if she didn't have a worry in the world.

"We need to talk, Hil," Chuck kept saying as he tamped his body dry.

Standing in the doorway, she thought for a moment about retrieving the Big Bertha driver—his birthday gift—hidden in her closet and bashing in both of their skulls.

Instead, she looked at the floor and said, "Get out. Both of you." What else, she wondered to herself, could you say?

She watched the blonde wrap the towel around her body and step out of the shower. Chuck stood there in the middle of the bathroom giving Hilary a pleading stare. Hilary walked back into the apartment and toward the front, setting herself down on a stool at the breakfast bar in her kitchen. A few minutes later, the woman walked wordlessly out of the apartment, Chuck about two minutes behind her. Hilary dissolved into tears and fury, and hadn't seen him since.

"Over at the Whitney School, they make the parents take a psychological test. If your kid gets in, it's $18,000 for kindergarten. That's when they should give you the damned test, to figure out if you're crazy for paying it!"

That was Erica, the coworker, a chinless, thirty-something woman in a Talbots' suit who was racing uncontrollably toward an early middle age.

Amanda, who seemed to sport not only her chin, but Erica's as well, said, "Well, Hilary will live all this soon enough." She looked at their younger, far more attractive coworker and asked, "What is it, six months until the big day?"

The big day, Hilary thought to herself. Right. The big day was last week, the day that changed her life, the day that would forever leave her jaded.

But to them, she nodded halfheartedly and said, "Yeah, six months." She hadn't told anyone yet of her relationship's horrific demise.

As Amanda launched into another question, the young bartender in black delivered Hilary another glass of wine. At that moment, a familiar man in a dark blue suit approached the three women, and Amanda and Erica greeted him as if they were in junior high, the former even shrieking his title—"Mayor!"—as she placed both hands on his wrist. Hilary, no great fan of the mayor's, turned toward the bar and rolled her eyes. This was not shaping up to be the escapist cocktail hour she had hoped it would be.

At that point, the night became a case study of one thing turning into another. Specifically, two glasses of wine turned into six, Amanda and Erica eventually, reluctantly, turned and headed for the door. Mayor Daniel Harkins turned from a loathsome egomaniac into an emotional crutch, and still later, a potential conquest, someone who could make a tattered psyche feel whole again, even if only for a moment.

All of which explains how Hilary Kane and the mayor ended up at his apartment on the twenty-eighth floor of the Ritz-Carlton at 2:00 A.M., drunkenly and awkwardly pulling off each other's clothes. She wanted to be desired, to be able to look in the mirror the next morning and know that this man absolutely had to have her.

After fifteen minutes of remarkably mediocre, alcohol-inhibited sex, Harkins placed a meaty forearm across his eyes and began to snore. Hilary climbed out of his bed, slowly and delicately, not out of any sense of courtesy, but for fear that if she woke him up, she'd have to spend another minute in his conscious presence. She pulled on her clothes—far quicker, she thought to herself, than the slutty blonde the week before.

She tiptoed outside his bedroom with her shoes in her hand, then sat on a high-back leather chair at a desk in his living room and looked at the blinking light on his computer. On the walls all around her were pictures of the mayor with various governors, senators, presidents, movie stars, and heads of state. She felt cheap in a way that she had never felt before: pathetic, insecure, and needy. She thought for a moment about quickly logging on to her email account to check one more time if Chuck had sent her a note of apology and explanation. She thought better of it, slipped her clogs on, and swiveled away from the desk.

But in a moment of weakness, standing before the desk, she flicked the computer mouse with her hand and the monitor came alive with light. Rather than a desktop, she was staring at a Word document, a file called Toby. She began scanning, and her hand instinctively rose to her mouth in fascination. She scrolled down, gripped by its contents, listening intently for any sounds from the bedroom. As she reached the second of what looked to be several pages, she struck the Print button.

The printer emitted the labored sounds of warming up, then began slowly churning out pages. As it did, Hilary clicked the Window field, saw another file called TOBY 2, and clicked on it. A new document, loaded with facts and names, filled the screen. She hit Print again.

She began collecting pages from the printer, when it suddenly froze up. A box appeared on the computer screen telling her she was out of paper. She looked in the printer basket and estimated she was about one page shy. A sound came from the bedroom, Danny the dolt rising to his drunken feet. She rolled the papers up in her hand, clicked on "OK" on the "Out of paper" box, and made for the door. The lights on the printer continued to blink a warning.

She pulled the door slowly shut behind her and bolted down the long hallway. What she needed was a taxicab. What she wanted was a shower. What she didn't know was that the beginning of the end was upon her.

Chapter One

The moment, or rather, the episode, might be the ultimate proof of that old sports axiom that only fools try to predict the future in that little jewel box of a ballyard called Fenway Park. The fool in this case: Me. I was sitting in a field box, third row behind the visitors' dugout, great seats courtesy of my editor, Peter Martin. Well, okay, it wasn't actually Martin's courtesy as much as my bribery that got me the seats. I offered him dinner at any restaurant in town for the company tickets, and Martin, having absolutely no appreciation for the consequences of this great athletic event, grabbed the bait. I've always believed it's food, not love, that conquers all.

So it's one of those crystal clear late September nights when Boston seems to be the absolute epicenter of the entire world. Suntans have faded. People have stormed back into town refreshed from a summer spent in Vermont, or Maine, or on Cape Cod. The city is filled with men in dark suits and red ties handing fistfuls of cash to young valets in front of swank restaurants with front doors lit by gas torches. Half the women on Newbury Street look like they just came from a Cosmo photo shoot. I swear, you could strike a match off their calves, if they let you, though they probably wouldn't, not, at least, until making more formal acquaintance.

Ahem, anyway. The leaves were just showing their first hint of color. The air had a slight nip to it, and the breeze a bit of an edge—enough of one, as a matter of fact, to take Nomar Garciaparra's lead-off line drive in the bottom of the eighth inning and turn it from a sure-thing home run to a sliding double that bounced hard off the left field wall, the famed Green Monster.

So Nomar's on second. The Sox are playing the Yankees. Need I say more? Well, yes, I do. They trail the Yankees 3–1 in the game, and they lag two games behind them in the East Division of the American League, with only a handful of games left in the season. To say this was an important game is like saying Jack Flynn only covers major stories. You don't need to; we're all too sophisticated for it; it's just one of those things in life that's automatically known among those accustomed to being in the know, and even those who aren't.

With Nomar taking a short lead, Manny Ramirez, batting cleanup, draws a walk, putting men on first and second, nobody out, David Ortiz coming to the plate.

Here's where the prediction stuff comes in. I turned to Elizabeth, my girlfriend, the brilliant, gorgeous one on my left with the pouty lips and the legs so achingly long it actually hurts her to fold herself into these seats, and I said, "My bet is, he bunts." I mean, of course he's going to bunt. Not only do you put both men in scoring position, but you take out the prospect of a late-inning, rally-dousing double play.

Elizabeth doesn't say anything, not because she doesn't have thoughts on this exact issue. I'm sure she did. But she's not there. I vaguely remember her telling me something about the women's room and heading out to look for a couple of those delightful Cool Dogs with the warm chocolate topping.

Instead, I'm looking at a short, middle-aged guy with stubby legs in loose-fitting jeans and a bored expression on his ruddy face. He looks like he took a wrong turn at the $2 window over at Suffolk Downs. I mean, he's the only guy within 200 miles of Fenway Park who's bored on this night.

"That seat's taken," I tell him.

He doesn't reply. Out of the corner of my eye, I see Rivera wind up and deliver. I turn back to the game, watch Ortiz lower his bat like he's going to bunt—I knew it—and the ball zip past him and into the catcher's mitt. Strike one.

"I said, that seat's taken."

Still, no answer. He's just kind of looking at me out of these deadened eyes, not even paying attention to the most pivotal game of the season, but hardly paying attention to me, either. Again, Rivera winds up, but this time Ortiz swings away—what the hell's he doing?—and misses. Strike two.

I watch Ortiz in disbelief. I look at the third base coach to see if maybe a signal was crossed or missed. Then I remember the clown beside me.

"Sir—" I begin. I hear the crack of a bat. Two men in the seats in front of me scream in unison. The entire crowd rises to its collective feet. The ball, a simple gleam of white, soars high into the air on its path toward nirvana, which in this case, is the right field bullpen. It's going, it's going, it's, it's—well, out of reach of the right fielder, bounding off the wall, squirting wildly around the turf. The damned wind knocked it down again.

Garciaparra scores from second. Ramirez comes chugging into third like he's running from a burning building with twenty-five pounds of firefighting equipment draped across his back. Ortiz stops on second: 3–2, nobody out, two men in scoring position.

I'm thinking that Elizabeth's going to be furious she missed all this. Then that thought is replaced by my abiding hope that she found the Cool Dogs. And finally it occurs to me that I've sat with her for three hours, seven-and-a-half innings, and the Sox scored a single run, and on a throwing error at that. This mute's been sitting next to me for five minutes and we're about to blow the game open. Now I don't want to sound superstitious or anything like that, but just to make sure he was in no unnecessary rush to leave, I turned to him and said, "Jesus Christ, pal, what a game, huh?"

He still didn't reply. The entire stadium is up on its feet, everyone clapping in an audible frenzy, and he's just sitting there looking at me, but really looking at nothing at all.

Undaunted, I said, "Great seats, no?" Read: Don't be rushing anywhere, there, MVP. You may be the entire reason for this turn of fortune.

Trot Nixon comes to the plate. He takes the first pitch for a ball. The crowd calms itself down and everyone takes their seats. Elizabeth is still down in concessions hell—exactly where I want her right now, bless her heart, not to mention the rest of her gorgeous body.

I leaned back in my seat, casually turned to my silent friend, and said, "Truth is, I think Trot's the best clutch hitter on the club."

He replied, "You Jack Flynn?"

Ding, ding, ding. I knew this was some sort of Christ figure, or maybe Christ himself, descending from the heavens to push the Red Sox to their first World Series win in 85 years, and he's about to let me in on his secret.

Nixon swung and missed. I turned to my seatmate and stared him up and down, allowing some of my reporter's skepticism to take hold. I asked, "Why do you ask?"

He was just sitting there, his eyes so dull we might as well have been sitting in the last pew of the Holy Name Cathedral on a Sunday morning rather than the box seats of Fenway Park during a one-run game against the Yankees in the middle of the best pennant race we've had in this city in twenty years.

"Because if you are, I have some information for you."

Well, there you have it, my biggest weakness—information, well, along with beautiful women, great food, and handsome dogs, specifically retrievers.

Crack.

I whirled toward the action to see an arching fly ball to center field, more shallow than I or anyone else in the park would have liked. The outfielder caught it. Ramirez tagged up and headed for home. It's a shame they don't have public transportation right on the playing field because it probably would have gotten him there faster.

As it was, the catcher caught the throw, completed half that day's *New York Times* crossword puzzle, then tagged Ramirez out. Double play. To Ramirez's credit, it took him so long to run home that it allowed Ortiz to tag up and get to third.

Back to the man beside me. I asked, "What is it you have?"

"You're Mr. Flynn?"

"No, my father's Mr. Flynn. He's dead, though. I just go by Jack. Jack Flynn."

I sounded like Bond, James Bond, when I said that, but not really.

My fellow fan said, "From the *Record*, right?"

I nodded.

"I have a group of associates who want to meet you after the game, in the Boston Cab Company garage. If you're not there within thirty minutes of the last out, they're gone, and they'll take the information somewhere else. We have a story of crucial importance that we'd like to give you."

His instructions were formal, rehearsed, as if he had gone over them many times in what I was starting to understand was his tiny mind. Deviation didn't seem to suit him well, as when I replied, "Not likely. But who are your associates?"

He fumbled for a moment, collected himself, and returned to the script, "You will see them soon enough. Mr. Flynn, people's lives depend on your getting this story. Life and death. It's in your hands."

Crack.

Again, I turned back to the infield and saw batter Jason Varitek racing toward first base. The right fielder was sprinting toward the foul line, heading directly at the Pesky Pole. I saw a blur of white disappear in the short right field stands. I heard a deafening roar. I began clapping along with the rest of civilization, stamping my feet, hollering my approval, until I couldn't clap, stamp, or holler anymore.

Then, flush with bravado, I turned back to my mystery man and said, "Tell your friends to go fuck themselves."

Elizabeth, standing beside me holding a Cool Dog in each hand, an impassive look on her utterly flawless face, held one out to me and casually replied, "Why don't you go tell them your-self."

I accepted the ice cream and said, "No, no, I wasn't talking to you."

She looked at me curiously. I cast a glance up the aisle, in search of my messenger, but he was nowhere to be found. Elizabeth said, "I had to go all the way over to the first base side to track these things down. You better like it."

Oh, I do. I do. I spread some warm chocolate sauce across mine. The Red Sox put New York down one-two-three in the top of the ninth, advancing to within a game of first place. But it ends up, now that the game was over, the night's excitement had just begun.

Chapter Two

I don't want to sound melodramatic and make this seem like I was meeting an unknown informant in an underground parking garage in the dark of an unfriendly night. That would be a lie. The garage was at street level.

The Boston Cab Company is located in one of those warehouse-style buildings on the outfield end of Fenway, tucked among the artists' lofts and sprawling dance clubs that encircle much of the park. Elizabeth and I filed out of the stadium with the rest of a happy humanity, and outside, on Yawkey Way, she grabbed my arm with both her hands in that affectionate way she has and said, "You pick the place, I'll buy the beer."

It was one of those increasingly common situations that required an ever so slightly delicate touch, for the following reasons: My name is Jack Flynn. If that's not enough of a description, and much to my professional chagrin, in most cases, it's not, I'm a reporter for *The Boston Record,* as the lucky messenger pointed out during the game. Actually, I'm the best reporter I know, though with a caveat. My editors often tell me I don't know a lot— jokingly, I think, or at least I hope.

Anyway, Elizabeth Riggs is also a reporter, though with *The New York Times*, her beat being New England and all the news that's fit to print about it. That's a little newspaper humor there. Admittedly, she didn't laugh the first time I used it either.

The point here being that because we work for two papers that might be considered rivals, I can't always share with Elizabeth every facet and nuance of my day, nor she with me. At least we both understood that, so I said to her, "Something work-related suddenly came up. Very suddenly. I have to go meet a guy. I don't have a clue about how long I'll be, but I suspect not very."

We were standing on the street outside of Gate A, with what felt like the entire baseball-loving world jostling past us. My emotions were admittedly mixed. On the one hand, the Sox had won. I had tickets to the next night's game. I wanted nothing more than to sashay into some bar with the most beautiful woman in town and celebrate what it means to be in the throes of an epic pennant race during the greatest month in the greatest city in the world.

On the other hand, this was Monday night, September 22. On Wednesday, the aforementioned Elizabeth would be boarding a flight that would take her to a new life in California, where she would become the San Francisco bureau chief for the *Times*. The prospect of her departure left me feeling somewhere between uneasy and morose, and standing there staring into the biggest, bluest eyes I might ever see in my life, I didn't like the fact that I was being dragged off on what would likely prove to be a goose chase, and one that probably wouldn't be all that wild. Good-byes are always tough, tougher still when you're not there to give them.

Elizabeth didn't ask any more questions. She had been as distracted as I had lately, wondering about her new job, wondering about her new life in a faraway city, wondering what the future held for us, as a couple, or not as a couple, whichever the case might be. All good questions, the last of which we had fastidiously avoided. She pushed her hair out of her face, kissed me softly on the lips, and said, "If I'm asleep when you get home, wake me up and fuck me."

Just one more reason why I love the woman.

Elizabeth and I went our separate ways, she heading to our waterfront apartment, me toward, well, I'd soon find out. Blind tips and unknown sources, by the way, aren't anything particularly novel in my business. In fact, this is how we get much of our best information—from people who care enough, or are angry enough, or hell, even vengeful enough—to reach out to reporters and push dark facts into the glare of publicity. The flip side is, most of these leakers and sources don't have much of a clue as to what comprises a great or important story. Their idea of a bombshell is often my idea of a New England News Brief, relegated to the middle of the second section if it deserves to be in the paper at all. But you never arrive at the occasional gold mine without slogging your way through so many veins of pyrite.

Which explains my thoughts as I arrived in front of the closed garage door of the Boston Cab Company, exactly thirty-five minutes after the game ended, meaning I was five minutes late. I didn't think it would be a problem, mostly because I had it in my mind that this wouldn't be a particularly useful excursion.

I walked past the garage, to an unmarked steel door with a simple knob, and pushed against it. The door, to my surprise, opened up into a dark room, which I assumed to be some sort of office or dispatch area. I stared around, looking for desks or computers or anything that might tell me where I was and why I was there, until my eyes slowly adjusted and I realized I was staring into the black expanse of the garage, completely still and seemingly empty. There wasn't a light on in the place, the only wan illumination coming from the open door just behind me.

The sound was that of utter silence. The odor was a dull potpourri of transmission fluid, motor oil, windshield wash, and engine coolant.

"Hello," I hollered. My voice echoed back off the walls and cement floors, then dissolved into the dark like sugar into black coffee. There was no response.

"This is Jack Flynn," I yelled. Normally I'd expect, or at least appreciate, cheering and hooting at such a dramatic proclamation. But again, only an echo, followed by silence.

Now mind you, the most dangerous thing most *Record* reporters encounter on any given day is lunch in the company cafeteria, especially on, say, Mexican theme day, what with Tony and Val at the grill making their version of a burrito or a plate of nachos. Even this didn't seem dangerous as much as foolish. Frustrated, I turned around and headed for the door, looking forward to waking Elizabeth, at her request, from her slumber.

Just as I did, a light flicked on in a distant corner of the sprawling garage, and I whirled toward it. Actually, it was two lights—headlights, of the soft, blue halogen variety, heading directly toward me, though not fast, and perhaps even slow. I leaned against the doorway and waited for what was to come, which in this case was the car and whomever and whatever was in it.

The vehicle pulled to within a few feet of me and stopped, its engine revving, then calming. I still couldn't tell the make, the color, who was driving, or how many people were inside. I didn't know if it was a taxicab. All I could see were the headlights, the high beams striking me square in my eyes. I continued to lean in the doorway, trying to look casual, though admittedly curious as to what the hell was going on.

The rear passenger's side door opened up, but nobody got out. The door just hung out there, beckoning, I suppose, but not really. I've always wanted my own driver, but the expectation if I ever get one is that I'd at least insist on knowing where he was taking me.

I heard the subtle sound of a purring motor, a power window descending, followed by the words, "Mr. Flynn, get in." The voice seemed to be coming from the passenger side of the car. I recalled a scene like this from *Lost in Space,* but I think it involved an alien craft, not a four-door sedan.

Still leaning, I asked, "Who are you?"

"We'll explain all of that. Please, Mr. Flynn. Please."

The voice was neither pleasant nor overbearing, neither tentative nor demanding, more earnest than I might have expected to hear in an otherwise barren garage under circumstances as undefined as these.

"Where are we going?" I asked.

"We're going to get you a story. A big story."

Good answer. Right answer. How does someone in my shoes, an admitted news junkie, say no to that?

"Why don't I meet you there?" I said this still staring into the teeth of the high beams, still seeing nothing at all.

Admittedly, that didn't make a lot of sense, considering I didn't know where "there" even was, but I was buying time, hoping they'd offer something more in terms of clues or agendas as I tried to delay the inevitable, which involved me getting into the rear seat of this mysterious car.

He replied with the magic words, "If you don't want to get in, that's your choice. We'll give the *Traveler* a call."

Well, he certainly knew what buttons to press. I mean, I've been shot at by assassins, kicked in the head by white supremacists, threatened by governors, lied to by none other than the president of the United States. If you think I have a good sense of danger, then you're right, and I was starting to sense it here. But all you have to do is tell me that *The Boston Traveler,* the city's feisty little tabloid paper, might beat us to the proverbial punch and all appropriate caution is thrown to the side of a potholed road. It's about how you want to live your life, and I like to live mine by getting to the story first.

So I walked around the headlights to the open rear passenger door. Outside of the glare, I saw that the car was some sort of dark-colored luxury model, perhaps a Lexus. I saw two men sitting in the front—the driver and the passenger who had goaded me into this act of stupidity—I mean, pursuit of a story. As I slid into the backseat, I couldn't help but notice another man sitting there beside me, mostly because he had many of the same physical characteristics as a gorilla.

I settled into the leather seat, looked around at the three silent men, and said, "Anybody want a stick of Juicy Fruit?" Nobody laughed, I guess for good reason, though they might have seen their way to being polite. All three, by the way, were somewhere in their fifties, dressed in black windbreakers and dark pants. None of them looked like they knew the way to the executive washroom, if you know what I mean. The guy beside me was one of those barrel-chested types with Popeye forearms who's either gone soft from age or forever retains his superhuman strength, though I wasn't in any real rush to find out which was the case.

The guy in the front passenger seat, wearing a dark baseball cap—a Red Sox hat, no less—slung low over his forehead jumped out and shut my door behind me. I heard the power locks go down in unison. The wide garage door ascended with a jolting roar. No one in the car spoke—no one but me, who asked, "You mind telling me where we're headed?"

Still, silence. I looked at the Cro-Magnon beside me. His face was wide and puffy, his nose broad and hooked, as if it had been broken in prior excursions. He had wisps of grayish-black hair, and his eyes, which stared back at me, were tiny and vacant. I could hear him breathe through his mouth.

I said, with a faint smile, "Lots of legroom back here." As I said it, I looked down at his legs, which were short and stubby, mere afterthoughts to his huge torso. He didn't reply.

Through the heavily tinted windows, I could see that the car was heading down Boylston Street, heading for downtown Boston. The car drove around the Public Garden, up and over Beacon Hill, and into the financial district, largely barren of people at this time on a Monday night, but for the occasional law firm associate trying to bill more hours than there are in a day.

I said, "I would have thought Ortiz would have bunted. Lucky he didn't."

More silence. Apparently no one felt like talking baseball, even after such a monumental win. Perhaps only their little messenger had been at the game. Or perhaps these guys were unschooled in the conversational arts.

By now, the car had driven through Government Center and pulled into a hulking downtown parking garage. I'll confess, I didn't quite get it. We left one garage only to arrive at another. The car kept circling through the building, heading upward toward the roof, around and around, past all the empty spaces. Finally, we pulled into a short section marked by signs that said, Reserved, Government Vehicles Only. The driver, who wore a baseball cap, glasses and the previously noted dark windbreaker, threw the car into park and hit the unlock button. The man in the passenger seat jumped out and opened my door.

Now I didn't exactly feel like a hostage, but nor did I feel free to come and go, either. As I was walking, I noticed that these Blues Brothers knockoffs essentially had me surrounded, their shoes clicking on the concrete floor as they guided me toward a steel door.

One of them, the driver, placed a security badge against the door, and there was an audible click. He pushed the door open into a well-lit hallway, and the four of us proceeded down a short, austere corridor amid our practiced silence.

At a second steel door, same routine. Inside, though, the hallways were carpeted, the lighting softer. We kept walking, took a left, then a quick right, and suddenly I found myself in an outsize office with a mustachioed man in a light blue windbreaker over a shirt and loosely knotted tie sitting behind an enormous wooden desk.

He stood up. The three men backed out behind me. The office door closed with a soft click.

"Good evening, Mr. Flynn," the man said, his whiskers twitching as he spoke in a gentlemanly farmer kind of way. "Nice of you to come out here at this hour. I appreciate that very much."

He came around the desk and shook my hand, all friendly and familiar, as if we knew each other, though I had never met him before.

I replied, just as breezily, "I'm not entirely sure I had a choice."

He gave me a low laugh while meeting my gaze. "Oh, you did. You certainly did. And you're free to go at this very moment if you'd like. I'll even have my"—and he paused here for a sliver of a second—"associates drive you right to your house." His mustache twitched again as he flashed a wry smile.

That's obviously not what I wanted for a lot of reasons, not the least of which was that I was within walking distance of my home, but no need to point that out. And I had come this far, arrived at this unusual sanctum. I wanted to find out who this was and what he had for me.

When I didn't respond, he said, "I'm Tom Jankle, special agent with the Federal Bureau of Investigation. I'm a fan of your work."

I said, needlessly, "Jack Flynn, reporter for *The Boston Record.*" I didn't mean to make fun of his introduction, though maybe I did.

Still in his windbreaker, as if he had just come in from raking leaves in the yard or, say, rounding up a collection of bank robbers, he beckoned me to a pair of upholstered chairs around a low-slung coffee table. Tom Jankle was, in a word, famous. I'll throw out another one: celebrated. He was arguably the most effective agent in the entire beleaguered Bureau, a one-man crime-busting squad who took down the New England Mafia, the Irish Mafia, politicians, bank robbers, white-collar criminals who thought they were above the law—anyone and everyone. And he did it all with a strangely unassuming air about him, as if he were an engineer in a struggling high-tech company out on Route 128, not an agent with the most powerful law enforcement organization in the world.

And there I was, in my first face-to-face with him, wearing faded jeans and a lazy navy blue sweater over an old tee shirt. My breath was a combination of the Italian sausage, Cracker Jack, peanuts and multiple beers I had consumed during the game, not to mention the Cool Dog. And yet, he made me feel perfectly comfortable.

He said, "Were my boys good to you on the way over?"

I nodded and said, "Here I am, so they got the job done."

He leaned back for a moment, taking me in, sizing me up, a look of mild amusement on his bespectacled face. Then he said, "Jack, if you don't mind me calling you Jack, you and I don't know each other, but right now, we can do each other a whole lot of good."

And with that, he leaned forward, his elbows on his knees, and he told me a story. What he neglected to tell me was how much bad we could do each other as well.

Chapter Three

Tom Jankle reached into a manila envelope that had been sitting on the glass coffee table before him and pulled out a stapled sheaf of documents. He read them for a moment as I watched his eyes descend the page.

Finally, he looked up at me and said, "Whoa boy. This is one heck of a story."

You don't hear the word heck a lot these days, especially among street-wizened agents. But he looked like just the kind of person who might try to revive its usage.

He looked back down at the sheets for a moment, then again at me. "What do you know about the Gardner theft?" he asked.

He might as well have just pulled his gun from his holster and fired a round into the bare white walls of his office. He might as well have just kicked me in the gut, or opened up a percussion grenade on the drab gray carpet of this windowless room. The entire world stopped short for a flicker of a moment. My vision blurred, my thoughts derailed, all sound, all motion, all sensory perceptions, ceased to exist.

And then I replied, unsure how I even scraped the single word from the far corner of my brain and out of the depths of my throat, "Some."

Forgive my drama, but the Isabella Stewart Gardner Museum remains the largest art heist in the history of America, a brazen robbery undertaken in the dark of a Sunday night thirteen years before by a pair of men dressed in Boston police uniforms who knocked on the massive front doors of the stately old museum and said there had been a disturbance nearby.

Once inside, the two imposters proceeded to bind and gag the two security guards, then methodically cut eleven art treasures from their frames on the walls, including works by Rembrandt, Vermeer, Manet and Degas. My tastes tend to run toward *Five Dogs Playing Poker*, but even I understood the import of this brazen act, and if I didn't, then the estimated price tag on these so-called priceless treasures made it quite clear. Experts said they were worth something in the neighborhood of $300 million, which, as the gossip columnists who write the *Traveler's* "Scene and Heard" column might say, is a very nice neighborhood indeed.

Most notable for the purposes of this conversation, the theft remained unsolved all these many years and so many thousands of infertile leads later. Nothing. Zero. Nada. Zip. When the two bandits were leaving the museum, one of them said to the bound guards, "Tell them they'll be hearing from us." But nobody ever had.

And now this. I had a very intense-looking lead agent with the Federal Bureau of Investigation sitting across from me in the urgency of a September night saying he wanted to talk about the Gardner Museum.

"But what should I know?" I asked.

He pulled his big frame up from his chair with a groan and ambled over to a tiny, beat-up old refrigerator that I hadn't previously noticed on the other side of his desk. He walked like he had just stepped off a horse.

"Beer?" he called out.

"Sure," I replied. I had already had enough for the night, and didn't want Augustus Busch impairing my senses any further, but to say no would have put me and him at a different place at a time I needed us to be nothing less than simpatico.

He came back with two bottles of Budweiser and absently handed me mine as he settled back into his seat. He took a long, thirsty pull, let out a quiet, pleasant sigh, and said, "I'd rather have a little bit of bourbon, but I've got work to do."

I didn't respond. He said, "We've had a pretty promising break in the case, but not enough of one to solve it."

The refrigerator rattled in the corner, or maybe that was my heart. Somewhere down the hallway, a door slammed shut. Then he added, "May we speak off the record, and we'll figure out what you can use when we're done?"

Seeing as I didn't even have so much as a pen and a piece of paper on me, I said, "Sure."

"And I mean, off the record," he added for emphasis.

"So do I," I replied.

For the record, off the record, in the vernacular of the information industry, means that any information provided to a reporter is unusable for publication or broadcast unless completely and independently confirmed. Some reporters, maybe most reporters, confuse this simple fact, and believe that off the record actually means the information is usable just so long as they don't identify the source of the information. They're wrong. What they're actually thinking about is "background" information, where a particular source will provide material on the condition of anonymity, meaning they are identified as, perhaps, an official familiar with the investigation. Two different things that most reporters can't get straight, though Jankle seemed to know full well the difference. I liked him for that already, or at least respected him.

He leaned toward me in his chair, took another short sip of his Bud, and, with the bottle still in his hand, said, "We have new information that Toby Harkins is linked in some way to the theft. We're in the process of trying to figure out how."

And there goes another percussion bomb. There's another round fired into the institutional-white wall. There's that foot-in-the-gut thing again.

Toby Harkins, in point of fact, is one of the biggest thugs that Boston has ever known, a coleader of an Irish Mafia that terrorized huge swaths of this city by running drugs, loan-sharking money and killing a sickening number of people who dared cross its path. Jankle had pursued him for years, finally with success. But Harkins had vanished a year earlier, precisely one day before the United States Justice Department announced its indictments on a litany of charges too long to list here.

By the way, it's also worth noting that Toby Harkins is the estranged son of the city's sitting mayor, Daniel Harkins. More on that in a while.

I stayed silent, listening to the quiet buzz of the overhead lights and the gentle ticking of a clock on a distant bookcase. I wanted to see where Agent Jankle was planning to take me before I even tried to alter his course with any questions.

"Now I'm not saying he stole the damned paintings. Seems too delicate an operation for a guy whose idea of sophistication is putting a bullet into the back of people's heads. But I am saying that he probably knows who stole them, and maybe he even has possession of them now."

He fell quiet, taking another long gulp of his beer. When he set the brownish bottle back on the table, I watched the bubbles within explode from the middle and rise toward the surface, all festive, even if the mood wasn't. When he didn't speak again, I asked, "How do we know that?"

Notice the word *we*, as in We the people, as in, Jankle and I, or is it me and Jankle, or Jankle and me. No matter. It was another subtle attempt to bond, to show that we were on the same side of the line, and that information shared would reap mutual benefits.

Without hesitating, he said, "We intercepted some correspondence, or rather, we had a piece of intercepted correspondence provided to us, that in some way links Harkins to the paintings. Unfortunately, I can't be any more specific than that."

"We're off the record," I said, meaning, tell me more.

"I can't be any more specific than that." He stared back at me, blank, then picked up his beer. Mine sat in front of me untouched.

I asked, "How seriously are you treating this new information?"

"Very. We now have dozens of agents in this office, in

Washington, and abroad, actively and aggressively looking into it. We're anticipating that the thieves or their representative might be prepared to reach out to authorities to broker the return of the paintings. That's the usual scenario in these kinds of cases."

"Meaning for money?" I asked.

"Most definitely."

"And where does Harkins fit into that?"

He shook his head ruefully and drained his beer. "We're still trying to figure that out. He may be the broker, skimming a huge percentage of the profits. That would be his way."

Admittedly, what he was giving me wasn't a lot, but in the news biz, not a lot doesn't always mean not enough. The journalistic processor that is my brain quickly kicked into overdrive, determining what I wanted to write versus what I could write versus what I needed to be able to write to get the information into print. And at that point, Jankle and I began the negotiation that precedes almost all source-driven stories of any worth. I borrowed a pad of paper, took down some notes and quotes, and when we arrived somewhere between his maximum offering and my minimum requirement, I stood up to leave.

As I gathered my borrowed belongings and pulled on my coat, I asked in as blasé a way as possible, "Why do you want this in print?"

Truth be known, the question was anything but casual. In the brokerage of information, everyone has an angle. Some people, often politicians and a few select investigators, just like the high of seeing their name or material in print. Others, natural pleasers, get off on befriending reporters, hoping that in some as-yet-unknown way, the relationship will ultimately pay dividends. Still others, those more vendetta-minded, liked to settle scores, and we provided a better forum than most to do just that. In this particular case, I harbored some suspicions that the frisky Feds were trying to spur an underworld war by putting information in play that Toby Harkins possessed several hundred million dollars in stolen treasures, or at least information on their whereabouts. With shootings or maimings or kidnappings come the endless possibilities of angry informants bringing information to federal investigators.

Not that I minded any of this. As in the law, motive in newspaper sourcing is interesting, though not necessarily important.

Jankle remained seated, and at this point, was taking a long slug out of my bottle of Bud, which I never touched. He put it down in front of him and looked up at me with newly tired eyes. He said, "Because right now, we don't have much of a case. I'm throwing out a line, seeing what I can reel back in. Someone's going to read what the *Record* has to write and they're going to call the FBI tomorrow morning with something more than we already have." Then, in a softer voice, "At least that's what I hope."

There was a moment of silence between us as I drank in just how bone-boring dry this office of his really was. The white walls were bare. The carpet was an institutional gray. His desk was only mildly cluttered. The chairs looked like they came from the waiting room of the Salvation Army. He was a man who cared about success, but not the trappings that go with it.

He added, "Jack, I can't guarantee you how long this information will remain out of the public realm. The FBI in Washington could call a press conference on this and issue a statement at any time, including tomorrow. This is a high-profile case. There are a lot of agents and assorted supervisors who want some mug-time on the tube."

I checked the clock on the wall—11:20 P.M.—and thanked him for his time. I declined the offer of a ride from his trained apes, jotted down his office phone number and headed for the door. It was, as they might say in journalism school, a killer story. I just didn't understand yet in what way.

Chapter Four

I walked into the newsroom carrying nothing more than a couple of scribbled pages of quotes in my hand and one of the more intriguing stories of the year in my head. At the far end of the room, the crazy, zany lords of the copydesk were spending the last minutes of deadline gloomily searching stories for punctuation and grammar mistakes that would no doubt cheer them up. Otherwise, the main part of the newsroom sat still and barren, nothing more than the sickly green haze of so many quiet screensavers waiting for tomorrow's daily frenzy.

I sat at my desk in the middle of the room and immediately began typing. I had already called Elizabeth on my cell phone on the cab ride over and warned her that I might be a while, and not to go hanging around with Toby Harkins tonight. Just kidding about that last part. I think.

More important, I also called Peter Martin, he of the Red Sox tickets, and flagged him on the night's events. As usual, he picked up the telephone on the first ring, regardless of the fact that it was after 11:00 and he was no doubt planning to be in his office by 7:00 A.M. the following morning, as he always was. Confident that my cabdriver could speak English as well as I could speak his native Ukrainian, I calmly told Martin what I had and from whom

I had it. He simply said, "I'll see you in the newsroom in twenty minutes."

Martin was my editor back when I was an investigative reporter for the *Record* in Washington and he was the paper's bureau chief. Since then, I've come back to Boston as a senior reporter, and in a recent and not uncontroversial shake-up, he became editor in chief. He's a diminutive guy, even weaselly in the wrong light, perpetually nervous, always pale, someone whose idea of outdoor activity was opening the sunroof on his Hyundai as he drove to work on a sunny weekend morning. But the truth is, he had the journalistic heart of a lion tucked into the body of a tabby cat, and at this time, on this night, I was glad to have him here beside me. Thrilled, actually.

As I said, we were hard against the paper's drop-dead deadline for what's known in the business as the Sports Final, known as such because it carries scores from games all over the country, including the late-finishing matches on the West Coast, and is usually the paper's last edition. It's distributed to subscribers in the city and the close-in suburbs.

I jumped onto my computer and quickly banged out a first paragraph which read, "Federal investigators have intercepted key information that links Toby Harkins, the fugitive mobster and son of the mayor, with the 1990 heist of more than $300 million in treasures from the Isabella Stewart Gardner Museum in Boston, the largest unsolved art theft in American history."

Okay, it's not poetry, but given the considerable constraints, it makes an unmistakable point.

Second paragraph: "A key investigator, speaking last night on the condition of anonymity, said agents were trying to determine if Toby Harkins was himself involved in the actual heist and if he is currently aware of the whereabouts of the eleven paintings and two artifacts stolen from the museum by two bandits dressed as Boston police officers."

And so forth, until I had a story that made it look, as these things tend to do, like I knew a lot more than I actually did.

I was typing so fast, concentrating so hard, that I never heard

Peter Martin breeze into the room and right up to my desk, until he finally said in a voice just north of an alarmed whisper, "Holy fuck."

He was reading over my shoulder, breathing quietly through his nose, not wanting to disturb me while I was on this obvious writing roll. He was one of the rare newspaper editors in this world who knew to never get in the way of a reporter on a good story. Others aren't happy until they've left what they might describe as "their imprint." In most cases, think of a goose shitting all over a dewy lawn.

A few paragraphs later, I took a quick break and pushed my chair back, rubbing my palms hard across my tired eyes. Martin continued reading the screen. He asked, "Tell me about the source again."

The rules of the road in newspapering require reporters to reveal the identity of their anonymous sources to their editors. Some editors, the best editors, always ask. Others don't. Martin's an asker.

I rolled back up to the computer. "Tom Jankle. FBI."

"Doesn't get much better than that. He a regular kneeler at the altar of Jack Flynn?"

"No. Truth is, I can't explain to you why he came to me, but he did. I was just sitting at the game minding my own business, or rather, the Red Sox's business."

Martin asked, "You have any sense of how this is going to affect the Dan Harkins nomination?"

Good question. He was referring to the fact that the senior senator from Massachusetts, Herman Harrison, was at that very moment being treated for a cancer that was known to be taking over a body already worn down by too much booze and too little attention. In the inevitable event of Harrison's death, the governor would appoint his successor to fill out the next year and two months of his term, until the next federal election. She had already leaked word that Mayor Daniel Harkins was her likely choice, though now, with more revelations about his son, she might reconsider.

"Don't know," I replied. "The mayor will keep denying contact, and his enemies will keep jabbing at him with it. Stay tuned."

"You'll mention this in print."

I would.

"Keep writing," Martin said. "I'll warn the copydesk that we're going to have to rip up the front page, and I'll try to buy you some time." With that, he literally jogged off to the populated part of the newsroom.

The man was beautiful, Martin was. Most editors these days dedicate themselves to what they commonly describe as "manicured news," stories that are conceptualized by their dim-witted underlings in morning meetings, assigned to willing reporters, edited over the course of several days, and finally paired with an artistic photograph on the front page. Put them on something resembling a deadline involving unwieldy issues like anonymous FBI agents warning of underworld figures stealing priceless paintings, and they start frenetically paging through the latest issue of the *Columbia Journalism Review* for answers they'll never find.

I finished, though you never really finish these stories; you just kind of acknowledge that you've run out of time. Martin returned. "Get up. I'll edit you right here," he said. And as I stood and paced the aisle, he sat in my seat, asked a couple of cogent questions as he read, made some small fixes in my story, and sent it on its uncertain way.

He leaned back in my chair in a position of faux relaxation—I say faux because Peter Martin, like most of the newspaper people I've ever worked with, was never truly relaxed.

"We're going to banner it," he said. "This thing's going to be the talk of the city tomorrow, the country maybe, and we've got it alone. Maybe we even end up doing some good by helping this thing get solved. You ought to feel great."

He was right, I should have. I mean, I broke the story of the week, the month even. As important, I broke out of something of a running slump. Journalism, specifically newspapering, is a business that requires constant reinvention and revitalization. Reputations are good, but they can get as old, as quickly, as yesterday's news. But truth be known, something nagged at me. It all seemed too easy, too pat. One minute I was watching the Sox stick it to the Yankees, the next minute I'm being handed a gift-wrapped bombshell destined for tomorrow's front page, and from there, the lead story on the network news. I'd have liked to think this is just what it meant to be Jack Flynn, but like I said, something nagged.

My desk phone rang, the sound crashing through the unsettled gloom of the newsroom—or maybe it was my unsettled mood it was crashing through. The two had become one, as these things tend to do. I fairly jumped through the drop ceiling. Martin, oddly composed, answered it.

"Yep." Pause. "Yep." Pause again. "Then fix it. Good. Good work. Let it go."

He hung up, looked at me and said, "That's the copydesk. You used *its* possessive as the contraction, *it's*, in your seventh paragraph. They fixed it."

Let me get this right. I have an exclusive story on a stunning new suspect in the most significant unsolved art theft in the nation, which happened to occur right here in my native city, and some bleached-out copy-editor is making sure all his friends on the desk and higher-ups know that he caught a second-tier grammar mistake deep into the jump? Maybe I really should have gone to law school.

Anyway, Martin and I stared at each other for a moment from our perches in the center of the otherwise empty room. Behind him, my computer flipped over to the screensaver, and even that minor act sent a little charge through my system.

He said, "You know we've chased down other false leads on this heist over the last few years. The Feds have tipped us off before. Most of them, I assume, involve rank-and-file ass-covering. But this one seems different. We have it alone, and they have an actual name they're putting into play, not vague references and unclear suspicions. I like this one a lot."

I should have too.

With that, he clasped his hands in front of him in that way he does and stood up from my desk. He slapped me softly on the shoulder, pretending, I think, that he knew how to take part in such fraternal acts. "We need to get right at this in the morning. Let's meet here by eight. This is going to be a wild ride."

A wild ride. One minute I'm at Fenway, an hour later I'm sitting in an FBI office being spoon-fed a story of significant proportions by an agent I didn't previously know, and an hour after that the thing is done and gone. Again, why didn't I feel better about all this?

Somewhere deep inside my psyche, in a place where instinct trumps common sense, I had the vague outline of a reason why. It was the core of the explanation that, at that point, I just didn't want to know.

Chapter Five

I sat at the wrought-iron table on our harborfront veranda staring so intently at the front page of the *Record* that the words seemed to meld into one giant block of meaningless black. Maybe it was the hour, which was 6:00 A.M., or maybe it was my condition, which was exhaustion. I blinked hard, took a long pull of fresh-squeezed orange juice, and looked again.

"Investigators Eyeing Fugitive in Gardner Heist," the headline read in a thick, appropriately foreboding font. Under that, in slightly smaller letters, "New leads create link to Toby Harkins."

My name, my byline, looked especially large up there on the left side of the front page, over a story that was stripped right across the top—a banner, as we call it in the news biz. On the far right side, the copy-editors cut in with a small photograph of Rembrandt's *Storm on the Sea of Galilee*, making it look like we put a whole lot more thought into this venture of reporting this story than was actually the case.

In general, I make it a practice not to read my stories once they've appeared in print, because all you can get is frustrated at some penny-ante change that some nickel-and-dime editor might have made along the line, entirely ruining the otherwise perfect rhythm and flow of your sentences and thoughts. This one I read, mostly because I barely remembered writing it, it all happened so quick.

And I was doing just that, reading it, when I heard the sliding glass door open behind me, and turned to see a topless Elizabeth Riggs, clad only in a pair of my white boxer shorts, her morning hair a tangle atop her beautiful head, step out onto the balcony and wrap her long arms around my neck from behind.

"I didn't hear you come to bed," she said in her thick morning voice, her warm breath filling my ear. "I didn't hear you get up. I don't recall getting what I asked for before you abandoned me last night."

It was true, all of it. I tumbled into bed sometime after 2:00 A.M. and a couple of cold beers drunk in the company of my dog Baker in the living room of our condominium. I had needed something to calm me down and help me get to sleep. Then I rose at 5:30 at the first light of early morning, unable to wait for the events of the day.

The *Record,* God bless the men and women in circulation, was already waiting on our doorstep, and I sat out here reading it in the growing light of a rising sun. It was cool out, yes, somewhere in the low 60s, but fresh, crisp, vibrant in that way that September is supposed to be.

"Where were you?" she asked, her mouth still directed against the sensitive parts of my ear. I felt her warm breasts against my neck, her hair against the sides of my face, and I'm not sure why it all made me feel so sad, so vacant, but it did. Actually, I lie. I do know why, it's just that I didn't want to confront it. The next day, Elizabeth would be gone, and despite anything on the front page of that day's paper, despite the whirlwind that was about to come, her departure was the major headline in the periodically sad life of Jack Flynn.

Without saying anything, I pointed to the story in front of me.

"Oh my God," she said. She said this as she pulled her arms back, came around to my side and sat on another chair silently reading the paper. By the way, it's important to note that our deck was completely private, inaccessible to any pair of eyes on land, though I've often been suspicious that voyeuristic yachtsmen, familiar with Elizabeth's penchant for topless and even naked lounging, drop anchor in the waters just off our building. I scanned the harbor but didn't see any on that morning.

She carefully read the story, turning from the front page to the jump—the part of the story that's continued inside the paper— then back to the front page again. Finished, she trained her enormous blue eyes on me and said, "How the hell did you ever get all this between the time I left you at Fenway and the *Record's* deadline?"

That was, to be sure, a compliment, presented in a classically journalistic way—with an incredulous tone, even a skeptical one, rolled into a question. Before I could answer, there was a knock, or rather a scratch, at our sliding door, and I turned to see Baker, his eyes at half mast and his fur fuzzy on top of his big head from what I'm sure was an unsatisfying half night of sleep, pawing at the glass to join the crowd.

As I opened the door to let him out, I heard an announcer on the Bose radio in the kitchen reading the news with one of those fake wire tickers sounding behind him.

"Federal, state and city officials are thus far offering no comment to this morning's *Record* report that investigators are eyeing the infamous fugitive Toby Harkins, the estranged son of the Boston mayor, in the 13-year-old, unsolved art heist at the Gardner Museum. The *Record* reports that authorities are still uncertain . . ."

I slid the door shut and the voice gave way to the tranquil sounds of a calm morning sea.

"It was one of those incredible, rare stories where everything falls immediately into place," I said to Elizabeth, sitting back down at the table beside her. I told her about getting picked up inside the Boston Cab garage, about the meeting with Jankle, about the rush with Martin to get this into print. She asked me a few typically intelligent questions, then focused on the story again.

In the silence, I looked around, at Baker already sprawled out on the cool floor of the deck, at the beautiful woman sitting beside me, at the harbor water glistening beneath us, and thought, in a couple of days, my little family—"our starter family," as Elizabeth liked to call it—would be no more. Elizabeth would be gone. Forever? I didn't know, but maybe. Maybe.

I should have been sitting there basking in triumph. Instead, I found myself climbing into a hole of emptiness, a feeling, a state of mind, hell, a state of being, that I knew all too well. I knew it, I lived it, after my wife and infant daughter died on the delivery table a few years before, leaving me with only memories of what I had and a forlorn void in place of what I never got to know, each day of fatherhood represented by another tear shed in that private hell called loneliness.

Did Katherine's death affect my relationship with Elizabeth? No doubt, there are entire teams of Harvard-educated psychiatrists that couldn't detail all the ways it did—about why I hadn't asked Elizabeth to marry me, about why we had split up temporarily the year before, about why, now, with twenty-four hours left in our time together, we couldn't even have a fully-fledged adult conversation regarding our future time apart.

She saw me staring silently at the water, saw, no doubt, the sad, even pained look that marked my face. She said, "I'm really proud of you, Jack," and I looked at her and she at me and I suddenly found my throat too thick to risk a response.

She stood up, still topless, always sexy, and she grabbed my hand and pulled me along with her. She left the door open for Baker to come and go at will, and on the rumpled white comforter of our sun-splashed bed, we became lost in an emotional stretch of silent sex. Afterward, as she looked down at me and pushed her face hard against mine, her tangled hair falling around my cheeks and ears, I felt her tears fall from her eyes into mine.

"I love you," she whispered, but the words, more sad than happy, carried more mystery than finality.

"I love you too," I replied, but I fear I sounded in some odd way resigned, though to what I didn't know.

Later, in the kitchen, she poured herself coffee. I ate fistfuls of Cap'n Crunch directly from the box. We avoided talk of her departure as if its very mention would set upon us an unspeakable plague. I knew she would be packing up most of her stuff that day, but what she instead said when I asked her plans was, "I have a lot of things to do around here."

That radio announcer was still blathering in the background, this time about the weather, then about the traffic.

"The surface roads are jammed all along downtown Boston as police have several major thoroughfares cordoned off for what we're told is a crime scene, possibly a murder or suicide scene, in the Boston Common. Boston police are confirming that the body of a young woman, in her late twenties, was found with a gunshot wound to her head a little over half an hour ago. . . ."

That's the first I heard of it. It didn't really register at the time, though maybe, in retrospect, it did. I flicked the radio off, rubbed Baker's ears and gave Elizabeth a long, silent kiss good-bye.

When I walked into the *Record* a few minutes before 8:00, Peter Martin was sitting at the desk beside mine scanning the wires, nervous as he's ever been, which is saying quite a lot. Here's a guy who drinks black coffee by the bucket just to soothe himself. His idea of a relaxing vacation is visiting the libraries of every twentieth-century president in two weeks' time. Once, when I had him temporarily convinced that there was more to life than newspapers and politics, he went to an upscale golf school in the Carolinas, one of those blessed places where you sip juice while sitting on a director's chair with your name hand-embroidered in the back while watching some young club pro demonstrate the importance of the interlocking grip on a pristine driving range. He claimed to love the experience, but he never played golf again.

Anyway, the newsroom looked almost the same as it had when I left a few hours before, only the copydesk was now vacant and a custodian—a cleaning engineer, I think they're now called—pushed an industrial-size vacuum down the empty aisles. Eight A.M. is at least an hour before most self-respecting reporters are climbing off their futons, and a couple of hours before they'd find their way into work.

"Thank God, I was sure you were going to be late," Martin said, looking up from his computer screen.

"Good, and you?"

He ignored my attempt at morning humor, stood up, and said, "Let's go into my office." I followed him through the mostly dark newsroom in silence.

Inside, the two of us sat across from each other at a small circular conference table in Martin's glass-enclosed office in the far corner of the newsroom. One wall of windows overlooked the traffic-clogged Southeast Expressway. The other wall overlooked the copydesk. All the furniture, the decorations, the lamps and the accessories, were exactly the way that the previous editor, Justine Steele, had them before she ascended to the publisher's office the year before. I swear, if Justine had left photographs of her children, Martin would have kept them on his desk.

Martin put his elbows on the glass tabletop and said, "The *Traveler* doesn't have a word on this. The three network affiliates are broadcasting our story, verbatim. The radio is quoting liberally from us and attributing everything. So far, we're all alone. But the whole world's about to crash our party. The *Times* is going to come in, the news mags, *The Washington Post,* the networks out of New York. This is big—huge—and we can't give anything up."

He was giving voice to what I already knew, but that's okay. This story, ours alone for the day, was about to turn into classic gang-bang journalism, the exact kind of story I hated most, when mobs of reporters trample across every possible bit of information, and every shred of context be damned. I nodded. Noticeably missing from Martin's soliloquy were words of praise for this morning's performance, but alas, he rarely had the patience for the triviality of commendation. I used to hold that against him; I don't anymore.

He continued, "So we have to figure out where we go from here." He looked anxiously out at the empty newsroom and continued, "When people find the time in their busy lives to wander into work today, I'll deploy as many as it takes to blanket every conceivable angle—the investigation, rewrite a tick-tock of the original heist, another lengthy profile of Harkins, the possibility of any connection to the mayor. What else?"

I remained silent. He knew he had everything covered. Martin resumed speaking.

"Jack, obviously you're the lead. Hit the investigation hard, do everything in your power to break more news. I don't have to tell you how to do it. Like all the other times before, just get it done."

Would that it were so easy. The problem with this business is that in every possible way, it involves constant reinvention, or at least restoration. If there's a formula, it consists of only this: Hard work—the extra telephone call, the added question at the end of the interminable interview, the long drive to some far-flung town to meet someone who you're not quite sure will be even the slightest bit of help. Hard work begets luck, and from there, the cycle continues.

"We will," I said, confident, but not really, and don't ask me why. Confidence is my trademark, but as I've said, these were strange times. Elizabeth was leaving. Something gnawed at me on this story, and as I looked out the window, I saw traffic at a veritable standstill on the highway, and even that inexplicably bothered me.

I stood up and said to Martin, "What do you know about the dead woman on the Common?"

Most editors in chief are big-picture people, probably because it's easier to be that way, just like it's easier to travel great distances by air than to drive in a car, though high above, you miss all the individual brushstrokes that go into the art of real life. Martin was decidedly different. To be sure, he could think big and ponder the most serious questions in the business, but he also had an insatiable curiosity for the details of even the smallest house fire in Dorchester.

As if to prove the point, he said, "First reports out say she was a young attorney, maybe thirty years old, found in her car in the garage under Boston Common by an attendant picking up the trash. Single gunshot wound to the head."

What the hell was the deal with parking garages lately?

"Suicide?" I mean, logical question, given that all the lawyers I knew were always saying they wanted to kill themselves.

"If it was," he replied, "then she managed to hide the gun."

Back at my desk, I snatched up the telephone, and pulled out the phone number for Tom Jankle, special agent of the FBI. My hope, my expectation, was that if he spoon-fed me the prior night when he only knew me by reputation, then now that we had a track record, he should be ready to spew any remaining information he had. No telling how much chicken I left on that journalistic bone, but my educated hunch was, a lot. A lot.

A rather imperious-sounding woman informed me, "Special Agent Jankle is not available right now. May I help you?"

A couple of points here. First, why don't newspaper people have the word "Special" in our titles? Actually, why don't we have titles at all? Why can't I say to someone over the phone, "Hello, this is Special Reporter Flynn calling from *The Boston Record* blah blah blah." Actually, here's why: Because we'd sound like asses, which is exactly how this secretary sounded now.

Point two: I hate when self-important secretaries and other assorted assistants ask, "May I help you?" as if my call, my concerns, must be so profoundly trivial that I couldn't possibly warrant the attention of their boss. Let me ask you something: Are you a party to the investigation? Are you prepared to be quoted in front of a million people in tomorrow's *Record,* or to leak sensitive information that will push the story along? If not, then just take a message.

Actually, I didn't say any of that. More politely, but not too much so, I said, "You could take a message."

"Is there someone else who could help you?" Okay, now this was getting rich. The night before, her boss sends a team of trained apes to pull me out of a ball game at Fenway Park. They chauffeur me to his office. He sits with me in private as the clock ticks toward midnight and provides me hitherto unknown details on the largest unsolved art heist in the history of the nation. He's in essence, actually, looking for my help. And she's thinking I don't warrant his attention, because this great man must absolutely be far too important to deal with anything or anyone so trivial as the largest, most respected, and most important newspaper in New England.

"I don't think so," I replied, my voice still surprisingly soft, even upbeat. "If you could just tell him —"

"His schedule is very full today."

"So's mine." Not quite as nice. "But if you could ask him to call Jack Flynn"—I gave her my number before she cut me off again—"I'll absolutely take the time to talk to him." I thanked her, almost overly pleasantly so, and quickly hung up, another border skirmish in the war on government imperialism successfully fought.

Then I proceeded to pound out another two dozen calls to various state, city and law enforcement officials who I knew or should have known or wanted to know, all in what the unkind might call a fishing expedition, but I'd prefer to describe as an informational dragnet. On a story of this caliber and magnitude, you leave no number undialed, no office unchecked. Hell, the truth is, most of the bureaucrats I was ringing up would take it as a compliment that I was even calling. Of course, all I got was equally officious secretaries and occasional voicemails, but the return calls would come soon enough.

All along, something still wasn't right. Intuition, while a gift, was not always a blessing. The pang in my stomach was slowly turning into a knot, and someone seemed to be tying it tighter, pulling on the strings, giving me a sickening feeling that penetrated my flesh and rattled my bones. I turned fully around and gazed out the far windows of the newsroom to see that traffic was still at a standstill. I absently flicked the On button on the portable television that sat on a corner of my desk.

As the screen came to life, I saw a familiar reporter standing in front of the Gardner Museum, a microphone held up to his uncommonly handsome face. "Behind me," he was saying, "is one of the world's great art museums, but most famous not for its paintings, but for being the target of the country's costliest heist." From there, it kicked over to a prerecorded segment that basically reiterated the guts of my morning story, with full attribution. I turned the volume down and made a few more calls.

Somewhere along the line, I noticed that the television image flipped from the Gardner footage to an open grassy space set against the backdrop of the Boston skyline. I quickly turned the volume up to hear a rather comely redheaded reporter saying, "Ham, police are saying that she was found at about 7:15 this morning slumped over the steering wheel of her Saab with a single gunshot wound to the left side of her head. The car doors were all closed, the doors locked, the windows unbroken. No gun was found inside. The twenty-seven-year-old victim was found on the second level of the garage. Her identity has not yet been released pending notification of her relatives."

The knot was starting to feel like a damned tumor. I bore in harder on the reporter. Behind her, detectives in suits came and went from a headhouse into the garage.

Ham, as anchors are wont to do, asked a stupid question. "Kelly, any suspects yet that we know of?"

Kelly shot him a look that melded disbelief and disdain. Then, composed, she replied, "Ham, the police are being unusually mum on this case. It has all the makings of becoming a very high-profile murder investigation, and they haven't tipped their hand to us as of yet. There is, however, a briefing scheduled for police headquarters later this morning, and hopefully I'll have more information to pass along after that."

It wasn't Kelly's rather colorless answer that sounded alarms, but what occurred at the crime scene as she gave it. Behind her, an enormous man in a dark windbreaker quickly walked out the glass doors of the headhouse, his mustache twitching with each step. He was in the frame for maybe two seconds, tops, but the sight sent a lightning bolt of recognition into my fragile brain.

Tom Jankle, special agent with the FBI, hanging around a local murder scene. It made not an ounce of sense. FBI agents don't investigate homicides, at least not run-of-the-mill ones, though I suppose none of them appear run-of-the-mill to the victims. They don't work with local police departments, at least not very well. They don't usually even offer their help. Cops and G-men are usually like cowboys and Indians.

Was it really him? I only caught the quickest of glimpses. I pondered that exact question as Kelly in the field answered yet another profoundly inane question from Ham on the anchor desk, and there, in the background, was Tom Jankle, once again hurrying back into the same glass doors in the near distance that he had just exited, his head down and a cellular telephone planted against his ear.

I snatched up my phone and called Martin's office. He picked up on the first ring.

"Who do we have on the Boston Common murder?"

"For right now, Mongillo. He's the only staffer up this early."

We both hung up, comfortable enough with each other that we didn't need time-consuming salutations or felicitations. I immediately belted out Mongillo's cell phone number, and he, too, picked up on the first ring.

"Mongillo."

"Flynn here."

His voice brightened. "Hey, hey, it's Fair Hair"—his nickname for me. "This is an unexpected honor. Hold on while I get rid of this call." That's the thing about Vinny Mongillo—he always had another call. About five seconds later, he was back on the line.

"So why on God's good earth would Jack Flynn, the author of the biggest story in America today, be calling a simple little reporting grunt like me?"

This, for anyone who knows Mongillo, even in passing, was an obvious dose of false modesty. He was as tenacious a reporter as I've ever met. He wielded his ever-present phone like a mallet and his pen like a jackhammer, and he had this inordinate, almost otherworldly ability to convince a coat of paint to share the secrets of the damned. This he knew, and so did virtually everyone who knew him.

"Why," I replied with a question of my own, as newspaper people tend to do, "would the FBI be interested in that murder you're covering?"

"I didn't know they were."

"I believe there's at least one agent on the scene, and maybe others that I don't know about."

He paused, then asked, "Why do *you* think they'd be interested?"

He's uncanny. He heard in my voice the whispery combination of faint knowledge and uncertainty, and was calling me on it.

I replied, "Why don't we get together."

"I'll call you after the police briefing."

He was about to hang up when I asked, "The victim, Vinny. What's her name?"

"Hilary Kane," he said, without hesitation. And then the line went dead, without so much as a good-bye.

Chapter Six

I was driving up and down Mount Vernon Street in the most historic—read: priciest—neighborhood of Boston, trying not to call attention to myself, which was no easy feat, considering my aging Alfa Romeo convertible was sending up plumes of black smoke from the decrepit exhaust. All parts of my life seemed to be breaking down.

It was, as I earlier mentioned, a gorgeous autumn day, temperate, with a gentle sun giving the entire city a clean glow—all of it, every bit, in direct contrast to my gloomy mood. Dog walkers in ponytails led bunches of Labradors and poodles up and down the steep hill. A few of the patrician elderly carried sacks of groceries from DeLuca's Market or Savenor's butcher shop. And in front of the apartment building in question, a three-story brick town house that butted up against the narrow sidewalk, a blue-and-white police van sat double-parked. This is where Hilary Kane lived until earlier this morning, and police were inside searching for clues.

I turned to my passenger, one Hank Sweeney, retired Boston homicide detective, now a shockingly pricey corporate security consultant, and asked, "How the hell much longer will they be in there?"

"Any moment," he replied. He said this distractedly, fidgeting, as he was, with a new Palm Pilot V he was trying to program. Actually, check that. I'm not sure if he was trying to program it, or just figure out how to turn it on.

"You use one of these things?" he asked me, his voice still uncharacteristically soft, like his mind was somewhere else.

"I've got a leather-bound datebook that does the trick."

"Does it have an On switch?"

"You just open the cover and flip to the page you need."

He said, "Yeah, that's probably the way to go." And he tossed his Palm Pilot down onto the carpeted floor.

Again, I drove by the apartment, and still, the van sat in the street. The outside apartment doors were closed. There was nothing to see but the clock ticking away toward my deadline.

Truth be known, I'm not sure what I was after. I had a pretty significant story unfolding on my watch, by my hand—new clues in the Gardner art heist—and here I was chasing my gut up and down Beacon Hill, waiting for a couple of numbskull cops to pack up their gear and hightail it back to headquarters with a few boxes of who knows what.

But something nagged. Actually, no, it didn't nag; it fairly well screamed. Something about that story last night wasn't quite right. Something about this murder this morning wasn't quite as it seemed. The feeling was causing a minor wave of nausea through my innards.

About an hour earlier, I had taken the simple step of looking up Hilary Kane in a legal directory. It said she graduated from Boston University Law School the year before and worked in a small firm in Cambridge. When I called the firm, the line had been disconnected. I called the BU Law School alumni office, and a curt woman there told me there was no record of where anyone by the name of Hilary Kane was currently employed. A police department spokeswoman told me, off the record, that they found a Massachusetts Bar card in her purse, but nothing that indicated where she now worked. This was just another reason why the police were inside her house at the time.

Which is why I was waiting to get in there as well. I needed to know if my suspicions bled into reality, if Hilary Kane was somehow connected to the art heist.

Hank, meanwhile, needed to know how to program numbers into his new cell phone, which he had pulled from his pocket and was regarding as if it were part of an elaborate communications experiment conducted by a team of professors at MIT. At a stop sign, I took the phone and punched my own name and phone number into his memory, and then punched his name and number into mine.

"It's like we're sweethearts," he said with that wry smile of his. And he tossed the phone down on the floor next to his Palm Pilot.

I drove up and down, again and again, Hank making almost unimaginably banal small talk, and me playing over the events of my life in my mind. A huge story breaks. Elizabeth and I are incapable of discussing her impending move. I inexplicably feel involved in the murder of a woman I don't even know.

And then the apartment doors opened. I quickly pulled into a rare Beacon Hill parking space to watch. A man and a woman, each wearing golf shirts, khaki pants, and sneakers, came walking out, each one of them balancing a sizable box in their arms. Their matching dress and rigid, humorless demeanor told me they were either tourists from the Dakotas or cops from Boston. Their shoulder holsters and shields hooked to their respective belt loops confirmed the latter. The fact that they had the Boston police insignia emblazoned on their jerseys actually screamed it. You don't need Bob Woodward here in Boston when the city is already blessed with Jack Flynn.

"Here we go," I said to Sweeney, who was squinting out the windshield at them. "Looks like they're cleaning her out."

"Routine, very routine," he replied, his voice low, flat, as if the detectives might be able to hear us.

They set the boxes down on the street, and, as the woman began placing the items in the back of the van, the man went back inside the apartment foyer and retrieved a computer monitor. He made one more trip back inside, and came out with what looked like the computer itself. They slammed the back doors, settled inside, and started the engine, the woman driving, the man shotgun. Justice for Hilary Kane was very much in the hands of the state.

Except, wait a minute. A shiny, gunmetal-black sedan came pounding up Mount Vernon Street, swerved around the van, and shot in front of it, screeching to a stop at a jagged angle that prevented the police vehicle from continuing in any direction but into the parked cars. A second car, identical in appearance, came racing up the hill seconds behind it and snuggled up close to the back of the van. Almost in unison, the driver's and passenger doors flung open on each of the cars, and four men in dark suits jumped onto the pavement and scurried to each side of the blue van.

I couldn't see the cops' faces, but I did see that the driver rolled down her window.

"We've got a courtside seat to an honest to goodness turf battle," Sweeney said, sounding at once interested and amused.

I looked at him quizzically.

"Feds verses Boston PD," he said, by way of elaboration, "right here in front of you."

This was somewhere far beyond intriguing, given that I hadn't said a word to Sweeney yet about my suspicions of FBI involvement, not because I was holding out, but just because I had no idea where this was going.

I asked, "How do you know those guys are Feds?"

He acted angry in that way he sometimes does, even when he's not. "Look at them, for chrissakes," he replied, his voice louder now. "Who the hell else do you know wears a suit jacket when they're driving in a car?"

Good point. I guess nobody. I said, "So they're FBI." It was as much a question as a statement of fact.

"Bet your ass," he said, his tone still angry. Then, calmer, "Straight out of central casting." I could all but picture him munching on a large bucket of popcorn as he watched the unfolding show.

I turned my attention back to the battle at hand. Nobody

looked particularly happy. This wasn't a collection of lawmen—and -woman—swapping war stories from the trenches, maybe giving one another the needle, talking about the fragile state of modern America when a pretty young woman can be savaged in a downtown parking garage. No, these people looked to have the personalities of professional golfers.

One of them reached into the breast pocket of his suit and pulled out—a gun? No—a sheet of paper. He deliberately unfolded it and handed it to the driver.

With that, the van doors opened. The driver got out and inspected the sheet. The second cop, the passenger, came around the vehicle, his two G-men escorts in tow. He, too, pulled a rumpled sheet of paper out of his back pocket, unfolded it in greater haste than his federal counterpart, and shoved it into the hands of a man who looked to be the FBI ringleader. For a long moment, everyone stood around reading the two sheets of paper. I wish newspapers attracted that much attention in the age of cable television. What we had was a certifiable standoff.

"What are they doing?" I asked Sweeney. Sweeney, by the way, is a man of monstrous proportions, not like a hippo, but more solid, like a bear. When I looked over at him, I saw he had a tiny pair of field glasses tucked under the bill of his Boston Red Sox cap and was peering intently at the proceedings.

"Dueling warrants," he said, the binoculars still pressed against his black, shiny face. "This could get real interesting."

I asked, "Why do they need warrants to get into a dead woman's house?"

"Maybe they don't, unless she's living in there with someone who might be a suspect—a husband, or a boyfriend, or a roommate of some sort. You know if she's married?"

"Don't think so. I checked the property records online before I came over, and she's the sole owner."

"Then like I said, boyfriend or roommate."

Outside, the female cop pulled the radio off her belt, turned her back on the assembled crowd, and made some sort of call, I assumed to headquarters. Not to be outdone, the FBI ringleader, virtually indistinguishable from his colleagues, pulled a tiny cellular telephone out of the breast pocket of his suit, took two steps in the other direction, and made a call to God knows where. It could have been the attorney general of the United States, the way this thing was looking. Now that would be a good story.

"Who they calling?" I asked.

"You think I read minds or lips?" Sweeney replied. Okay, good point. I just thought he might have been in a similar predicament at some point in his long law enforcement career.

Sweeney, you see, is of the Boston Police Department homicide unit, retired, a lieutenant when the gold watch finally came. I met him a year ago, when my newspaper was under a takeover threat and my publisher was shot to death. We did each other an enormous favor, and from that, I think we're entwined for life. He moved back to Boston from a retirement home in one of those wretched little towns in Florida, and is now making a small fortune telling people things about police departments that they wouldn't otherwise know. For me, he does it for free. He thinks he owes me. I do nothing to dissuade him of the notion.

"Here we go," he said.

As he said this, another unmarked cruiser gunned up Mount Vernon Street and jammed on the brakes behind the FBI sedan, which sat behind the police van. A man in a shirt and tie, carrying a sport jacket over his shoulder, got out and walked determinedly into the crowd.

"Fed or cop?" I asked.

Sweeney put his glasses down and looked over at me like I had just fallen face-first off a beaten-up turnip truck.

"He's carrying his jacket," he said loud, his voice soaked with aggravation. "Of course he's a cop."

As if to prove the point, the cop in question grabbed the federal warrant, read it for all of nine seconds, and handed it back. Immediately, he began jawing with the FBI ringleader.

Do they have free refills here on the large sodas?

Then came another car from the other direction. Two guys wearing their jackets—Feds, I'd hazard a guess—got out and walked into the crowd. People were pointing fingers, raising voices, gesticulating wildly.

Sweeney said, "You mind me asking why you give a damn about this murder?"

"Can't tell you," I replied. "Not because I can't tell you, but because I don't really know. I think it's connected to something else, and this whole scene confirms my beliefs."

Interesting as all this was, it wasn't getting me what I needed, which was to find out if Hilary Kane could have in some way been connected to the heist. And if she was, then did my story in that morning's paper get her murdered? It was nearing noon. I had a lot of work to do, and the sands of time were pouring through the hourglass of life.

"I'm going over," I said, putting my hand on the door handle.

"You're what?" Sweeney asked me this loudly, but he was more amused than upset.

"Public street. I'm allowed."

"Why?"

"I'm not sure."

With that, I opened the door and stepped out. We were about ten cars down from the action, so nobody took any notice. I walked down the middle of the street toward the assembled crowd, which now consisted of precisely six FBI agents and three Boston police detectives, not to mention the two patrol officers who were at that moment pulling up in a cruiser, though I guess I just did. I had a legal pad in my hand and a pen in my pocket.

"Possession is nine-fucking-tenths of the law, and we've got it." That was the Boston PD detective in the necktie, fairly shouting his lucid analysis into the reddened face of the FBI ringleader.

"The other tenth is this warrant, and that fucking trumps it." That was the FBI agent, providing his equally lucid response.

Several of the underlings on both sides of the warrant divide looked over at me warily as I approached, probably wondering if yet another agency was about to get involved.

I gave them my most sheepish, party-crashing smile and said,

"Morning. I'm Jack Flynn from the *Record*. Just trying to get the lay of the land out here."

I heard an FBI agent, the late-arriving supervisor, mutter, "Fuck." Two of the other well-dressed agents cut me off as I continued to walk, such that we were chest to chests.

I caught the gaze of the Boston supervisor, who gave me some sort of knowing look, and already, without knowing why, I was on his side.

"We're going to have to ask you to leave," an FBI agent, one of the guys in my face, said.

"Ask away," I said, "but unfortunately, until I get some information, I don't think I can really go."

He didn't take too kindly to that and said, "Get the fuck out of here."

My tax dollars at work. I'm trying to remember what the good faculty at the Columbia School of Journalism advised in these situations. Of course, since I instead matriculated at the School of Hard Knocks, I had absolutely no idea.

So I said, "Sir, it's a public street." I said this dismissively, as if I was running out of patience, and I was. I was.

"It's a crime scene."

"The crime," I replied, "occurred down the street, in the parking garage. The only crime going on here are all the bad haircuts."

Actually, I didn't really say that last part, not because it wasn't true, but because if I did, I probably would have been the recipient of a deserved haymaker from this antsy agent hanging all over my space. What I did say, though, was, "The only crime going on here is the waste of public energy."

"Move!" he screamed, drill-sergeant style, right into my ear, so that I could feel not only his bad breath, but his warm spittle, on my lobe.

I ignored that too, hard as it was becoming, and called out to the ringleader and the late-arriving supervisor, "Can I get your names, please."

They looked at each other. The boisterous agent in front of me didn't know what to do next. I knew, and he did too, that one push, and he'd be working the switchboard of the FBI's field office in Omaha.

The two supervisors traded nervous glances. It's part of the majesty of this great profession that we can make men bearing arms afraid. The senior FBI agent turned to the ranking cop and said, "We're going to follow you to headquarters."

The cop snorted and replied, "Well, you sure as hell ain't getting in."

And just like that, in seconds, actually, everyone jumped into their cars and drove off. Suddenly, I was standing in the street all by my lonesome. I walked back toward my car and said to Sweeney, "Please, call me Henry Kissinger."

He got out, wide-eyed and said, "What in the hell did you say?"

"I told them my name and asked them theirs."

He laughed. I added, "Come on, we have work to do."

He followed me silently to the front door of the apartment building. We both saw four mailboxes, meaning one apartment on each floor. He pulled some tiny device out of his pocket—for all I know, it might have even been a key—and had me inside the front door in a matter of about three seconds. We walked up to the second floor, and he used the same tool to unlock the door to Hilary Kane's condominium. This was illegal, this break-in, and nothing I found in this search could be used in print. But someone was playing dirty with me, I feared, so I needed to play dirty back.

"Get out of here before you get in trouble," I said to Sweeney at the door. "I have my phone on vibrate. Call me if a cop or Fed is trying to get in." He nodded, turned and silently walked down the flight of stairs.

And I opened the door in search of my own worst fears.

Chapter 7

The first thing that struck me was the light, loads of it, pouring through the back windows, splashed across her rumpled queen-size bed, speckled across the dark hardwood floors that were casually draped with discarded clothes. The second thing to strike me was the airiness of it all. The apartment, from front to back, from side to side, was wide open, like an artist's loft, no walls, except in a far, rear corner where I assumed the bathroom must have been.

This was unusual for Beacon Hill. Apartments here are usually closed and cramped and dark as the night in the middle of the afternoon, and the architecture usually ranges from the uncreative to the dowdy. This one was stylish even, chic, and I liked the owner immediately. Apartments and houses can do that. They have a reflected personality, an ability to acquaint and comfort. Having never actually met her, I already knew that Hilary Kane was my kind of woman. Actually, check that. She was much too good for me.

I called out, "Hello," the single word, happy at its core, just drifting into the vacant air of the room. I thought to myself what a shame it was that she couldn't answer. Of course, if she could, I'd be facing imminent arrest, so I guess I wasn't in any great position to complain.

The entry was in the middle of the apartment. To my right, the back end, was where she slept, so noted because that's where the aforementioned bed was, with a soft down comforter tossed haphazardly on top of it, as if she had overslept that morning and rushed into a day that would unknowingly be her last. I walked back into her bedroom area and looked at the fashionable clothes that lay about the floor—a pair of stretch jeans, a few flimsy tank tops, some rayon running pants—and shoes, everywhere, shoes, various types of clogs and boots and sneakers and high heels, some pointed and refined, others chunky and rugged. What is it about women and their shoes?

I wandered over to her small desk a few feet from her bed, painted white, and saw from the dust marks where the confiscated computer monitor had been. Various papers sat in careful piles, likely placed there by the uncharacteristically thoughtful police. About eight or ten framed photographs sat on a shelf on the desk—mostly women friends smiling into the camera, often arm in arm, at various celebratory events. Three photographs were carefully tipped over, turned down on their faces. I reached out a hand to grab one of them, to see the image, when a jolt went through my arm—Sweeney's vivid warning: "Look but don't touch, not unless you're wearing these gloves."

I yanked his latex gloves out of my back pocket and pulled them on, golf-glove style. I felt somewhere between ridiculous and ominous, but the alternative—winding up arrested and hauled into court to explain my actions and plead an innocence that wasn't really mine—was enough to prod me on. I picked up one of the photographs and held it in my hand.

It was of a man, reasonably handsome, with blue eyes and a strong chin and a full head of black hair that tumbled down onto his neck. He wore a blue blazer and he stood on what appeared to be a dock hanging over somewhat churlish seas. This picture could have been torn out of a Ralph Lauren catalogue. He carried the classic look of an ex-boyfriend—a little too smug, far too pleased with himself, in total, not a keeper, not for someone with the style and taste of Hilary Kane.

My suspicions were confirmed when I picked up the second picture, this one of the same guy, his hair a little shorter, a too-cool formless sweater covering his torso with a white tee shirt showing underneath. He was wearing a pair of perfectly faded jeans, sitting on the front steps of what appeared to be an extraordinarily expensive house, a mansion even, that I immediately suspected was that of his parents.

But he's not what caught my breath short. It was her, Hilary. She was sitting one step beneath him, and his arms were wrapped affectionately around her neck. I wanted to punch him in the head.

To say she looked beautiful would be like saying that eagles know how to fly. Yes, on one very simple level, it's true, but it gets nowhere near the glorious heart of a wondrous reality. She was blonde, with soft hair that no doubt flowed like silk down beyond her shoulders. I wouldn't know, because in the moment of the photograph, she had it pulled back in a casual ponytail that highlighted the perfect lines of her chiseled face. Her features were small and sharp, except for her eyes, which were big and grayish-blue. She was wearing an old baseball-style undershirt, navy blue arms, baggy, down to her elbows, and a white body. She had on jeans that were smudged with dirt on both her knees. She wore a controlled smile on her face, her lips pursed, as she looked upward as if trying to see her boyfriend who lurked above, though not really. She had on worn track sneakers. In sum, I think I was in love.

But onward. I put both photographs down, my heart now even heavier with the events of the day and the suspicions of the moment. I picked up the papers on the desk and flipped through them, looking for any clue as to her employment. But mostly they were old bills and flyers. I checked through her two desk drawers, looking, perhaps, for a pay stub or an ID card, but there was nothing of any worth inside. I began walking out toward the living room part of the sun-splashed loft when something on the floor caught my eye. It was just a corner of white paper, wedged behind the desk. I hunched down, pulled on it, and was suddenly holding another photograph, this one an image that stunned me.

Oh, it was nothing vulgar or pornographic or even remotely compromising. Black Hair wasn't even in it, thank God. I was sick of him already. What it showed was the mayor of Boston standing with his arm around Hilary Kane, various clingers-on in the background, at some ribbon cutting ceremony somewhere. Scrawled across the bottom of the picture were the words, "To Hilary, the best lawyer at City Hall. With all my gratitude, Mayor Harkins."

A couple of points worth making here. First, what kind of jughead calls himself "Mayor" even to his own staff? At least he doesn't have the title "Special Mayor." Second, it obviously meant that she was in the employ of the city, probably as a lawyer in the corporation counsel's office. Third, it might well indicate that the reason the FBI was investigating her death was because the Feds were probing the mayor on some other issue and were searching for a link to the Kane murder.

All of it was interesting, but not terribly conclusive. Still, the nagging got louder, almost to the point of shrillness. The photograph in my gloved hands was one of those pictures that only politicians and their pathetic groupies love. Hilary Kane obviously wasn't one of them, given that it had slipped unnoticed behind her desk. She probably never missed it, forgot she had ever even had it, or maybe she had even tossed it toward the trash can and hit the rim. It was meaningless, to her and any normal-thinking person.

But not now. Now it was an important clue that I held in my own sweaty hands. Now it broached some terrifying questions. Now it whispered truths that I couldn't quite hear. I came here because my very refined reporter's instinct told me that Hilary Kane was in some way linked to the Gardner Museum heist. This picture indicated that I might well be right.

But when does intuition give way to facts? When does fear turn to anger? Did I cause someone to die? And not just anyone, but did I help end the life of the young and beautiful Hilary Kane, for reasons that I didn't yet know?

I tucked the picture back behind the desk precisely where I

had found it, happy—though that's probably not a good description of the moment—to have it out of my hands. I picked up another photograph on the desk, this one of Hilary and two other women with remarkably similar features—one about her same age, the other older, no doubt a sister and their mother. They were standing outside of this very building, not posed, but candid. Each of them had a box of some sort in her hands, probably on the day Hilary moved in. I suspected that the lazy no-good boyfriend was the one behind the camera, his way of sneaking a break.

I looked hard into Hilary's eyes, big and blue-gray, dazzling, knowing. She was a smart woman; you could tell that from even the quickest glimpse. She had that same somewhat practiced smile on her naturally beautiful face. Her hair was pulled back. She wore a tank top and a pair of short-shorts showing legs that were long and carefully formed.

I shook my head. I put the picture back down. I cursed, and the sound of my own voice jolted me from my dark reverie. Well, my voice and the faint rattle of a key in the door on the other side of the room.

With no great embarrassment do I confess to being relatively new at this whole burglary venture, though it does seem that whenever I commit one, Hank Sweeney is somehow involved. This time he apparently let me down in his role as chief scout. The plan had been for him to ring me if anyone was coming into the apartment. My phone, set on vibrate, hadn't moved.

No time to assess blame. I placed the picture on the desk and bolted for the nearby bathroom door, the only place to take shelter in the entire apartment unless I were to have done the clichéd hide-under-the-bed thing, but it was probably packed with more shoes under there.

I got into the bathroom and pushed the door halfway shut just as I heard the apartment door open and a set of jangling keys pulled from the lock. The lights were off in the medium-size bathroom, but sunlight poured through the one window, showing a fashionable design in tile and slate. The sleek, black slate was in the walk-in shower, beyond the pristine glass doors. I mean, I've soaked the *Record* for enough $300-a-night hotels to give me a some fair standing as a designer, and I never came across anything this nice.

I slowly, silently pulled off the rubber gloves, so as to look slightly less menacing to whoever happened to catch me in there, and shoved them into my back pocket. I glanced out the window to see if there was a balcony, a fire escape, anything that would allow me to get out, but there was barely even a ledge. So I pushed my head closer to the door and listened to what was left in the proverbial store.

There were footsteps, somewhat light, like that of sneakers, moving across the floor away from the bathroom, toward the front of the apartment. It sounded like just one pair, which was a good sign, better, anyway, than half the homicide unit or a bunch of bruisers from the FBI. Why, I wondered, hadn't Sweeney called?

Then silence. Nothing. Just dead air that lasted several minutes long. I wanted nothing more than to peer through the opening of the door to see who was on the other side. Short of that, I wanted to call Sweeney out on the street and ask him who the flying hell had just come by on his watch. But I couldn't risk either. I was, in fact, in the act of committing what I think must be a felony—breaking and entering. I'm sure the Feds could add a host of other charges to it as well, like tampering with evidence, just to name one of the bigger ones.

All of which is to say, I remained still and silent and wondering. I strained so hard to hear any foreign, unusual sounds that I felt like Colin Montgomerie on the first tee of the U.S. Open. My senses, on hyperalert, caused me to take in just about every little detail of the bathroom.

On the vanity, she had a container of facial cleanser, a couple of bottles of moisturizers, a tube of some sort of hair product that was something other than mere gel, and a bunch of what I believe younger women call scrunchies—elastics to pull back her hair, in various shapes, colors and sizes. There was a bar of plain old soap, a tube of Colgate toothpaste, a single toothbrush in a white cup, and a floss dispenser. The only makeup I saw was a cylinder of lipstick. This was, as Aretha Franklin might say, a natural woman.

Still, on the other side of the door, silence. I inched closer to the opening, but didn't dare take a look. I heard the cry of a baby far outside of the bathroom window, and beyond that, the distant sound of a siren, probably that of an ambulance. But inside this apartment, just the unsteady sound of my own breathing, and even that I tried to keep quiet.

And then, footsteps again, coming from the front of the apartment to the back, where the bathroom was located, and more important, where a well-known, otherwise highly regarded reporter from one of America's truly great newspapers, remained in hiding. As my mind raced and my body braced, the sound of the steps stopped several feet away from the partially open door. Then I heard the scratch of furniture moving along the wooden floor—the chair to the painted desk where I had been a few minutes earlier, I assumed, sliding outward.

I heard a drawer open, papers being ruffled, then the drawer closing. This happened again, and again after that, and then I heard more papers being shuffled on what was probably the top of the desk. And then, once again, I heard nothing at all.

Well, almost nothing. I heard the faint sound of objects being lifted, then silence, then put back in place. And I heard what sounded like sniffling, and the sniffling turned into a low-level sobbing, which then took on the sound of someone actually convulsing in tears, shaking, crying, gulping for air, then exhaling sorrowful, uncontrollable moans. Man or woman, I didn't yet know, but if this was an FBI agent or a homicide detective, they might have been taking this newfangled victim-compassion thing a little too far.

For at least five minutes, I listened to the heart-wrenching sounds of this person gasping and crying. They blew their nose. Their cell phone rang, but they didn't answer. They just kept crying, apparently unable to pull themselves together again.

And I simply stood inside this door, leaning against a vanity, feeling both helpless and heinous, not to mention voyeuristic. At this point, it was all I could do not to cry myself, like a single cough in a movie theater setting off a fit of the same.

The person's cell phone rang again—once, twice, three times, four, and then stopped, the sound echoing around the open expanse of the apartment before disappearing into a canyon of silence. Well, not silence, but sobbing.

And then a voice. It was low, somewhat husky, obviously thickened by all those tears, jarring in a room that hadn't heard a voice in all this time. It was that of a woman, who said, "Hil. Hil. I should have been there to help you —" As she tried to continue, her words trailed off into a fresh round of tears.

The chair scratched abruptly on the wood floor. I heard a couple of abrupt steps toward the bathroom, then the door pushed quickly open as I stepped back to avoid it. Although I had many minutes to prepare for what was probably an inevitable confrontation, I hadn't thought it through. I didn't know what I was going to say. So as she looked at me and I looked at her, I held my hands up in the air in front of me and hurriedly said, "I'm not here to hurt you. My name is Jack Flynn. I'm a reporter for *The Boston Record*."

She screamed. Well, maybe it wasn't quite a scream. She yelped, one of those panicked sounds when a shocked person already under great duress doesn't exactly know what to do. I could appreciate the feeling right now.

She backed out the bathroom door. I said, firmly, but hopefully not ominously, "I'm not here to hurt you. I will leave immediately if you allow me."

I heard her sifting around for something, then saw her figure in the door again, this time with a steam iron in her right hand, which she held up as if she were going to fire it at me. Me, I don't personally use an iron. I send all my shirts to the cleaners. Now I kind of understood why. This thing looked dangerous—sharp and hard, and of course, at times, incomprehensibly hot.

"Please," I said, taking a step back against the far bathroom wall, the one with the window. "Please allow me to explain what I'm doing here. Again, my name is Jack Flynn. I'm a reporter at the *Record*. I had a story in this morning's paper about the Gardner Museum heist. When I heard about Hilary's death, I suspected she might be in some way involved, so I snuck into"—well, broke into, but this seemed an appropriate time to draw fine lines—"her apartment to find out if I was right."

We locked gazes, but I had no idea what it is that she saw. How much like Hilary Kane did she look? Enough that I had absolutely no doubt this was her sister, the same woman I saw in the photograph of moving day in front of the apartment. Same eyes, same high cheekbones, same blonde hair except this woman's was cut much shorter. And here in person, same long, lean body. I'd even call it a killer body, except right now, I'm the one she was in a position to kill. If she did, she'd even get away with it in court.

"Please," I said. "I know it's a sad and frightening time for you. I know I shouldn't be here. But I'm trying to help. Please trust me."

And still, she stood there in tears. She looked at me and I looked at her, and in the pounding silence, she slowly lowered the arm that held the iron. She said in a very husky voice, "Show me some ID. Don't make any fast moves."

I deliberately reached into my front pocket and pulled out the kind of press card that old-style reporters used to wear tucked into the front of their hats. I held it toward her in my left hand, and she took a step closer and took it from me.

With communication established, which in my business is almost always a good thing, I said, "I can give you a business card. It's in my wallet. My wallet is in a car across the street."

She looked carefully at the laminated *Record* ID card in her hand, then up at my face through her teary eyes, then back down at my picture, which, I should point out, wasn't a particularly flattering one. I vividly recall that Elizabeth and I had a heated argument that morning, and an hour later there I was standing before a white backdrop, snap, snap, getting shot.

"How did you get in?" she asked.

There are basically two types of people in life: Those who hate reporters, and, well, those who don't. The haters, they're not always rational people, I've found, or for that matter, particularly likable. Ask them what they so disdain about the news media and they'll tell you we're all a bunch of lying, parasitic, sensationalistic pigs sucking off the body public. So what's their point?

Actually, they're likely to say all this with a rolled-up copy of a tabloid newspaper in their hands, or with plans to get home and watch that ever soothing 11 o'clock news. They hate us, but they watch and read us. They hate us because that's just what they do in life, and we've given them too many good reasons for it. Turn on the TV news and we're inevitably pictured as an unwieldy horde hollering stupid questions to politicians or criminals—sometimes one and the same—who conveniently ignore us until they hear an inquiry that suits their needs. Cop shows portray us as bumbling nuisances insensitive to anyone or anything but our own dead-lines. And the haters, lemmings, just go along, thoughtlessly, hating us because they think that's what they're supposed to do.

But then there are others who get it, those who understand that the vast majority of reportage is a solitary endeavor important to the public realm, not to mention the public good. At our best, we provide the public information that it should have, or need to have, or want to have, and on our best days, all three at once. We shine attention on politicians, business leaders, and other notables who go wrong. We keep countless others right out of the simple fear of landing on the front page of the *Record's* next issue. We do it seven days a week, fifty-two weeks a year, every year for as long as I've been alive, and that's not about to change.

Do we make mistakes? God yes. Do we occasionally embarrass ourselves? Yes again. But in sum and substance, we are a crucial contributor to the common cause, and smart people, most people, recognize that fact free and clear.

Now let me dismount from my high horse and try to figure out on which side of the chasm the striking blonde with the iron proficiency will stand.

"I broke in," I replied.

"Why?"

"Because I think I might have been used. Because I was afraid that something I wrote, something somebody leaked to me for this morning's newspaper, might have caused Hilary Kane to be killed. I needed to find out right away, rather than wait for some official statement from the cops that probably wouldn't tell me nearly what I needed to know." I added, "So I broke in. It's wrong. It's against the law. It's an invasion of privacy. I understand all that. But I needed to find out what went wrong, and I needed to find out if I caused it."

There was a long pause as I stopped talking, and she simply looked at me.

"You did," she finally said, and with that, she turned around and walked out the bathroom door. I heard her footsteps keep going. I heard the apartment door open, then close. She was gone, but my reporter's instincts, already in overdrive, told me it wouldn't be for long.

Chapter Eight

It was the teeth of the lunch hour, so to speak, when an unapologetic Hank Sweeney—"I just assumed she lived in the building"—and I breezed through the front door of the University Club and took a table in the far corner of the half-filled dining room.

This wasn't the leisurely, wine-soaked lunch that the other diners—mostly stockbrokers and institutional investors who already had the flavor of the day's Dow—were sharing. I needed information and I needed some counsel, and I needed it fast. The clock was pounding toward 1:00 P.M., an hour when all good reporters already had a rough draft of the next day's story in the computer monitor of their minds. Me, I had only questions to ask of people I hadn't yet called, as well as a sense of gloomy guilt so large and ominous it could envelope an oversize cow.

Still, I'm not a good reporter. I'm a great one. Just ask me. Which is why the passage of time didn't bother me as much as it did, say, Peter Martin, who kept ringing my cell phone approximately every nine seconds, no doubt, in his words, to find out where the flying frick I might be and did I have the time in my busy day to bother writing a follow-up story about the biggest theft in the history of the fricking world?

Or something like that. I couldn't be sure of the exact verbiage because I didn't answer the calls. I'd get to him soon enough.

My favorite waitress, Pam, glided over to the table with menus and I pointed at Hank, who, by the way, was the only black in the room not carrying a tray or wearing an apron, and said, "Burger?" He nodded, looked at Pam and said, "Medium, please."

"Same," I said, and added, "And bring a third one for our late-arriving friend, rare, with extra everything. And we're in something of a rush, Pam."

As if he sensed a countdown toward good food, Vinny Mongillo appeared in the distant doorway, spotted us without trouble, and sauntered through the room like he owned it, even stopping and chatting with a couple of the more familiar captains of industry along the way. It makes no sense that a man of his considerable girth can actually saunter, and yet he does, he does. He makes every motion seem so natural, right down to the clap he gave me on the side of my shoulder as he said, "Jesus, Fair Hair, your voice-mail was so dire it made it sound like one of the mean third-graders stole your Halle Berry lunchbox."

I ignored that, which I do with so much of what Mongillo says. He exchanged greetings with Sweeney, calling him, unless I heard wrong, "Brother Hank."

I said to Mongillo, without elaboration or any need for it, "Spill. I need everything you know and everything you suspect on the Kane murder."

He shook his head, not in a way that denied my request, but more like how a kitchen contractor immediately searches out the negative in even the simplest undertaking. "You want a faucet in your sink? Oh, boy, I don't know, especially with the way the tile is cut and the pipes are shaped and the light fixture hangs down." And then he comes up with an answer that he knew all along.

Vinny's like that as well. He always has the answer. He just wants to make sure you know the obstacles he overcame to get it.

So here we go. "You want to talk tight-lipped," he began. "Jesus mother of an unforgiving Christ. The press release was a total of one paragraph. One. The homicide cops never came over to the tape to talk to us hacks. The briefing at headquarters lasted all of two-and-a-half minutes, and involved the commissioner reading a statement that said nothing and walking away from the podium without answering any questions."

I glanced over at Sweeney, retired homicide lieutenant with the Boston PD, and he seemed enraptured by his view from the other side, actually leaning over the table, his big chin resting on the back of his right hand. He wasn't completely familiar with the whole Mongillo extravaganza quite yet and this probably wasn't the time to warn him.

Mongillo kept talking as Pam filled our water glasses and placed a basket of bread on the table.

"Here's what they want you to know," he said. "They want you to know that the victim's name is Hilary Kane. She's twenty-nine years old. She's a lawyer for the city. She was shot once in the temple and once in the back of the head as she sat in the driver's seat of her car, a 2002 Saab 9-3 four-door. She was dead virtually immediately." He paused here for effect, then added, "And the police, of course, also want you to know that they're pursuing numerous leads."

That last bit is a line, and a rather ridiculous one, written into the end of every police press release. I looked back over at Sweeney, who seemed to take no offense.

Mongillo reached over for a hunk of bread, spread a heaping wad of butter on it like it was good for him, and took a longing bite. After he chewed for a moment, he said, "Here's what the police don't want you to know." And with that, he looked at the two of us conspiratorially.

"They don't want you to know that they're in some bizarre shit-fight with the FBI over the evidence in this thing. The city beat the Feds to the girl's apartment by about an hour, then they argued so hard about where the evidence should go that bosses had to be called in from both sides. My understanding is that there's a U.S. attorney preparing to walk into U.S. District Court by three this afternoon seeking a temporary restraining order against Boston PD from mucking with any materials, meaning possible evidence, pulled from the victim's apartment."

Mongillo paused for another bite of bread. I took the opportunity to pose a question, the answer to which I already pretty well knew, at least partially. Or maybe not. "Why the hell is the Bureau getting involved in a local murder?" I asked.

Mongillo looked at me in that way an impatient teenager might look at his tagalong little brother.

"Gee, good question. You ever thought about being a reporter?"

Luckily, the hamburgers arrived at that exact moment, and any prospect of tension gave way to the joys of gastronomy—and believe me, with Hank Sweeney and Vinny Mongillo involved, virtually any gastronomy is a joyous occasion, and when the food is on someone else's tab, namely mine, it's nearly transcendental.

Mongillo took a monstrous bite into his burger, chewed methodically, then said, "It's the question of the hour. I've got about two dozen calls out on it. I'm not getting any answers back, at least not yet, anyway. Obviously, either the victim or a suspect that we don't yet know about is in some way linked to a federal case."

Yeah, the Gardner Museum heist. So I told him, in utmost confidence, of my visit to her apartment that afternoon. Sweeney sat there eating, taking it all in.

When I was done with my soliloquy, Mongillo looked at me bemused and said, "A B&E on Beacon Hill. Christ almighty, Fair Hair's turning into quite the bad boy."

As he made reference to my lawbreaking ways, I felt my insides begin to churn, until I realized it was actually my cellular telephone vibrating in the breast pocket of my jacket. I glanced at the number—Peter Martin's, again—and ignored it.

I shook my head sadly and said, "I wish I could laugh about it. The fact is, I think I caused an innocent person to die."

Vinny was midbite as I said this. He stared at me as he chewed, and when he was done, he said in an uncharacteristically soft tone, "You're serious, aren't you?"

I nodded. "Unfortunately, I am."

"Tell Vinny."

"I'm not sure yet what there is to say. I get leaked information, spoon-fed, really, by a senior government official I'd never previously met. I get it into the paper under the crush of deadline. I wake up the next day and a lawyer with the city, a young woman, is shot dead in the Boston Common garage. Sorry, Vinny, but I don't believe in coincidence. I work for a newspaper. I'm not allowed to. That story triggered something, and in this case, it was a gun."

Vinny shoved a couple of Chef Kelly's handcut French fries into his mouth, which inexplicably made me wonder why chefs get this lyrical little title that precedes only their first name. Reporter Jack. I just can't picture it.

Vinny was quiet. Check that. He wasn't speaking, he was chewing, which is anything but quiet. I looked at Hank, who stared back knowingly at me, though what he knew I wasn't sure right then. In the absence of anything else, I said, "I may have caused a young woman's murder."

That hung out there like a storm cloud before a hard rain. It hung out there until Hank audibly cleared his throat and said, "Jack, if all this worst-case scenario jazz is right, you didn't cause anyone to die. You didn't leak the story. You didn't pull the trigger. You don't know what the story behind the story really is."

I replied, in a sharper tone than I intended, "So what you're saying is that I was probably just used."

Hank nodded.

I pounded my closed fist on the table, so that the plate with my mostly uneaten hamburger rattled against my water glass, and a few of the nearby diners, fearing some rapid downturn in the NASDAQ, reached in unison for the Palm V's to check the latest numbers.

Hank Sweeney had just given voice to my unspoken fears, and I looked at him hard and all but hissed, "That's worse. That's much worse. I'm too good to be used. I've been doing this too fucking long to be used. I'm supposed to use people. I'm not supposed to be the one who's used—especially not in the death of a young woman."

Vinny started to say something and I cut him off, looking from one to the other, then out into an empty expanse of dining room at nothing at all.

"I've invested my adult life, my entire career, my very sense of identity, in pursuit of the truth. Sometimes it's unpleasant. Sometimes it gets downright nasty. Sometimes the truth isn't anything that you ever want to have anything more than a passing familiarity with. But still, you have to learn it. We have to let the public know it. Even at its worst, it's a bedrock, an immovable foundation, a place from which to build or mend.

"And now, by doing what I've always done, believing what I've always believed in, I might have caused someone to die. I pursued truth, and Hilary Kane is dead. So tell me this: How do I ever justify what I do for a living now?"

Silence, at least at our table. In the background, you could hear the idle chatter of the working rich as they bade each other fond farewells until the evening cocktail hour would bring them together, perhaps in the very same place.

I looked at Hank, who stared complacently back at me. As we did this, it was Mongillo who absently pushed his plate a few inches toward the middle of our table and said, "Suppose you have it inside-out, Jack." He paused here for a moment and we locked in on each other's gaze. "Suppose," he said, "that you didn't print the truth at all?"

Did someone just pull the pin on an old-fashioned hand grenade? His words seemed to explode across the linen tablecloth, through the thick bone that needlessly protected my brain, and into that tiny part of my body, my nature, that occasionally commits an act called thought.

"Suppose," Mongillo continued, knowing full well he was on something of a roll here, "that you were used so bad that it wasn't even with truth, but with lies."

I didn't know whether to throttle him or hug him. I didn't know whether to embrace what he was saying, or be repulsed by it. I didn't know which was better, or more accurately, worse: to have the truth lead to someone's death, or to have been set up with a deadly lie.

I felt my phone vibrate again, and then I felt it stop. I felt a pit in my stomach, and then I felt it go away. I felt all eyes staring directly at me, then I felt like I was very much alone. More than anything else, I felt the need to peel back the layers, to uncover the deceptions, to clarify the distortions, to confront the lies in search of an immovable truth.

"I need your help," I said, hitting the edge of the table with my open hand, softly, not hard. As I said this, I looked from Mongillo to Sweeney. Each of them looked back at me and solemnly nodded.

"Someone's going to pay," Mongillo said, "And I want to be there to collect."

Spoken like, well, Mongillo.

Sweeney said, "I've got more time than a turtle crossing the Mojave."

Speaking of time, I checked my cell phone and saw it was close to 1:30 P.M., close to panic time for ordinary reporters.

"Thank you," I said to each one of them, more sincere than I usually sound, which probably isn't hard. "Then this would be the point in the life of a story when we make a plan."

Right then, the nattily dressed Jason Buick, the appropriately obsequious manager of the club, approached our table with an air of apologetic urgency, as well as a cordless telephone.

"Jack, sorry to interrupt, but I've got a call here from a Mr. Peter Martin, who says he has an important news matter to discuss with you."

"Mr. Peter Martin thinks that a change in the weather is an important news matter."

"I heard that," Martin said when I put the phone up to my ear.

"How are you, Peter?"

"I might be better if my best reporter might take a fricking moment and answer his fricking cell phone when I call him on it to talk about the biggest story in the nation today. Short of that, I'm not doing all that fricking well."

I hate the word frick, by the way. I mean, be a newsman. Just say the real thing.

"I've been in meetings."

That last line came out weak, the tone even weaker than the words. Reporters don't go to meetings, at least this reporter, though I did meet the victim's sister, or at least someone who I believed to be the sister, at the apartment. I was meeting Mongillo and Sweeney at the time of the call.

Martin said, his words and voice less accusatory: "I've got all hell breaking loose." He paused for a flicker of a moment, then added, "And not just in the usual way." That's Martin's code for: Jack, listen closely.

"Go ahead," I said.

"I got a call a short time ago, a few minutes, maybe five minutes. It was from a young woman. She sounded really afraid, but coherent, not frantic or anything. She said she had tried to call you several times but only got your voicemail. So she called the switchboard looking for you. Barbara tried you on your cell phone, but you didn't pick up. She thought the call sounded important, so she sent the woman to me."

Barbara has an eye for news like Dean Martin had a taste for whiskey. She runs what's known as the *Record*'s message center, sitting behind a big, circular panel in the front of the newsroom, answering phones, sending out pages, patching calls through to reporters traveling out of state and abroad. She hears sob stories from the public, tales of utter woe and incomprehensible tragedy. Then she makes sense of them, either blocking liars or searching out reporters for the callers who she believes are telling important truths. All this is to say, I listened even harder now.

Martin continued, "So the woman says to me that she's in danger, that someone is stalking her. I'm thinking, yeah, give me a piece of news there, honey. Then she says, 'I can't go to the police. I need to speak to Jack Flynn. He'll know why.'"

My mind was racing at a million miles an hour, but the problem was, my thoughts weren't heading anywhere in particular. I didn't know a stalking victim. I didn't know anyone who couldn't take their problems to the police. Before I could say anything, Martin added, almost as punctuation, "She said to tell you that this morning's situation never really got ironed out."

Get it? My sister; well, not my sister. Either one of my sisters would have clocked me with the iron and asked questions when I came to at Mass General Hospital. But the sister, Hilary's sister, the one who could have put me out of my misery but instead chose only to add to it. Maybe she knew what she was doing after all.

So I got not only attentive, but deadly serious, pardon the overuse of the adjective. "How'd you leave it?" I asked, unable to conceal my urgency. "Where'd she say she was?"

"Wouldn't tell me. She said she'd only deal through you. So she gave me a number that she said was to a pay phone and she told me to have you call it at exactly 1:45 P.M."

Martin read me the number. My first thought was that some pay phones, maybe most pay phones, don't take incoming calls. Martin being Martin, he said to me, "I told her, most pay phones don't take incoming calls. He'll try to call, but he may not get through. So she took down your cell phone number. If she doesn't hear from you by 1:50, she said she'd call."

A pause, as I collected myself and read the number back in my mind. Martin added, "So you may want to answer your fricking phone."

Touché.

I hung up. Mongillo and Sweeney had not only ordered dessert, but the ever-efficient Pam had just delivered it. I told them I had to run—an emergency, a possible break in the story. I'd let them know what happened as soon as it did.

Mongillo looked at me with unabashed concern. "Are you still going to sign the lunch away?" he asked, fully cognizant—as well as appreciative—of the University Club's policy of no cash transactions. I nodded. Sweeney looked at me with equal concern. "You want me to come along?" he asked. To that, I shook my head.

Many, many years ago, I used to think the most important woman in the world was my mother, and later, it was, of course, my wife. More recently, it was Elizabeth, but it was a feeling that was fading faster than I knew how to explain. Walking out the dining-room door, it occurred to me that this woman, at least for now, at least for a while, had become the most important woman I knew. It was yet another one of my finely honed reporter's premonitions that was to become sometimes painfully and occasionally blissfully true.

Chapter Nine

She answered the phone on the first ring with an abrupt, "Yeah," though given the situation, the grieving, the fear, the unknown, I excused her obvious and understandable lack of etiquette.

"This is Jack Flynn," I said, trying to sound calm, reassuring, more confident than I was in the bathroom when faced with the prospect of a Sunbeam iron across the upside of my handsome head.

"I know," she replied. Her voice was taut. She wasn't being rude, just concise, as if she didn't have the emotional capacity just then to say much more.

I was standing on St. James Street, my cell phone planted against my left ear, pacing back and forth along the brick façade of the University Club. She was on a pay phone at an undisclosed location, though I immediately knew she was hard by a busy street because of the noise from the loud traffic that threatened to overwhelm her voice.

"Tell me your name, who you are, and what I can do for you," I said, still trying to sound confident and competent, not always an easy trick to pull off, especially in my current state.

She hesitated on the other end of the phone. I heard the revving engine of a truck gaining speed as it passed her, telling me that she was at an intersection, probably with a traffic light. I heard the beep of a thin horn, like on one of those tinny Asian imports that come from countries like Korea that you associate more with madmen than cars. I heard muffled voices in the near background, perhaps people at the same bank of pay phones.

"I'm being followed," she said, responding to precisely none of my questions. She threw that line out there as if it were a dart, simple, direct, and more than anything else, pointed.

"How do you know?"

"I was so shaken after I saw you in the apartment that I pulled over on Beacon Street because I thought I was having an anxiety attack. I could barely see. I was hyperventilating. And this car that was behind me pulled over a little ways in front of me. When I pulled out, the car pulled out. So I went around the block, like they do in the movies, just drove a nonsensical route, and he followed me all the way."

"Where are you now, and is he still following you?"

"I don't know. I'm at a pay phone, obviously. I double-parked in the street. I haven't seen his car, but I assume he's out here somewhere. I'm just trying to stay around other people so he can't get to me."

I tried asking the most important question again in the same exact way. No sense in playing tricks on her: "I need to know, where are you now?"

"I told you, at a pay phone, in Boston. I can't tell you any more. I'm too afraid."

And at that moment, she truly sounded it, her voice becoming even more strained with fear, that fear nearly spilling over into a fit of emotion.

I said, trying to sound less like the inquisitive, opportunistic reporter that I am and more like the stable presence that I can occasionally be, "I want to help you. You tell me who you are."

Again, silence from the other end, but this time not the result of her putting herself back together, but rather gauging whether it would be wise to provide me, a newspaper reporter, with this kind of information. That silence rounded the corner toward an eternity before she said, "I'm Hilary's sister, Maggie." And she left it at that.

I said, "If you feel threatened, why don't you go to the authorities—the police or the FBI or somebody?" Truth is, I'd rather have her come to me, because once she was in the hands of detectives, I'd probably lost any shot at getting any decent information out of her. Police disdain the same public realm that I thrive in, for a lot of logical reasons, and some rather illogical ones as well.

But the greater truth was, I felt like I'd already caused the death of her sister, and wasn't exactly of the mood or mind to be cavalier with her life next. So I added, "They could protect you."

She laughed a rueful laugh, her mouth pressed hard against the phone, and replied, "Yeah, just like they did with Hil."

I calculated that last comment in a gathering silence. Then I heard bells go off, not around me, not on the phone, but in my own head, like the ceremonial opening ring of the New York Stock Exchange. Information was starting to come in.

"Tell me what you mean by that," I said, trying to maintain the veneer of control.

As she began to reply, an ambulance hurtled toward me on Stuart Street, it's blaring siren echoing off the ancient stone buildings and smacking against the sleek glass side of the John Hancock Tower. She was talking, but I couldn't hear her, so I said, trying to control my frustration, "Hold on, I can't get what you're saying." Then I added, "Is there any chance we can just get together?"

Again, I heard her voice in the phone, but not the words formed by it. At that moment, the Boston Emergency Medical Services ambulance streamed past me and took a right on Trinity Place, heading toward Copley Square. As the blare faded, I said to her, "I'm sorry, I couldn't hear a word you were saying."

And then I heard it again, the siren, and angrily looked down the street to see if another one was on the way, or perhaps a fire truck racing to the scene of a disastrous crash. But my street was barren now—no ambulance, no fire truck, not even any traffic, really.

The siren, I realized, was coming through the other end of the phone. Unless my ears and all that empty space between them were playing tricks on me, Maggie Kane was standing somewhere in Copley Square, less than a few hundred yards from where I was then.

So with the phone up to my ear, I began walking, first tentatively, then quickly. I moved fast around the corner, down Trinity Place toward the square, somewhere between a stride and a jog. Still, I heard the ambulance in the phone, and as I got closer to Trinity Church, the live blare filled my other ear as well. Any reporter worth the ink in their Bic Click has been accused of being an ambulance chaser at some point in their illustrious career; I will say, though, I don't think even the best of them has taken the concept quite this literally.

But Maggie Kane was around here. She was near me, and I needed to find her.

I arrived on the grassy stretch of the Copley Square park, panting slightly like Baker might and scanning intently around in search of any public phones. Because of the sirens, Maggie couldn't speak, or if she did, I couldn't hear her. The sounds of the ambulance faded, both in the phone and in my open ear, and I looked across the park, onto Boylston Street, and saw the tail end of the actual vehicle vanish down the block. I wonder if she heard what I heard in the phone, if she put sound and sound together and came up with the possibility of discovery.

I said to her, trying to catch my breath, "Look, Maggie, I really want to help you, but I can't if you insist on hiding from me."

She replied, in a voice even more shell-shocked than before, "Jack, I don't know what to do." And then there was silence— actual silence, without so much as the siren, which was fine, because it provided the opportunity for exploration. I set off across the park in search of a pay phone and the woman on it.

"She's dead," she said, her words now dissolving into tears. "Hil's dead. Someone killed her. Now they might kill me."

"I can help you," I said. The problem with pay phones is they tend to fade into the cityscape. We tend to just assimilate them, overlook them, see right through them.

I crossed Boylston Street and jogged east along the wide sidewalk, past the Copy Cop, the CVS, the various financial institutions with nonsensically spelled and descriptively meaningless names like BancNorth. I kept my mouth shut tight and breathed only through my nose so she wouldn't hear me straining. And I searched, as hard as my eyes would allow me, boring into the buildings and the crystal clear autumn air that marked another September afternoon.

I saw a homeless man, gray-haired and bearded, pushing a grocery cart filled with plastic bags of beer cans. I saw men by the dozens in business suits returning from another expense account lunch. I saw women young and old darting about during a lunch hour filled with the routine administration of their busy and sometimes difficult lives. But no Maggie Kane.

"How am I supposed to trust anyone?" she asked. She asked this sincerely, like she wanted an answer, needed an answer, before we could consummate any relationship or deal.

I said, "You need to tell me who your sister trusted. That will help us find out who killed her."

My eyes raced around the sidewalk, even as I stood frozen in silent agony. More men and women in suits. More kids in loose jeans. Another homeless guy, this one lugging a torn trash bag over his right shoulder.

And then I saw it. No, not Maggie Kane. That would be too easy, too ordinary. I could have just walked up to her and said, "Maggie, hi, it's Jack. We met at your sister's place. Yeah, that's right, in the bathroom. I'd really like to help you." We could have walked up the street to the Starbucks, had ourselves a nice cup of coffee, maybe some biscotti, and she could have explained to me in minute detail all that she knew about her sister's life and what she suspected was the cause of her death, and I could then have taken that information and put it on the front page of the next day's *Record* and brought an end to the tragedy that was overwhelming my otherwise perfectly pleasant career.

But no, it wasn't her that I saw, not at first, anyway. What I saw was a dark green sedan double-parked on the north side of Boylston Street. I saw it because the rear driver's-side window was rolled down, and a metal object barely protruding from it caught the afternoon sun in such a way that the gleam seemed to poke me in the eye. I realized it was some sort of scope, and below the scope I saw the long, black barrel of a rifle, and I followed in the direction of the rifle, across the sidewalk, and saw nothing but passersby making their merry way to places unknown.

But beyond the sidewalk, I saw the shiny glass front of a store, a bagel store called Finagle-a-Bagel, to be more specific, and through the reflecting glass, I noticed the hazy outlines of a female form leaning on a wall with a telephone up to her ear. And thus I found Maggie Kane.

"I think I'm just going to run, to get the hell out of Boston for a while. Maybe I'll call you from wherever I go." That was her, still talking into the phone, having no idea of what was unfolding outside. The door to the store was propped open, which explained the street noise and the ambulance silence. There were a few customers flitting in and out. The situation, the scenario, the utter unlikelihood of a rifle here in Copley Square, of a woman talking to me on the verge of death, took a moment to register, and once it did, the next few seconds seemed to unfold in that proverbial slow motion, though rapidly so.

I yelled into the phone, "Duck, Maggie. Duck!" To emphasize that I wasn't just some proselytizing member of the Audubon Society seeking to fill our ranks, I hollered, "Hit the floor!"

I don't know if she followed orders or not, because the next thing I did was pull the phone away from my ear and fire it in the direction of the car. Now's as good a time as any to relive the past, so I want to remind anyone and everyone that it was a scant few decades before that I pitched a no-hitter in Little League, and a talent that immense doesn't fade all that fast. I'd also like to note that this wasn't the first time I threw a telephone in what seemed to be a life or death situation. A few years before, in the Washington bureau of *The Boston Record*, I struck a derelict FBI agent named Kent Drinker in the wrist with a desk phone that had never before made such an important connection, but more on that topic some other time.

I watched the mobile phone scream through the twenty feet of afternoon air between me and that green car. I think I was still on the line with Maggie Kane when I made the throw, and the thought briefly occurred to me that the phone might end up inside the car, Maggie might fall to the ground in escape, the car might drive off, and I might get a cell phone bill for about five thousand Benjamins because no one on either end ever bothered to hang up. I'd like to see Peter Martin's reaction to that.

Instead, the phone struck the scope dead-on, not to use that word too loosely here. I saw the gun twitch to the right. I heard it fire, the report thundering off the walls of the nearby buildings and echoing back onto the street. People screamed. Some ran; others dropped to the ground, everyone no doubt believing they were amid one of the biggest nightmares of modern America: the mass murder. Six dead, two injured, gunman commits suicide. Film at 11.

I glanced over at the store and saw that the bullet had taken out a plate glass window many feet to the right of where Maggie Kane had stood. I tore after the car, which was in the process of pulling back into traffic. I was running off the curb and into the street when the driver leaned on his horn and accelerated through the intersection. The image of me as roadkill flickered into my mind, and then out. I grabbed the last three figures off the license plate—JF1, as in Jack Flynn has the number one arm—and ran another thirty or so yards down Boylston Street until I couldn't see the car anymore.

I jogged back to the bagel shop, sweating like a hog in heat by now. All the customers, all the staff, were gathered on the sidewalk, some in tears, others in small groups talking among themselves while they waited for the television cameras to arrive and make them famous, if only for the night. I walked through and among the groups, looking for Maggie, then around them, and then I scanned the sidewalk and park on the other side of the street, but saw nothing of consequence. I asked a few people if they saw a pretty woman with short blonde hair leave the scene, but no one had. When they realized I had no microphone or klieg lights, their interest seemed to wane significantly.

It was then that I heard the familiar ring of my cell phone and reflexively reached into my back pocket to answer it. But the ring came not from immediately behind me, but from a short distance in front. My phone, sitting in the gutter, was chiming, and I immediately thought of Maggie Kane, standing at a nearby pay phone, urgently trying to reach me.

I bolted toward the sound, saw my severely dented phone resting atop an empty, bleached-out Doritos bag, and answered it. I mean, I was on what Verizon calls the "Do Anything plan," but I had no idea it allowed me to literally throw my phone around. God bless Japanese engineering.

"Finally, you pick the frick up." It was the annoyed and annoying voice of Peter Martin. Let's quickly review: I think I'm responsible for a woman's death. I just saved another woman's life. I chased a murderer down one of the main avenues of downtown Boston. And Peter Martin, sitting in his comfortable office over at the *Record,* is severely put out because I haven't answered the phone every six minutes when he's been on the other line.

I bit my tongue, and my lip, and the inside of my cheeks. Finally, I said, "I've had a few things going on."

Martin replied, his tone now one of complete sincerity, "You're going to want to get over here, and fast. There's a hand-delivered package sitting at your desk, and if it's what I think it is, all hell is about to break loose."

"What? What is it?"

With that, the phone made some funny squawking sound, like two horses mating on a Wyoming ranch, and went completely dead. When I pressed the On button again, the battery fell loose in my hand. Goddamn Japanese engineering.

As the sound of sirens filled the air all over Copley Square, I stepped off the curb, flagged a cab, and headed for the newsroom.

I was alone, and so was Maggie Kane, and somewhere in the city, a killer was on the loose with a motive that I didn't yet know.

Chapter Ten

I occasionally wonder what it would be like to walk through the sleek lobby of a downtown office tower every morning, ride the elevator to, say, the twenty-eighth floor, and report to work in a windowless cubicle at a job in which the tomorrows are indistinguishable from the todays. A bad day at the office is when the markets dip in the triple figures or that surefire client decides to take his business to Acme Whatever down the street. A good day is when your best stock announces a split or when you lock down a sale you never really expected to make. It's a tribute to the human psyche that you're able to contain the euphoric onslaught of unmitigated joy.

Truth be known, it's why I went into newspapers—that and the fact that my father worked for the *Record* as a pressman and newspapering is the only business that I have ever known. As a reporter, you can be sitting at Fenway Park one moment watching the Red Sox make an improbable journey toward the pennant, and the next moment, you're being led by a pride of hairy thugs to a meeting with one of the most senior law enforcement officials in the city—all in the name of front-page news. You can challenge authority at will, make even presidents sweat, and tell people, regular, normal, God-fearing people, that which they would never otherwise know. All this, and no license required.

And yet, on days like this one, I looked longingly on those downtown towers, pining for the relative predictability and obscurity contained within—at your desk by 8:30, out by 5:00, all aboard the 6:07 to Wellesley Farms. Honey, sorry I'm one-and-a-half minutes late, but Mr. Talksalot wouldn't let me go.

By way of explanation, my situation: One young woman dead, another likely on her way, an editor informing me that, in his words, all hell was set to break loose, and a colleague espousing an uncannily insightful theory involving my utter imbecility. And of course, add to this the fact that my fabulously intelligent and beautiful live-in girlfriend, one Elizabeth Riggs, was at that hour home packing her belongings to depart not just my house, but I suspect, my life.

"Tell Agent Jankle, please, that I am planning to post a story on our website very soon about the murder of a young woman in Boston that I think he will be very interested in."

That was me, essentially lying to Special Agent Tom Jankle's secretary. Look, someone was obviously lying to me about something, so I'm not going to sit back and be purer than a virgin snow. I was in the taxi, talking on the cabbie's cell phone that he was nice enough to loan me because he knows I'm Jack Flynn and the urgent business of daily journalism never takes so much as a momentary break.

Well, actually, a loan might be something that would happen in St. Louis or Denver. This being Boston, I was paying to use it for the duration of the ride. And Jack Flynn, Jack Ass, no difference to him. He didn't understand English when I initially inquired, but became well versed in the intricacies of capitalism when I pulled out a crisp $20 bill.

Anyway, the particularly ornery woman on the other end of the line seemed unimpressed. "Even if he cared," she told me in a tone so dismissive it made me more jealous than angry, "I couldn't reach him at the moment anyway. He's on a flight right now to Washington."

Ding, ding, ding. That, ladies and gentlemen, would be news

we've just spotted there. Washington, D.C. is, last I checked, capital of the United States of America, home of, among other things, the White House, and more pertinent to the situation, the headquarters of the FBI. Someone wanted to see Jankle about something—and quickly. I punched out a couple of more numbers on the rented phone, tossing out lines to FBI officials I knew in Boston and Washington. That done, I placed a call to my condominium, to see how Elizabeth was faring, but got only the voice machine.

The phone rang in my hand and, without thinking, I answered it with my usual, "Flynn here." A raspy voice on the other end of the line began a machine-gun-fire conversation in a language I had never before heard. I handed the phone up to the driver in the headdress and tunic.

I leaned back and closed my eyes and listened to his end of the indecipherable conversation and thought about how big this world we live in really is. This driver had fled his homeland, perhaps leaving a family behind, to journey across an enormous ocean to the mysterious shores of America, all in the name of freedom. Perhaps it was political freedom, perhaps financial. Didn't matter, he had set out in a brave search for a better way in another part of the globe.

So if this world around us was so big, then why, I wondered in my current state of exhausted angst, did mine seem so suddenly small? Everywhere I looked, there were walls of misery and an impenetrable haze of helplessness. I thought of Hilary Kane's parents, probably planning her burial. I thought of desperate Maggie Kane running for her life. I thought of Elizabeth, home sadly packing up her things, maybe drying the inevitable tears that streamed down her cheeks on the top of Baker's soft head. Everyone and everything seemed to be going away.

Before I came to terms with any of it, the car stopped. I opened my eyes and saw the familiar and sometimes friendly front doors of the *Record*. The driver said, "$18.75." With tip and the phone bill, the ride cost me $45. As Martin would probably point out, it wasn't so long ago that you could fly from Boston to Washington on People's Express for about the same amount. But no matter. Time now to head inside and peer into the looseness of a broken hell.

As I strode through the newsroom, I could see Martin pacing along a distant aisle, his head down, his hands moving as if he were carrying on a conversation with himself, which he probably was. I stopped at the reception desk and asked Barbara, my surrogate mother and the chief gatekeeper of all things *Record*, if she could see her way to finding me a replacement phone.

"Honey, I don't know which looks worse, you or this Nokia," she said in her thick South Boston accent when I handed it over. I tried to think of a witty response, but that rather large part of my brain had apparently ceased to function, though hopefully not for good.

When I got to my desk, Martin was already standing there, accompanied by Edgar Sullivan, the paper's longtime director of security—and when I say longtime, I'm talking in multiples of decades. Edgar couldn't catch a cold these days, never mind a thief, but he's always been our security director, thus he always will be our security director until the day that he decides not to be, which is just one more reason why I loved this newspaper so.

I said, "All right, Edgar, you've got me. I refilled my Coke in the cafeteria last week and forgot to pay."

Edgar, a longtime friend, laughed an appreciative laugh and replied, "Up against the desk, Jack. Don't make this hard on either one of us."

Martin, ever impatient and equally humorless, said simply, "Why don't we turn off the laugh track while we get down to business."

And business, I suspected, was this rather large tube wrapped in brown butcher's paper that sat propped against my desk, with an envelope taped to the top that said in handwritten letters, "Jack Flynn."

We all looked at it together, silently, until Edgar said, "I already scanned it once downstairs, through a machine, but I brought the handheld up with me to show you it was safe." And with that, he produced a portable magnetometer that he flicked on and casually waved around the perimeter of the package.

Around the room, reporters were openly peering in our direction. Some had actually wandered by to watch. Subtlety isn't a trait of even good journalists. Martin, standing directly beside me, rubbed his hands together and said, "Let's have a go."

Not quite yet. Edgar pulled a pair of latex gloves from the breast pocket of his ancient and wrinkled blue blazer, and handed me a second pair of the same. "I'd advise that you wear these, Jack," he said in his soft, gravelly voice. "We might be dealing with important evidence here."

Indeed, we might. Now's as good a time as any to note that this would be the exact kind of package in which a painting might be shipped, which had been Martin's unstated point since he reached me on the phone in Copley Square. You don't need Carl Bernstein kicking around the newsroom to know when news might be about to hit us flush in the face.

Finally, Edgar, who had already exhibited more knowledge of protocol than I ever would have imagined that he had, gently pulled the envelope off the package and handed it to me, unopened. He then pulled a letter opener out of his coat pocket—what the hell else does he keep in there?—and said, "Keep it as intact as you can."

And I did, which wasn't easy, given how many sets of eyes were on me. It was about four o'clock, rounding the corner from the casual ease of another newspapering afternoon to the full tension of deadline. But everyone in the room seemed to have nothing but time.

I pulled the note out, sat down in my chair, and read.

"It's real," it said in the same crude, almost childlike handwriting that was on the envelope. "We have the others." And then, in a direct quote from what the thieves told the Gardner Museum security guards that night, the note concluded, "Tell them they'll be hearing from us." It wasn't signed, as these things usually aren't. It just ended, unceremoniously so, right there.

I turned around to show Martin, but he had already read the entire thing over my shoulder.

I began rereading the brief note, when Martin said in a tone as taut as a rope, "Open it." He knew, I knew, what was very well inside.

I reached for the tube, when Edgar put up his wrinkled hand and said, "Let me do it." My old friend Edgar was suddenly equal parts Dirty Harry and Sherlock Holmes. He flipped a box cutter out of his breast pocket and, like a surgeon, cut the paper wrapper off the tube in one precise stroke of his gloved hands. He pulled off the top and handed me the package.

I reached inside and pulled out a heavy piece of scrolled paper and handed Edgar the empty tube. It had the odor of age to it, of history, something significant that had been passed through the years, studied by scholars, and in this case, perhaps hidden for too long in a dark corner of a distant safe. I pushed the old newspapers and used legal pads and assorted books off the top of my desk and unfurled the canvas. Before I could fully synthesize that which I saw, I heard the familiar voice of Vinny Mongillo, who must have arrived on the scene with uncharacteristic silence, utter the following memorable words: "Holy fucking fuck."

I was looking at what seemed to be an oil painting, though in truth, how the hell do I know these things? It could have been done in Crayola pastels and I wouldn't have known the difference. Anyway, the painting showed three people—two of them sitting, the third, a woman, standing—on the far side of what seemed to be a checkered-floor conservatory, with two of them playing some sort of musical instruments and the third leading them in song. It reminded me of one of those incredibly complicated thousand-piece puzzles that my grandmother used to assemble over the course of weeks on her dining-room table.

"Vermeer," Mongillo said, stepping forward, in a distant voice that made it sound like he might be under a hypnotic spell. I looked at him for a long moment as he stared wide-eyed at the canvas. *The Concert.* You're looking at one of the great art works of all time, the most valuable painting stolen from the Gardner

Museum thirteen years ago, a priceless treasure too great for words, too beautiful for anyone to ever assign mere human emotion."

By now, my massive friend was standing directly beside me, hovering over the painting like a Yellowstone bear regarding a finely sculpted piece of Nobu sushi. It's important to have a full appreciation for the aesthetic—as an art dealer might call it—of Vinny Mongillo. He is big in the way a mountain is big, with an unwieldy girth that sprouts oversize limbs coated in a constant sheen of oil and sweat. His hair is thick and black and always matted down—and not just on his head. His odor is that of Italian cold cuts. His clothes—rugged khakis, flannel shirts, heavy shoes—are bought from specialty shops that supply outsize construction workers making an honest day's wage for a hard day's work. In short and sum, he looked like the type of guy that would collect various renditions of Elvis on felt, but here he was ready to fall to intellectual pieces over a painting by this master called Vermeer.

"What do you see?" he said to me, still in that faraway tone. He said this as he continued to drink in every last detail of the canvas, never taking his eyes off the muted colors of the paint.

"I see three women in a room—" and here I borrowed off the title to make what I thought was an impressive-sounding assumption—"giving a little concert in the way they used to do."

"Yeah," he said. He repeated that, saying, "Yeah," softly, slowly, and then in that same absent voice, "You really are an ass, aren't you?"

I didn't think so, but mine is a subjective view. Before I could reply, Mongillo said, "First off, that figure in the middle with his back to us, that's a man."

I peered more closely at the painting and saw from the robes and possibly the long, flowing, Christlike hair that Mongillo was indeed correct in his gender identification.

"And you're right, there is a, ahem, little concert going on, but there's so much more. It looks so innocent, doesn't it, but it's not."

He paused here to stare harder still at the painting, and I did as well, though he seemed to be seeing things that I couldn't find.

He glanced at me for a flicker of a moment and said, "Look at the depth of light, at the richness of color, at the enormous meaning."

I saw a few people playing a song.

"It's so serene on one level, isn't it? And yet, the serenity is a mask for the turbulent, sexual undertone that nearly engulfs the entire work."

I, again, saw a few people playing a song.

I asked, "How the hell do you know all this?"

"I know," he said, "because it's beautiful." He paused for a moment and added in words that were now hardened by some frustration, "You don't see the meaning, do you?"

"Well, I, I think—"

"Look," he said, cutting me off, "at the Van Baburen on the wall, *The Procuress.* Look at what it tells us about these three people. Look at the sexuality it exudes."

At that point, Mongillo reached out his hand as if to touch the part of the canvas where The Procuress was depicted, and poor Edgar, standing sentry, slapped his arm up and barked, "No touch."

Martin, seeing an opening, piped in, "Can we can the art history lesson while I ask just one very plebeian question: Is it real?"

Mongillo looked at Edgar and then at Martin and finally back at the painting. All around us, reporters stood on tiptoe or climbed up on desks for a view of the proceedings. Ringing phones, including mine, went unanswered. Emails sat unread. All eyes were now on Mongillo as he was set to explain whether one of the most significant treasures ever stolen in the refined world of art sat right here in the *Record* newsroom.

He said, "Only experts, trained chemists, could tell you for certain. They'll test chips of paint scraped from the perimeter. But I've got to tell you, it looks real to me."

There was an audible buzz in the room. Edgar, God bless him, moved closer to the painting, as if to protect it. Martin called out for all to hear, "People, we publish 365 days a year, and tomorrow would be one of those days. Don't you have stories you need to write?" And then he added, "No one, and I mean absolutely no one, is to tell anyone anywhere outside of this room what we correctly or incorrectly believe we might or might not have. That's a job-dependent order."

Then he looked at Mongillo and at me with a cross of anger and intrigue. "You two, in my office. Edgar, please carry the canvas in with us." And the ever-efficient Peter Martin turned and walked away.

Roughly six years before, a reputable reporter for the rival *Boston Traveler* was driven along a "circuitous and somewhat paranoid" route under the cover of dark by an informant who was never named in print. He was taken to what he would only describe as a "run-down warehouse" in a "barren and forsaken" district somewhere in the Northeast.

There, the informant opened a pair of airtight caps at each end of a heavy-duty poster tube, then unfurled what he claimed was Rembrandt's *Storm on the Sea of Galilee,* another treasure stolen in the Gardner heist. The only illumination in the warehouse was the informant's flashlight. No photographs were allowed, no fragments of the painting could be taken, and within fifteen minutes, the reporter was sent on his way.

At the time, it was widely believed that the informant was working for a pair of convicted swindlers and thieves who were trying to broker the return of the stolen paintings and drawings in return for legal immunity and the $5 million reward posted by the museum.

A couple of months later, the *Traveler* obtained photographs and some minuscule paint chips which, when tested by art experts, were deemed not to be from the stolen Rembrandt. At that point, the negotiations dissolved into a fit of accusations and name-calling.

And now this. Edgar had placed the canvas back into the tube, sealed it up, and sat in a chair in the corner of the office with the tube between his legs. The three of us—Mongillo, Martin, and myself—sat around a cheap, circular conference table. Martin immediately broke the ice with this memorable line: "What the fuck."

"Five minutes," Mongillo said, apropos of nothing. "Just let me hang that thing in my apartment for five minutes. Let me revel in it. Let me luxuriate in its presence. For Christ's sake, let me die a happy man, and this is the only thing that can possibly allow for that."

Martin looked at Mongillo, opened his mouth as if to say something, then thought better of it. Instead, he looked from one of us to the other and said, "Okay, before we get lawyers and all the bullshit involved, let's just hash things out for a moment. From my quick review of our situation, we have two broad options. First, we keep the painting and figure out what to do with it. Second, we immediately turn it over to authorities."

He paused and looked down at a legal pad he had in front of him and scratched out a couple of notes in the brief quiet. "Under Option One, we run a story in tomorrow's paper saying this painting—what the hell did you call it, Vinny, *The Concerto?*"

"The Concert," Mongillo replied urgently, as if Martin had just mispronounced the name of his girlfriend. "Vermeer's *The Concert.*"

"Right. Okay, so we can run a story saying that someone delivered this canvas to the *Record* and we're trying to ascertain if it's real. Or Two, we wait and have it tested and base any story—if it warrants one at all—on the results."

I nodded. Martin locked in on me for a moment. Then he continued, "Under Option Two, we lose control of the painting, but legally, we're probably on safer footing, no? And if we're good doobies and relinquish control, the FBI and the museum might feel the obligation to play ball with us as the story unfolds. And whoever sent us the painting, we should assume, will still continue to use us as a conduit, giving us better bargaining power with the Feds."

You know, you go through too many days listening to too many ridiculous ideas from too many self-indulgent people who know far less than they could ever possibly imagine, and half the time protocol requires that you sit there and nod with an occasionally murmured "Sure." And then every once in a rare while, you come across pure genius like this. Understand, Martin can be as skittish as a rodent. He can be shortsighted, recklessly impatient, and just plain aggravating. But time and again, in the toughest of situations, he can distill the most complicated situations down to their most basic ingredients, always with a mind toward getting the story into print.

He looked at me here and said, "What's your take?"

My take was that the first half of Option One wasn't a viable option at all, and I sense he knew that. You can't ramble into print with raw speculation, especially when you're putting the good name of the newspaper on the line in more ways than one. Option Two wasn't much to my liking either because of the level of control that we'd lose. I'd rather be the one gunning for birdies than sitting in the clubhouse hoping that the final players on the eighteenth green miss their putts for par.

That left Option One-b, so to speak, which I liked very much. Find out what we have or don't have. Keep our hand on the wheel. Be the public's agent in a case that the government has failed to solve for thirteen years. Have we received stolen merchandise, in this case, a priceless painting? Maybe, but we can't and won't know that until we get it tested. There would be a proper time to turn the canvas over to authorities, but right then wasn't it. For all we knew, the canvas we had contained little numbers beneath the paint.

So I said all this, and concluded, "Keep it and test it."

Martin nodded and turned to Mongillo, who said, "What he says. And I'd be glad to hold on to it until you find a suitable expert."

Martin, looking down again at his legal pad, said, "I'll run interference with our company lawyers. We'll run no mention of this in tomorrow's stories." He turned and looked at Edgar. "You'll stay with me and the painting will stay with you. Do you have relief who you can pass it on to?"

Edgar replied with great certainty, "I don't pass this on to anyone. I'm with it until I'm ordered to give it up."

I never again looked at him in the same way. Before I could

stand and make my escape, Martin said to us, "So what do we have for tomorrow's paper?"

My mind flashed back to the scene in Hilary Kane's apartment, to my lunch at the University Club, to the single gunshot in Copley Square. No sense in lying to him, so I explained to Martin how I had essentially squandered my day in pursuit of a hunch that hadn't yet panned out.

Barely able to contain his frustration, he said to me, "Well then, I guess we'll just lean on Smitty and Hasbro"—our federal court and FBI reporters—"to write the investigation story. Let me know if something falls in your lap."

That last phrase, for anyone keeping track at home, is an insult in my business, implying that to break something on this story, it would have to just be effortless luck. Ah, the difference a day makes.

Vinny and I walked out of the glass office together, and halfway toward our respective desks, with the buzz of deadline all around us, he said to me in a tone of uncharacteristic earnestness, "Fair Hair, I really need to talk to you. Today."

"Vin," I replied, not even looking at him, "my whole world is caving in. Don't get too close or you'll be gone with it."

And I kept walking, knowing the enormous pit in my stomach had less to do with Vermeer or the Kane sisters than the events of the night ahead.

Chapter Eleven

We pulled up to the airport, Elizabeth sitting stone-faced in the passenger seat, Baker sprawled in the back with his chin resting on the seat between his front paws. He was, the dog that he is, taking his cue from us in regards to his mood, and the cue was—very decidedly—to be forlorn.

The ride from the waterfront to Logan, in terms of total miles, encompassed about three of them. So why then, one might logically wonder, did I feel like a member of the Donner Party who had just eaten one of their relatives on their endless journey across the snow-covered cliffs of the Continental Divide?

Along the way, we tried to keep the sparse conversation on completely safe terrain—when would the movers arrive in San Francisco with her stuff, when would she report to work, what might her first story be, where was the art museum story headed. But during one of the many lulls, I said to her, sincerely but incorrectly, "I love you." I paused and added, "You know that, right?"

The polite answer, the easy one anyway, would have been for Elizabeth to say, "Of course I do, Jack. And I love you too." But Elizabeth, being every inch a woman, and a wonderfully strong one at that, instead replied, "Sometimes I do. But mostly I don't—

not anymore." She said this while blankly staring out the front window as the narrow environs of the Callahan Tunnel slapped past.

I remained quiet for a moment, partly in contemplation, partly to make sure this farewell didn't ignite into unnecessary trench-to-trench combat.

She stepped into that cold and barren expanse and said, "But I understand."

To the uninitiated, this might be cause for celebration, a woman, a good woman, essentially saying that it's okay to act the way I have, to be the person I've been, because she in some way understands the forces behind it, the very cause. But by now, I knew that would be a gravely naïve, even stupid read, an invitation to a much more strident fight.

I said, "Then I should tell you more often." Notice the effective use of the present tense, keeping everything forward-looking and harmonious and all that other good stuff.

"You should love me more." She said this without a moment's hesitation, her words coming out flat and plain like distant rifle fire.

We were heading out of the tunnel now into the dusk of a September night. The lighted billboards along the side of the ramshackle highway pictured exotic places like Paris and a sugar-sand Caribbean beach, including one with a slogan, Closer Than You Think. . . . Yeah, maybe, but not even the recently retired Concorde could have effectively whisked me away from the helpless moroseness of this farewell scene.

I stayed quiet again as I pulled into the airport. My eyes absently followed a jet silently ascending above the terminal buildings and floating toward destinations unknown, all those lucky passengers rising to the clouds, leaving so much of this behind, looking down at this world in all of its relative inconsequence.

She said to me, for the second time now, "But I understand."

I knew where she was going. I knew where she was going because we had both been there before, and I'll readily admit, I'd rather be on my way to Paris or the Caribbean.

"You tried, Jack, you did, and I appreciate that. I love you, and you know that. There was a time, a long time, when I wanted to marry you and make babies with you and grow old and spoil grandkids and travel the world, and to always come home to a place, a big old drafty house, that we liked more than anyplace else. And we'd like it because we were in it together, always."

I'd never actually been kicked in the stomach by a shod horse, but I imagine this is how it might feel. I lost my breath for the briefest of moments as my mind raced toward a scene involving an eternally shapely, fashionably dressed and graying Elizabeth Riggs picking up a grandchild in the kitchen of our suburban home and resting her on the counter while she cooked the type of dinner that she never even considered in her first forty years on Earth.

She said, "You tried, Jack, but you can't do it, at least not with me. You lost more than your wife and your baby in that delivery room a few years ago. You lost a part of your soul. It makes me love you even more, but it also makes me crazy that there isn't a damned thing I can do to help. I always thought I'd be able to, but now I've come to terms with the fact that I never will."

It's funny what happens in these fights. The optimistic part of me, which I'd like to think is the biggest part of me, thought that by opening the door to a confrontation, what I'd find on the other side was something so simple as a back and forth over why we had been noncommunicative over the past few weeks. We'd talk about it, we'd both apologize, we'd make plans for me to fly out there in early October for a quiet weekend of relationship rebuilding by the Bay. Big kiss, have a good flight. Maybe we didn't get at the core of the issue, but the core of anything is often too hot a place to be.

And then this. The door flings open and what you find is a veritable cauldron of unfathomable female emotion—stunningly practical at one level, devastatingly complicated at another, all told with Elizabeth's admirable economy of words. She might be tough, but she was never melodramatic.

We were pulling into the garage by now. This was not an occasion when I could zip right up to the terminal, yank her luggage from the trunk, and tearfully kiss her good-bye, all as a pesky state cop hollers something about me idling in a no-parking zone. So I found a space and said, "I don't agree with that."

That's what I said; the reality, I'm not so sure. Elizabeth had a knack for being right in these things, and tended to be a scholar of all things Jack. I had a tendency to block so much of the emotion out, mostly because if I didn't, I feared it would swallow me whole.

It was four years before that Katherine and I rushed through the doors of Georgetown Hospital on the day that we were to have our first baby, which was going to be one of the truly great days in our already blessed lives. Six hours later, I staggered from that hospital completely, unequivocally, incomprehensibly alone, in many ways forever changed, in other crucial ways always stuck in the awful moments of that single day. Katherine died that afternoon, of what the exhausted doctor explained to me was a placental tear. The baby, our daughter, died as well, literally drowning on the blood that had nourished her for all those pregnant months.

When I got back to our empty town house that afternoon, if I had owned a gun I probably would have loaded it. If I had a garage, I would have pulled the doors shut and sat in my car. I'm not saying I would have killed myself. In fact, I can reasonably say that sound judgment would have prevailed. But never in my life had I ever felt such utter, inconsolable loneliness, not just for what had just happened, but for the ache of what did not.

Instead, I sat on the couch, Baker mournfully, nervously at my feet, and cried like I never have before and hope never to again. I cried until I couldn't see. I cried until I couldn't think, until I didn't have any tears left to shed. On my way to bed, our bed, I pulled the door shut on the nursery that we never got to use. I opened the pocket doors of Katherine's closet, and her familiar smells, calm smells, beautiful smells, gently wafted out. I ran my hand down the back of my favorite black dress of hers, the one she wore to our favorite restaurant, La Chaumière, the night she gave me the news. We had ordered dessert and were waiting for it. I leaned over the table and told her in no uncertain terms what I was planning to do with her once we got home.

She said to me, "Jack, I owe you an apology for being something of a bitch lately, but it's all your fault."

Truth is, she had been something of a bitch lately, somewhat short, tired, put upon. I said with sincere curiosity, "What the hell did I do?"

"You got me pregnant."

She said this as the biggest, happiest smile filled her entire stunning face. She was still smiling when tears dripped simultaneously out of the corners of both of her eyes. She just kept looking at me, letting the drops roll slowly toward her exquisite mouth, with this expression that spoke to our greatest dreams. It's a look that I never want to forget, and never will.

I slowly shut the closet door and Baker pulled himself up off the floor and warily followed me over to Katherine's dresser, where he settled back down onto the carpet with a long, loud groan. There, I opened her top drawer and found an envelope resting on her wool socks and delicate nylons, and on that envelope was just her name scrawled in handwriting that was jarringly familiar: mine.

I opened it up and, with trembling fingers, unfolded a note that I had written a month before. "Katherine," I said to her, and thought it unusual that I didn't use the word "dear." "Our entire lives are about to change in the next few weeks, always for the better. But there's one thing I never want you to forget, one thing that I've felt in every cell of my being since the day we met. You were put on this Earth to be with me, and I was put on this Earth to be with you, and that will never change, even as our life together does. I love you more today than yesterday, and I'll love you more tomorrow than today. Jack."

I staggered over to the bed, our bed, before the storm of emotion overwhelmed me yet again. I burrowed my head into her pillow, smelling her wonderful smells. I somehow fell asleep to a dream that Katherine was in the kitchen when I walked downstairs, making waffles. I said to her, "In your whole life, you've never made breakfast like this," and she gave me a pouty little look of faux regret and said, "I know."

So getting back to Elizabeth's point about what else I lost in the delivery room that day. Yes, I probably did lose part of my soul along with everything else. But if broken bones can eventually heal on their own, if cuts can scab over and return to real skin, if bruises can give way to pink flesh, shouldn't a soul be able to regenerate? Shouldn't time heal even the deepest wounds?

I thought it did, or it would, or it had. I mean, don't get me wrong. I didn't spend my life reliving the look of pain and panic on Katherine's face as the doctor brusquely ordered me from the room, or the unnatural coolness of my wife's forehead when that same doctor pulled the sheet away and I tearfully bent down and kissed a face that I had kissed a thousand times before, but this time for the final time. I thought of it enough, but couldn't, wouldn't, let it engulf me. At least I didn't think I had.

Rather than elaborate on my disagreement, I got out of the car and walked back toward the trunk. Elizabeth got out as well, but she then opened the rear door and slid onto the backseat, beside Baker. I saw through the rear window Baker run his enormous, grainy tongue directly across her face. Most women would have screamed about their makeup or the germs of the general grotesqueness of it all. Not Elizabeth. She cupped Baker's big furry head in both of her hands and planted a massive kiss on the bridge of his proud nose, and then held her head against his. When she got out and shut the door, she was running her palm across her face, but it wasn't Baker's slime she was wiping off, but fresh tears.

In that one moment, it occurred to me that the entire world, my entire world, was simply a constant succession of good-byes.

"I'll miss that dog like I don't even want to imagine," she said, softly, more to herself than anything. Then, to me, she said, "Remember, I made him an appointment at the vet for Friday to get some of those fatty tumors looked at. I left you a reminder on the refrigerator door."

We were walking through the garage, toward the American

Airlines terminal, when she said to me with her tone stiff and her eyes still straight ahead, "So what is it that you disagree with?"

Good question. She ought to think about becoming a reporter. By the time I answered, we were out of the garage, traversing one of those wide crosswalks with the angled stripes. A couple of rental-car shuttle buses had stopped to let us pass. I was carrying one of her bags on my shoulder and another in my hand. She had a knapsack and a shoulder bag. All of which is to say, it was an awkward situation, physically if not emotionally.

"This is a long conversation," I said. "You really think walking through the airport as you're getting ready to leave is the right time to have it?"

"I think it's the only time we have left," she replied. *The only time we have left.* Those words fell out of her like heavy stones and sat there between us in all their cold, deliberate hardness.

That line, admittedly, caught me short. We were in the terminal now, waiting in line for her to check her bags, people in front of us, people in back—no time to dissect the emotional shortcomings of Jack Flynn. She, though, didn't seem to mind.

We stood close and she stared down at the floor and she said in her low, husky voice, "I love you, Jack. I know you love me. But it's not enough. Not anymore."

I looked over at a balding, middle-aged guy, a million-miler, according to the tag on his carry-on, and he was looking back at me, either thinking I'm a lucky bastard for being with this knock-out woman, or a poor slob because of my inability to make it work.

I looked back down at the floor. A moment later we were beckoned to the counter by a terse woman in a uniform who cared not a whit that both of our lives were about to irretrievably change. She ticketed Elizabeth with barely a smile or a word, and we walked over to the security screening area and stood silently in the middle of the hallway. There was a Dunkin' Donuts cart behind us, a bank of Fleet 24-hour tellers beside us, and aggravated travelers jostling past us for places that were better than here.

Elizabeth looked sadder than I had ever seen her, but oddly resolute. She said to me, "Jack, I mean it that I don't blame you. I don't know what I'd be like if what happened to you ever happened to me. But I've tried to help you, and I don't think I can anymore. I need something that I don't think is yours to give."

She leaned in and kissed me in that warm, familiar way of hers, her hand on my shoulder and then on the back of my neck. We locked gazes for a moment, and then she turned and walked away with a barely audible, "Bye." I suppose I could have called out to her, run after her, somehow blocked her way. But for reasons that I may never fully understand, I didn't.

Maybe she was right. Maybe I just didn't have it in me.

Chapter Twelve

On the way back into town, my new cell phone, courtesy of Barbara, chimed from its hiding place in the center console, and I had a fleeting wish that it was Elizabeth telling me that she had skipped her flight and wouldn't leave until we had refashioned our relationship into what it once was. Such are the pathetic thoughts of another perfectly helpless man.

The caller ID told me it was a restricted number, and as I got ready to answer, I imagined that it might be Maggie Kane, looking for help on the run, or Tom Jankle, special agent with the FBI, looking to shed light on what the flying fuck was going on in my professional—as opposed to my personal—life.

"Flynn here."

Silence. Well, not exactly silence, but a muffled static, as if someone was holding their calloused hand over the receiver and scraping it around.

I said, slightly louder. "This is Jack Flynn."

Still nothing more than that previously mentioned sound. And then my phone started beeping a little warning sound and unceremoniously went dead. It was out of juice. Barbara had given me a warning that I didn't heed, and I didn't have a car adapter yet. No big deal, just people's lives on the line.

Back on the better side of the tunnel, I drove past the turnoff for my condo, drove straight through downtown, and parked a few minutes later in a space near the Boston Public Garden. It's where I came to think and to walk and to gulp fresh air, and God knows, I needed to do all three of those things in no small way right now.

Baker was somewhere far beyond, thrilled at the prospect of circling the duck pond a time or two, and immediately went into prowling mode in a futile search of nocturnal squirrels. I walked alongside him, happy to be outside, even as I was devastatingly sad within, thinking of all the memories I had from this twenty-three-acre patch of green in the center of town.

It's where I first told Elizabeth that I loved her, on a snowy Christmas morning when we were the only two people in the park. It's the last place I saw the beloved *Record* publisher, Paul Ellis, before he was murdered in the newspaper parking lot two years before.

We walked once around the elegant duck pond, Baker probing the bushes and groves of trees for possible prey, my eyes attracted to the glittering lights of the downtown skyline to our east. My thoughts inevitably drifted to Katherine, as they so often do, and I wondered what she would tell me to do. I imagined her walking right here beside me. I imagined her telling me with a smile forced across her perfect lips that I had to move on, that life is for the living, that I didn't have time to keep trying to hold on to something that wasn't mine anymore.

"But I thought it would always be mine," I told her.

"It is, Jack, and it isn't." And what was that supposed to mean?

Well, maybe it meant that I was crazy, because there I was in the dark of a September night talking to myself on an otherwise barren expanse of the Public Garden. Even Baker looked back at me with an expression that said, My guy is going over the edge.

So I shut up and thought of the look on Elizabeth's face, how her soft brown hair framed her beautifully shaped cheeks, the pain in her eyes, the way she despondently turned and walked away, this time, probably, forever.

I thought of Maggie Kane, so frightened and confused, telling me, accusing me, of causing the tragedy that had just overwhelmed her life. Maybe she, too, was dead.

And then I thought of the noise, the mysterious rustling, coming from behind a bank of rosebushes, a thought that had already fully engulfed Baker, who was in an uncharacteristic state of high alert. He stood in front of me on the path, his legs locked, the gold fur standing straight up on his back, growling the growl of a tough dog, like a German shepherd.

"What is it?" I whispered to him, and hearing the tension in my voice, he let out a loud warning bark. Who, by the way, was this guard dog?

It was a moonless, windless, and cloudless night, meaning the stars shone in the sky but the still Earth was bathed in a murky, inky black. Again, more rustling, so I called out, "Who's there?"

As is so often the case in these situations, the question was a rather obvious one, but still, it seems like it would get the job done. Not here though, not now. There was no response.

And then I heard a man's voice, soft and low, followed by more rustling. After that, I caught an inexplicable whiff of a pizza delivery boy—the odor of a fresh-baked pepperoni pizza mixing with the plainness of the cardboard box and the sweat of the person delivering it. And then I thought to myself, pepperoni pizza and sweat. Pepperoni pizza and sweat.

"Mongillo, that you?"

An enormous silhouette appeared from the side of the rosebushes. I watched the outline of a beefy arm pull something away from his face, and heard the unmistakable voice of Vinny Mongillo reply, "Jack, that you?"

Baker went running toward him, his tail wagging like the propeller of an outboard motor. Mongillo called out, "Don't go anywhere. Let me just get rid of this call."

Then he said into the phone, "If I think you're leaking to the *Traveler*, I'll personally squash both your testicles and present a scientific analysis of your impotence on the front page of the *Record*. Got it?" And he hung up.

He came walking across the grass and onto the cement path, Baker happily in tow, and said to me, "Jesus, Fair Hair, if I didn't know any better, sometimes I'd think you don't really love me anymore."

I wanted to strangle him even as I wanted to hug him. Instead, I simply said, "What the hell are you doing out here?"

"Looking for you. Trying to get a damn cell phone signal out here at night. Passing the time, you know?"

No, I didn't, though I did recall him telling me that afternoon that we urgently needed to speak.

My nerves were starting to calm down by now. Baker lay down and chewed on the end of a fat stick. I said, "What do you need?"

"Some friendship. A little bit of love. But I'd settle for a drink."

"At the moment, I think I can only give you the first part."

"Well, I brought the third." He walked over to the rosebushes and came back carrying one of those Igloo coolers just large enough to hold a six-pack of beer or the appetizer course of Vinny's typical lunch. He opened it, pulled out two icy Sam Adamses, and jovially said, "You remember that great commercial when we were kids that went, 'If you've got the time, we've got the beer?'"

I nodded my head as we both took a seat on a lone wooden bench. I replied, "The slogan I always liked was the one that went, 'The one beer to have if you've having more than one.' You can't really get away with that campaign these days."

He chuckled, and so did I, but beneath the very thin veneer of friendly frivolity lay something of great import. I could sense it, but I didn't know what it was, so I cut to the chase and said, "Tell me what's going on."

"You're not going to like it, Fair Hair."

"Tell me."

I had fears of them finding Maggie Kane's bullet-ridden body in the trunk of a Lincoln Continental parked at Logan Airport, or visions that Tom Jankle had just announced his resignation at a hastily called Washington press conference and wouldn't have anything to say to anyone about the events of the day. In other words, I wasn't in the mood for stalling or games, so I added, for emphasis, "Now."

"I'm leaving."

"You just got here."

"No, I mean, the paper."

"So do I."

He smiled and took a long swig of his beer, so long, in fact, that he drained it. He opened his cooler and pulled another one out and methodically put the empty in its place.

He looked at me without an ounce or a trace of humor and said, "I'm serious, Jack. I'm leaving the *Record*."

He let that hang out there in the dark of that September night, let the words form into the concept and then drift toward an unthinkable reality. From the first day I walked into the *Record* newsroom, Vinny Mongillo was already there. I never remember him taking a sick day. I don't think he ever went on vacation. I never heard him give voice to an ambition that involved anything beyond his next major story. The thought, the departure, was pure lunacy.

"You get an offer from the *Times*? The *Post*?"

We were sitting side by side on that bench, each with a Sam in our hands, looking at the other through the dark with our heads cocked and our minds racing to points far beyond the serenity of this gorgeous park.

He shook his head and said, "No newspapers, Jack. I'm getting out of the business. I'm done."

Well, this just went from the lunatic to the imbecilic. I looked at Mongillo, at all of him, from his enormous head with the heavy mop of thick black hair to the fat cheeks to the puffy neck and the barrel chest and the wide girth and the bulbous, stubby legs. I asked, "What the fuck are you talking about?"

He simply shook his head and repeated those bizarre words, "I'm done."

I said, "You're going to get a job at a Home Depot, are you?" And immediately I regretted my pallid attempt to make light of either him or his situation. So quickly, I added, "I mean, what the fuck."

He finished off that beer as well, opened the cooler, pulled out a fresh one, and tucked the empty inside. It was growing cool outside and there were crickets all around us and Baker continued gnawing on a good-size stick in the damp grass.

Mongillo took a healthy—or perhaps unhealthy, depending on the perspective—gulp, peered at me hard with his newly sad brown eyes, and said, "Look at me, Jack. Fucking look at me." With that, he set his gaze downward at the patch of dirt beneath the bench, his shoulders hunched, his head forward, the beer bottle looking miniature in his catcher's mitt-size hand.

"I'm obese, Jack," he said, his face still pointed down. "I'm a fucking pig. I'm a hundred pounds overweight. My cholesterol is double my IQ. My blood pressure is racing faster than the NAS-DAQ in the late nineties.

"I eat when I'm stressed and I eat when I'm lonely, and these days, stress and loneliness are the only two emotions that I know." He paused and gulped his beer and looked at me and then down again and said, "It was okay in my twenties and early thirties. You're immortal then, you know? You have your whole life ahead of you, at least what's supposed to be the best of it.

"And now I'm supposed to be in the middle of it all, you know—a wife and a couple of kids and a cute little house and a lot more responsibility than what's in tomorrow's paper and what little factoid in the twelfth graph that the *Traveler* might have got that I probably missed. I'm supposed to mow a lawn, Jack, to change a fucking diaper. But instead, all I do is eat and drink and write about other people while my own life passes me by.

"One day in the not-too-distant future I'm just going to keel over from a heart attack, Jack, and my only mark on this earth will have been a few exclusive front page stories with some nice turns of phrase that not a soul could possibly remember two days after I wrote them. That's what my obit will say: Wrote for *The Boston Record*, survived by his mother. Poor, lonely stressed-out bastard."

He stopped and finished his beer with another ferocious gulp and this time just let the bottle fall from his hand and clank down onto the dirt, the sound one of forlorn emptiness not unlike the sum and substance of his little speech.

Let me be clear: Vinny Mongillo was the best, purest, most dogged reporter I had ever known, relentless in pursuit, flawless in execution, gloating in the aftermath of a page one break. So I asked in as straightforward a tone as I could muster, "So what do you propose to do?"

"P.R."

"That's fucking absurd."

"I've got an offer to make three times the coin I make at the *Record* doing crisis consulting with Gregor/Sunhill"—the largest public relations firm in Boston—"beginning next month. Jack, this is real."

Three times the pay. I thought of that scene chasing the gunman down Boylston Street a few hours before and wondered if they might have any more slots to fill. But I abstained. Instead, I said, "Vin, you sound like a typical victim, blaming your job for your weight and your health. You can shed some pounds without walking out on the one true thing that you love."

He shook his head and said, "You might be right, but I don't think so. I have to get away from the stress of daily deadlines, the worry about always having to re-prove myself, every damned day of the year in front of a million unforgiving readers. I'm gone, Jack."

Baker trudged over and dropped his muck-covered tennis ball onto the lap of Vinny's extra-strength khakis. Vinny picked it up without a thought and lobbed it across the nearby lawn. Baker walked after it in slow pursuit.

"When?"

"I'm going to give notice Friday and, if they'll keep me, hang in there for two more weeks. I'd like to help you through the Kane story and the Gardner heist."

I nodded, ruefully. Vinny lifted himself to his giant feet, and so did I. He embraced me in a tight bear hug, his massive, oily arms squeezing me into his pungent-smelling chest. What can you do besides love the guy?

"I'm not done with you yet," I told him.

He smiled as he walked away, the cooler in his hand. "I'm taking control, Jack, and it feels pretty fucking good."

He disappeared into the dark as I sat back down on the bench. I thought of Hilary Kane heading to her car that sun-splashed morning, having no idea it would be the last walk she would ever take. I thought of the panicked voice of Maggie Kane and wondered where she was, how she was. And I thought a bit too long about Vinny Mongillo, and wondered a bit too long about whether he was right about much of what he said.

Chapter Thirteen

Wednesday, September 24

The sun was streaming from a pale autumn sky as I trundled down Hilary Kane's front steps, turned left down Mount Vernon Street, left again on Walnut, and headed toward her parking garage, all as part of my workmanlike attempt to commune with the recently dead.

It was 6:45 A.M., an hour that most self-respecting reporters have never actually seen, not unless they happen to stumble through it at the tail end of the night before. But I couldn't sleep very well in a bed as newly empty as mine, or lounge around an apartment that now seemed to have all the hominess of a highway-view room at the Dew Drop Inn. So here I was, in search of what I did not know.

They don't necessarily teach this at the esteemed Columbia School of Journalism, this thing called empathy. But I wanted to see what Hilary Kane saw on her last few moments alive, to walk where she walked, to smell what she smelled. Homicide detectives, I'm told, do this as routine, to better understand the victim and perhaps the act that caused their death. Would it give me answers? Probably not, but it would lend itself to the cause.

So I wondered if she looked at the newly planted, brightly colored chrysanthemums in the window boxes at the corner of

Mount Vernon and Walnut, or if she happened to smile at the handsome young man in the navy blue suit who came bounding down the steps of his town-house condominium building just as I was walking by.

So I asked him, "Sir, did you happen to see an attractive young blonde woman come down this street yesterday morning when you were on your way to work?"

"Who wants to know?" he asked, answering a question with a question in that way I so dislike. What I disliked even more was the prep school accent in which he asked it.

"Jack Flynn from *The Boston Record*." I find myself unable to say these words without a certain sense of pride, which I guess is good, but maybe not.

"Go back under the rock you crawled out from, maggot," he said, and walked off.

For this I went to college.

I considered, for the briefest of moments, lighting after him, accosting him, maybe even punching his too-pretty rich boy's face. But I quickly decided, why bother? In this day and age of conservative talk show hosts blasting away at what they deem the "liberal media" from their cable television soapboxes, there's a certain dim-witted percentage of the population that actually buys into their overly simplistic cause. Rich Boy was obviously one of them. The ultimate irony, though: He was carrying a copy of that day's *Record*, home-delivered, under his right arm. Go figure.

At that exact moment, the vision of Vinny Mongillo sitting in a private office in a high-rise building earning in a week what most reporters make in a month suddenly had an even a greater visceral appeal.

So I went on my way, down the hill toward the Boston Common Garage, where Hilary Kane met her maker. A few doors down, an older woman—perhaps in her sixties—with a pretty face and long, grayish-black hair stood on the street with an ancient chocolate-colored Labrador retriever who seemed to be doing an in-depth olfactory study of the base of a sign pole. The dog's muzzle was entirely white, she had bare spots along the side of her coat, and moved like she was riddled with arthritis. Her owner was ever patient and appropriately adoring, even saying to her in a singsong little voice, "What'd ya find, Bonnie? What'd ya find?"

There was a flicker of a debate in the journalistic calculator that was my mind over whether to approach her as well. The downside was that she, like the, ahem, gentleman before, might tell me to take a flying fucking hike. Not likely, though. Dog owners are something of a different breed, pardon the weak pun. And more important, they, along with their animals, are creatures of habit. If she was standing here at 6:50 in the morning today, bet the leash that she was out at virtually the exact same time yesterday.

"Very pretty old girl," I said, and could have been talking about either one of them. They both looked over at me with appreciation. Bonnie's tail began furiously wagging and her owner smiled kindly at me. "I've got a five-year-old golden at home. How old's yours?"

"She's fourteen," the woman said proudly. "I got her the day I retired at sixty-five, and we've kept each other busy ever since."

I gave her my whole I'm-Jack-Flynn-with-the-*Record* spiel, and before I could say anything else, she interrupted with, "Goodness, I've been reading your byline for years. I'm a big fan."

From a maggot to a saint in about two minutes. This job has more ups and downs than a roller-coaster repairman. I thanked her and asked, "Did you happen to see a young woman come walking down this same street yesterday morning, an attractive blonde?"

Without hesitation, she replied, "Hilary, yes, it's awful, tragic. I cried myself to sleep last night. Such a beautiful girl with a bright future."

"It is tragic, it is." And she didn't even know the half of it. Hell, I didn't even know the half of it. I said, trying to control my sudden urgency, "So you saw her yesterday?"

The woman nodded as she took a big swallow. She got a far-off look in her big brown eyes and said, "She was crying. We walk by each other almost every morning, and Hilary loves Bonnie, and Bonnie loves Hilary, so they always spend a few minutes with each other while the two of us make small talk. But yesterday, she was in tears and didn't stop."

"Did she say anything?"

"She just kept walking. She was crying, like I said, and she kind of blurted out, 'Sorry Rita. I'll see you tomorrow.' But she'll never see us again."

"Did she say anything else? Did you notice anything different, aside from the fact she was crying?"

As I asked these questions, it occurred to me that the homicide detectives should be doing precisely what I was doing here. I would think it would be standard operating procedure. Was there a breakdown? Was there neglect? Were they just not here yet? Did they already come and go?

"I remember that she was carrying the newspaper in her hand, your paper, all kind of folded up and wrinkled, which she usually didn't do, and she was really rushing. I called out to her, 'What's wrong, honey? Is there anything I can do?' You know, I don't know her all that well. I mean, I didn't know her that well. I just see her in the street every morning. But sometimes you just form a kinship with people, especially over a dog."

I know. Believe me, I know. The woman was a good interview in that she had a good mind for detail and a good sense of recollection, but she required some prodding, so I asked, "Did she answer you?"

"She said the strangest thing, and I don't want you to take this personally. She was past me, rushing down the hill, and she just barely turned around and said, 'Don't believe everything you read.' And she just kept walking. I don't know what she meant."

Don't take it personally. Is murder personal? Is being a colossal fuckup and causing someone's death personal? Is transforming from truth-seeker to dupish, lug-headed fiction writer personal?

I got her name—Rita Wicker—and thanked her in as kind a tone as I could possibly muster through the crud of self-condemnation. I asked her if she had spoken to police and she gave me a surprised look and told me no. So I made my way off, off on what seemed an increasingly futile search for some form of control.

I was sitting at a stoplight in the Theater District remembering the time that Vinny Mongillo was propositioned at a nearby bar by a transvestite prostitute with hairy legs when my new cell phone chimed an unfamiliar ring.

"Flynn here."

"It's original."

It was Peter Martin, who's also an original, maybe too much so. His tone was tinged with excitement, but when he gets excited, he has this enviable capacity to become remarkably serene, almost Zenlike. The more things are popping, the calmer he becomes. He'd probably fall asleep in the middle of a nuclear war. It's when there's nothing happening that he turns into the proverbial basket case that he so often seems to be.

"The painting?" I asked.

"The painting."

The light turned green and I accelerated past the Wang Theater, heading toward the *Record* newsroom. It was a few minutes after 7:00 A.M., and it wasn't even remotely a surprise that Martin was already attacking not just the story, but the day.

"How about you and I sell the damned thing this morning and be sitting in our own Tahitian mansion by tomorrow night?"

As I asked this, I thought of Peter Martin complaining to the Polynesian houseboy that the tropical fruit picked from our own trees hadn't been properly cleaned, or that he didn't like the feeling of sand between his toes, or couldn't something be done about the chirping crickets that were keeping him awake at night. I mean, there he'd be, peeling off his black socks on the beach, lathering his ass-white legs in Number 40 sunblock, wondering why we couldn't get a faster Internet connection so he could keep up with *The New York Times*.

"How about you haul your ass out of bed and get the hell in here before the entire day slips by."

"I'm already on my way, and I've already worked what the union would describe as half a day."

His tone, still calm, turned less belligerent and more confiding. He said, "The Harvard profs worked all night. They say the microscopic paint chips they scraped from the canvas match the chemical composition of oil paint used in that era. It's either the original, or a reproduction from the exact same time, which doesn't really make any sense. We've got our hands full with the best story in town."

"Provided," I said, "that we don't get arrested."

He didn't really acknowledge that, so I added, "And I've got an entirely new layer to add on to it. I'll be there shortly." It was time to share with him my belief that I somehow caused the death of Hilary Kane.

I hadn't been off the line for more than a minute when the phone chimed anew, and assumed it was just Martin again wanting to play out the glory of the upcoming day. The Caller ID, though, said Restricted Number.

"Flynn here."

There was silence, though again, not exactly silence. I heard traffic. I heard the audible mush of urban life. Then I heard the familiar voice of Maggie Kane, sounding at once very close but also very far away, her words echoing into the phone.

"Jack, it's Maggie."

"Where are you?"

"Where are you?"

Those were my own words, echoing back at me in that way that sometimes happens during foreign phone calls. That prospect—that this was a foreign call—certainly put a chill in me. Maggie Kane, not just on the run, but outside of America.

She didn't respond, so I repeated, "Maggie, where are you?"

"Maggie, where are you?" My voice was slow and dull, even moronic.

"Europe," she finally said, sounding as if she had to force it out in a rush.

"Europe?"

"Europe?" God, I hated the sound of myself. It was as if the otherwise good people of AT&T were somehow, in some way, mocking me.

"I jumped in a cab yesterday. I told the driver to take me to the airport. We came all the way around to the last terminal"— Terminal E, the international terminal—"and I bought a ticket on the next flight. Here I am."

"Where?"

"Where?" I mean, I sound like a fucking moron, unable to even ask a creative question.

"I don't want to get more specific. What if your phone is bugged?"

Good point. Check that: Excellent point. This was a shrewd woman on the other end of the line, exercising more caution in a stressful situation than I even thought to have.

I swerved to the side of the road and jumped out at the local White Hen Pantry, which is your basic 7-Eleven-style convenience store, though with a better, albeit illogical, name. I checked out the grungy pay phone in the small parking lot and said to her, "Do you have a pen?"

"Do you have a pen?" I've really got to learn to talk sharper, quicker. I wonder if there's such a thing as voice lessons for plain, everyday speaking.

She did, and she wrote down the number, and I told her to call me immediately, and if it didn't take calls, to telephone me back on my cell phone. Within seconds, the pay phone rang and we were in business.

"Where are you?"

There was no echo this time, which was good. And no caution.

She replied, "Rome. I took an Alitalia flight from Logan to here."

"Do you think you were followed?"

"I didn't see anything suspicious. I switched cabs once on my way into town."

She sounded not just weary, but outright exhausted, possibly to the point where she was destined to break apart. And who could blame her? The morning before, her look-alike sister was murdered. She was shot at by a gunman in the light of day on a busy city street. She took an overnight flight to a foreign land. Three thousand miles from home, she was now suspicious of everyone and everything that flitted in and out of her tenuous life.

"Look," I said, trying to sound soothing, "you sound like you're doing well, given everything that's going on. I want to help you. I really do. You have to let me."

Her voice started quivering then as she said, "I am so scared . . ." Her words trailed off toward a muffled sob, and I pictured her at one of those newfangled European phone booths quaking over the receiver as fashionably dressed men and gorgeous women came and went in the art of another Roman afternoon.

"Let me help."

She sighed loud in the act of composition. I could visualize her wiping her hands across the smooth regions of her pretty face, her short blonde hair probably matted down in front and tousled in back from the long flight.

"I need help," she said, talking now without tears. "I'm afraid of what I know, and even more frightened by what I don't."

"Do you want to come home?" I asked.

"I can't. I'll have to use my own passport to get into the country, and people will know. I'll be killed."

Again, her making more sense than me. "Then I'll come to you," I said. "I'll fly out tonight. We'll meet tomorrow morning. Have you checked into a hotel yet?"

She was crying again when she said, "No."

"Where are you?" I had a passing familiarity with Rome from a long-ago work trip and a more recent weekend away with Elizabeth, an extraordinarily good weekend, actually, but no reason to dwell on that just now.

"Piazza Navona," she said.

"Get a room at the Raphael. It's not far from where you are right now, toward the Pantheon. I'll meet you at the rooftop restaurant at the hotel tomorrow morning, ten A.M. your time. If there's any problem, call my cell phone. If you can't get a room there, go to the Albergo del Sole on Piazza della Rotunda, near the Pantheon."

We were both quiet for a long moment, just the muted sound of transatlantic static on the line. Finally, she said to me, "Do you have any idea what it's like to lose someone you love so suddenly? Do you have any idea what it's like to be shot at?"

These weren't asked so much in the hypothetical, as by way of explanation for her emotional state. The answers were yes to both questions, which have inextricably defined not so much who I am but what I've inevitably become. We are shaped to a greater degree than we probably care to admit by forces, occurrences, far outside of our control.

I didn't answer. Now was not the time for conversation or comparison of our respective tragedies. I said to her, "Stay safe now. Tomorrow, we'll get to the bottom of all this. Call me if you need me."

She mustered the normalcy to say, "Have a good flight," and the two of us hung up.

I walked back to my car thinking of what Martin was going to say when I told him of my mission. "What," he'd tell me, "she couldn't have fled to New York?"

Chapter Fourteen

When I walked into the virtually uninhabited newsroom a few minutes after 7:30 on what was already shaping up to be a dismal morning, it appeared that the front line of the New England Patriots was holding an Egg McMuffin eating contest outside of Peter Martin's corner office.

There were four, maybe five of them. It was tough to tell because they all seemed to blend in with one another like boulders on an Arizona desert. They wore golf shirts stretched so tight across their massive biceps that the fabric wasn't angry as much as it was furious, absolutely livid, borderline out of control. There were fast-food bags all over the secretary's desk and the men were eating these breakfast sandwiches like they were potato chips.

"Don't move," one of them said to me as I walked toward Martin's office.

"Don't talk with your mouth full," I replied. I thought that was pretty good. He didn't. Rather, he came walking up to me like he might turn me into the cafeteria's lunchtime hash, and the thought crossed my mind that I'd probably be tastier than their usual fare, though if it were the case, I wouldn't be around to try it. I could see Martin and Edgar through the glass panels of the office, and just in the nick of time, the former walked toward the doorway and called out, "He's okay."

Thanks, Peter. Just what I strive to be: okay—though given that in this particular situation it may have saved my life, I guess I was once again the beneficiary of low expectations.

"We hired a private security firm," Martin explained to me as I stepped past this mountain range of manhood into the office. The painting, by the way, was sitting unfurled in all its glory on the conference table, one of the greatest art treasures the world has ever known and lost, right now sitting in the control of a couple of chuckleheads—me included—whose aesthetic appreciation usually carries no further than a woman in a pair of tight jeans.

Truth is, when I looked at the canvas, I didn't so much see a few people playing a song or even the sexual reverie that Mongillo had described. What I saw was me living a life of unadulterated leisure that would result from the black market sale of this little work. Alas, I'd probably get bored with the beach after twenty-five or thirty years of constant sea and sun.

Martin, for what it's worth, was so serene it appeared that he might have ramped up his medications for what was doubtless going to be one of the most memorable days that either one of us would spend in the wacky realm of the written word.

I said to him, "Are you all right? I imagine you've been up pretty much all night."

He replied in a somewhat distant tone, "We have a priceless work of art sitting right here in this office, and tomorrow morning, we're going to tell the entire world that it was returned—not to the Boston police, not to the FBI, not even to the museum, but to you, to us, to the institution that is *The Boston Record.*"

He added, "Through great reporting, we got it back, the *Record* did. Maybe we're going to get them all back."

Perhaps. Or through shoddy reporting, the *Record* got an innocent woman killed. And maybe it was about to cause the death of her sister. This was a symmetry that I did not like.

I was about to tell him just this when Barbara's voice beckoned over the newsroom public address system, "Telephone call for Jack Flynn. Emergency telephone call for Jack Flynn."

There's something about the word emergency that makes me think of red hazard lights flashing, the sound of a siren, the wrenching feeling of a tightened gut. Without bidding adieu, I bounded from the office, past the Muscle Beach crowd, and motioned Barbara to send the call to my desk. I had a feeling I was about to hear the panicked voice of young Maggie Kane.

"Flynn here."

The next second seemed to extend across an eternity. In that time, I watched Mongillo walk into the newsroom carrying a box of Dunkin' Donuts. I saw the portable television on my desk cut to a commercial for hemorrhoid medication. I felt my own fingers tingling as they tightly gripped the phone.

"You're a tough guy to reach."

It was a man's voice, loud and gruff, vaguely familiar. And then my mind caught up like the clicking chains on a road bike, and I replied, "You'd actually have to try to reach me to know if I was tough."

Touché, maybe, but on second thought, I really wasn't trying to prove any point. It was Tom Jankle, special agent of the FBI, on the other end, and the sound of his midwestern accent caused relief to swell from my stomach into my chest.

He ignored my comeback, which was just as well, and said, "We need to talk."

That's an understatement. We had talked precisely once already, and the casualty rate from that particular conversation stood at one and appeared to be growing. Perhaps he more than anyone else might explain to me why. Or just as likely, maybe he was the direct cause and I was about to get a spoonful of lies. Either way, I needed him.

"I'm listening," I said.

"Not on the phone. I'm worried about bugs."

What is this? The whole world was engaged in spy games while my life was a hearty rendition of Chutes and Ladders. So I asked, "When and where?"

"In twenty minutes, at the clubhouse at the Franklin Park Golf Course. You know where that is?"

Know where it is? Which particular inch of it?

The sun was shining, the breeze was light, and the air seemed as soft as calfskin when I made my way from the parking lot toward the clubhouse of one of the greatest public golf courses this world may ever know. Franklin Park spread through the broken heart of some of Boston's most crime-ridden neighborhoods, yet it served as a sanctuary of good sport and better cheer, a magnet for golfers dressed in old tee shirts and tattered jeans who had swings so smooth and pure they could make a willow tree weep. I'll take the five best players here in a match against the five best from Myopia Country Club anytime. I'll even give out strokes.

I watched from a distance as four old black men stood on the first tee in their daily dispute over handicaps, among them an old friend called Sal, which is short for Salvador, though his real name is actually Eugene. He happens to be from El Salvador, and thus his assignation. Out here, the guy from Oakland is known as California; Omaha comes from, well, Omaha. The exception is Idaho, who really hails from New Haven but happens to have an insatiable appetite for potatoes. At Franklin Park, like the bar on *Cheers,* everyone knows your name; it just rarely happens to be your own.

"Hey Keebler, you slumming today?"

That was Sal. I'm Keebler, so named because my father began bringing me out here when I was a kid of about ten years old, a little elf, except one the regulars, who more polite society might describe as "vertically challenged," already possessed the nickname Elf. You take what you're given and Keebler's what I got. Luckily, it never spread beyond these hallowed grounds.

"Doing some undercover work for the paper on illegal gambling," I called back.

The four guys laughed and someone made the requisite first tee joke about Jose's (San Jose) pencil being the best wood in his bag, and they laughed again. Three of the guys were retired from their respective jobs as a bus driver, a cop, and a City Hall janitor, and the fourth, Sal, still worked as the short-order cook in the clubhouse, though no one can actually remember the last time he cooked. He commuted to the course by subway, devoted himself to laughing, spent his time hustling, and life, all in all, was pretty damned good.

Imagine, I thought to myself, what it would be like to have it so easy, so simple, these days.

A police car and an ambulance screamed past, their sirens in full blare, and Europe—formerly Georgia until he took an overseas vacation—said, "Ah, another free concert from the Franklin Park Philharmonic." Everyone laughed again and they all hit their drives—each of them straight and long—and I made my way up to the cement patio outside the fortresslike clubhouse and took a seat at a plastic table.

That morning's *Traveler* was on a nearby chair so I scanned the first few pages until I assured myself that they weren't reporting anything that we didn't have. Then I contemplated what was to come, which, very specifically, was Tom Jankle, but in a broader view, answers, I hoped, to some of the nagging questions of the day.

To wit: what the hell did I write, and what had he fed me, that would possibly cause the death of Hilary Kane? Was I correct in the fundamental point of the story, which was that authorities were now viewing infamous fugitive Toby Harkins as either a significant suspect in the theft of the paintings, or more likely, that he had some connection to them now? Or was I completely duped, as Vinny Mongillo had suggested over lunch at the University Club?

And while we're at it, why me? Why had Tom Jankle, a senior FBI agent who I had never had the pleasure or displeasure to previously meet, specifically approached me, even sending hired thugs out to Fenway Park to escort me back into his office in the dark of a pennant-race night? And what was the rush? Why had he warned me so sternly that this information might not hold?

As I pondered these questions and still a few more, I thought of

Peter Martin sitting back in the newsroom in a full-bore belief that we were on the brink of a coveted Pulitzer prize. And here I was, sitting in a shower of sun, wondering if I'd ever be able to wash this blood off my incompetent hands. I took one of those hands, balled into a fist, and absently hit the table in frustration, which is when I heard that upbeat voice call out, "We better get a waiter before you start in on the chairs."

It was Tom Jankle, a proud but tired smile lurking under his twitching mustache. He was wearing that same blue windbreaker over a wrinkled navy suit and a striped tie that was already loosened along his neck. His bespectacled eyes were as alert as cold water, even if the rest of him looked like it was in dire need of some sleep. His full head of hair was brushed flat in a style that would best be called Boys Regular, or maybe Law Enforcement Standard. All in all, when you take heed of Hank Sweeney's comparisons, Tom Jankle had more the look of a farm-belt tractor dealer than a suave agent of the federal government. He was easy to underestimate, which I'm betting worked in his favor every day of his illustrious career.

I stood up, slightly embarrassed but not really, and shook his hand. When we both sat down, I said by way of setting the tone, "I really could have used you yesterday."

He met my gaze head-on in a neutral but unflinching stare and said, "I've got a job to do, and it's not always answering to *The Boston Record.*"

I reflexively smiled, but not out of any amusement. We weren't off to what anyone would call a good start, not unless you're Bill O'Reilly trying to make enemies like the Woman in the Shoe made babies. But give me a break. He put me in a bind, and then wasn't there when I most needed him to get or help me out. That didn't exactly thrill me, even if I was sitting on a priceless work of art because of his original story.

"Maybe not," I replied, "but you certainly seemed a whole lot more accessible before Hilary Kane died."

Waste no time, test his reaction, see if he tried to pull off some sort of lame kind of lie. I wanted him to fully and quickly realize that he wasn't dealing with some rookie crime and grime reporter from the *Beaufort Bugle*. Of course, I thought to myself, that cub reporter probably wouldn't have careened into print the way I had with a sketchy story that caused an innocent's death.

He looked away, off toward the first fairway, where Sal and his foursome were putting on the distant green. He put his manicured hand up to his carved chin in thought, looked back at me, then away again. The momentary silence had now filled the space in between us and was seeping all around. I had apparently thrown him for a loop, and wasn't entirely sure if this was a good thing or not.

Finally, he smiled a thin and shallow smile and said, "You're right, I was."

And just like that, he fell quiet again with a look of contemplation on his face. I refused to speak in the time-tested reportorial belief that you never occupy a void that a source might fill with information. But he didn't talk either, and the silence grew from awkward to stubborn until I finally said, and forgive my lack of eloquence, "Why?"

He gave me that same smile, turning his glance from the fairways to my face.

"Are we on the record or off?"

Last time I went off the record with Tom Jankle, we essentially sat in his office and negotiated Hilary Kane's death. I didn't much feel like doing the same thing all over again, this time with Maggie Kane's life on the proverbial line. That said, to insist on journalistic purity and remain on the record, I'd probably be costing myself crucial information, and the bottom line was, at the moment, I was in search of answers more than I was a newspaper story.

So I said, almost dismissively, "Either way."

He leaned forward in the bright sun, his elbows now resting on the white plastic top of the cheap table. He said to me, "Off the record, I think I've been played like an overfed steer in a Nebraskan slaughterhouse, and consequently, so have you."

He let that sit there for a long moment while he searched out my eyes with his own. Then he continued: "I brought you that story with every good intention. I'll be honest. The Bureau got a tip. It was our first sign of progress on this case in a long, long time. I think you realize, I'm obsessed with Toby Harkins's capture. I sought the indictment against him that drove him out of town, and now I spend every waking moment wanting to see that piece of garbage behind bars. I thought I could leverage more information by having something in the newspaper."

His voice trailed off some as he talked. His eyes, at first, focused on mine, then flitted off to points unknown. And he finally said in an entirely different tone of tired resignation, "And now I don't know what the hell went wrong."

Reflexively, even obstinately, I replied, "Bullshit. Of course you do."

I must have sensed weakness on his part, and thus the opportunity to bully more than cajole information out of him. He looked at me with no surprise and said, "It's not bullshit." And then he looked down and so did I.

Collecting my thoughts, I asked, "What's Hilary Kane's involvement?"

He put his fist up to his mouth, his thumb under his chin, and looked down at the table between us. Still looking down, he said, "The official answer is, absolutely nothing. That's what you'll get if you call one of our spokesmen in Boston or Washington. The real answer is, I'm not sure yet. I just don't know. Me and you, we're like two hungry hens in a wire coop."

Enough with the barnyard analogies. He was basically telling me that he was harboring the same suspicions I was, and had no more information than I did, which I knew couldn't be true. If that was the case, how to explain his early-morning appearance at Hilary Kane's murder scene just hours after he had tipped me about the Gardner Museum heist. He knew something that he had yet to share.

So I asked him about it pointedly, asked him why he raced to the Boston Common Garage early that morning when a city murder was so far out of his jurisdiction or common field of interest.

He looked at me square and said, "Still off the record?"

I nodded.

"The tip I got from my superiors in Washington was that a young woman had intercepted information about the Gardner, valuable information. I don't know how, I don't know where, I don't know who. I just know it incriminated Toby Harkins. They wanted me to get to him. So I leaked to you. You wrote. A young woman is murdered. And I shot down there to find out why."

I asked, "You think she was the one who intercepted the information and passed it along?" An obvious question, but I wanted to make sure we were operating under a floodlight rather than sitting in a dim corner of implication and intuition.

"Nobody's told me that, but I do, yes."

He shook his head absently as he looked at me. Truth is, Tom Jankle appeared worn, not just from lack of sleep, but from a deprivation of information. It's a look that any reporter, any investigator of any sort, knows all too well. Information is energy. It's like that wonderful can of spinach. You eat and you flourish. And the lack of same is exhausting, even debilitating, causing you to question everyone and everything around you, including yourself. Right now, especially yourself.

He added, as something of an afterthought, "I believe I may have acted too quickly, and consequently, so did you."

We both looked at each other hard amid this communion of the tragically flawed. He was obviously trying to form an alliance, but whether I could believe he had told me everything he knew about Hilary Kane was entirely unclear.

He said to me, "There's something else," and then fell quiet, as if to build expectation.

I didn't bite, which I have a feeling aggravated him to some small degree. Rather, I simply maintained eye contact with him until he said, "It's the mayor—Mayor Harkins. We have reason to investigate the possibility that he's had some level of contact with his son, though I'm not in a position to be more specific about the type or nature of the contact. I just know it is in contradiction to his public statements. That's all off the record for now, but it's something to keep in mind."

I would. Believe me, I would, despite his accusation, which was so carefully worded—"reason to investigate the possibility"—as to be absurd. Bill Clinton was more reckless in front of a grand jury than Tom Jankle just was with me. Still, the very notion intrigued.

He asked me, "What have you learned that would be helpful for me to know?"

If we were in a sci-fi movie and he was wearing those thick goggles that allowed him to view images that were flashing inside my significantly sized brain, he would right now be looking at the beautiful and frightened Maggie Kane sipping a cappuccino or maybe picking at a tartufo in a shaded café on Piazza Navona. Or maybe he'd be looking at the three musicians in Vermeer's painting, *The Concert*, sitting there as it was in Peter Martin's office.

Instead, I met his gaze and said, "I don't have anything for you yet. But I'm working it every minute. By my estimation, I caused Hilary Kane to die. You're telling me nothing to dissuade me of that. You're also giving me precious little else to go on."

He nodded regretfully at me, telling me, in essence, that all of what I just said was true. He said, "Jack, we can work together, or we can compete —"

"Last time we worked together didn't turn out so well," I said sharply, cutting him off.

"Which is why we need each other now."

"You used me, Agent Jankle, or your Bureau used me. You set me up so that a young woman, an innocent, died. Now you offer nothing in the way of making amends. When you decide to give me something, let me know, and maybe at that point we can help each other out."

I knocked my fist on the table, much as I had done when the conversation started. I stood and walked away, catching a last glance at his enormously sad eyes as I made my way past him. He just sat there, still resigned, making no attempt to stop me. A voice called out to me from the practice green, "Hey Keebler, have time for a quick nine?"

Would it be that life was so easy, a leisurely little round of golf, straight drives, the occasional five iron onto the green, make a few putts, have a beer in the clubhouse before heading back to work. Instead, my job, my life, my world, seemed ready to explode, if it hadn't already.

It was Juan, from San Juan, who had extended the invitation. "Soon," I called back, never breaking stride for my car.

As I was pulling out of the lot, the music on the stereo stopped and the news began at the top of the eight o'clock hour. There wasn't a farmer in the nation that had anything on me in terms of early-morning work today. Anyway, the anchorman all but called out my name when he said, "Police have questioned the estranged boyfriend Charles, better known as Chuck, Hamlin, in yesterday's Boston Common Garage slaying of his former girlfriend, Hilary Kane, sources tell WBZ News . . ." I listened for more, but there wasn't any, this being the soundbite way of drive-time radio.

I thought of poor Chuck, probably that dislikable soul from the turned-over photos in Hilary's apartment, his hair all thick and his chin strong and his face too pretty in a prep school kind of way. I thought of him getting arrested—printed and photographed down at headquarters in Roxbury, tossed into a holding cell without the dignity of his leather belt or the laces on his Kenneth Cole shoes, his $400 an hour family lawyer rushing in to threaten civil rights violations at a bunch of cops who wouldn't bother stifling their collective yawn.

Chuck wouldn't do well in the Big House, despite the fact that I'm sure he lives in one now. Lucky for him, he's got nothing to do with the murder. I knew that. He knew that. The federal agent I had just left behind at the Franklin Park Golf Course knew that. Question was, did the Boston police know that? At a time when it suddenly seemed that anything goes, when shots are fired in Copley Square, when newspaper stories lead to the slayings of young women, when sisters are forced on transatlantic runs for their lives, how was anyone to know? All of which placed yet another burden on the already strained life of Jack Flynn.

"Chuck," I said to the radio dial, "be nice to those detectives, or you have no idea what you may get yourself into."

Chapter Fifteen

The Isabella Stewart Gardner Museum is one of these uniquely Boston places that we all claim as our collective own, but truth is, precious few of us ever knew we had—at least not until we woke up to the headlines screaming of the brazen heist of some of our most beloved treasures.

I was working in Washington at the time of the crime, in the paper's D.C. bureau, and I remember having two questions the day the news broke: How dare they, and where the hell's the Gardner? It's not easy to feel a loss over something you never knew you had, but still, you manage. It's another part of the human condition.

More than a dozen years had passed—more than a dozen years of hopes and frustrations and sweat and tears, a dozen years of dogged search and inevitable failure, a dozen years that either froze the trail toward the suspects or periodically reignited the possibility that somewhere, somehow, someone would tire of the wait and say something that would lead to the return. Paintings couldn't be spent. They'd have no currency if they were destroyed. They were stashed someplace, the optimists always said, and at some point, they would find their way home.

Who knew the route home would come through the *Record* newsroom, specifically my desk, at least for Vermeer's *The*

Concert? Certainly not Stephen Holden, the chairman of the board of trustees of the Gardner Museum. He met me on the top steps of the ancient brick building, shook my hand as if it were a piece of molten rock too hot to grip, and led me inside the enormous double doors. For a guy who lives for life's aesthetic, who derives all his purpose, his raison d'être, as he might say, from the visual world, he wouldn't look me in the eye for even a passing fraction of a single second, a fact that quietly, inexplicably, infuriated me. But I kept my anger in check as we walked into the cavernous lobby, gazed up at the tall ceilings, and said to him in an unintentionally rubish kind of way, "Quite a place this is, Stephen."

"Steph-an," he said, nearly looking at me, but not quite. He pronounced his name like a Newbury Street hairdresser might. I'm sure I saw in the *Record*'s old clips on him that it was spelled Stephen, and I'd bet some pretty good coin that his parents intended it to be pronounced Stephen, but what are you going to do? Well, here's what I did: When he introduced me moments later to the museum's media affairs director as Jack Flynn, I smiled and said, "Jacques."

The director, an accessibly pleasant-looking middle-aged woman named Betsy, smiled curiously back at me. I caught Steph-an staring me full in the face for the first time with something that actually resembled respect. Then I said, "Just kidding. My mother was a big Cousteau fan, but she wouldn't make me pay the price."

Steph-an, by the way, was an elegant guy of about sixty years of age in the kind of perfectly tailored black suit that you don't expect to see outside of the fashion capitals of New York, Milan, or Paris. He was neither large nor small, tall nor short, fat nor thin, but someplace in the comfortable middle of all that and more. His close-cropped hair wasn't so much white as colorless, almost like the pallor of his skin. Maybe he was gay or maybe he was straight or maybe like so much else, he fell somewhere in between. I just know that he appeared to exist so seamlessly in this museum life that he made me feel conscious of every one of my inevitably human traits. This was one of those rare times in an otherwise confident existence that I actually wondered what someone must think about my very practical shoes.

Now I'm not saying all this is necessarily bad, or that I felt a visceral dislike for the man. To Steph-an's considerable credit, he had won raves as the extraordinarily passionate and tireless overseer of one of the world's truly great institutions of art, and for that, he deserves a city's appreciation, including mine. I also needed his help here, which was the purpose of this little sojourn. Just like I wanted to see the street that Hilary Kane walked down on her way toward an unacceptably early death, I wanted to see the scene of one of Boston's most infamously unsolved crimes. Steph-an, for the latter, was a key to a proper understanding of the depth of loss.

Betsy handed me her business card and pleasantly peeled off. Steph-an, walking a couple of paces in front of me, led me from the museum's lobby into one of the first rooms. I asked, conversationally, "What's the price of admission?" and regretted the question even as it was coming out of my mouth.

"Ten dollars, but you don't have to worry. We'll cover you today," Steph-an said coolly.

I wasn't worried, I could have told him. My paper would pay for it, and even if I had to, I had an equity stake in the damn company from the time I almost brought down the president of the United States, so a ten-spot wasn't really going to hit me all that hard. Instead, like a chastened boy, I said, "Thanks," and vowed to myself to be good.

As we proceeded onward, he was silent, much as if he were walking his dog. I followed just behind him, much as if I were his dog. I finally said to him, at considerable risk of further embarrassment, "Like I said on the phone, I was hoping you could show me where the paintings once hung so I can get a visual image in my mind."

"That won't be hard," he said to me cryptically, and I wondered for a moment if I should be in some way insulted. Probably, but who really cared? Well, me, kind of.

A moment later, Steph-an slowed down to allow me to catch

up, and said to me, "The walls where the paintings and sketches once hung are still bare. Mrs. Gardner's will specifically stipulates that if any treasures are inappropriately removed from the museum, the space from whence they came shall remain as was until the occasion of their return."

He paused here before adding, "I don't know if she intended it this way, but it serves as a daily reminder of the enormous loss that we in the art world all feel. It pushes us constantly to secure their recovery."

I didn't like the way he talked, very, for lack of a better word, uppity, his words too carefully chosen. At the same time, I saw no compelling reason to share this with him, so instead, I asked, "You mean, the walls simply stand bare where, say, *The Concert* used to hang?"

Condescendingly, he replied, "That's what I just said."

I wondered if any of the nice, pearl-wearing patrons of the museum would rush to his aid if I walloped him so hard in the face that he knocked over an ancient Chinese vase on his way to the floor. This was no time to find out, though. Not until I got more of what I needed.

He stopped in one of the ornate rooms, in front of a bare spot on an off-white wall and said, "This is where *Storm* was presented." As he said this, he hung his head in sorrow like a church-goer at Good Friday services.

We repeated this exercise another half a dozen times, each one of them in front of a blank space on an unassuming wall. I don't know why it reminded me of the way I kept my infant daughter's nursery intact for a full year after she died at birth, but it did, and consequently, it made me terribly sad, this loss of something so irreplaceable. It made me realize, viscerally as I disliked him, that these treasures were Steph-an's adopted children, and lost in the theft was a big chunk of his heart.

It also made me think of Elizabeth, made me realize how she was so careful not to leave a damned thing behind in her move west, as if she'd never, ever have a compelling reason to return. I mean, she even took clothes that she never wore out of a storage closet. She took photo albums of her childhood stored in boxes that we rarely opened. She took some of the kitchen utensils that were hers that she knew I liked to use. She hadn't just moved away. She was gone—forever. I knew it, and so did she, and damned the both of us for being incapable of having an adult conversation about what had gone wrong.

I thought of all this as I stared at the blank spot on the wall where Vermeer's *The Concert* was supposed to hang. I should have felt something of a rebirth, knowing, as I did, that the painting had been returned, that it would grace this space yet again, sometime very soon. But all I really felt was loss—for Hilary Kane, for Maggie, for Katherine, for Elizabeth, for the great Mongillo who was leaving the sanity of journalism for the intellectual corruption of public relations. The world seemed filled at the moment with the hollow echoes of an irretrievable past, sad at a core that couldn't actually be touched.

Steph-an looked at me and said, "Do you want to go talk?"

I thought for a passing moment he meant about my life, about my deep sense of unshakable sadness, and I almost hugged him, but not really. He instead meant the paintings and the museum's efforts to recover them, so before making an ass of myself again I nodded my head in the affirmative and we made off for his upstairs office.

It was, by the way, a grand little enclave, graced with a richly colored Oriental rug and an ornate desk that surely hailed from some long-ago French period marked by a king's name and followed by a Roman numeral that I undoubtedly wouldn't be able to guess. Autumn sunshine streamed through the tall windows, and graceful modern paintings adorned the cappuccino-colored walls. The dentil moldings alone seemed an independent work of art.

Old Steph-an removed his black suit coat and settled behind his desk in an absurd position of authority. I took my place in an upholstered chair.

"Your story," he began, "did not come as a surprise to us."

Of course not. What would a peon like me be able to say to him that would ever be original, let alone surprising? Actually, how about this: *Here's your Vermeer back.*

Here in the realm of the interview rather than in the world of art, I felt more comfortable, and replied with a rediscovered confidence, "I'm not sure I understand what you mean."

"What I mean is that our private investigators have been pursuing an underworld connection in Boston for the last year. The FBI is fully aware of this. I was surprised that they'd leak it like they did to the news media."

He said this last sentence, especially those last two words, with a coating of disdain all across his tongue. The truth is, they didn't leak it generically to the news media that he so despises. They leaked it to the *Record,* specifically to me, with an alternative purpose that I now needed to learn—and quickly.

There was nothing for me to get out of a fencing match with him, or by putting forth a defense of my chosen profession, so I said, "You have private investigators?"

He gave me that look like I had just traveled east from one of the Dakotas and replied, "Since the day the paintings were stolen."

"They work with the FBI?"

"They're former FBI."

"That's not what I asked."

He hesitated here before answering, "Sometimes, our objectives are different. Government authorities, specifically the FBI, would like to make arrests and punish the perpetrators. Of course, we would like to see punishment meted out as well, but our principal goal is the return of the treasures. We view that as necessary beyond everything else."

He was talking in a code here that I was supposed to understand, but I wasn't 100 percent sure that I actually did, so I asked, "So how are you trying to achieve your—" and I paused for a fraction of a second here, not entirely on purpose "—objective?"

"Money." Steph-an Holden, arrogant to the core, especially around a troglodyte like me, had no problem admitting that he was shirking the public code.

I asked, masking my surprise, "Ransom?"

"This is all, what is it that you people say, off the record."

You people. He was just dripping with charm now. But more important, he was giving me information that I was sure would prove crucial; I just wasn't so sure yet in what capacity.

He continued, "We've amassed a little more than $10 million in private donations from wealthy benefactors of the museum, and have made it very clear within known organized crime circles in Boston and New York that we're willing to pay that amount for the safe return of the paintings."

I remained silent, as I'm wont to do, waiting, hoping, for more. In an uncharacteristic bit of defensiveness, Steph-an added, "It's a known and accepted practice among museums, paying ransom for priceless works. Insurance companies encourage it, and government authorities are quietly complicit in it."

I wanted to point out that the works weren't so priceless once you paid for them, but decided to hold fire. Instead, I asked, "So the FBI knows that you're looking to pay for the safe return?"

"Some members within the FBI. The agency doesn't necessarily work as a unified organization."

Thank you, Steph-an Holden, for the lesson in the ways of the law enforcement world. I once again wanted to level the guy, but instead asked, "Is it Toby Harkins who you're looking to pay?"

"Toby Harkins is a fugitive. We wouldn't know how to pay him even if we tried. But we do know people who might be connected to him who are taking part in the negotiations."

I asked the obvious question, as I'm also sometimes wont to do: "Who?"

Steph-an looked at me long and hard across his antique desk as he slowly, firmly shook his head. It occurred to me at that precise moment that he had already told me more than he wanted me to know—not necessarily because of my exquisite reporting skills, though those should certainly never be underestimated, but more because of his base conceit, that he could thrust and parry with a bovinelike reporter and never possibly come out on the losing edge.

I didn't think that Steph-an Holden had necessarily done anything wrong, but I wasn't so sure that what he was doing was actually right. The moral high ground upon which he believed he stood, the intellectual plateau, seemed to be sliding decidedly downward. Suddenly, we were eye to eye, and he had a newfound recognition of it.

For kicks, if only to subtly remind him that he had put himself in a precarious position, I asked again, "Who?"

He abruptly stood up and said, "I've had quite enough here. I'll have my assistant show you to the door."

He didn't so much as offer me a shake of his flaccid hand. I wonder if he'd be as reticent the next day when he learned about the return of his famous Vermeer.

When I walked outside into the brilliant day, I couldn't help but notice a rather large man in a black suit—this one looking like it came from the bargain rack at JC Penney—leaning against the passenger door of my car. He, too, was eating a lunch from McDonald's, making it a little bit difficult to buy into the news reports of the tough business times in McDonaldland. I mean, these monsters I've seen today probably consumed the right side of a Nebraskan steer.

Anyway, he allowed a cheeseburger wrapper to float aimlessly away in the autumn breeze. I stooped and picked it up as it skittered past me, handed it to him and said, "You dropped this."

He took the last bite of his burger and with a full mouth, said, "I'm about to drop more than that in a minute."

Now that wasn't a bad little comeback, as these things go, and no doubt as intellectually taxing as could be. Probably better than what I said next, which was, "Don't put your greasy fingers on my new paint job."

I began walking around my prized Alpha Romeo, which hadn't been painted since I owned it, which had been a long time, to get into the driver's side when Orca stepped into my path. Anyone who has ever witnessed a solar eclipse might relate to the situation. In addition, he was so close to me that I could smell not only the onions on his breath, but the pickles, the mustard and the ketchup as well. Actually, they weren't just on his breath, but crusted in the corner of his thick, dry lips.

Chest to chest, he asked, "Where's the girl?"

I squinted. "Girl? Which girl you talking about? Goldilocks? Little Red Riding Hood? Man, I think someone was taking you for a ride, hotshot. Those people don't really exist."

He seemed momentarily perplexed by that, so I tried making my way around him as he attempted to figure things out. Again, he cut me off and said, "The Kane girl. Where is she?"

The mere mention of that name—and the profound, personal failure it represented—from a moronic thug like this inspired a flash of rage in me. I controlled the physical part, mostly out of self-defense, but the intellectual reins weren't so easy to hold. I said, "She's dead, asshole. I read it in the morning *Record*."

That perplexed him as well, standing there on Huntington Avenue in a ridiculous suit with a gray shirt and a monochromatic tie, bits of his lunch stuck around his mouth and his eyes all tiny and beady like those of a cow. Then he said, "The other one. The sister."

"No clue, shitbrain. Now get the fuck out of my way before you regret ever being in it."

Truth is, I rather like the line, which almost sounds like something out of a movie with an unassuming hero who emerges from a life of relative pacifism to finally face down an evil, bullying enemy. That said, I knew the results of the words—and their accompanying sentiment—would have anything but a Hollywood ending, even as they were just drifting forth from my mouth.

Wouldn't you know that I was right. Indeed, here's what happened next:

He punched me.

Oh, I don't mean to imply that this was some ordinary punch marked by that sickening sound of knucklebone on flesh. No, this was the Lincoln Navigator of punches, inefficiently big and hugely unwieldy but filled with an almost indescribable power. If this punch were a dog, it would be a Great Dane; if it were an airplane, it would be a Boeing 747; if it were a book, it would be *War and Peace.*

He struck me in the stomach, directly in my navel, with a downward thrust that was even worse for the fact that I saw it coming. I felt the air lapse out of my entire body in a single split second. I saw the stereotypical stars, followed by—and I'll admit, this makes no great sense—Ginger of *Gilligan's Island* fame in a tight gown beckoning me toward a desolate lagoon. It doesn't make sense because I've always been a card-carrying fan of Mary Ann. And then, for the briefest of times, I saw nothing. When my eyes reopened, I was looking up at the bumper of my car. A city meter maid, though since he was a man I'm not sure what his proper title would be, was standing over me, asking if I was all right. Sure, I'm fine. I thought I'd just take a quick catnap here in the gutter of Huntington Avenue.

He helped me to my feet and as I leaned on the hood trying to gather my wits, handed me a bright orange parking ticket. "I didn't see you down there when I wrote this out," he said. "Sorry."

Yeah, I bet he was. I struggled over to the driver's door, walking hunched over and bowlegged. I looked around for the Neanderthal assailant but didn't see him anywhere. It was then that I vaguely recalled him speaking to me as I lay on the ground, his words filtered through my ears like the sound of an old record set on a speed too slow.

"You ain't felt nothing yet," he told me in my pain-induced haze. And indeed, for a guy so obviously, visibly stupid, he sure as hell had that part right.

Chapter Sixteen

First thing I did when I walked into the *Record* newsroom a little after noon was head straight toward Peter Martin's office, where the Beastie Boys continued to reign supreme. Fear not, these guys couldn't possibly throw a punch harder than the one I had just taken, though it was good of Martin to come to his doorway again and make sure I didn't have to find out.

Inside, we both sat down at the round table—free and clear since the Vermeer, I noticed, had been placed atop a cabinet behind his desk. With no time to waste, I said to him, "I think we really screwed up. Check that. I think I really screwed up."

He still had that calm and collected thing going, and asked me in an assured tone, "You told someone about the painting?"

I shook my head. Outside, the September sun had ducked behind a thickening cover of afternoon clouds. Midday traffic on the Southeast Expressway was oddly light. A washed-out, postpubescent model wearing a pair of uncomfortably tight jeans watched it all from a roadside billboard for the Gap.

I said, "I think we might have caused a woman to die." And with that, I provided the scant details that I had, from my initial gut instinct when I heard about the murder to Maggie Kane's first vague warning to the shot fired in Copley Square to the frustrating conversation with Tom Jankle a couple of hours before. I concluded by telling him that I both wanted and needed to head to Rome that night to cut through the consuming haze.

He listened intently, nodded his head occasionally, and when I was done, looked down at the table for a long moment of absolute silence. Finally, he asked softly, "She couldn't have fled to Hartford?"

Then, looking me square in the eye, he said, "So we rushed a story into print that caused the death of a young woman while at the same time helping to retrieve one of the most valuable stolen paintings in history." It was part question, part summation—and a typically pretty good one on both counts.

I pursed my lips and slowly nodded. Before I could say anything, he asked, "How do we know Hilary Kane was so innocent?"

Um, good question, because the fact is, we didn't. She certainly would have been too young to play any role in the initial heist, though she could be involved in some way in the return, or the negotiation over the possible ransom that Stephen Holden seemed to think was so inevitable. I replayed for Martin some of Jankle's suspicions that she might have been the conduit of intercepted information, but the nature of the information and the way in which she came across it was entirely unclear, making it potentially dubious.

"Look, Jack, we've got to do one thing at a time here," he said. "So go write the story about the return of the Vermeer. It's going to be the talk of the nation tomorrow. I've emailed you an official statement from the newspaper on how we plan to turn the painting over to authorities, having deemed it authentic.

"And then go to Rome. It might even be better that you're out of the country, because once this story hits, the FBI is going to want to grab you for what could be a whole day of interviews. Just take it easy on me. No frescoed ceilings in your room and twelve-dollar bottles of mineral water from the minibar."

When I came out into the center of the newsroom, Vinny Mongillo was fully reclined in his chair, talking to the environment reporter, Todd Balansky, aka the newsroom Romeo, who was leaning on his desk. When they say a reporter is in bed with his sources, Todd takes it to its most literal extreme. There's not a tree hugger in New England he hasn't tried to date—date here being a gentlemanly euphemism.

"Seriously, I had her screaming for over an hour. Screaming." That was Todd, never one to be discreet about his exploits, talking in something less than a low voice.

"Yeah, I can hear her now," Mongillo replied. "'Todd, Todd, I can't feel a damned thing! Todd, I can't feel anything!'"

Mongillo laughed his big, full-throttle laugh, his stomach actually heaving up and down. I did as well, and Todd, not graced with the self-deprecation gene, stalked away. Such was life in the *Record* newsroom for those who hadn't caused the death of Hilary Kane.

I leaned on Mongillo's desk where Balansky had just been and asked, "What do you have?"

It's important to understand, Mongillo always has something, and I don't mean crabs or heartburn or any of the various maladies that I'd normally accuse him of. No, I mean in the reportorial sense. He spends twenty of the twenty-four hours in a day with the phone to his ear, always hustling, horse-trading information, "What do you got; why I no have; hey, did I tell you about so-and-so; no, I can't until I get something from you." If reporters really were the animals that we're often made out to be, then Vinny Mongillo would be the great white shark of the *Record* newsroom—a pure fact-gathering machine, always looking to devour another piece of information.

He hesitated here, which meant a couple of things—first, that he had the nugget of something, but second, that he hadn't yet moved it from the realm of the probable to that of publishable fact. He looked at me with those big brown eyes that I was going to miss so much, and I looked at him with a half nod intended to loosen him up. How many times had we played out this game before?

He said, softly, "I hear the mayor's antsy."

"About what?"

He shook his head slowly. "Trying to figure that out. I'm just told he's been following both these stories—Kane's death and the FBI leak on the Gardner heist—with unusual attention."

I asked, "But why would that be so unusual? Hilary Kane was a city employee. And the Gardner heist is in the heart of his city, and now involves his fugitive son. It could simply be that he's scared to death about how this might hurt his standing in the polls, if his kid gets tied any further into this."

Mongillo nodded again, taking it all in, betraying little that was already there. "That might all be right, but I'm told he's not acting just attentive, but nervous. He's worth keeping an eye on."

Well, enough of the devil's advocate. I said, "I'm hearing from a reasonably well-placed source that the Feds might be probing him for ties to his son. I don't know a lot more than that, but we ought to get in to see him sooner rather than later."

He nodded and asked, "You want to double-team him?"

"I do. Problem is, between us girls, I'm on a flight to Rome tonight. I'm hoping it's a real quick turnaround and that I'm back here as early as tomorrow afternoon."

He looked at me incredulously. "You're going to Rome?" Then he repeated himself, this time less a question than an assertion. "You're going to Rome. I wonder if you could go to Rome if you were, say, bleeding profusely from your fat skull?"

Interesting question, though not one that I currently had the time to ponder. Before I could respond, he asked, "Why?"

The problem with an answer is that it might prove to be little more than currency for Vinny Mongillo to trade upon with someone else. Like I said, he's a shark, constantly in search of what else is there, always about to make the kill, and sometimes, even with the best of intentions, he can't help himself.

So I shook my head and said, "I'll tell you when I get back."

"You'll tell me right now or I'll bitch slap you until you're on your knees crying from a pain that you can't really feel."

How postmodern of him. I looked at those needy eyes and that wonderfully puffy face that I loved so much and decided not to withhold, not now, not with him gone from the newsroom in a couple of weeks' time. I said, "This can go absolutely nowhere, and I really mean that." I stared him hard in the eye and he stared back at me.

"It will go absolutely nowhere," he said, "just like your career."

Isn't that the truth? So I told him about the shooting in Copley Square after I left him at lunch the day before, and Maggie Kane's flight to Italy, her phone call to me, my belief that she probably talked to her sister before the murder, and that she had something vital to add.

"Good luck," he said somberly. "Get the story, drink the Chianti, and feast on the spring lamb. God, are Roman women beautiful. They all look like me, only a little thinner and more fashionable."

The phone was ringing when I got to my desk and I paused for a moment before I picked it up with the standard, "Flynn here."

There was a hesitation on the other end of the line before I heard a familiar voice say, "Riggs here." My heart reflexively lightened for the flicker of a moment, then quickly became weighed down by the reality of the day, the relationship, the incongruity of it all.

I pressed the phone hard against my mouth as if the receiver was in some way an extension of her face and said in a surprisingly thick voice, "How are you?"

Another hesitation, before Elizabeth said, "I'm okay. I'm okay." She said this word—okay—in that cute way she always did, as if it were a mouthful. Then she added, "I just wanted to hear your voice for a minute, if that's all right." With that, she fell into silence. I didn't, or maybe couldn't, reply.

After a long moment, she suddenly said, "On the ride into work this morning, I was thinking about that weekend we had in Bermuda. Do you remember how hard it was raining?"

I did, and a small smile reflexively spread across my lips.

She continued, "We couldn't even step outside, the way those big drops were slamming against the stone patio. We'd go to dinner and everyone would be complaining, but you and I just put the Do Not Disturb sign up and couldn't keep our hands off each other and read books and had sex and talked about everything and drank wine in the bathtub. We didn't see the sun once. I don't know if the hotel even had a beach. And it was the best vacation I've ever had. It always will be."

"It was on that trip that you told me you loved me for the first time," I said. "It was the middle of the afternoon and we were in bed and we forgot to put the sign on the door and the damned minibar guy comes walking in and we hid under the covers, me still inside of you, and you whispered into my ear, 'I love you, Jack Flynn.' And I had to lie there, my entire body about to explode from the sound of your voice and the feel of you against me and the meaning of your words, and I couldn't move."

She gave me that little giggle of hers, but I heard her sniffle and knew that tears were rolling down her face even as it was crinkled into that wonderful smile.

After a pause, she asked, "What went wrong?"

Life. History. The past nagging at the present, altering the future, making me a very lonely man, at least for now, maybe always, a burden I couldn't shake.

This was all undoubtedly true, and she was surely as aware of it as I. But instead, I said, "I don't know." Pause. "I don't know." Another pause. "Do you?"

As I asked this, I emerged from my hazy angst to notice Vinny Mongillo pacing along the aisle beside my desk, munching loudly from a bag of especially crispy Tostitos. He was also talking on his cell phone, saying, "Yeah, the guy's a sleezehog, but he's my sleeze-hog, my helpful sleezehog, so if you don't leave him alone I'll have your name in print in the most unflattering possible way within twenty-four hours."

I met his gaze. On the other end of the line, Elizabeth was saying, "I've been thinking a lot about this, and I've come to the conclusion that this is just our unfortunate way. I don't mean to sound cosmic, but maybe it's just our destiny, to love each other, but never completely have each other."

"Get off the damned phone." That was Mongillo, hanging up from his call and talking directly to me.

I said, "Wait a fucking minute."

Elizabeth, suddenly alarmed, said, "What? What did I say?"

I put my fingers up to my forehead in absolute frustration.

"Not you," I said into the receiver, still pressed hard against my mouth. "Mongillo. He's standing here telling me to get off the phone."

I pulled the handset back and whispered to Mongillo, "Get the fuck away."

Problem was, good friend Hank Sweeney, once a Boston PD homicide detective, now a well-paid security consultant, had just walked in and held up two videocassettes with his right hand while giving a thumbs-up with his left. Mongillo grabbed both of Sweeney's shoulders with typical exuberance.

"It's always something. It's just the way it is with us." That was Elizabeth, on the other end of the line, her tone more resigned than aggravated. "I don't even blame you, Jack. It's just that life is always getting in our way."

As I was listening, Mongillo hit me on my arm and gave me an urgent wave. "I'm going to call you tonight," I said to Elizabeth. Then I realized I'd be on an airplane, but didn't have the time to explain.

"We can finish this whenever you want," she answered, her tone now more sad than resigned. The word *finish*, by the way, is the one that stuck out in my mind. It sounded to me like she stressed it, but maybe not.

I said, "I love you."

"I love you too, Jack. I just wish, on both our parts, for both our sakes, that it was somehow enough."

The receiver wasn't even in the holder yet when Mongillo, his face so close that I could smell the Tostitos on his breath, said, "Come with me, my concave-chested friend. Our first big break."

"I thought the return of the Vermeer was our first big break."

"It was, but on the Gardner. This one's on Hilary Kane."

I fairly well jumped out of my rolling desk chair, not to mention my skin, proving to me how much more important the Kane murder was in my mind than the return of *The Concert*, which would automatically rank as one of the biggest blockbusters in the history of the *Record.*

Mongillo led us into the conference room. Inside, Sweeney handed him a tape and explained to both of us, in his most businesslike voice, "Off the record, this was sent anonymously to the homicide bureau of the Boston Police Department. In turn, it was provided to me by a homicide detective, with the intention of getting it to the two of you. The boys over there are chomping at the bit to use it, but for reasons that will become obvious when you see it, they're fearing for their jobs, their pensions, their families."

Sweeney and I were leaning against the U-shaped conference table. Mongillo walked over to one of five televisions hooked up to VCRs that are used to record the nightly news on all the affiliates. The room, by the way, is where the *Record*'s so-called braintrust holds a pair of meetings every weekday—the first at 11:00 A.M. to discuss the stories that were being pursued and the news that was breaking, and the second at 3:30 to update everyone else on whether those stories had been successfully pursued and the relative worth of the broken news. The top half-dozen editors gathered again at 5:00 P.M. on the newsdesk to read story tops submitted by reporters and view photos and graphics all in an effort to choose the content of the front page.

As Mongillo fumbled with the VCR, I asked Sweeney, "What are they looking for from us?"

"They want you to ask the questions around town that they don't think they can ask right now, maybe even get it into print. Once it's in the public eye, headquarters will have no choice but to give them the go-ahead to pursue."

Not often do detectives deign to put reporters out front on a story. This, I told myself, must be fairly juicy, or perhaps disconnected, so sketchy, so far-fetched, that the homicide bureau was looking for the *Record* to take long-shot risks that they couldn't afford to take. As I pondered this, the screen came to life. Mongillo stepped back and joined us against the table. All three of us stood with our arms crossed and our eyes riveted on the television.

We watched the almost stereotypical countdown—3 . . . 2 . . . 1—before an image appeared of what looked like an office lobby, captured by one of those cameras that was focused down at an angle, as if it were shooting from high against a wall, like something in a bank. The lower left-hand corner carried the stamp: "02:33, 09/20"—2:33 A.M., on Saturday, September 20, five nights before. All was still, empty, such that it could have been a photograph rather than a video—that is, until a distant silhouette appeared from around a blurry corner and hurriedly walked toward the camera, closer and clearer, closer and clearer.

"Stop," I said.

Mongillo hit the Pause button on the remote control. I walked up to the television, fairly well putting my fat face against the screen. The frozen picture had waves rolling through parts, but remained clear in others.

"Roll it for another second," I said.

Mongillo hit Play. The figure walked from the center of the screen toward a corner, in real life, toward the door. "Stop," I said again.

This time, in the still frame, the figure was outside of the static, and I was standing there staring at the heartbreaking, breathtaking image of Hilary Kane.

Her blonde hair was mussed to the point of being unkempt, as if she had just jumped out of bed, and given the time, that's probably exactly what she had done—a fact about her last days on earth that I didn't really want to know, but maybe I needed to. She had a nervous look on her face, frightened even, and the way she moved was anything but the relaxed and satisfied gait you might expect from someone who had just spent an enjoyable hour or two in someone else's apartment. She carried a bag over her left shoulder and what looked like rolled-up papers in her right hand. She put her head down and didn't acknowledge the uniformed security guard who was visible in the far left side of the picture, sitting as he was behind a paneled desk.

"It's Hilary Kane," I said, still staring at the screen. The silence behind me spoke to the fact that these two already knew. "She's coming out of a building at 2:30 A.M. on Friday night/Saturday morning, but where and why and what's it have to do with anything?" With that, I turned around and faced Sweeney and Mongillo. Mongillo hit Play and Hilary walked out the front double doors. The video then gave way to blackness.

Her image in motion, this woman who I knew only in still pictures and then dead, and whose life, for me, took place in the abstract, was nothing short of jolting, a stark and almost cruel reminder of how recently she was among the living, of how great this loss had been, a vibrant person feeling real fear just a few days before. And then my story appeared in print, and some lives changed for reasons I couldn't yet understand, and hers was over.

I got no answers from my two compatriots, so I asked again, firm to the edge of anger now, "What's the significance?"

Sweeney spoke, directing his remarks from one to the other of us in that easy, mossy voice of his. "The building is the new Ritz-Carlton complex, the lobby of the north tower, which is exclusively high-priced condominiums. And I mean real high-priced. Mother of Christ, are they expensive. You could buy my entire retirement complex in Florida for the cost of the penthouse here, but maybe that's saying more about where I lived in Florida—"

"Hank," I said, cutting him off, urging him toward a point. "All we have here is a video of Hilary leaving the Ritz alone five days before she was killed. What's got the cops so scared?"

He looked at me pointedly, maybe offended at the rush treatment of his presentation, but maybe not. He was, after all, a pro, one of the best homicide detectives the city of Boston had ever known.

"This," he said, and he handed Mongillo the second tape.

Mongillo placed it in a second VCR, right beside the first, and the accompanying television came to life. The time stamp this time said "02:01, 9/20"—thirty-two minutes prior to the last tape. The lobby was the same, but the image was recorded from a different direction, apparently from a camera posted on the opposite wall. Again, all was still, until a pair of silhouettes appeared on the other side of the outer glass doors. The doors flung open, a man and a woman walked inside, the man's beefy arm slung over the woman's shoulder, drawing her toward him as they walked toward the camera, closer and clearer, closer and clearer.

"Stop," I said, and again, Mongillo hit the Pause button of the remote control. I stepped toward the screen. Both faces were outside of the static, and right there, on the television in the conference room of *The Boston Record,* I saw frozen footage of Hilary Kane five days before her death in the intimate company of Mayor Daniel Harkins. My heart felt like someone tied a piece of lead to it and dropped it off a cliff. My chest immediately had the sensation of being empty. My stomach rolled into an immediate knot. Even in death, women can break your heart. I suppose I already knew that all too well.

"Roll it," I said, and Mongillo hit Play.

The pair—I refuse to use the word couple in regards to Hilary Kane and any other man, let alone a politician twice her age—walked wordlessly past the guard at the front desk, and when they were out of his view, but still within the range of the lens, they stopped in a groping embrace. Harkins put both his hands on the back of her blonde head and pulled her face sharply into his. They kissed awkwardly, even angrily, at least on his part. She pulled back some, and when they began walking again, he stumbled ever so slightly, and then they were out of view. A few seconds later, the screen went dark.

We all stood there in silence for a long moment. I thought of the guard at the front desk, and immediately assumed that he was the likely source of the shipment to Boston PD. Maybe if the mayor had just said hello to him that night we wouldn't be sitting here looking at this tape now. Who knows?

Outside the glass walls of the conference room, I saw Peter Martin walking from the vending machines with a can of Tab and a bag of pretzels. I heard Barbara announcing phone calls on hold for this reporter or that. I watched Todd Balansky corner an exquisitely mediocre-looking copy editor from whom he was no doubt seeking a date.

"This is why the mayor has been so nervous over the last couple of days," Mongillo said in a low, serious voice.

Sweeney quickly said, "Where I used to work, this is what's known as a break in the investigation."

"Even," I asked, "in an investigation in which they've already made an arrest?"

Sweeney replied, "This might explain why they moved so quickly, maybe too quickly, to make that arrest."

I looked at Mongillo and without a word exchanged between us, he nodded back at me. I picked up the phone on the table beside the TVs and punched out the number to the mayoral press secretary down at City Hall, Grace Flowers. Her name, both the front and back ends, was an outright lie.

"Gracey," I said in the most cheerfully fake voice I could muster when she picked up the line. She hated me. I already knew that. But she still had to talk to me. It's another reason that makes this job so great. "Listen, I was looking to chat up the mayor a bit."

"He's out of touch," she said, flat and unhelpful. No kidding. If she had her way, that was the extent of the conversation and the pursuit. Luckily, as is usually the case, the way would be mine and the tango had just begun.

"That's a shame," I said, still cheerful, still fake. "You know why? Because we're looking to put a story in tomorrow's paper that involves the mayor, and my bet is, given his potential appointment as a United States senator, he'd be real interested in what it's about. He'd probably even have something to say about it, either him or his lawyers."

His lawyers. I threw that in for dickish good measure.

"Jack," she said, her voice bristling with frustration, "why don't you tell me what it's about so I can make sure that he returns your call."

"Awfully afraid I can't do that on this one, Grace. It's very personal for the mayor. But I can do this. I can be available to talk to him. Just tell him it's about who he's keeping company with over at the Ritz, and to give me a call and I'll go into it some more."

I could hear her shouting "Jack!" as I hung up the phone.

Chapter Seventeen

I'm at the point in my illustrious newspaper career where you can impose virtually any act of rudeness on me and it will roll off my back like water off a duck's behind, or however that phrase goes. Call me names. Call me stupid. Call my journalistic bluffs. Just call me back. I think I speak for every reporter everywhere when I say, if you don't, you've just made an enemy for life, and as that old saw goes, why pick a fight with someone who buys ink by the barrel.

All of which is to say, an hour later, no word from the mayor. I had a flight to catch to Rome, a woman to save, a murder to solve, a salvaged masterpiece to publicize, and as I said to Mongillo when I wandered over to his desk, "The fucking fuckhead in City Hall doesn't give us the respect to pick up the phone." I was, in a word, angry. Of course, I was other words too—harried, stressed, uncertain, and here's one I rarely use in self-description: nervous.

"I haven't heard from him either," Mongillo replied as he held the receiver of the phone away from his head to show I was interrupting a call. "You want to just show up where he is?"

Just show up. I love just showing up. It takes people off guard, gives them no time to prepare, doesn't allow them to scribble notes to their nervous press secretary as you're awaiting an answer on the other end of the line and they're pretending to be lost in statesmanlike thought.

"Let me find out where he is," I replied.

It was nearing 5:00 P.M. Time was an enemy, not an ally. And it's not necessarily good to link a sitting mayor—or a standing one, for that matter—to a murder investigation on deadline. After the fall-out from the Toby Harkins story of two days before, I'm not sure I was qualified to do anything on deadline anymore.

Fortunately in life, I'm blessed with friends in low places, people whom I find much more valuable than the invariably self-important types who ascend to loftier heights. I punched out the number to the mayor's office in City Hall and asked to speak to a woman with the appropriate name of Rose, a former neighbor of mine going back to my childhood days in South Boston.

These days, she was the mayor's official scheduler and gatekeeper to his inner office. Like any denizen of Southie, she was loyal to a fault, meaning her first loyalty would always be to me for one simple reason: She knew me longer, from the old neighborhood. So I engaged in our usual banter and then dropped the question without apologies. "I'm trying to track down the mayor. Is he in his office?"

"With the door shut, and Grace Flowers inside."

Rose, Grace Flowers. There's a woman named Daisy who runs the Parks Department. I've always wanted to host a garden party for the mayoral staff, but don't know if anyone else would get the joke. Anyway, she gave me more information than I initially sought, which was typical, and good. I asked, "What's his schedule like?"

"He's not due to leave the building for thirty minutes. I don't think there'll be any changes."

Within five minutes, Mongillo and I were armed with note-books and pens, weaving through rush hour traffic, on the verge of accusing Mayor Daniel Harkins of being involved in Hilary Kane's murder, at least in person, and eventually, hopefully, in print.

The woman at the reception desk in Mayor Harkins's outer office was not, as they say, any kind of rose. Well, let me amend that. She did seem rather thorny. She looked like she had been sitting here since James Michael Curley was running the show, what with her beehive hair getup and what looked to be a polyester pantsuit, which, for all I know, might have been back in style. I do know this: She wasn't buying any of the Jack act.

"Good afternoon," I said, in my absolutely most cheerful voice, as Mongillo and I innocently approached her desk. I saw her nameplate and smiled at her stern face and said, "Mildred, I'm Jack Flynn. This is Vinny Mongillo. If you could send our apologies to the mayor for running a little late, we're ready to see him now."

She looked from me to Mongillo and then back at me, her expression never changing from that of casual, bureaucratic scorn. Just a guess, but I think if she smiled, her entire face would crack and crumble all over her spotless, empty desk. She looked down at a sheet of paper in front of her, ran her fingers along what appeared from my upside-down perspective to be a list of names, and said, "I don't see that you have an appointment with Mayor Harkins."

"Last minute thing," I replied, still smiling.

"Your names again?" She asked this as if we were about to tell her they were Crap and Phlegm.

"Jack Flynn," I said.

"Spell it."

"F-U-C-" Just kidding. I spelled my name quickly and clearly. Mongillo's took a little bit longer, given that I don't think she knew any names—O'Hara aside—that ended in a vowel.

She said, "And you're from?"

"Boston."

Look, if I said we were from the *Record*, she would have immediately called down to the press secretary, Grace, who would then have tried to escort us out of the mayor's office, and failing that, would have warned the mayor to use some sort of back entrance. I mean, you think this is easy, this street reporting?

She shot me a look as piercing as a bullet, and believe me, I know of what I speak. Not only was she not buying the act, she was outright tiring of it—and fast. I snuck a look at the wall clock, which indicated that it was exactly thirty minutes after my good friend Rose had told me that Harkins would be leaving the building. The goal here was to stall, then ambush—a strategy they don't necessarily teach at the Columbia School of Journalism, but they should. Believe me, they should.

"I mean," she replied curtly, "what organization do you represent?"

"NATO." Well, okay, that's not exactly what I said either. I didn't have to. At that exact moment, the mayor himself, the Honorable Daniel Harkins, came walking through a set of double doors behind this nice woman's desk and ran full-on into Vinny Mongillo. I'd like to bottle the look on his face and keep it on my desk as a daily reminder of why I should stay in this business. He was, to put it mildly, shocked.

I said, in an overly upbeat voice, "This is really fortuitous running into you, Mayor Harkins. We were just trying to get in to see you."

I smiled. He scowled at me. He also kept walking, straight through the windowless outer lobby toward the bank of elevators, in the company of a clean-cut, plainclothes Boston police officer who serves as his driver and security detail.

So I called out again, but this time not so happy about it, "Mr. Mayor, it's very important that we talk to you."

And he kept walking. The cop pressed a button to call the elevator. I said, louder this time, "Mayor, we'd like to ask you about your relationship with Hilary Kane and the visit she made to your apartment a few nights before her death."

I heard a little crash behind me, which I think was Mildred's jaw smacking against her desk. I think I heard Mongillo emit a low little chuckle, almost prideful. I watched as the mayor whirled around. His eyes were on fire and his cheeks were red and his nostrils were flaring like some sort of feral, furry animal. He was accustomed to people groveling, not challenging, which in very short form explains why I became a reporter rather than a political aide.

He stared at me in loud silence, until I said, "Your choice: We can follow you through City Hall shouting the questions out to make sure you can hear them all crystal clear, or we can talk about it civilly and privately in your office." I was going to smile, but I didn't. No need to rub it in.

He stood there indecisively for an interminable moment. If the elevator arrived and he leapt on it and shut the door, I'm not quite sure what Mongillo and I would have done. But he had to know that if we didn't corner him at that exact moment, in this precise place, then it would be later that night at a fund-raiser, or maybe the next morning when he dedicated the new wing of a downtown hospital. So he stepped toward me and kept coming, his stride fast and purposeful. He brushed past me—his shoulder literally touching mine—as he sneered, "Come with me." The look on his face was more of hatred than fear, which was fine. It allowed me to believe for the flicker of an unconsidered moment that this man was indeed capable of murder. Mongillo and I met eyes—he actually gave me a big goofy smile—and we followed him through the double doors and into potential trouble.

I first met Dan Harkins a decade ago, back when he was a junior varsity developer who had leveraged himself to his nose hairs to build what turned out to be a thoroughly bland hotel in Boston's Back Bay. The most notable thing about the hostelry was that there was absolutely nothing notable about it at all, but in the high-tech and biotech booms that defined the city through much of the 1990s, he made a not-so-small fortune gouging businessmen who didn't know there was another way.

His problem was, he wasn't bright enough to build another hotel. Or check that. Maybe deep down, he was shrewd enough to know that he couldn't possibly replicate his success. So in a fit of whimsy, in a flood of money, he threw his proverbial hat into the political ring, splashed his business credentials all over his television commercials, sucked in millions of dollars in campaign contributions from other developers and businessmen, and one odd day woke up as the newly elected mayor.

The most vexing issue he faced in the campaign was that of his estranged son. Toby Harkins had served some jail time in his late teens for stealing cars and selling drugs. In his early twenties, he was rumored to be an up-and-coming mobster, a Dorchester king-pin who ran an elaborate criminal enterprise that took a piece of every drug sale and loan sharking deal in the most active neigh-borhoods in and around Boston. That's when I first met Harkins, the elder, during the campaign. We sat down for a long interview focusing exclusively on his son. He repeatedly said that his boy was a challenge from a very young age and that he had failed miserably as a father to meet it. He said their contact now was nominal and growing less by the week. Still, he stressed, he had hope that he could somehow play a role in turning his son around. He added, though, with no small amount of sadness, that he had no idea what that role might be.

The public didn't seem to mind. How many parents are there in the world who wished their kids turned out better, who saw in their children's failings some failings of their own? I suspect he carried that vote by a wide margin, and on Election Day, he swept to easy victory all across the city.

Once in office, word of his son's growing prominence within the Irish mob became more prevalent. It wasn't long before Toby Harkins's name was linked to gangland killings, major drug traf-ficking operations, and the occasional spat with the Italian Mafia based in the city's North End. It proved to be an appealing story for the networks, the heavyweight newspapers, and the national news magazines—the successful mayor and his criminal son, each operating with a sense of impunity on different sides of the spec-trum in the same city. Still, the mayor survived, always with the explanation that he had lost control of his son, that he was filled with regrets over his parental shortcomings, and overcome with sorrow for the people who were affected by his son's crimes. He loved the boy, he'd say, in the inevitable way that a parent always loves a child. But he had been completely shut out of his life.

The year before, the U.S. attorney's office in Boston obtained a twenty-seven-count indictment against Toby Harkins that included charges ranging from heroin trafficking to murder. When FBI agents knocked down the door to Harkins's $3 million condominium in Back Bay, he was gone—with luggage, untold amounts of cash, and his passport. Every few months, a new tip was publicized that he was spotted in a Dublin pub drinking a black and tan, or at a hairdresser in one of those dusty Central California valley towns that no person with any sense would ever think to go. But there's no tangible sign that the Feds were any closer to catching him now than the day he left.

All of which was fine for his father, the mayor. With the son out of town, he was also out of the headlines. And this was no doubt exactly where he wanted his son to remain in the run-up to his potential Senate appointment. New publicity could easily deep-six his prospects with a governor who was nervous about alienating the electorate.

And then along comes Agent Tom Jankle to leak word to me that Toby Harkins is a suspect in the Gardner heist. Then we obtain a videotape showing that Hilary Kane had been in Mayor Harkins's apartment. The morning of my story linking Toby to the Gardner, Hilary winds up dead.

Which brings us to the mayor's office. It is a cavernous space with towering ceilings and exposed concrete beams. A wall of windows overlooks the famed Quincy Market and Faneuil Hall, one of the most popular tourist destinations in the world, though a place that no one from Boston would ever consider visiting, except for a weekday lunch.

The mayor stood in the doorway until Mongillo and I walked in behind him, slammed the door shut, and raged at us, "That's the most obnoxious, underhanded, sensationalistic stunt that I've ever had a reporter pull on me in ten years of politics."

Mongillo, aimlessly walking around the office, turned to him and tersely said, "I've done worse than that. This week." Well, this was really turning into some interview.

Harkins smashed his fist against the closed door. He stalked over to a sitting area and took a spot in a leather club chair without extending an invitation to us to join him. We did, anyway, side by side on a leather couch that looked like a throwback to when Mildred had just started on the job.

I said, "Mr. Mayor, nice as it would be to make small talk, you don't have the time, and truth be known, neither do we. We have a problem. We have videotape of you and Hilary Kane entering your apartment together at two A.M. on Saturday, and of Hilary leaving alone thirty-two minutes after that. Three days later, she's dead, shot in the head. We'd like you to answer some questions."

If a man, if a mayor, could actually foam at the mouth, I think he'd be doing it now. His entire face was crimson, and not because he graduated from Harvard. He didn't. It appeared that blood vessels were about to burst in his nose.

When he finally spoke, it was with a surprising clarity and sense of calm that belied his appearance. Carefully enunciating every syllable, he said, "I don't have to speak to either one of you or to your fucking stupid newspaper about this or anything else in my personal life. You understand that?"

Mongillo, God bless him, said, "We're on the record here."

I shook my head and said, "No, I don't understand. A woman, a city worker, is dead. You were with her in unusual circumstances three nights before. It's a fact worth reporting, and we're going to do just that in tomorrow's paper."

Were we? Probably not, not unless we got something more to go on. Harkins may or may not have realized that his refusal to speak would put enormous pressure on us to justify rushing the story into print. On the other hand, a detailed denial would somehow give it credibility, or news value. If that seems warped, it's probably because it is, but I never said the news was an entirely rational business.

He looked at Mongillo and said, "I'm off the record."

Well, he's wrong about that, really. A subject doesn't go off the record unless the reporter agrees to it. The default setting is always on the record, which means that anything that's said can be used in print—kind of like the Miranda thing, only for the media age.

Mongillo was about to say something that was no doubt terse, if not incendiary, so I quickly cut in and said in an even voice, "Sir, we're not going to talk off the record to the mayor of Boston about his possible involvement in a murder investigation. This isn't about your campaign strategy for reelection, in all due respect."

No respect intended, really, but I didn't think it wise to tell him that.

He looked at me and said, "I don't specifically recall being with Hilary Kane in my apartment. I would tell you that any tape that you claim to have is probably a dupe, doctored in some way by the many opponents I have who seek to discredit me. You're just a tool. I'd be careful if I were you."

Good points, all, and believe me, I'd felt like a tool lately, somebody's bitch, if you will, racing into print with a story that I wasn't completely comfortable with, watching the news unfold of a young woman's death, being told by her sister that I in some way was linked, now watching that sister running across another continent for her life.

Mongillo furiously jotted down his quote in one of those pocket-size reporter's notebooks that bad actors carry in movies when an obnoxious scribe with an invariably bad haircut plays a bit part.

I replied, "Sir, we're authenticating it right now." A lie, but a damned good idea. I'd have to jump on the phone with Peter Martin to do just that as soon as we left. "We're also confirming the story with actual witnesses." Another lie, another case of needing to get on the horn with Martin and sending a team of reporters to swarm the Ritz and its environs.

Outside, the light grew pale and bluish, sending the office, which faced east, into shadows. Harkins hadn't bothered turning any lamps back on when he unexpectedly returned.

He said, "Well, I tell you what. When you test the video and realize it's a fraud, when you fail to find a single witness that puts me in that building with Hilary Kane, then you can give me a call and apologize for that repulsive exhibition in my lobby and these demeaning questions in my office. Meantime, stay the hell away from me."

He stood, meaning, I guess, that he was through. I wasn't. So from my vantage on the couch, with the very angry mayor towering above me, I asked, "Sir, when's the last time you've had contact with your son?"

He glared at me even harder than he had before, and I didn't think that was possible. If his eyes were lasers, I'd have a face full of holes. He seethed, "What the fuck does that have to do with anything?"

Interesting answer, informative, even while it wasn't. Before I could speak, Mongillo stood up beside me and said, "It has to do with the story in the *Record* yesterday morning about your son being a suspect in the Gardner theft. When's the last time you spoke to him or saw him?"

He looked at the floor, as if calculating his response, thinking back through time, not wanting to misstep or misspeak. He looked at Mongillo, and then at me, and said, "Too long to clearly remember." He shook his head in sadness, relieved of some of the anger that encompassed him just a moment before, and added, "Far too long, and that's the shame of it all." And then he turned and walked out.

Mongillo and I followed behind him at a respectable distance. We allowed him and his police escort to ride down in the elevator alone while we waited for the next car. Once we got on it, I looked at Mongillo and him at me, and he said, "You're a father. Your son's an accused murderer, one of the ten most wanted fugitives in America. Can you really not remember the last time you spoke?"

I shook my head. The doors slid open and a pair of bureaucrats, Mildred's sister and cousin, from the looks of it, stepped on. We had a lot, but nothing fit for print. In the newspaper business, it's called gathering string. At this point, I still had no idea where it led, I just knew we had to get there fast.

Chapter Eighteen

The Boeing 777 landed at Leonardo da Vinci Airport as if it had descended on the wings of angels, making me wonder why it always is that the larger the plane, the smoother the touchdown. In fact, the entire flight had been utterly flawless, a sentiment attributable to the lovely young woman at the ticket counter in Boston who had the generosity of mind and spirit to upgrade me to business class. My only concern was the fact that the pilot, an unceasingly handsome fifty-something man with a voice as deep as well water, kept strolling through the cabin. Two people I never need to see while I'm in their care: the chef and the pilot. And yet, all of them seem to think that they're the next Bill Clinton.

I racked my brain wondering if da Vinci had any inventory in the stolen treasures from the Gardner Museum, because if so, maybe I'd be seeing his work literally come across my desk in quick time.

I was tired, exhausted even. Back in Boston, I had punched out the tell-all story on the return of the Vermeer, raced home to pack an overnight bag, and left the keys under the mat for Melissa Moriarty, a delightful senior at a nearby college who regularly sat for Baker. She'd probably have sex on every surface in the house, throw wild parties with keg beer spilling all over the rugs, and have college guys hanging off my balcony screaming for their lives, which was all fine, just so long as Baker got his three long walks and his two square meals a day. And then I made my way to Logan Airport with about nine seconds to spare.

These European flights are like those college all-nighters spent writing the final research paper of the term. You land, and all you want to do is sleep the soundest sleep you've ever slept, and yet something pushes you onward in the face of physical and mental adversity, some unknown facet of the human soul.

In my case, on this trip, I think it's called disgust, and no, not angst-ridden disgust, for what I'd already done to Hilary Kane. This was an even more urgent, pointed disgust for what I suspected I had unwittingly done to Maggie.

To wit, refer back to our telephone conversation of the previous morning. I dispensed what I thought was reasonably sound advice on something that's always of the utmost importance to me and many others, and that's superior accommodations, especially while journeying through a foreign land. I provided her a rendezvous spot with me. I gave her a precise time. I recommended a pair of very nice hotels.

What I didn't give her, I realized on the long and restless plane ride over the ocean, was even a speck of thoughtful advice on how not to be found. I didn't tell her to avoid her credit cards or her bank cards or her calling cards. I didn't instruct her to get cash, or offer to wire her any currency. I didn't advise her not to check into the hotel under her own name. I didn't order her not to call home.

And I kept thinking of that errant shot fired by an unknown gunman in Copley Square.

In essence, I came to realize somewhere in the skies over Newfoundland, that if she checked into the Raphael under Maggie Kane, laid down a Visa card issued to her name, withdrew money from a local automatic teller machine, and called home on her AT&T account, then she and her sister were about to spend eternity together, both pretty much on my dime. Let's just say that by the time I got off the plane, I was sick to my stomach, and not from the four-course meal that the nice people of American Airlines see fit to serve in their premium classes.

It was 8:15 A.M. Our meeting on the rooftop of the Raphael was set for 10:00 A.M. Walking through the bustling airport, I stepped into one of those newfangled Italian phone booths with plans to call Maggie's hotel and then Elizabeth, before realizing that I had a better chance of personally piloting the jet airplane back to Boston than I did of figuring out how to make a call in Italy. For kicks, I picked up the receiver and pressed 0. A woman's distant voice came on the line. I panicked slightly and said, *"Je ne parle pas Français."* Hey, it's the only line of any European language that I knew. She said something in what I presume was Italian, knowing full well now that I couldn't speak French. I said something loud in American involving the acronym AT&T. She said something that seemed to end in a question mark. A moment later, I just hung up the phone.

On the cab ride into the old part of the city, to the Albergo del Sole, I thought back to my last visit to Rome, a couple of years before, a weekend getaway with Elizabeth Riggs of Boston, Massachusetts. She had just finished a series of sensational stories for the *Boston Traveler*—sensational in the good sense, not the common journalism criticism sense—on a shady real estate scheme presided over by the president of the Boston City Council. It cost him his job, those stories did, and later, his liberty. It made Elizabeth one of the hottest reporters in town in more ways than one.

I met her at home under the guise of an early, celebratory dinner at our favorite Italian joint in the North End. Instead, I packed bags for both of us and hid them in the trunk of my car. Our passports and tickets were concealed inside my coat. She thought we were going for pasta. We were, just on a different continent. I'd be lying if I said I wasn't a little more than a little proud of myself.

"You missed the turn, goofball," she said with quasi-urgency when I drove into the mouth of the tunnel for the airport.

"Damn," I said, and kept driving. "I'll turn around at Logan." It wasn't until I parked the car, popped the trunk and handed her the overnight bag that I told her we were going away. She didn't know where until we got to the gate. It was and will always remain one of the best weekends of my life.

Funny thing, though. On that weekend, I recall thinking back to my previous time in Europe, on a honeymoon with my wife in the south of France, and I remember, even feeling as close as I did to Elizabeth, that constant ache for Katherine. A couple of years later, here I was again in Rome, this time alone, longing for the relationship I once had with either woman. Some people squander their whole lives dreaming of things that they'll never have. Maybe I'm wasting mine by longing for things that are already gone. Rare are the good soldiers of life who can devote themselves to the present.

I was in this thorough state of depression when the taxicab rounded the corner of an ancient alley and pulled right into Piazza della Rotunda, one of the most inviting squares in the entire world. The sun shone brightly on the cobblestones. Beautiful Italians lolled in the outdoor cafés sipping cappuccinos and espressos. A few tourists in matching windbreakers and sneakers—I'm going to guess Americans—filed into the McDonald's across the way. If I wasn't so tired, I might have been ashamed.

I traded pleasantries in rudimentary Italian with the nice man at the hotel's reception desk, and to his considerable credit, he neither laughed in my face nor carried the conversation any further. Rather, he began speaking better English than half of the copy editors at the *Record* are capable. I was assigned a room on the third floor, facing front, and when I pulled open the floor-to-ceiling shutters, and then the enormous French doors, I walked onto a step-out that looked directly down on the hulking gray edifice of the Pantheon.

The morning sun shone brightly. Italians buzzed past on mopeds. Others chatted at tables shaded by hunter green umbrellas at the half dozen trattorias that lined the square. Delivery drivers gunned their trucks as they waited for room to park. It was, all in all, the very vision of chaotic Italian charm. It should have put me in a wonderful mood, instilled me with that sense of worldly calm that takes over when I'm dispatched to various corners of the globe. Instead, looking down from my perch, a small part of me saw Elizabeth, at the good times we had here that were no more, at the finality that she had come to represent, at the gloom in her wake.

I left the doors open so the soothing street symphony could fill my room as I jumped into a cool, refreshing shower. I toweled off and changed into fresh clothes. At various points over my once-bright career, I had confronted corrupt governors and lying presidents. I had coaxed deep secrets from killer mobsters and untrusting militiamen. I had been the target of fists and bullets. But never before had I felt so helpless—frightened even—over a meeting with a potential source. Actually, scratch that. It wasn't the meeting that I was so afraid of. It was the pulsing likelihood that the meeting wouldn't take place, that she had been snatched or killed, all because I provided her with recommendations on where to stay rather than how to stay alive.

Years ago, breaking into the business, I once had a fat old city editor—a guy with ink in his veins—who told me that some stories involve an endless series of worst-case reporting scenarios. If it can go wrong, it will. In those cases, he said you're no longer the lion, but the trainer, trying to beat back circumstances with a whip while you protect yourself with a turned over chair. That's how I felt now, only the whip was lost and the chair was broken and I was left with my own questionable wiles to fend for myself and those who needed me.

I checked the clock beside the bed and saw it was 9:50 A.M. I walked out of the room, down the wide stairs and into the plaza. Very rarely do you ever say this, but the unfolding circumstances of the next ten or fifteen minutes could determine how I viewed my entire worth.

Chapter Nineteen

The first thing you notice about the Hotel Raphael is that you barely notice it at all. It sits demurely on a classically crooked Roman side street a minute or two from the haunting glory of Piazza Navona, a blocky building drenched in cascading green vines, as if it's incognito, in hiding, much like the woman I was hoping—praying, really—that I was about to meet.

I stepped into the kind of garishly opulent lobby that hoteliers simply don't design anymore for reasons that are quasi-obvious, yet this one portrayed itself with a timeless pride. There were extravagantly cut sofas with fringe, and curved buffet tables, and gilded mirrors everywhere the eye could settle. The ceilings were high, the rugs a deep maroon, the mood one of refined disorder, much like the city itself. I looked about the space nervously and purposefully, searching for Maggie or anyone who looked like they might want to kill her—or me, for that matter. I didn't necessarily see any killers, though I did note something of a theme. Everyone was dressed in black, the men and the women—black suits, black turtlenecks, black shirts, black ties, black belts. Black seemed to be the new black, as my fashion-conscious friends in Milan might say.

I found my way to the elevators—what the locals, I believe,

quaintly call lifts, though maybe I'm confusing European Union members. I pressed the button for the Bramante Rooftop Terrace. Just as the double doors were sliding shut, a forty-something man dressed in, well, black, jumped onto the elevator, gave me an up and down look, and said in an accent more reminiscent of Rome, N.Y., than Rome, Italy, *"Buongiorno."*

"Good morning," I replied, trying to smoke out his nationality. He didn't reply, nor, more importantly, did he press a button for a different floor. The plot thickens. Maybe.

We stood in opposite corners of the elevator, he and I, like boxers awaiting the starting bell for another round. At least that's how I saw it, but admittedly, I was exhausted to the point of being nearly delusional, not to mention as tense as a tuning fork. I kept looking up at the floor numbers slowly gliding by on the old-fashioned dial built into the elevator wall. Out of the corner of my tired eye, I could see my fellow passenger looking—staring, actually—directly at me.

Be calm, stay rational, I told myself. I tried to picture the young and beautiful Maggie Kane sipping a fresh-squeezed blood-orange juice at a wrought-iron table shaded by a green umbrella from the warm September sun. She'd spill her guts to me, she would. She'd give me answers to questions that I didn't even know to ask. I'd find out why her sister died, and more importantly, who was to blame. We'd fly back to the United States together. We'd dig to the bottom of the pile of garbage that was now strewn across both of our lives. We'd get stories in the newspaper. We'd force authorities to take action. Maybe I'd never feel vindication. Maybe I'd never escape the blanket of guilt that felt wrapped around every thought in my head. But I'd at least understand what went wrong, and do whatever was in my power to make some of it right.

Unless this clown on the elevator tried to stop me.

The elevator moved as if we were in a hospital or nursing home, which is to say, slowly and arduously, every inch seemingly a mile. Finally, unable to ignore his probing stare, I shifted my look from the wall to his stubbled face and met his gaze head-on. He said, without hesitation or embarrassment, "I know you, don't I?"

A couple of thoughts raced through my mind. First, that this was a very sophisticated mind-fucking by the people who wanted Maggie Kane either dead or within their control. By staging a faux recognition, they might have believed that they could scare me away, and then lure Maggie out of a public restaurant, perhaps follow her to her room, and dispense with their problem.

Second, maybe he was just making idle small talk before sticking a forearm-length knife into my heart. Maybe he was one of those hired guns you read about who got off on having interaction with the victims he was about to lay waste. My own arms tensed in reaction to this thought, as if being put on alert for the possibility of attack.

Third, hell, maybe he really did recognize me. Years ago, I was shot in a failed assassination attempt on President Clayton Hutchins at Congressional Country Club outside of Washington and my handsome face was splashed all over the network news for day upon endless day. The fame, fortunately, was as fleeting as the wounds. But maybe he was one of those devotees who look worshipfully on the pseudo-celebrity that television laughably bestows. Maybe he actually remembered me.

"I don't think so," I replied, polite, my eyes still meeting his.

The elevator arrow moved from five to six. I mean, Neil Armstrong flew to the moon faster than this cube is hoisting me to the Bramante Terrace.

"I'm sure I do," he said, staring so hard at my face, even squinting, that I almost in some small way felt violated. Not that violation is a bad thing, though here it was.

I shrugged.

He asked, "What's your name?"

"Jack."

"Jack who?"

If this guy wasn't a killer, then he certainly knew how to murder everyday etiquette. I simply shook my head and muttered, "Not important."

The arrow hit floor number seven. The elevator jerked to a stop. The doors slid slowly open. Everything seemed to be operating at a snail's pace, except my mind, which was operating at hyper speed. I stepped toward the doors and graciously paused, saying, "After you." Both my arms gathered subtley in front of me preparing to ward off an attack, though I knew deep inside my head that if one was coming it would have already arrived.

He smiled as he walked out, shaking his head and saying, "You look so darned familiar."

I stepped off the elevator and, in order to get this clown away from me, knelt down to tie my shoe. Problem was, I was wearing loafers, so I instead pulled the right one off to awkwardly shake out a pebble that wasn't actually there.

It was then, kneeling down like that, that I heard the chime on the next elevator and instinctively looked in that direction. The doors, already open, were in the process of sliding shut. Inside the elevator, I spied a patch of short blonde hair on a woman whose face I couldn't see. It was hair the same length as Maggie Kane's, the same color as Maggie Kane's, but I couldn't tell if it was Maggie Kane. I mean, you put yourself in a room where you fear there are mice, and you see little flashes of motion along the periphery of the floor. It's known as human nature, even if it doesn't seem all that natural. I jumped up for a better look, surged toward the doors, then furiously pressed the call button, but the elevator was already on its slow descent. I was fairly sure that I was fairly sure about what I saw, but how was I to know?

I considered for a fleeting moment climbing on the adjacent elevator and speeding down to the lobby—speeding being a relative term here. But I worried that if I left Maggie waiting too long in the restaurant, either she'd grow worried and leave, or the goon who rode up with me would lure her out. Why, I asked myself, would she have been on that elevator down? Why would she have come, then left at almost precisely our assigned time, and if it was her, surely she would have seen me kneeling down and remained. She wouldn't have. That's what I kept telling myself. The glimpse I had was not of Maggie Kane.

By now I was as brittle as frozen glass. I quickly made my way to the maître d' stand, where an officious gray-haired gentleman—

presumably the maître d' himself—asked in reasonable English, "May I help you?"

"Meeting a friend," I absently said as I made my way past him and onto the terrace. I stopped and did a quick scan of the crowded tables, but failed to see her. That's all right, I told myself. She's in hiding and wouldn't put herself on prominent display. So I walked—trotted, really—among the tables, like some American madman. Half the place probably thought I was packing heat and was about to take the whole restaurant down. I looked from one table to the next. I searched the far corners. I retraced my steps. There were many women in attendance, Italian women, beautiful women, but I didn't see a blonde among them. And yes, it occurred to me that she might have dyed her hair, so I was probing the faces of even the brunettes, but nothing. There wasn't even a woman sitting alone.

By now, the maître d' had caught up with me on the middle of the terrace and asked with greater urgency in a thicker Roman accent, "Sir, may I help you?"

I stopped now and replied, "I'm looking for an American woman, a young blonde, maybe thirty years old, five feet nine inches or so. Have you seen her?" I have no idea if he actually understood a word I was saying, so I added, *"Très magnifique."* Hey, look, you do what you can, and what you can't, you just raise your voice.

He nodded his head furiously, as if I had just ordered the spring lamb. He gave me a little underhand beckoning wave with his hand and led me to an empty table in the far corner of the terrace with an amazing view down upon the medieval buildings of ancient Rome. Upon the table, there was a quarter-filled glass of blood-orange juice, and a half-drunk cup of café au lait.

"There was such a woman as you describe sitting right here," he said, nodding at a cushioned wrought-iron chair that was pushed away from the table, as if whoever was in it had left in a rush.

So I was right, that was her in the elevator. "How long ago did she leave?" I asked.

He simply shrugged. "I did not see a woman depart," he said. He gazed across the table and added, "She has not yet paid the bill."

I didn't want to tell him that he had just been stiffed, especially given the outrageous prices that Roman hotels charge for virtually anything. Poor Maggie was probably already into breakfast to the tune of 67 million lire, roughly the equivalent of $19, and that's before she was served anything that required the use of a fork. These places are Peter Martin's biggest nightmare.

I asked, "The woman's room?" But what I was thinking was that at that very moment, Maggie Kane was inexplicably fleeing through the lobby of the hotel, but from what, from whom, I had precisely no idea. Why would she have come here and then failed to wait? Had she seen something? Did she get a menacing sense from someone? Had she been followed? Had I?

I was trying to be low-key, but people were watching. The kind maître d' had called over a female in civilian clothes, black of course, and, speaking in his native tongue asked that she check the woman's room for my friend. At least that's what I imagined he had told her. More likely he warned her about this stupid American with the fashion sense of a trained ape and told her to lay fresh newspapers along the floor in case I wasn't properly trained.

As she made off to either check the bathroom or call authorities on me, I looked about the restaurant again, this time for anyone who might look like they wanted Maggie Kane dead. At this point, everyone did. Either Italy had turned into a terribly unfriendly country, or I had long ago burned through my last sane thought.

The woman reappeared a moment later with a shrug of her shoulders and put her hands up in the air in the international sign of failure. Such a gesture could have aptly described my current life. I quickly turned and headed for the exits. On my way, I saw my elevator mate sitting alone at a table near the entrance, looking at me while he apparently spoke into the cuff of his black shirt. This rather alarming observation prompted me to break into a full-out run, and when I did, I heard chairs scrape against the hard floor. I heard footsteps behind me. I bolted past the maître d' stand, past the elevators and toward a red sign that proclaimed, Exit.

I slammed through the heavy door and bounded down the narrow stairs three at a time. If I tripped, I assumed I was dead, and it wouldn't be from the fall. When I had descended a floor and a half, I heard the door fling open above me, then the sound of voices speaking a foreign language, which I assumed was Italian. Again, you don't need the investigative skills of a Woodward or a Bernstein when you've got me around to provide a reasonably accurate account of events.

This wasn't the most agile group in pursuit, thank God. If they were Romans, that might help explain it. I mean, they're a beautiful people, yes, but when's the last time you heard about the Italian national team sweeping through the Olympics? As I leapt down the stairs, the gap between us seemed to grow bigger, to the point that I could barely hear them speak. My fear was that they had comrades stationed on lower floors who would slam through the doors and deck me. I flinched on every landing, but the coast remained thankfully clear.

Five turned to four, turned to three, turned to two. On the ground level, I paused momentarily, remembering the man speaking into his wrist, calculating who might have been on the other end of the line, and calmly pushed open the door from the stairs into the lobby. If I had thought it through more, I probably would have been more wary than I was, but I didn't have the luxury of such caution.

Everything here was oddly calm, almost unnaturally normal. My body was the picture of serenity, the waterfall of sweat descending down my forehead aside; my mind, on the other hand, was an utter frenzy. I scanned the few passersby and the lobby lollers, looking for that which I didn't yet know and couldn't then see. There was a middle-aged couple checking out of their room at the reception desk. Another older man leaned against the marble concierge desk while a prim woman behind it—presumably the concierge—talked on the phone. People came, people went, and then my eyes settled on a lone figure sitting on a sofa by a potted fern.

It's that whole flash-of-motion-at-the-fringes-of-the-room syndrome. I suspected Maggie was around, therefore I believed right to the core of my soul that this person in a skirt with the *International Herald Tribune* shielding her face had to be her. My mind immediately settled on the theory that she had come downstairs, spotted someone sinister outside, so settled calmly on a couch and took refuge behind a newspaper. I'd like to think it wasn't the first time in life that an innocent was protected by the published word, but these days, I couldn't be so sure.

I heard voices behind me in the stairwell—the exact nudge I needed to go racing toward the *Herald Tribune* reader. I had a vision of grabbing Maggie by the wrist, leading her quickly to the front door, having the bellman beckon us a cab, and disappearing into the ancient streets of Rome, not to be found again until the true story of Hilary Kane's death was told on the front page of *The Boston Record*.

So I bolted across the lobby, narrowly missing a Japanese businessman dragging a hefty piece of rolling luggage. I grabbed the top of the newspaper and said in my firmest, lowest, voice, "Come on."

She screamed. I mean, she really screamed. The larger problem was, it wasn't Maggie at all, but some absolutely luscious-looking blonde-haired, blue-eyed German model of a woman. Have I mentioned that she was beautiful?

Anyway, she shouted something at me in a foreign language. Allow me to say, every normal guy's fantasy is to someday have sexual congress with a German model, preferably on a white sand beach with a horse tied to a nearby tree, though maybe that last part is just me. But anyway, no part of that fantasy involves the woman actually speaking in her jarring native tongue, what with all the hard "acht" sounds that could drive a sex addict to outright celibacy.

I apologized, but on the run. The door from the stairwell burst open. Everyone everywhere was looking toward the three guys who just rammed into the lobby, then at me, then back at them.

Over by the entrance, I saw another lone figure sitting on a settee throw a newspaper down on the floor and bolt for the door. Maggie Kane. I was right, dammit. She had been hiding in the lobby. She did, in fact, take refuge behind the written word. I just picked the wrong figure.

Before anyone could say anything, the German model aside, I raced for the door in hot pursuit. The three men hesitated, got their bearings, and set out after me. I charged outside, caught a glimpse of Maggie to my right, rounding a corner to her right, and hightailed it in that direction.

Rounding the corner, I saw it was a short block and Maggie wasn't on it, and at the end was another busy street teeming with traffic. I raced the thirty or so yards to the intersection, looked to my right and saw no one who looked like her, then looked to my left and saw that elusive mop of blonde hair pushing and pulling through the thronging mob.

I went to cross the street, but three cars beeped while simultaneously whizzing past. Romans made Boston drivers look like Milwaukeeans—all polite and patient, waving people across the street, calling out "You betcha" for no reason at all. I watched helplessly from the curb as she got farther and farther away. The three jamokes behind me rounded the corner on the short block and were about twenty-five yards away. That's when I stepped off the curb and got hit in the face.

It happened like this: There was an opening in the traffic, so I bolted. Along came a moped with two men riding double. The vehicle stopped right beside me, blocking my way, the guy on the rear got off, and kicked me in my proudest parts. I doubled over in obvious agony, and he leaned down and punched me in the face, causing me to straighten back up before I slowly, surely, collapsed to the pavement of the busy street.

On my descent into darkness—which I assume coincided with my fall to the ground—I remember having hazy regrets that I hadn't had the chance to have even a forkful of homemade ravioli at my favorite Italian restaurant, Romolo; that I'd yet to have a sip of Chianti, an order of tartufo, a free afternoon to while away in a breezy café near the Spanish Steps. I remember wondering how Baker was doing without me, how American health insurance would work in a foreign land, whether the hotel would know enough to check me out or if they'd bill me—and consequently, Peter Martin—thousands of dollars for a stay that I didn't really have. Look, I'm not proud of any of these thoughts, but they're the ones that I had.

And then I felt a shod foot, a Gucci, I would bet, though you can't count out Prada either. Anyway, that foot came into hard, intentional contact with my lower chin, and after that, I remembered absolutely nothing at all. A Roman holiday this was not, not for me or for the elusive woman named Maggie Kane.

Chapter Twenty

When I opened my crusty eyes, I was immediately struck by just how right Vinny Mongillo was in at least one regard—that half of Italy really does look like him. I was thinking this as I dreamily stared at a countenance that was a dead ringer for my old reporter friend, soon to be former reporter, though never former friend. I was lying in a bed at—well, truthfully, I don't know where the bed was at, nor, consequently, where I was at. Likewise, I don't know why I was wherever I happened to be, or who this figure was in front of me who looked so much like someone he couldn't possibly be.

Then I heard him say into a cell phone that I hadn't at first seen, "Oh boy, got to run. The damned patient just woke up and I've already spent my inheritance money. Get that info I need or I'll rip your scrotum off and shove it down your throat." He flicked his phone shut, peered down at me with that sadistically loving look of his and said, "Jesus, Fair Hair, you might have a lot of spirit, but you really do have a glass jaw."

I had the odd sensation of an elderly Italian woman with a kerchief around her head and a broom in her hands sweeping thick cobwebs from the far recesses of my mind. I gradually noticed the light flooding into a large window, the rails on the side of my bed, the institutional TV bolted to a far wall, the cheap commercial furniture in the tiny room, and realized quickly enough what I was in—a hospital—though not yet where.

"Vinny?"

"You were expecting Marcus Welby?" He paused and added with a wheezy laugh, "Or perhaps Marco Welbino?"

"Vinny."

"Yeah," he said, the laughter dying and his face growing more serious as he approached the side of my bed. I think it started to dawn on him that I might be in pain.

When he drew near, I said, "Shut the fuck up. Just stand there and explain to me where I am and what the hell is going on."

And he did. He told me how witnesses reported seeing a moped stop on a busy street in old Rome, how the man riding double methodically stepped off the bike, kicked me in the groin, punched me in the face, then, as I lay sprawled on the pavement, kicked me again in the chin. The man, on the slightly younger side of middle age, dressed entirely in black, then got back on the bike. The driver took a left-hand turn and hadn't been seen since.

He concluded with, "Justine"—Steele, the publisher—"and Peter"—Martin, our fearful editor, but not really—"wanted me to extend their best wishes for a full and speedy recovery." As he said this, he was making an obscene stroking motion with his right hand close to a set of private parts that no right-minded person would ever want to contemplate. Then he added, "I translate that to mean that we can spend anything we want and go wherever we want in this, the world's greatest city."

"Not so fast. First, how'd I get here?"

"Fair Hair, this is Rome, not Paris. We're a helping people. Someone called authorities. Police came. They summoned an ambulance. And here you are, at the San Giovanni-Addolorata, one of the greatest medical centers known to man."

He remained standing beside my bed. I was getting not only my wits back, but my wit as well, and said, "I thought the safest hospital waiting room in all of Italy was the lounge at the Leonardo da Vinci Airport." I mean, from the little I had heard of

Italy's state-run health care system, they were probably slaughtering horses halfway down the hall.

"Well, okay, sure, but have you had a hospital meal yet? They have veal on the damned menu."

I put my hand up to my chin and the coarseness of my skin scared the hell out of me, until I realized it was a bandage. By now, that little old lady with the broom was throwing open windows and doors, and thoughts, questions, fears, were rushing into my previously muddled brain.

With a start, I leaned forward and gave voice to the words as the thoughts rushed through my head, "What's happened with Maggie Kane?"

Mongillo took a seat in the plain wooden chair behind him and stayed quiet for a moment too long. My heart sank, and I could feel my entire face fall with it, as if the blood, the life, was flowing from my body. I quickly pictured the worst—me recovering in a hospital while the woman I failed to protect lay somewhere in this city in the public morgue, an identification tag wrapped around her toe, her parents back in Boston inconsolable over the news of losing two daughters in a single week. How could I live with myself? How could I carry on in a business that either I had badly betrayed, or it had badly betrayed me? How could I ever pull the trigger on another important story when the last one caused the deaths of people who should never even have been hurt?

"Tell me," I said, more urgently now. At this point, I was leaning on both elbows, and my head was starting to throb.

Vinny slumped forward in the straight-back chair and simply said, "We got a call."

He paused again. By now, I was sitting up and it felt like that once-kindly Italian woman had traded in her gentle broom for a meat cleaver and was swatting me in the front of my skull.

"Vinny," I said, the words coming out like a hammer striking a row of nails, "tell me what you know."

"That's the thing, Jack, it's not much. A call came in to your desk in Boston last night, to your work phone. I was already on my way over here. Martin was having all calls monitored round the clock. It came from Maggie Kane's cell phone. We traced the number. But it was all muffled. Martin believes he heard someone crying. It could have been a struggle or it could have been a bad connection. We just don't know, but it's on tape, and you can hear it for yourself. I just talked to Martin ten minutes ago, and there have been no calls from that phone, or any other unusual calls, since."

I fell back into the bed and my head pounded so hard that I thought about summoning a doctor for either a frothy cup of hemlock or a bullet in my brain and take me out of a misery that was unfolding at too many levels to contemplate. But I wasn't sure if Italians condoned mercy killings, though they're a warm, generous people, so probably they do.

Instead, I regarded Mongillo for a long moment. He was sitting beside me in a flannel shirt with the sleeves rolled halfway up a pair of meaty forearms that had the look of butcher's paper with hair. He seemed worn, no doubt from traveling through the night to get to my bedside. His thick black hair was matted in front against his oily forehead. His deep brown eyes were rimmed with red. He carried the distinctive odor—pepperoni, perhaps—of someone who hadn't yet showered that day. Then again, he carried that odor when he was still damp from the shower.

Didn't matter. I loved the guy. I'd miss him in the newsroom more than I could ever say. I was thrilled that he was here with me now, though maybe thrill is the wrong word. The emotion, more accurately, was relief.

I said, "We've got to find her, Vin. I've fucked this story up more than anything else in my life. We've got to find her."

He shook his head casually and replied, "Naw, you've fucked things up worse than this." He smiled at me, that big toothy smile, and I just stared back at him. Then he added, "And Martin's panic-stricken. This Vermeer story is bigger than you can imagine. He wants me to bring you stateside as soon as you can walk onto a plane."

I thought that over for a brief moment, the almost unthinkable concept that I was going to fly back home while a desperate

Maggie Kane traversed the foreign cultures of Europe with a group of killers following closely behind her.

"That's not going to happen," I said. "I ain't leaving without the woman."

"Sounds like a line in a Meg Ryan movie," Mongillo replied.

I ignored that and instead asked, "By the way, am I all right?"

He stood up, picked up a clipboard adhered to the end of my bed, and said, "Well, the chart here says that you have a strain of sexually transmitted disease indigenous to apes in southwestern Africa and a commune of female midgets in Tibet. Public health officials are very curious as to how you contracted it. Other than that, there's a lot of fancy Italian talk that says you have a bruised chin and a mild concussion, the latter from when you hit the street."

He read for a moment longer, put the chart back into the slot, and said, "You're fine, Fair Hair."

I didn't quite feel it, but knowing I was made me feel better, if that makes any sense. I was convalescing in a hospital four thousand miles from home. My wife was dead. My girlfriend didn't give an apparent damn. My newspaper career was in shambles. My best friend was leaving the paper. My head hurt to its brainy core. I was lonely, I was tired, I was for all practical purposes, defeated.

I hesitated and asked, "Did you tell Elizabeth I was here?"

He hesitated as well and replied, "I did." Another pause, then, cryptically, "She told me to send you her very best."

Like a distant cousin, a loose acquaintance. Send along my best. My life, in the last second, had just grown a shade darker.

So I did what I always do at such depressing times, and believe me, they've been many. I devised a plan of action, not necessarily full of thought, but something to get me going. Better to move than wallow, which was my guiding philosophy when I spent a year jetting around America in pursuit of news right after my wife had died in childbirth.

I swung my bare legs over the side of the bed and sat up for the first time in what must have been nearly a day. My head throbbed so bad that I had to squint through the pain. I leaned down, my elbows on my knees, facing Mongillo, who had sat back down on the chair, and I asked the most pertinent question you can ask him, which was, "What else do you have?" Mongillo, as I've noted, always has something else.

He reached into the case of his laptop computer, pulled out a folded-up newspaper and unfurled the front page on my lap. It was the prior day's *Boston Record,* and the banner headline read as follows: "Stolen Treasure Returned." The subhead said, "Priceless Vermeer painting taken in Gardner Museum heist anonymously delivered to *Record.*" Right beneath it, the left side of the upper half of the paper contained a giant photograph of *The Concert,* with none of the obvious obscenity that Mongillo had described. Beside it, on the right side, the top of my story unfolded in two wide columns.

I looked it over for a long moment. I should have been somewhere far beyond ecstatic. I mean, seriously, I had a front page, above-the-fold newsbreak about a painting that had gone missing for more than a decade personally delivered to me at the *Record* newsroom, as a possible prelude of more to come. The story was undoubtedly the talk of the city, maybe of America. It was probably even in the pages of the *Herald Tribune.* They love art, those Europeans.

And yet, I felt precious little of the adrenaline rush that comes with such a huge hit. Yeah, sure, it was pretty, this front page; I love telling people—namely, readers—that which they wouldn't otherwise know. But this story had the feeling of a distraction at best, a decoy a worst, like hush money, something good that is supposed to overcome something uniquely awful. I tossed it on the bed beside me and said to Mongillo, "What's the reaction back home?"

"Bedlam. You haven't been this sought-out since you got stuck in the ribs out at Congressional Country Club that morning. Every TV news crew is parked in our front lot. Every network has flown an A-list correspondent to Boston. Every expectation is that there's more on the way.

"And the FBI is livid. The case has gotten completely away from them. They have agents up from Washington running around the Boston office with lie detector equipment, much more concerned with who leaked you that first story than in finding who stole the paintings. Oh, and they got a subpoena to haul your ass before a federal grand jury for questioning. The paper put out a statement that you were out of the country on assignment. We just haven't told anyone you're sleeping one off in Rome."

I shook my head at it all, and that hurt as well, not the events, but the simple motion. I thought of Tom Jankle, special agent with the FBI, and more important, my personal sieve, and how he was withstanding the pressure. Was he acting independently? Was he under orders to set someone up? Who was telling the truth, and who was it that wanted Maggie Kane dead?

And then the image of the mayor popped into mind, staggering through his own lobby in the dark of a drunken night, his arm folded around the beautiful Hilary Kane. Hilary was gone within half an hour, dead within three days, and me, Mongillo and my trusted friend Hank Sweeney were the only ones who knew of his possible—check that, likely—involvement. Mayor Daniel Harkins, a killer. Now there's a story that would kick a city on its side.

I glanced over at the paper one more time, and back at Mongillo. I said to him, "You still going to bail out on the business?"

He replied, "Look at you, Jack. Look at you. Get up and look in the damn mirror. You have a hurt head and a broken heart. You're exhausted. You feel like you've been used. You want nothing so much as to take a break, and yet there's nothing within your body or soul that will allow it. You have to find a truth that may well leave you dead, that already killed one, maybe two women. And as soon as this is all wrapped up for good or bad, another story's going to break, another leak or a crash or a stupid act by a ridiculous politician, and you're going to have to climb back on that horse all over again."

He paused, looked at me hard, and said, "Yeah, I'm still getting out of the business, and the way you look, you should come too."

The creaky door slowly opened and a nurse came walking into the room. She was young, maybe twenty-two or twenty-three years old, with olive skin and full lips and jet black hair that flowed past her shoulders to the middle of her back. Her uniform, white, seemed to be cut inappropriately short, which was terrific. She flashed me an enormously alluring smile and said, "Mr. Flynn, I've come to give you your sponge bath."

Actually, I lie. The door did open, a nurse in fact walked in, but she looked like she had eaten her share of rigatoni with shaved Parmesan cheese, if you know what I mean, older, stern as a high school vice principal, and she said to me something to the tune of, "What the hell are you doing up?" Add an "a" to the tail end of each word for effect.

I told her I really needed some aspirin, preferably extra strength, and she stalked off, clearly unhappy with the idea of aiding a patient. I looked at Mongillo hard and said, "We've got to get out of here. These people could kill me."

"You wouldn't be the first," he said.

I struggled to my feet. My legs were wobbly, but not necessarily weak. I just hadn't stood in a while. I found my clothes in the drawer of a cheap dresser. I thought of my overnight bag sitting on the bed of my room at the Albergo del Sole. Probably the same guy that punched and kicked me had already riffled through the few belongings that I had brought. I put my clothing on, looked aghast in the mirror at the dark circles around my eyes, at my hair standing on end, and at the dressing that covered all of my jaw. I slowly, delicately pulled the bandage off, and saw that the huge black and blue welt was on the underside of my chin. So at least my male modeling potential was still intact.

As we stood ready to leave, Florenza Nightingale walked back in with a bottle of medicine in her hand, presumably aspirin—I hoped. She saw me fully clothed and yelled something in Italian, flapping one arm while she wagged a finger in my direction. I was going to get detention, I just knew it. She fled out of the room with obvious plans to quickly return, probably with reinforcements, and I looked at Mongillo and said, "Let's go." With that, we strode out into the hallway. After a couple of steps, the agony of motion lessened into excruciating pain. Mongillo pushed through a heavy fire door into the kind of stairwell that got me into so much trouble before, and down three flights. In the landing, I paused with my hands on my knees and said, "Hold on a second," as I tried to catch my breath.

I was always running lately—running from somebody, running after somebody, running away from my own sorry life. It was never-ending, the motion, the sense of fleeing, as if once again I had arrived at the point where I couldn't bear that which I had, so I chased something that I didn't know. I thought of bolting down Boylston Street in Boston a couple of days before after the gunman who had shown a brazen predisposition to firing his weapon. Could it be my own mortality that I was shagging down? Was I in some odd way suicidal?

My mind flashed back to a scene many years ago that I wouldn't have had any good reason to ever remember. It was a Sunday afternoon. I was living in Washington, in a house in Georgetown. Baker was but a puppy then. Katherine was my wife. It was one of those rare snow days in the capital when an entire panicked city seizes up and shuts down.

I had fallen asleep on the couch reading *The New York Times*, stretched out and impossibly comfortable, the light from the snow casting a warm glow through our tall windows all about the room. Katherine had taken the dog for a cold romp, and came walking back in with a movie from the video store. I don't even remember what one. But she woke me with a kiss, her nose freezing cold, and when I opened my eyes, the dog ran his grainy tongue across my face. I lay there stunned, smiling, light with a feeling that what I had, all these wonderful things that were mine, would continue until the end of time. It was one of countless moments of pure, stable bliss, until one day all of it was gone.

I looked up at Mongillo, who had no idea, in the most figurative sense, where I had just been. Maybe he was right for leaving this business, for searching for a stability that I had loved and lost.

Maybe I should do the same, chuck it all, become a consultant, maybe go to business school. It's true, I had been dealt a miserable hand, but maybe it was my fault for not doing something more with my cards.

I was about to say something to him, but what, I didn't know. I had no idea how we would find a woman who might already be dead in a capital on another continent. I had no idea how to even begin, what calls to make, who to go see. But it was then that Mongillo's phone rang, a Hungarian marching song or something like it. He reached into the back pocket of his khaki pants and flipped it open with a simple "Hello."

He looked into the dark, vacant air of the stairwell for a moment, then emotionlessly and without warning, he handed me the phone, saying only, "It's for you."

For me.

I took the phone, placed it against my ear as if this were all normal, and said, "Flynn here." In retrospect, I don't know what I expected. Probably Peter Martin. Maybe Tom Jankle. Possibly Elizabeth Riggs.

It was a woman's voice. She sounded distant, surrounded by noise, a little panicked. "Jack," she said, "it's Maggie Kane."

She paused here, giving me enough time to regroup and say, "Are you okay?"

"Am I okay?" she said, and then she laughed a low laugh. It wasn't a funny laugh, or mocking, but almost as if she were losing her faculties, as if life had taken so many turns for her in the past couple of days that she didn't have the capacity to do anything else, so she laughed. She added, "I'm in trouble. They found me in Rome. I think I got away. I took a flight to Paris." Here, the laughter turned to tears. It's amazing how close the two can sometimes be—laughter and tears, not Paris and Rome, though those too. "I need your help," she said, her voice trailing off into emotion.

"Are you on a cell phone?"

"No, a pay phone."

"I'll be there this afternoon. Where do you want to meet?"

She paused, then said, "At the entrance to the Louvre, there's a pharaoh. Meet me near him, five o'clock."

"Maggie," I said, my voice rising, "listen to me. Don't use your credit cards, your calling cards, your cell phone, anything. I will bring you cash. But do not do anything that can lead people to you."

By now, she was fully crying, convulsing, the fear overtaking the strength of her good intentions. "Five o'clock," she said, and she hung up the phone.

I handed the cell phone back to Mongillo and walked toward the outside door. Maybe it was a ruse, some sort of setup, an attempt by kidnappers to get us out of town. But I didn't have time to overanalyze. Usually, there are twists and contortions and distortions, but sometimes, life is what it is, and this time, it was time to go to France.

"Where we heading?" Mongillo said, bounding after me as we hit the parking lot of the hospital.

"Paris, on the next flight."

"Oh, man," he said. "I come all the way to Italy and don't have so much as a bowl of pasta. It's like going to one of those strip joints in Rhode Island where you're not allowed to touch the girls."

Yeah, something like that.

Then he said, "Martin's not going to like this."

"Tell me about it. Have you ever stayed in a Paris hotel room? They're about $400 a night."

Chapter Twenty-one

There's nothing quite like a bad economy to make the persnickety French a whole lot more amenable to loathsome American visitors and the wallets full of money that we freely toss around.

I came to this realization on the Air France flight from Rome to Charles de Gaulle, when Vinny Mongillo, God bless him, told the flight attendant, who I swear must have been a finalist in the 2002 Miss Universe pageant and would have won if her lips weren't so succulently swollen, *"Mon chat est un blanc chapeau."*

What he wanted was a rum and Coke. Now I don't want to be showy about the two years of intensive French studies that I undertook at South Boston High, but what I believe he said was, "There's a fetid moose in your medicine cabinet." So I pointed at the Coke can and one of those tiny bottles of rum that sat on her cart. She smiled, nearly causing the plane to do a loop-the-loop, and said in a delicious Parisian accent, and I quote, "That's what I thought he wanted."

Ah, love.

On the ground, it was much the same story. We made an effort to speak French, they rushed into English. Not once did I feel even the slightest need to remind anyone of how the US of A bailed out an entire continent back in WW-Two, their sorry little country included. Even the new currency, the Euro, seemed so wonderfully American, unlike the nine million drachmas to the dollar or whatever it was that they used to use.

It was only two in the afternoon, three full hours until our intended rendezvous, so at Mongillo's insistence, we immediately made our way from the airport to the Louvre. It was, I should probably be embarrassed to add, my first trip to this fair city, and as such, my eyes were about to fall out of my head, not just from all the beautiful women, but from the stunning palace architecture, the flowers, the narrow streets, the patisseries, the boulangeries, the glaciers. I mean, how is it that the entire cigarette-smoking, cell phone–gabbing nation seemed so wafer-thin with temptations like these along every gently curving street?

We got out of our cab at the top of the U-shaped complex, though complex is entirely the wrong word because it implies something new, like a suburban office park. No, this was old, ancient, rich, and textured, carrying the type of history that wasn't measured in decades, but centuries. It made me feel at once young and completely insignificant.

Speaking of which, I insisted that we case the pharaoh statue before we headed inside, so we could get the lay of the land. Ends up, the pharaoh wasn't a statue at all, but a live human being dressed entirely in a shiny pharaoh costume, head-to-toe, available for hired photo opportunities, which seemed to have a strong appeal to Japanese tourists. I don't know why this bothered me, meeting at a person rather than a monument, but it did, probably because my mind was now entering the realm of spy games, wondering who was inside that getup, and were they part of some larger, dangerous conspiracy. Could I be killed by someone who was dressed up as someone who was dead? Would that fact be the first paragraph of my obituary?

Mongillo assured me that the pharaoh was a fixture, that anyone of any decent breeding knows all about him, and that it was time for me to get a grip. Yeah, well, tell that to Hilary Kane, though it's too late, which is exactly my point. So, inside we went.

They say it takes four days to properly tour the Louvre, see everything that needs to be seen, and appreciate everything that demands appreciation. And maybe that's true if you happen to be an amputee or bound for any number of other reasons to a wheelchair that needs to have its axles properly greased. Me, I could probably make a few bucks teaching people how to see the entire place in under two hours, an idea that I ran by Vinny Mongillo, who in turn muttered for the third time in an hour, "Philistine."

The first time, it's worth noting, was in front of the *Mona Lisa*. After we fought through the crowd for an up-close look, I turned to him and said, "I thought it would be bigger." The second time was when I tried ordering a Budweiser in the concourse snack bar, but I was only kidding there, having a little fun with my newfound friends, the Fronch.

Anyway, Mongillo was having more fun than I ever would or could, expressed at times in the oddest of ways. As he stood silently staring at a painting entitled *Venus and the Graces Offering Gifts to a Young Girl*, a Botticelli, I watched in confusion as he wiped a tear from his olive-colored cheek. He stared and he stared and he stared as a veritable United Nations of tourists had to walk around the hulking figure for their own look at the work.

Later, when I was denied my Bud and instead stood in the snack bar sipping on a four-Euro Coke, I asked him, "I'm not giving you a hard time. I'm actually curious. What made you so emotional over that Botticelli?"

"Jack," he said, calling me by my given name, which meant that he had left the realm of the joke. "Did you look at it? Did you really, really look at it? Did you notice the soft colors and the light brushstrokes? Did you catch the earthiness of the young girl, the symbol of our youth, yet the essence of our mortality, our very mundaneness?"

Actually, I didn't, or couldn't. Or maybe, given who I am, just plain wouldn't. What I saw was a bunch of pale-faced, virtually identical looking women and wondered how hard it would be to put together in one of those 10,000-piece puzzles that my grandmother used to spread across her dining-room table.

He went on, "The contrast, the heaven and earth, endless virtues faced with natural vices. It's all there, right in front of you, the work of a master with a brush. And I couldn't help it, looking at the raw beauty and all that it encompassed, so I cried."

He paused and added, "Don't tell the newsroom, asshole."

He was kidding about that last part, I think. I said, solemn-toned, feeling a little self-conscious now, "No, I didn't see it. Maybe I didn't look hard enough." My own pause here. "Or maybe I didn't know how to look."

We both stood in silence in one of the snack bars at the Louvre, Vinny eating a turkey sandwich on what I would imagine was French bread, though I guess any kind of bread you get in this country could be so described. I continued sipping on the Coke, my stomach tight from the meeting ahead.

I asked, "How long have you followed this stuff?" As I asked, it occurred to me that *follow* might be the wrong word. You follow the Red Sox or the Celtics or weather patterns that come across the Great Lakes and wreak havoc on your shallow little weekend plans to sit your fat ass on a Maine beach. You don't follow Renaissance artists, assuming that's what Botticelli was, and obvi-ously, with me, that really is only an assumption.

Vinny, kindly, didn't call me on it, though he did hesitate a bit before answering.

"Since I was a kid," he said softly, looking down at his nearly eaten food.

Surprised, I said, "You were interested in Renaissance artists as a kid?" I mean, you look at Vinny and you picture him in his youth spattered in mud, his fist slammed inside an oversize bag of potato chips, a baseball cap cocked sideways, maybe trying to hustle a few pals in a game of jacks.

He nodded, but didn't speak, and it was obvious that he didn't want to. Didn't matter to me. I asked, "What got you interested?"

He took the last bite of his sandwich and wiped his hands on a napkin that said The Louvre on it. All around us, tourists from every possible country and culture came and went, excitedly talk-ing in languages that I didn't understand, like Australian. We leaned against a metal counter that separated the shop from the hallway that ran past it.

Vinny met my gaze and said in a suddenly determined voice, "There aren't a lot of things in my life, then and now, that are particularly beautiful. You know what I mean? I look in the mirror and—" he held his hands around his face now, as if presenting it— "this is what I see. I'm obese. I'm a greasy wop. I have to buy special clothes. People look at me wondering what the hell went wrong. I see some of them shaking their heads as if I did something wrong, as if me being me was somehow offensive to them, like I invaded their aesthetic just by crossing their line of sight."

He kept the same tight-jawed tone throughout the monologue. I don't know who he was most mad at—himself, the world, me, whomever—but an inner anger that I had never seen revealed in him was suddenly pouring forth.

He said, "I didn't suddenly get fat; I've always been fat, as a baby, as a schoolkid, a teenager, a young adult, now. I've never had a beautiful woman in my bed, Jack. I've barely had any women in my bed. I don't see what you see. I don't get the looks that you might get, that any normal person gets. I have all the same hopes and God do I dream those same dreams, but it ends up being sad because I know deep inside that they'll never be fulfilled.

"But just because I'm a fat slob doesn't mean I can't appreciate beauty or want it all around me. So when other kids were going off to the school dance or flirting with the girls in class, I looked at art. It was a beauty that I could have, right at my fingertips. I got to understand it, to live it, to appreciate it more than most people ever will. And to no small extent, it's kept me going through all these many years and insults and insecurities. I love art, and it's mine."

What an utter, unambiguous, unadulterated ass I am. You think you know someone well. You're around them virtually all day, every day. You do the same basic job. You respect their abilities to no end. You assume you understand their very core. And then you realize over a damned turkey sandwich and a Coke that what you've been looking at all these many years is not a person but a mask, and what's underneath is probably more attractive, more interesting, than anything you could have imagined.

I didn't know what to say, so what I said was this: "I wish you had told me these things a long time ago."

"What, that I'm a fat fuck?" Vinny said. More jovial now. "That I'm depressed? That I'm in a cycle I can't bail out of? That I'd like to nail a decent-looking dame?"

"So you'll lose the weight now. You'll knock your blood pressure down. Your cholesterol will fall." I said this in a tone laced with almost too much determination, making the feat seem somehow harder than it should have been. I mean, come on. The entire world was on the Atkins Diet, eating a pound of bacon five times a day and somehow watching weight melt off them.

"I will," he replied. "Problem is, I lose my career ambitions with it. But maybe it proves a small price to pay."

With that, he looked down at the watch stretched tight across his wrist and announced, "Four-fifteen. We need a plan, and we need to get outside. Time to salvage what's left of your sorry little career."

The last time I sat outdoors watching a life-changing event unfold before my eyes, I was blissfully planted in Fenway Park, and the Red Sox were high-stepping toward the pennant. Four days later, I'm in the courtyard of the Louvre, watching any sense of professional pride, personal confidence, and self-esteem slipping toward the proverbial door. What a difference a few days makes.

Here, in a nutshell, is what happened. Vinny Mongillo and I took the long escalator up through the glass pyramid entrance. Outdoors, in a cloudy September chill, we separated and walked around the famous pharaoh in different directions, Mongillo to the left, me to the right. He stopped around thirty, maybe forty yards away, in an open expanse with an unimpeded view. I slowly made my way toward the costumed creature and pulled up about ten yards short. It was 4:30 P.M., thirty minutes to showtime. I was utterly without so much as a whiff of a guess as to where it all might go from there.

So I stood and I stood and I stood. Minutes moved slower than water through a drain at a men's hair-loss clinic. The sky went from gray to slate. Waves of tourists flocked from the museum at closing time. The damned pharaoh, blessed with endless energy, kept beckoning to people, serving as a veritable magnet for virtually anyone of Japanese descent. They'd smile, place an arm around his shoulder, pose for a photograph, and they were off, another uniquely French moment to tell friends and families all about in the suburbs of Nagasaki.

The air turned from chilly to cold, and believe me, the Parisians are not to be confused with frontiersmen, not unless you consider a trip to Provence with a stay at a Relais & Chateaux inn in the company of a toy poodle to be the frontier. So they were all bundled up in black peacoats, the men as pretty as the women, and I watched them, wondering what was to come, waiting for it to arrive, fearing the results.

I thought back to that night at Fenway and how innocent life had been not all that long ago. Elizabeth and I were in those last clingy moments of our inevitable good-bye. The Sox were in the pennant race. I was in a slump, but I knew I'd break out of it; I always do.

Not this time, though. I killed a young woman, or rather, a story I dupishly wrote led to her death. Same thing, really, or maybe worse. And now another woman, an innocent human being, was being stalked by a killer or killers who wanted her dead. And what was I doing to help? Nothing, really, except putting her in harm's way, forgetting to give her advice on how to save her life, in effect using her as I had used so many others before to try to get to the heart of a publishable truth. I've heard it said that newspaper reporting is like war, meaning that innocents will be hurt in the name of a common good. Even if that's the case, this story of Toby Harkins was certainly an extreme.

I thought of Jankle, so confident the first time I met him, so confused the second. Was it an act? Was he behind any of this? I thought of Peter Martin back in the *Record* newsroom, relatively immune to all that was going wrong. He had a front-page story detailing the return of one of the world's most valuable stolen paintings. To him, for him, death and destruction were the justifiable means toward a stunning, perhaps Pulitzer prize–winning, end.

I was, quite literally, more than an ocean away from anything that previously mattered in my life—a girlfriend who was no longer mine; a fluffy golden retriever that would be my best friend until the day he died; a career that seemed always on the incline. And here I was in this forlorn courtyard in a foreign capital with dark descending faster than an April tide watching it all flitter away and wondering why. Why?

Because I, Jack Flynn, should be renamed Jackass. That's the glib answer. I needed more.

And more important than any of this, more important than the sad details of my own life, was the following question: Where was Maggie Kane?

At 4:55 P.M. I looked over at Vinny Mongillo, about half a football field away. He was taking in the scene through a small pair of opera glasses that I had no idea where or when he acquired. He was scanning the periphery of the park, refocusing back on me and the pharaoh, then to the edges again. He kept his face partially concealed with a folded-up newspaper, *Le Monde,* I believe, which I also believe stood for, "You're screwed, vulgar Americans."

I, too, looked around, but saw nothing—no pretty blondes, no shadowy killers lurking with a cache of deadly weapons, no great hope. I guess, in retrospect, I don't know what I expected to happen. Did I really believe that as I stood near this bizarre pharaoh in a crowd of tourists within the shadows of the Louvre that Maggie Kane would come walking across the Jardin des Tuileries, tap me on the shoulder, and say, "I've been looking for you, Jack. Let me tell you everything." And that at that point, we'd steal away to a French restaurant with a tuxedoed sommelier and order a fixed-price meal involving tender beef and a buttery Bordeaux and never would we hear from the would-be killers again.

In other words, which Dakota do I think I'm from?

Instead, five o'clock came and went with nary a tap, whisper, or flutter—my heart aside. I stood virtually frozen, trying to look any-thing but, glancing to my sides, occasionally turning around, trying to get a lay of this foreign, potentially dangerous land. Mongillo had my back, and my front, for that matter, perched across the way trying to blend into the scenery as well as a 300-pound American in a flannel shirt and khaki work trousers can in the heart of Paris, France.

Five-ten turned into 5:20, and nothing. At 5:30, a car pulled over at a nearby circle and a man in a black raincoat emerged from the passenger side. He walked in my general direction, took a long look around, then headed back to the car with neither an expres-sion nor a spoken word.

By that point, the flow of people emerging from the Louvre had receded to a small trickle, then to barely nothing at all. At 5:40, the pharaoh picked up a canister of money from the cement path in front of him and walked slowly off toward the Tuileries, another day at the office behind him. At that point, Mongillo, now sitting on a bench in the distance, began walking toward me. I made a subtle motion with my hands that told him to stop, and he did. We stood awkwardly like that, forty yards or so apart, for another ten minutes, until I beckoned him over. By then it was 5:55, and we were alone in the cloudy cold, save for a few stragglers making their way toward the bridge over the River Seine.

When he drew close, Mongillo asked simply, "Now what?" and the very question, as well as the vacant tone in which it was asked, caught me oddly off guard. Vinny Mongillo, bereft not just of answers, but of ideas. We were exquisitely screwed, and his two words forming one question gave voice to just how badly.

Sternly, I replied, "Maybe she meant six o'clock. Maybe she's messed up in the time zone changes. We wait longer." I knew I was probably wrong, but how was I supposed to know for sure, so we sat on a bench in the middle of a stretch of park with grass and hard-packed dirt and some cement paths, and we waited some more, mostly in silence, but for the frequent sound of Mongillo's cell phone vibrating. After a particularly long patch of nothing, he said, "We should eat well tonight." But the line, the sentiment, would never be fulfilled; he knew that and so did I.

By 6:30, it was mostly dark—so much for Paris being the city of light—and I said in desolate frustration, staring at the perimeter of the park around us, "Where do you want to stay?"

"Don't know. What's that place Princess Di stayed on her last night, the Ritz?"

And for some reason, the thought of Diana's death in Paris made me sad. Everything at that point made me sad—the mournful look of the darkened Louvre, the lack of a sunset over the Seine, the breeze that carried no good tidings.

"We stay at the Ritz, Martin will make sure its *our* last night alive."

"No matter to me."

Probably no matter to me, either, except I needed to be around to get thoughts into print to pull myself—and hopefully Maggie Kane—out of this mess. But for the latter, I suspected it was too late. If she wasn't here, she was probably dead—a thought that thrust me into deep depression.

The breeze blew up off the river, the last bits of easy gray faded from the ceiling of clouds, and I said to Mongillo, "Let's get out of this place."

"Unfortunately," he replied as we both struggled to our feet, our bones stiff from the cold, "I'll never look at the Louvre the same again."

We set off, down some wide steps, across the Tuileries, and veered right down Rue de la Paix, toward Place Vendôme, past one fabulously expensive boutique after another. We cut across the beautiful square and arrived at the door of the Park Hyatt Hotel, at which time Mongillo pointed to the sign and said, "Martin can't get upset over a damned Hyatt."

Five minutes later, when he plunked down his credit card for both our rooms—I didn't want to use mine—at $450 a night, Mongillo said, "All right, so he can get upset. Thank God I'm leaving the paper."

We must have looked like quite a pair, the rotund Italian-

American who hadn't had a wink of sleep in two days, and the beaten-up hero with a bruise on his lower chin, despondence in his deep blue eyes. Or something like that. I grabbed a copy of the *Herald Tribune* from the concierge desk, told Mongillo I'd meet him in the lobby champagne bar in an hour, and made my way upstairs.

Once in my room—my *chambre,* I think they might call it in France, I drew a bath. Truth be known, those are words—I drew a bath—that I never thought I'd utter. I mean, the only thing I'd ever drawn in my life was a king-high flush in a poker game at the University Club one night, but the damned thing looked so inviting, with brushed chrome handles on the deep soaking tub, a clever little spigot that was more like a waterfall, and a fluffy bath mat waiting to soak up the warm water from my tired feet.

I pulled a large bottle of Evian out of the minibar. As I opened it, I gazed at the little menu card and saw it cost $12. Too late now. I peeled off my clothes and climbed inside the tub, feeling much like I did during my Saturday night baths at our South Boston home when I was a kid. I picked up the *Herald Tribune* and scanned the front page—a corrupt finance minister in Italy (Stop the presses!), a squabble over NATO expenditures in Brussels, a bevy of cops indicted on brutality charges in Los Angeles. Ho-hum. I flipped inside to get more U.S. news, and scanned a column of brief stories from the States. It was the fifth one down that didn't just grab my eyes, it all but poked them. "Masterpiece Returned to Boston Newspaper." It mentioned *The Concert* and the Gardner and the damned thing had Vermeer and Flynn in the same sentence. Artists, both, at different times, in different ways, with different instruments. Who would have thunk?

I leaned my head back and, for reasons that I can't properly explain, I thought about my father, a career pressman before he died, sitting at the kitchen table every morning eating a bowl of corn flakes with a sliced banana, still in the ink-stained hunter green apron that he wore through every one of his shifts, proud to be a part of an enterprise as great as the *Record.* He never lived to see my byline in his paper, but what would he think of me now?

After that, I thought of all those nights lying in my single bed in my tiny room in South Boston, the transistor radio under the pillow broadcasting the late innings of a Red Sox game or the final quarter of the Celtics playing at the old Boston Garden, Jo Jo White passing to Havlicek, Havlicek faking left even though everyone knew he couldn't go that way, then driving right, another shot, another score. It was in the middle of these games that the train would invariably glide by in the distant night, sounding a horn that to some might seem forlorn, but to me was a beckoning—an invitation, the audible manifestation of an abiding desire to break the bonds, to be a part of a larger world, to shed the expectations that were never set high enough.

And here I was, a well-known newspaper correspondent, the bane of some famous people, the confidant of others, out there in that world that I so wanted to embrace. And now, all I wanted was a home that I could call my own, and at this very moment, the modest rowhouses on the ramrod-straight streets of my native South Boston would have been more than enough. Oh, to be able to go back in time.

This, of course, caused me to take a census of the important women in my life—Katherine and Elizabeth and Hilary and Maggie. Two of them were dead; one was missing by her own volition, the other by someone else's. This is some life, Jack Flynn. So I shut my eyes in a marble bathroom in Paris, France, and I thought of Baker, odd as that may seem, loping across Columbus Park on the Boston waterfront in simple pursuit of a tennis ball, bounding back, dropping it at my feet, doing it all over again until it was time to go home and he'd happily tag along at my side. After Katherine died, I tried to convince myself that I could only miss what I still actually had, and right now, Baker was pretty much it.

Finally, I thought about the knock on the hotel door, three firm bangs, followed by a muffled announcement. I tried to holler back, but my throat was so thick that I couldn't get the words out with any volume or velocity. The door immediately flung open and a man with a tray came walking in.

He saw me through the opening and said in the unapologetic tone that pretty much characterizes his country, *"Pardon, monsieur."* Then he said something that sounded like "Free," but after just a few hours in Paris, I knew that the concept didn't exist in French culture, so the word probably wasn't a part of their language. As he said it, he held up the tray, which bore a silver bowl containing apples, oranges and a bulging bunch of red grapes. At that point, my sophomore high school French came trickling back. Free was fruit. The fruit, hopefully, was free.

"Merci," I said, and he placed the basket down and carried on his way.

Now I was left to contemplate the growing roll of the dead, and proceeded to how I would find Maggie Kane in a city of more than nine million people, a place where I had no friends to help me, no cultural knowledge to guide me, nothing so much as an English to French translation dictionary to assist me. Should I fly home the following day, or return to the Louvre and wait yet again, or simply wander the streets hoping for a stroke of blind luck?

I stepped out of the tub as I contemplated these miserable options, and though I'm honestly not prone to talking to myself, said aloud, "Where the hell are you, Maggie Kane?"

"Right here," she replied. I looked up, and there she was, Maggie Kane, leaning in the bathroom doorway, her arms crossed, her legs long. She looked a little worse for the wear of the last few days, but perfect nonetheless. And there I was, naked as a walrus on an Antarctic iceberg. When I lunged for a bath towel, I actually heard her laugh—a sound no exposed man wants to hear.

"What the fuck," I said, as much to the situation as to the woman who had created it.

"We have a thing about bathrooms, you and me," she said, her eyes not even flinching from mine. I wrapped a towel around my waist. I shot her an angry look, but truth be known, I was anything but. What I really wanted to do was hug her, though in my present state of undress, reverted to Plan B, which is, when in doubt, get dressed.

"Give me a minute," I said, and she turned and walked out.

I wrapped myself in what all the hotel brochures inevitably describe as a "plush terrycloth robe," and grabbed my overnight bag from the bed. She had already begun feeding herself some of the grapes. I returned to the bathroom to get dressed and tried to control my feeling of unabashed elation. The return of the Vermeer aside, this was the first reasonably good thing to happen to me in a week.

Maggie Kane was sitting here in my hotel room, after seeing me naked, which I suppose was little more than a metaphor for this whole entire story. And now it was time to do what I do best, which is to push through the layers of intentional haze in pursuit of a clear and unimpeachable truth.

Chapter Twenty-two

After she finished the grapes, she started in on the red pear, which, truth be known, I had my eye on myself.

"You want me to order us some room service?" I asked.

She nodded her head. I had dressed quickly in my one remaining change of clothes, combed my wet hair, and emerged into the bedroom. She was sitting in an upholstered chair next to a small café table. I handed her the leather-bound room service menu that had been resting on a nightstand, and then I sat on the edge of the bed.

Make no mistake, this was one striking woman, even in her current state. Her short, moppy blonde hair was ruffled in the back. Her cheeks were streaked by tears and slightly stained by dirt. Her pretty blue eyes, unusually deep-set, were rimmed by red. And yet she carried an unmistakable look of relief, as if she had finally found a sanctuary right here in the Park Hyatt Hotel, in the company of Jack Flynn. I wish more attractive women adopted this exact attitude.

Five days ago, she had led what I suspected was a relatively unremarkable life, a description that isn't intended to be in any way a slap or knock. Suddenly, her sister is dead. She's shot at on the streets of Boston. She escapes on a flight to Rome, runs for her life on the crooked byways of that ancient city, and then finds herself in Paris.

And here's what she had to say: "I'll have a hamburger, medium, cheddar cheese, extra fries, with a glass of Pinot Noir, oh, and a Coke." She said this while scanning down the menu with her index finger, then looking at me without a hint of embarrassment. I think that might have been the point at which I began falling in love.

"No dessert?"

"The chocolate mousse cake."

So I ordered two of everything, just to make things easy, create some camaraderie—a pair of like-minded people dining on the same things as they move toward a common goal. That and the fact that I also craved a juicy burger, and if the French don't know how to make fries, then who the hell does?

She put the menu down and looked around the room, which I began noticing for the first time. "Nice place," she said, and she was right. It had tall ceilings, maybe twelve feet high. The palette was one of total neutrality, various shades of tan melded with touches of dark wood, all to create a chic, minimalist feel that flies in the face of most things Parisian. The place whispered luxury rather than screamed it.

"Thank you," I said, and she looked at me oddly, almost as if she were looking through me.

As we waited for the room service, I asked her how she had found me and where she had been, and she walked me through the hell that was her last few days. She had fled Copley Square by subway, got off at the airport, grabbed the first flight out of town, which happened to be to Rome. Once there, she holed up in a room at the Raphael, paying by her own credit card, which was undoubtedly the source of the problem. She stayed inside until breakfast, but as she sat on the roof terrace, she saw a familiar face that she couldn't quite place. So she left. In a hurry.

She bolted safely through old Rome as I was serving the quasi-useful purpose of being someone's punching bag. She jumped into a taxi and headed back to the airport and jumped on a flight to Paris. She had no choice, she said, but to pay by credit card, so someone somewhere surely knew that she was here. Fortunately,

Paris is a big town—a fact that I was ruing just a few moments before.

Once here, she hid out in the Louvre, watching our rendezvous location through an upstairs window with the help of a pair of cheap binoculars. She left the museum when the pharaoh did, and followed us through the Tuileries, across the Place Vendôme, and to the hotel. She snuck into my room when the server delivered the fruit basket, which she had arranged.

All in all, this was one resourceful woman.

"What's your day job?" I asked out of raw curiosity when she finished her tale.

"Third-grade teacher," she replied. Of course.

The food came, and I've got to admit, those French chefs know their way around the old Gaggenau, if you know what I mean. The French fries were so good I was ready to strip off my clothes and lie on the plate next to them, though maybe that's just me. Actually, it's not. I looked over at Maggie and she was outright moaning as she took bite after ravenous bite of her perfectly seasoned burger. I mean, never in my life had I been alone in a bedroom with a woman in this state of advanced ecstasy.

She saw me looking at her, shoved the last of her food into her mouth, and laughed a complicit laugh. "I haven't eaten a thing in two days," she said.

She put her napkin up to her face, and then pressed the palms of her hands against her temples, pressed them hard, and when she let her arms fall back on her lap, the light seemed to have left her eyes, the softness gone from her mouth.

"You know," I said, jovially, "we can always order more food."

She shook her head, smiling again, but it was a wan smile now. Then she stopped smiling and looked down at the patch of taupe carpet in front of her and said quietly, "My sister was buried yesterday."

"I'm sorry," I replied. "I can't even begin to tell you how sorry. Which is why I want to start finding out what the hell went wrong, and if there's any small part of this that we can still make right."

She looked up at me with those blue eyes, but said nothing. I began to speak, but was interrupted—startled, really—by the ringing phone. Nobody knew where I was except the people who were already here, and then I realized: Mongillo, waiting for my arrival down at the champagne bar.

"Let me grab this," I told her. "I think it's my colleague."

Picking up the phone: "Yeah."

"I come all the way to the city of eternal love to get stood up by the likes of you?"

"Listen, change of plan. I'll fill you in on everything very soon. But I don't want you to leave the bar just yet, in the event that you're being cased. Stay put. Have a plate of foie gras and I'll call down there in about twenty minutes."

Sitting back down, I said, "We don't have the luxury of a lot of time, so I'm just going to ask you to tell me everything you have. I want to know why your sister is dead, and I want to know what I did to cause it."

She looked back down at the floor for a long moment. The room, by the way, was illuminated by a single low lamp, and light from the street that filtered through the floor-to-ceiling windows cast odd shadows across the walls.

"It's someone very powerful, very dangerous," she said, staring up at me, her arms on her knees. She was wearing a pair of raggedy old jeans and a navy blue sweatshirt—a kind of Honey-I'm-just-going-to-grout-the-bathtub-before-I-haul-you-back-in-bed-and-have-my-womanly-way-with-you look. Trust me, it works.

"That's what we do at a newspaper. We take on powerful people."

"Not this time," she shot back. "This time you helped them kill my sister."

Valid point, perhaps, and even if not, I wasn't in any position to fight back. She still had some anger in her, and it wasn't my place to fight it. It might never be my place. I also couldn't afford to have this be an argument. I needed it to be a congress. And this is what I did, better than just about anyone I know—I got people to talk, whether politicians or professional crooks, or as is so often the case, a combination of the two.

So I said again, "Yes, it's my fault, but now we're in it together, and I need information to get us out. Tell me what you know, Maggie. Please."

She looked at me again with those piercing eyes, not frightened or angry now, but determined. The look turned into a stare. I told myself, warned myself, to forget her aesthetics, as Mongillo might say, and concentrate on her knowledge. I met her gaze, flat, intentionally needy, helpful, apologetic, some odd combination that I wasn't sure I could actually pull off.

And then she started.

"My sister had a fiancé," she said. "This schmuck who's been questioned, though I'm sure he didn't kill her. She was ready to be married. And one morning she caught him—well, anyway, she broke it off. And then she made a mistake a week or so ago. She was confused and vulnerable and she was at a bar, drinking, and she ended up with the mayor, Dan Harkins."

Maggie hesitated, looked back down at the floor, and said, "This is embarrassing for Hilary." She paused again, searching for polite words, no doubt.

I interjected, "Look, if it makes you feel any better, there are people out there who've accused me of being in bed with the mayor for a long time." It was a little reporting humor—too little, it ended up, because Maggie just stared at me expressionlessly for a long moment.

Then she said, as if relieved to get it out in one long exhale, "They went back to his place. He has a condo at the new Ritz-Carlton complex there. You probably know that already. She didn't spend the night or anything.

"When she was leaving, he was asleep in the bedroom, and she logged on to his computer, she says to get her email, and I believe her. But when she moved the mouse, a file was already on the screen."

She paused here, this time as a frightened look drew her face even tighter than it had already been. She put her hands up to her temples again, as if steadying herself, before she went on. I remained quiet, part of that old reporter's rule about never getting in the way of someone who is telling you an important story.

After a long moment, she said, "The file, like a Microsoft Word file, was slugged 'Toby.' That's the name of his son, the fugitive. You know that." She said this last sentence as a declaration, not a question. And she was right, of course. I did know that.

"It had some telephone numbers, foreign numbers. It had the name of a bank—Barclays, and what Hilary thought were account numbers and maybe some routing numbers. It had an address in Ireland, County Cork or County something. I have most of this stuff written down."

That ringing sound, like a pinball machine recording a particularly hefty bonus score, I hoped was only in my head. This is what my good friend Tom Jankle had been driving at in our meeting on the patio at Franklin Park. This was also a perfectly plausible motive for the mayor of Boston, Daniel Harkins, to kill this lovely young woman. If he hadn't, she would be able to tie him to his fugitive son. My mind immediately began racing to and fro determining exactly what else I would need to land a story naming Harkins as a prime suspect into print.

Of course, none of this explained any connection between my leaked story about Toby Harkins and the paintings to Hilary Kane's death, or why the Vermeer had been delivered to my newsroom three days before. My head was starting to hurt again, even as my heart pumped harder in unseen celebration.

I stopped her here, asking, "What do you mean, it's written down? Do you have a printout of the documents?"

"No, but there is a printout. Hilary thought that's maybe what would get her in trouble, and I suspect it did. She made a printout, and got a few of the pages, but then the printer either jammed or ran out of paper, and she got the fuck out of there."

We'll excuse her vulgarity for now, and as important, we'll excuse me being turned on for the slightest flicker of the briefest moment by said vulgarity. Anyone who saw her looking like that, dressed like that, talking like that, would completely understand. I asked, "Do you know where the printout is?"

She held my gaze with those piercing eyes. "No," she said. "I was poking around in her apartment, looking for it, but couldn't find it. She never told me what she did with it."

"But what do you mean you have something written down?"

"When Hilary was killed, obviously I realized this was life and death, so I jotted down what I remembered of what she told me. I stashed it in my locker at the gym."

Again, this was one resourceful woman. After I leave the news business, which would probably be sooner rather than later, she could have my job.

I said, "All right. Sorry to interrupt. Keep going with what you know."

She looked off into the dark expanse of the hotel room, collecting her thoughts. Then she refocused on me and said, "There's not a whole lot more. Hilary opened another file that she said, I think, was slugged 'TOBY 2.' It had the names of a couple of law enforcement types written down, their phone numbers, maybe a lawyer or something. I don't have their names. I don't think Hil ever gave them to me. They're on the printout."

I nodded. I was sitting on the edge of the bed in a darkened Parisian hotel room as the realization crashed over me like cold seawater on a March day that Daniel Harkins, the longtime, much respected mayor of Boston, had probably had a young woman, a complete and total innocent, killed, for the sole purpose of protecting his own career and the flight of his murderous son. Forgive me for saying this, but in a strictly journalistic sense, I loved it.

That same mayor, despite regular denials, had apparently kept in close contact with this fugitive son, to the point of either sending him money in Europe—or maybe taking money in return for some favor. Could he have been blackmailing his own child?

And did this mean that my story didn't cause her death? That thought, that question, was the nicest one to ponder.

Maggie Kane looked at me and I looked back at her. In the distance, I heard an ambulance siren, which always sounds a little more frantic in Europe, and it reminded me of the afternoon I had hidden out in her sister's bathroom only four days before. Seemed like an eternity ago.

I asked, "How do you know all this?"

She didn't hesitate, as if she had been waiting for the question. "Hil was panicked. She wanted to go to the authorities, but she was afraid she might end up going to someone listed on Harkins's file, and that they'd try to cover the whole thing up—or worse. She didn't know what to do, so she told me all about it. And together we decided that she should hire a lawyer, and hopefully the money she spent would someday be repaid to her in some way. She had made an appointment to see someone Monday morning, but before she got there, she was killed."

She gave me the lawyer's name, which I didn't recognize, and I made a mental note to have Peter Martin send a reporter over to the office ASAP.

Normally, I get an elaborate adrenaline rush when I come into information like the stuff that Maggie Kane was giving me now. I begin writing the top of the story in my mind, I sketch out the questions that I'll ask the targets, I anticipate the pathetic answers I'll get in response, I envision how it will look in print, the glory of seeing it above the fold on the front page, the impact it will have as the knowledge rains down on an unsuspecting city.

But I felt none of that now, just a headache as I tried processing all that I knew in contrast to the more that I didn't know in the journalistic calculator that was my brain. The question of the moment: Why was FBI Special Agent Tom Jankle leaking to me about the Gardner heist just as the mayor was thinking he might be caught aiding and abetting his own son? Was it coincidence? Did Jankle know? Were they somehow in cahoots?

"What aren't I asking you that I should know?" It's the standard, mop-up question at the end of any friendly interview. Sometimes, oddly enough, it's where you get the best information, because the subject starts free-ranging thoughts in a stream-of-consciousness kind of way.

Maggie shook her head, as if to say there wasn't anything else, only she kept shaking her head, slowly, and after a moment, almost imperceptibly. She just kept looking at me while I looked back at her, her eyes frozen, her face the very picture of resigned fear, and finally she asked a seemingly simple question that might have been the most complicated one I've ever heard: "What am I going to do?"

The first city editor I ever had used to tell me that when a story, and by extension, life, got too complicated, you had to plot a strategy that began with a string of basic, even minute, actions. Complexity breeds inertia, and inertia is the father of defeat, he used to say. So do anything to create the aura and perception of movement, and it will feed on itself.

So even though I had no idea yet what in God's good name we were going to do, I said, "First thing, you're going to get some rest. You're going to sleep right here on this comfortable bed. We're going to triple-lock the door, bolt the windows, pull the curtains, and I'm going to push these chairs together for my bed and make sure that nothing in here goes wrong.

"Then we're going to wake up and get back to Boston. We're going to get some protection, professionals, who'll get us in without incident. We're going to put you somewhere safe. And we're going to find out exactly who was behind your sister's death, and publish all the reasons why. At that point, the authorities will have no choice but to take action, even if it's the mayor."

Sounded good, no? I mean, well-thought, confidently delivered, a real honest-to-goodness plan. Too bad I didn't believe it myself.

I kept thinking of Jankle. What did he know that he wasn't telling me? Why did he reach out to me that first night? Where did the Vermeer come from, and why? Was it merely a ruse intended to take my mind off what I privately believed was the real story?

Maggie stood up, and as she did, she stumbled, maybe from an exhaustion that I, too, was starting to understand. I jumped up and caught her before she could fall. She was heavy against me, as if she had lost some of her motor control. Rather than pull away, she buried her face in my neck and I could feel the moisture of all of those tears. She wrapped her arms around me and was stone-still. I put my hands on the back of her neck and pressed her tight against me, whispering, "Maggie, you're going to be fine, and we're going to catch the bastards who have done this to your family."

After several minutes, she pulled softly and slowly away. My mind, like a slide projector, flipped to a scene of too many years before. Katherine had just gotten a call from her sister saying that their father had died of a heart attack. She hung up the phone and whispered the news to me, then buried her face against my chest in utter silence, standing there for five minutes, ten minutes, fifteen minutes, before she reluctantly pulled away. "This is the saddest thing that's ever happened to me," she said through her tears, "but I know I can get through anything as long as I have you."

To be loved like that, and to be needed, and to need. And look at me now.

Maggie began to say something, but the phone rang, the sound crashing through the murky angst of the room.

"You should lie down," I whispered to her. "You need the rest."

When I got to the phone, I hesitated over the receiver, realizing that every conversation seemed to be spinning me in directions I hadn't even considered a few moments before. I picked it up with a curt, "Yeah."

"Fair Hair, tell me the single best thing you've ever had to eat."

It was, indeed, Vinny Mongillo, and from the background sounds, it seemed he was still at the hotel bar.

"I don't know," I said, unable to conceal my frustration. Truth is, I knew perfectly well. It was called la bête noire, a flourless chocolate cake served with a warm chocolate drizzle in a deep pool of crème anglaise. I had it at a restaurant in Boston called L'Espalier about twelve years before, and have thought of it every day since. But none of that is really the point here.

"You've got to get your ass down here and try this foie gras."

My world was spinning out of any semblance of control. Normalcy wasn't merely foreign, it was outright alien. But there would always be Vinny, unchanging, the rock.

And then it struck me with no small amount of renewed melancholy that even he was about to take leave.

"We've just had a good break," I said. "I'll fill you in in the morning." Before he could throw out any large number of questions, I gently hung up the phone.

Chapter Twenty-three

Saturday, September 27

We gathered in the glass-walled conference room of *The Boston Record,* myself and Mongillo fresh off the flight from Europe, though I use the word *fresh* rather liberally there, as well as Peter Martin, former editor turned publisher Justine Steele, and Edgar, our crack director of security, a tiger in lamb's clothing. I wanted Hank Sweeney to be a part of things, but couldn't raise him on the phone.

We spread ourselves out around the horseshoe-shaped conference table. Several large containers of Mexican take-out food, Martin's idea of largesse, sat at a side table. One quick question: When editors send for ethnic food for their charges, why can't it ever be French?

It actually felt damned good to be back on American soil, and specifically on the commercial carpet of this wonderful newsroom. Some reporters, the worst reporters, never leave the building. They spend all their time on the phone, rarely glimpsing real life, the travails and the triumphs of the people we write about. I tend to spend an inordinate amount of time either on the street or on the road, with a front-row view of the mess that defines so much of modern life. It's when I come back into the newsroom that I'm best able to make sense of what I've seen and work it into a form that the *Record* readers will understand.

Anyway, Edgar started us off. "I had a private contractor comb this room two hours ago for bugs, and they found nothing. I've had Peter's, Jack's, and Vinny's phones tested for any form of listening or tracking devices, and detected none. Ms. Steele, I can have yours examined as well if you'd like. We've doubled our full-time, round-the-clock security detail in the lobby, and the same applies for the parking lot. Ms. Maggie Kane is currently in the presence of a team of trained security guards at an undisclosed location."

"Would you tell her to give my best to Dick Cheney?" That was me, Jack, trying to draw a laugh with a little levity, in what I regret to inform turned out to be a dismal failure. In fact, I knew that Maggie was at that very moment in a downtown hotel, along with the former front line of the Nebraska Cornhuskers. Is it normal that I should feel jealous about that?

Martin, stone-faced, said, "Jack, why don't you tell us what happened on your all-expenses paid European vacation this week."

Yeah, it was just great. I went to Rome and got kicked in the balls and punched in the face and fled to Paris, where a woman laughed at my nudity and I had a room service hamburger and escaped the city with the specter of death looming every which way we looked. But it is, I determined for all of humanity, possible to do the Louvre in under two hours.

Well, that's not what I really said. What I did was ignore his attempt at humor just as he did mine. I mean, I was exhausted, harried, impatient, and sore. I had slept in a chair the night before while Maggie Kane was stretched out in all her womanly splendor on the big, firm, king-size bed that dominated not just my room, but my thoughts. I was tired of chasing that which I didn't yet know, and being chased by a villain who I couldn't identify.

So instead, all businesslike, I launched into my spiel. I explained, because Justine hadn't heard them before, my initial suspicions that I had been set up or duped in the original story portraying Toby Harkins as a suspect in the Gardner heist. I showed them the videotapes of Mayor Harkins and Hilary Kane. I described the bungled breakfast meeting, the assault on the Roman street, the flight to Paris, the unrequited rendezvous at the Louvre, the visit in my hotel room in the dark of a French night. I omitted the precise details of the bathtub moment.

And then I told them of Maggie Kane's assertions about what her sister saw in Harkins's apartment that night that caused her to be so worried when she left, and that probably brought about her murder within a few days.

When I stopped, I looked from Martin to Steele and said, "So that's what I got. Sorry I didn't bring back any souvenirs, but I was tied up trying to save the world as we know it, not to mention something even more important, which is myself."

Maybe it's worth noting for no other reason than random kicks—though I don't like that word much since the encounter on the Roman street—that Martin was attired in a shirt and tie on an autumn Saturday afternoon in a mostly desolate newsroom. Truth is, I don't ever really recall seeing him in anything but a shirt and tie, as if that's all he owned. Justine, a well-preserved middle-aged woman of relentless style, was wearing fashionable and casual jeans and what was no doubt an extraordinarily expensive top, even if it looked like you could get the same thing at the Gap for ten bucks. Vinny and I looked like last week's laundry.

Martin said, as he's prone to do in these situations, "So give me the lede as you have it now."

A lede, by the way, is newspaperese for the first paragraph of a hard news story, usually a down and dirty summation of the points that will follow in the body of the work. I thought about that for a moment. Vinny used the time to help himself to more ranchos huervos or quesadillas or whatever it was that was over there. Edgar seemed ready to keel over from boredom, but I think he was just giving it his Columbo act.

I said, "The way I'd write it now is something to the effect of, 'The city attorney slain earlier this week in the Boston Common Garage had been involved in an intimate encounter with Mayor Daniel Harkins days before her death, according to the victim's sister.'

"Second graph: 'During that encounter, the sister said, the

attorney happened across seemingly confidential information in the mayor's personal computer listing telephone numbers and other information about his fugitive son.

"'The mayor,'" I said with a little more drama here, "'has previously maintained that he has not communicated with his son in any way in at least ten years.'"

Martin gave that kind of exaggerated head nod that said, "Not bad." He asked, "Now when Harkins wins a libel suit against us, do you think he'd convert this building into a casino or just outright level it and make a parking lot?"

Mongillo laughed, despite himself. Justine stared at me without expression. Edgar looked out the window at the Southeast Expressway. I got Martin's point.

"I'm not saying we're there, yet. I'm saying that's what we're striving for."

"I understand," Martin replied. "Do we have anything besides the sister's word to go on? You've considered, I'm sure, that this could be a setup. She might not be a sister at all, or assuming she is, she might have some vendetta against the mayor. Maybe *she* had an affair with him."

My head hurt again, and not from the fall in Rome, which is not to be confused with the fall of Rome. I said, "She says that Hilary took the printout of the information, or at least the sheets that she got her hands on until the printer malfunctioned. She doesn't know where they are. My best guess is that the Feds or the Boston cops came across them in the sweep of her apartment last week."

Martin: "Can't your pal Sweeney call in some chits over at homicide and tell you that?"

I nodded and was about to say that I was trying to reach him when Martin, smartly, added, "But if they had found it, what's that ex-boyfriend doing sitting in the slammer?"

I nodded again. I can't say it enough, Martin knows how to cut to the quick faster, with more accuracy, than a plastic surgeon in Beverly Hills.

Out of nowhere, Edgar said, "Let's see that video of her walking out again."

We all looked at him for a moment, and without comment, I got up and hit Play again. I mean, at this point, Edgar could have said he needed me to disrobe while he pierced my nipples and I probably would have done it. Anyway, on the screen, there was the image of Hilary again, walking through the lobby alone on her way out the door. Edgar ordered me to stop, and he got slowly out of his chair and ambled toward the screen and pointed at the shoulder bag that she was carrying.

"This could be it, those papers," he said, and sure enough, what looked to be a couple of sheets of white paper were protruding from her unzipped bag.

"Go to her entrance," he said. And I did, and there was the bag again, but with no papers sticking out.

Edgar, in a moment of low-key triumph, said as he sat back down, "She took something out of that apartment."

We all considered this in silence. Well, near silence. Mongillo was eating away, making his usual Vinny sounds. Martin was spooning Mexican food from the serving containers onto a plastic plate.

Justine said, "Well, I think we can agree that we're not where we need to be. We have video footage, and we have the account of the sister, which entirely involves what a judge would describe as hearsay evidence, though that's perfectly usable in print. But it is entirely necessary to have some sort of corroboration, and that computer printout would be pretty damned good. Short of that, even a police source saying that they're investigating the mayor would help us."

Martin, himself sitting back down now, said, "The question we're not asking, though, is how do these two unfolding events tie together? At the core, we have Jack's story naming Toby Harkins as a suspect in the Gardner heist. But that spawns two different stories. First is the return of the Vermeer. Obviously, someone is trying to signal to us that we're on the money, or not, and I have a good feeling we haven't heard the last of them.

"Second, we have the death of Hilary Kane and the constant threats to her sister. Why," and he looked around at each of us here with an uncharacteristically dramatic flair, "would it be in anyone's best interest to have the Kane sisters dead after—after—the story has already been in print?"

And right there, floating out there above the table, hanging in that gloomy conference room on this otherwise brilliant autumn afternoon, was the question of the hour, of the day, the week even, maybe the month. We all sat in a stumped silence mulling what Martin just said, trying to grab on to the moving parts of the stories and fit them into some semblance of a proper place. I'll admit, I was frustrated.

And then Mongillo spoke. He took a giant bite of guacamango or whatever the hell they call that green gunk that looks like it came from a dying cat's intestines. He swallowed, sipped on a bottle of Coca-Cola, and said, "Because maybe Hilary Kane saw something that night in Harkins's apartment that we don't yet know about. Maybe the mayor or whoever else is behind her death is afraid that she told Maggie. And maybe it's on those printouts that we haven't yet found."

At that exact moment, I heard the sounds of pieces coming together, fitting snug into preconceived slots, like doors kissing shut or the hood of a car falling closed, as if suddenly, there was a design to what we needed, a rhyme and, if you will, a reason.

I nodded and looked down at the expanse of the shiny table and said without looking at anyone, "Mongillo's right. Maybe what we already have isn't what we really need."

Martin spoke up. "Well, gentlemen, you're going to have to put this to Harkins. There's a good chance that we're essentially about to accuse the mayor of Boston of murder. Much as I like the element of surprise, it would be nice to give him a little bit of notice and maybe see what he has to say."

He added, "He's at a nondenominational prayer breakfast in City Hall Plaza at ten tomorrow morning. That sounds as good a place as any to ask him if he's killed anyone lately."

Mongillo looked at me and I looked at him and we both nodded. Another classic double teaming in the making, courtesy of *The Boston Record*. The mayor wouldn't know what hit him.

And at that point, I had no idea that misfortune was about to give way to catastrophe.

Chapter Twenty-four

It began with a voicemail. Melissa Moriarty, my dogsitter, or rather, Baker's dogsitter, left a message on my work line saying that she had been trying to reach me on my cell phone without any success. She said she needed to talk to me—soon. My mobile phone, it's worth noting, wasn't working in Europe, and given my roving ways, she wouldn't have had any idea where I was staying.

I called the house but got no answer. Mongillo had strapped himself in at his desk with the leftover Mexican food and begun working the phones. Martin returned to his office to mull our plight. Justine went wherever it is that publishers go on a Saturday night, which I'm sure was better than anyplace I had in mind. Edgar was protecting all things *Record*. So I bolted for the parking lot. I didn't like the tone of Melissa's voice, and especially didn't like that she failed to say at the end of her message, as she usually does, that there was nothing to worry about, or that everything with Baker was great.

In the car, my cell phone rang, and it was her. As soon as I heard her unusually taut voice, I said I was on my way home.

"Get here quick," she said.

"Is he all right?"

"I, I, I don't know. I've never seen him like this before." And with that, she started to cry.

I soared along the Southeast Expressway as if I were trying to take flight. I descended into the new tunnels of Boston's infamous Big Dig, exited downtown, zigged and zagged along some waterfront streets, and screeched to a halt in my condominium building parking lot, all in what I would imagine was record time. I bolted from my car, up the stairs two and three steps at a time, and I thrust the key into the door lock as if I were trying to slay it.

Inside, Melissa stood in the living room with both her hands covering her mouth in fear as the tears rolled down her cheeks. Baker was flopped across the couch, his head down and his brown eyes open as he emitted a constant, low moan that seemed to be emanating from the base of his throat. Trotting through the room, I looked hard at Melissa and she shook her head in silence as she tried to collect herself.

I knelt down on the floor in front of the couch, saying in a soft and soothing voice, "I'm here, pal. I'm here. Everything's going to be all right."

Baker acknowledged me with a start. His body seemed to spasm once, and he slowly lifted his head, his big brown eyes glazed over in what was undoubtedly pain. His tail pounded several times against the cushions of the couch—*Whump, whump, whump*—as he focused his vision on my face.

"No, no, no," I said softly, smiling at him, though it was a smile as forced as anything I've ever done in my life. "Put your head back down. Put it down." Everything soft, smooth, reassuring.

His head still up, he let out a long, dramatic moan, his lips parting and his snout pointed directly at my nose—his way of telling me about his excruciating pain. I was just inches away from him, and I leaned in even closer and kissed the side of his muzzle. He then gave me a long, laborious lick, the grains of his enormous tongue slowly rubbing against every pore on my face.

His gums, I saw, were discolored white. His tongue was oddly dry. I calmly pressed his head back down on the couch and kissed his ear, whispering, "You're going to be fine, goofball. You're going to be fine." Actually, I wasn't so sure.

"He hasn't eaten since you left." That was Melissa, having gathered her wits, coming up from behind me, speaking in the type of low voice usually reserved for hospital rooms and funeral homes. "He's barely touched any water. He doesn't go to the bathroom much; he hasn't really wanted to go out."

I looked back at her, but before I could say anything, she knelt down beside me and added, "This dog loves you, Jack. A lot of times, when you go away, he gets depressed. I never wanted to tell you that before because I didn't want you to worry. It usually just takes a day or two for him to perk up and be playful and want to eat. So at first, I just thought it was normal. But by yesterday, when he was still dragging around, I thought it was strange. And then an hour or so ago, he started with this moaning stuff, and hasn't picked up his head until you arrived. If you didn't call, I was about to take him to the vet."

"Thank you," I said to her. I didn't know what else to say. Baker's always had a weak stomach, and I was still hopeful, though not really, that he had a bad ache or a cramp. But I couldn't get past the knowledge that I had never seen him act like this.

As Baker moaned and Melissa quietly wept and my entire life seemed to be caving in around me like sand into a formless hole, I gently ran my hands all across his furry body, not knowing what I was looking for until I found it, which was when I reached the soft, pink part of his stomach. There was a protrusion that wasn't there before. I could touch it, feel it, and when I did, Baker moaned louder and tried but failed to lift his exhausted head.

I said, "I'm going to get him over to Angell." I was referring to Angell Memorial Hospital, arguably the best animal hospital in the world, located in the Jamaica Plain neighborhood of Boston about twenty minutes away. "You'd be doing us a huge favor if you stayed here and called ahead. His doctor's name is Lisa Stoles. Maybe she's there and you could talk to her and explain the symptoms, and if not to her, then any doctor on duty."

With that, I scooped Baker up in my arms and carried him out the door and down the steps. Melissa came outside with me and opened the passenger side door to my car and I gently placed the dog on the seat beside me. He groaned and shot me a frightened look with those enormous brown eyes that were more familiar than anything else in my life, and then he put his chin down against the center console and moaned anew. This, I knew, was not good.

I caressed his head for the entire, tense ride, caressed around his neck, all over his floppy ears. His eyes were at half-mast. I think he was exhausted from the pain. He kept his eyes trained on me, wondering what was wrong, waiting for me to make it better. I kept telling him again and again and again, "You're the best dog. You're my best friend." I'm not embarrassed to say that more than a couple of times, my voice caught with emotion. I could withstand a lot in this life I lead, but seeing my dog in this kind of pain was a little bit more than I could handle.

Baker kept moaning. I kept talking. He had been a massive part of my life for seven years now, sometimes, in my darkest days, the focus of my life, a reason to exist, making me laugh, always pulling me toward that elusive emotion called happiness.

He was my constant companion, introducing me to people, making me appreciate things that, but for him, I never would have otherwise—the smell of fresh turf on an early spring day, the warmth of the March sun, the sunsets over the Charles River, the crunch of leaves on a chilly autumn night.

He was with me the night that my wife and infant daughter died in the delivery room and I returned from the hospital in an uncomprehending daze. He saw me through girlfriends, new apartments, a move from Washington to Boston, huge stories, endless slumps, bouts of sickness, and the occasional job-related wound. He was trained to walk off-leash, to never jump, not to beg, to wait politely outside stores. He loved kids, and as such, would search out mothers pushing carriages along city sidewalks, then calmly walk beside them, always glancing back at me with a look that said, "Why can't we get one of these?"

He was a scholar of all things me. He would carefully, quietly, read my moods. When I was happy, he would engage me. Those times I was sad, he would entertain me, run his tongue over my nose until I laughed. Always, every day, his entire philosophy could be broken down into three simple words: Count me in. If I was doing it, whether it was errands or a car drive or a day at the beach, he wanted to do it as well. And usually, he did.

When I pulled up to the hospital emergency room, I bolted around the car, opened his door, and lifted him out onto the pavement. When I put him carefully down, his legs buckled and he fell slowly to the ground with a long, loud moan. He stared at me through those frightened eyes with an odd mix of embarrassment and pain.

I said to him, "I'm so sorry. I'm so sorry." I whispered this into his ear, hoisted him back up, and carried him through the automatic doors. Inside, a young man in those pale green hospital scrubs met me in the lobby with a rolling gurney.

"Mr. Flynn?" he asked. I nodded. "Put the dog right down here," he said, tapping the cold top of the metal cart. I did, and he immediately took off with Baker, me trotting along beside them. Even with all the commotion, Baker's head remained flat against the surface and his gaze never left mine.

We hurriedly moved through a waiting room filled with people sitting on hard plastic chairs and holding small cages in their laps containing anything from sneezing cats to whining birds. We made our way down a long hallway with painted pale yellow cinder-block walls and the type of shiny linoleum floors that are typically reserved for parochial high schools.

The orderly stopped outside a plain wood door, knocked once, and pushed it open. Inside was a small, bland examination room, with a sink and counter in one corner, a metal table in the middle, a chart that showed various pictures of tapeworms and heartworms on the near wall, and a light fixture for X-ray shots on the far wall. The young man pushed the cart next to the table and was about to lift Baker from one to the other when I cut in and said, "I'll do it." For whatever reason, I didn't want anyone's hands on him right now but mine.

Baker sprawled on the table in the same position he had assumed on the couch—stretched out, his head down, his glazed eyes open, a guttural sound emanating from within. The kid asked me a series of typically stupid questions—stupid because the vet would walk in any moment and ask me the same things all over again. I impatiently answered them until I think he began to fear that I might do him some harm, at which point he backed toward the door and said, "I'll go find the doctor." And he was gone.

"You're the best boy in the world," I whispered into Baker's ear. "The very best boy." His tail thumped against the hard surface several times. He had a look on his face like he had done something wrong, so I caressed his forehead and his muzzle and repeatedly said, "You're going to be fine, pal. You're going to be just fine."

A few minutes later, the door opened and Lisa Stoles came in with a concerned look on her well-preserved face. She was a woman of about sixty, with an unkempt mane of grayish black hair that flowed down beyond her shoulders, a true Cantabrigian who I suspect lolled away endless hours in Harvard Square coffee bars reading a much dog-eared copy of *Moby Dick* or *War and Peace*. Of this I had little doubt: She loved animals, Baker particularly, and she was every inch as smart as she looked.

"Jesus, I'm glad you're on tonight," I said as she made her way into the room.

"So am I," she said, her tone concerned. She kept walking right toward Baker. The dog whacked his tail a few more times for good measure when he heard her voice. His eyes opened wider. He liked Lisa, despite himself, though he knew that the things she represented—needles and pulling and prodding—he could live without. Or not.

"What is wrong with my Baker?" she asked in her dog voice.

Thump, thump, thump.

I showed her the bulge. I explained the symptoms. She felt around, put her stethoscope up to his heart, looked at his gums, probed inside his mouth, peered into his big brown eyes one at a time. All along, he kept his head down on the cold metal and his gaze focused on mine.

"I'm going to need X-rays, immediately," she said, and I lifted him from the examination table onto the cart and she began rolling him out. I followed her until she said, "You stay here, Jack. I don't want him distracted by you. We'll be back in ten minutes."

As she pulled him out the door, he lifted his head up with a monumental struggle, his eyes focused like lasers on mine, and let out a long, soft, moan. "Good boy," I said, but the words didn't really get out, and by the time I cleared my throat enough to speak, the wood door had clicked shut and I was standing in the spare room all alone.

Standing there with nothing more than my fears, awful memories rushed into my addled mind, first and foremost, the vision of Katherine staring panicked at me on her delivery room bed as her doctor ordered me in no uncertain terms to get out of the room. It is a look that will haunt me the rest of my life.

Then better ones, of Baker, the way he'd sit obediently in front of me to take his arthritis medicine, how he'd paw at tennis balls that rolled under the couch, chewing on sticks in the park while I shot baskets, proudly stalking squirrels in the Public Garden that he never actually caught. "That's 0 for 7,943," I used to tell him, and he'd give me a sidelong glance that said, "Whatever."

He was my last link to a way of life that was never supposed to end—a gift from my late wife, a puffy little ball of blonde fur presented in a hatbox a few days before Christmas as we sipped red wine on the couch and looked at a newly purchased tree that wouldn't stand straight in its stand. To lose him now was to lose a little bit more of Katherine. No, make that a lot of Katherine, because Baker, physically speaking, was the last remaining tie that binds, and I often pictured that wonderful woman somewhere in the Great Wherever looking at us with a smile on her face as we walked through the park or wrestled on the living-room floor, and saying to herself, "My two boys." What would happen if I were to lose that?

Not to be overly dramatic, but put it this way: My life is his life. He is there every morning when I wake up; sometimes, he's the one who wakes me by licking my hand or my chin as a gentle reminder that I'm cutting into his daily routine. If I rose too early, he would fake being asleep, not quite ready to rouse before his desired time. I would hear him have little dreams in the still dark of the night on my bedroom floor, small yelps as he shuffled his paws as if he were in hot pursuit of a neighborhood cat. If I read too late on the couch or got caught up in a show on television, he would stand up with a long, dramatic sigh, pad back to the bedroom, and flop down on the L. L. Bean bed that Katherine had gotten him years before.

We had walked thousands of miles together, had made tens of thousands of throws of the dirty tennis balls that he constantly carried around in his mouth, maintained a running seven-year conversation. If he could actually speak, he'd probably be constantly telling me to shut the hell up. Most important, to borrow that line from the great political novel *The Last Hurrah:* How do you thank someone for a million laughs?

I was so lost in thought that I jumped when my cell phone rang. I was still standing, leaning with my back flush against the cinderblock wall, and I peered at the incoming number long enough to realize that I didn't recognize it. At that moment, as the phone continued to ring, the door opened up and the male orderly backed in with Baker following on the cart. The ringing stopped and the kid pushed him toward me and said, "The doctor said she'll be back in a few minutes." He quickly got out of the room.

Baker was still moaning, but he thumped his tail again when he saw me, and I buried my face into the soft fur on the side of his neck and told him that nothing would ever go wrong as long as I had any say in it. The question is, did I?

A few minutes later the door opened again, and Lisa Stoles walked in. She wore a flowing peasant skirt beneath a bright white laboratory coat, and her unruly hair was now pulled into a loose bun on the back of her neck. She carried an oversize manila folder. She leaned back on the examination table facing Baker and me and said in a no-nonsense voice that will be forever lodged in that worst part of my mind, "Jack, things don't look very good."

Those words hit me like an uppercut. Emotion began to wash from my chest up into my head, as I told myself to stay clear and remain calm.

"Tell me," I said, swallowing hard. My hand was absently caressing Baker's ear. His head was still flush on the metal.

She pulled the X-rays out of the folder, walked around to the lamp and flicked on the light. "Push him over here," she said. I did, and she turned the overhead lights off in the room. She placed a print up against the lightboard and pointed at it with a retracted pen.

"I've already gone over this with the head of oncology at the hospital, who happens to be on tonight, and she is in complete agreement over what we see. This is a side view of Baker's stomach. You can see this unusual mass down here, very large. It's a tumor, a very rapidly growing one, hemangiosarcoma, and it's opened up and bleeding into his stomach. It could fully burst at any moment now, and if and when that happens, he will die of shock or loss of blood."

My head went light. I lost all feeling in my body—my hands and my feet and everything else. My eyes were open, but I couldn't see anything, until I turned my face and looked down at the fabulous animal stretched across the gurney beside me, still moaning, still scared, still in deep pain. Now I knew why.

"We could operate," she said, and I quickly cut her off, saying, "Then do it."

She didn't respond. Instead, she pulled the print off the lightboard, placed it on the table, and picked another X-ray from the folder. She adhered that up against the pale glow.

"Except for this, Jack. Except for this. Here's a view, straight-on, of Baker's chest. Take a look at all these little masses. They're called metastases, and they're lodged into his bones, his lungs, and I'm sure in his other vital organs as well. This was a brutally fast-moving tumor, and it's spread throughout his entire body before you or I or probably even Baker realized it was there."

I shook my head. I was trying to focus on the X-ray, but couldn't make out what she was telling me that I needed to see. I blinked hard, stared harder, all as my hand kept rubbing the side of my dog's face. "What are you saying?" I finally asked.

She folded her arms across her white coat and replied, "I'm saying that, yes, I could do the surgery. We could do it right now. We'd try to pull the tumor from his stomach, and sometimes we get it and it works, and sometimes it doesn't and the patient dies during the procedure. But even if it was a success, he's still riddled with tumors everywhere else. He's never going to fully recover. He's never going to be healthy again, to run or even walk, or eat, or play. Jack, I hate to tell you this, but I have to. Even if we do the surgery, Baker's probably going to be dead within a few weeks, best case, and those aren't going to be comfortable weeks for him. He's going to be in real pain."

She paused. I sucked in the stale air in that tiny room, trying to maintain composure, keep my balance, hold on to some vestige of clear thought.

"If you decide on the surgery," she said, her gaze tight on mine, "it's for you, not for him. I know how much you love that dog, Jack, and I think I know why, and I love him too. He's a wonderful animal, my favorite patient. But I have to say, the most humane thing you can do right now is to put him out of his misery and have him pass gently."

My left hand instinctively covered my eyes as my right hand stayed on Baker's face. I fought back tears with every ounce of will that I had, and once I found the composure to speak, I said, "Can you give me some time with him in here?"

"Whatever you need."

She flicked on the overhead lights, shut down the X-ray board, and walked over to the cupboard by the sink. She pulled out a blanket and spread it on the hard floor. She placed a medicine bottle on the counter next to a catheter and a syringe. Every move seemed to be in slow motion, every sound lumbered through my head.

She said, "Just open this door up whenever you two are ready, and I'll be right along." And she walked out, clicking the door shut behind her.

I picked Baker up, set him gently down on the blanket, and sat beside him on the floor. I tried to remember every one of those miles we walked on the coldest winter mornings and the softest summer nights. I tried to recall every one of those balls that he fetched, the cookies that he ate, the rawhides that he chewed, the countless times he'd whack me with his paw in an indication that he wanted to be rubbed.

The crying started not in my eyes, but my chest, a quaking rumble that rolled up my throat and into my face until I began to shed a storm of tears—little droplets that rolled down my cheeks and onto his. He struggled again to lift his head and gave me a short lick, but he put his cheek back down on the wool blanket with a painful groan.

How, I wondered to myself, could a grown man who had lost his wife and infant daughter be this upset over the death of his dog? Then I realized: It's partly because I lost my wife and daughter that I was this upset. Baker was all I truly had.

"Seven years, pal. Seven years of laughs. Seven years of fun. Seven years of stability, of responsibility, seven years of faith, seven years of the best friendship that I'll ever have." And I cried anew, kissing his ear, his muzzle, his cheek below his eye. He wagged his tail again, but I knew he wasn't happy; he was scared, and so was I.

I collected myself. I rubbed my palms along my face as I thought of a random morning seven years ago when I got up early to make waffles and Baker fell sound asleep in bed with Katherine, his paws draped over the back of her neck. When I came into the room to wake her, the two of them lifted their heads in unison.

I thought of him earlier in the week, on Tuesday morning, when he pawed at the glass door to the balcony because he wanted to be outside in the sun with Elizabeth and me. He had the tumor then, and I had no idea.

"You're the best friend in the world, pal. My very best friend." I rubbed my hands up and down his sides, trying to bring him some comfort in a time of tremendous pain. He moaned and thumped and kept looking at me, and the thought struck me like a bolt that maybe he knew what was happening, and maybe he had some innate understanding that it was his time to go.

As I rubbed his head, I heard laughter coming from outside the door, two technicians cracking jokes. Someone else yelled something about going on break, their voices bouncing off the walls. I heard a squeaky cart being wheeled down the hall. Life went on, but for the two souls here in this room, everything had just changed.

"I love you," I said. "I have since the day Katherine brought you home, and I'll love you until the day I join you wherever it is that we go. Hopefully they'll have a crate of tennis balls there." And I kissed him long and hard on the bridge of his nose. I stood up, steadied myself, and opened the door.

A moment later, Lisa walked back in. "You're ready?" she said in a low voice. I wondered how many times she had done this before, put dogs down, comforted emotional owners. Probably every day of her career.

I nodded. I was back on the floor, sitting beside Baker, my hands caressing his head. She said, "I'm going to put a catheter in his front leg, then administer him a dose of barbiturates that will overwhelm his system. He'll be very peaceful. There won't be any pain. And in a moment, it will be done."

She looked at me with pursed lips and I nodded again. She knelt on the floor and put the catheter in his front leg. Baker and I stared at each other. I told him, repeatedly, "You're the best boy in the world. You're the best friend I've ever had." I fought back tears with every ounce of energy that I had.

She put a blue solution inside the catheter and I watched it out of the corner of my eye flow down the tube and into his leg.

"You're the very, very best boy," I said, putting my face directly against his. "You're my best boy."

He gave me a half lick. His eyes went from open to half-mast, and then they closed. I kept rubbing his ear, his forehead, his neck. Lisa pressed the stethoscope to his chest and pulled it away.

"He's gone, Jack."

I kissed him one final time, letting my face linger on the top of his head, feeling his warm fur tickle my eyes, my cheeks, the sides of my nose, as I had so many thousands of times before.

And that was it. I got up and looked down at the most beautiful animal that I will ever know. And at that moment, I was in every way alone.

Chapter Twenty-five

So now what? Now what happens when virtually anything of any emotional value in your life is stripped away, one thing, one person at a time, slowly, tragically, after a while, almost mockingly. My wife is long gone. Elizabeth is on the other coast and doesn't bother to call. My career is in shambles. Mongillo is leaving the paper. My most trusted friend, my dog, is dead.

Well, here's what happens. You shift into automatic pilot. You dull your emotions, something I've had no choice but to practice over the years. You think practically, address the obstacles one at a time, and always strive toward a goal, which in this case was finding out who killed Hilary Kane, and why.

With those answers, I might well save Maggie Kane and salvage what was left of my own damned reputation.

First things first. I pulled my cellular phone out and listened to the message that was left for me as I comforted my dying dog. It was an unfamiliar voice, gruff and grainy, emerging amid a din of background noise that sounded like a restaurant or bar. "Jack Flynn," the voice said. "Call this number—" and he gave it to me. "Your friend Hank needs your help, quickly."

I didn't like the sound of that. One death in one day was enough. So sitting in my parked car in the lot at the Angell

Memorial Hospital, I punched out the number as quickly as I could, which wasn't very quickly at all, given that my unsteady hands kept striking the wrong keys. When I finally got it right, a man picked up the phone on about the fifth ring with an abrupt, "Mulligan's."

"This is Jack Flynn. Someone left me a message saying that Hank needs my help." I said this in as firm a voice as I could muster.

"Hold on," he said, and the phone clanked on a hard surface. In the background, I heard the tinny sound of jukebox music, the loud laugh of a drunken woman, then a man's voice, close by, asking for a pack of Winston's. A moment later, that same man got back on the line and said, "Yeah, he's still here, drunk as a skunk, sitting by his lonesome over in a corner booth. You better get him out of here before he says the wrong thing to the wrong person."

"Where are you?" I asked.

"In Southie, 840 West Broadway, World-famous Mulligan's Bar and Grill." He was giving me a whiskeyed laugh as he slammed down the phone.

Great. This is just what the doctor—or rather, veterinarian—ordered, a night of playing caretaker for a drunken friend just a few minutes after putting my dog down. I didn't think I would ever again feel anything but sad, but an inner anger began to weave its way to the forefront of my thoughts.

Regarding Hank, he had been a friend of mine for a couple of years now. I quite literally showed up on the doorstep of his Florida house one morning looking for help on a case that he had handled in homicide back before he retired. And did he ever help me. He flew to Boston. He guided me through a labyrinth of obstacles and deceptions toward an elusive truth. He risked arrest. He got shot. Once, he even plunged into the icy harbor in a needless bid to save my life. And I've got to say, I've loved the guy ever since.

That said, a couple of things were noteworthy about that call from Mulligan's. First off, in all the time I had known him, I had never witnessed Hank Sweeney drink anything more than a single beer or, if I bought it for him, a glass of red wine. He just plain wasn't a drinker. A smoker? Yes. An occasional pain in the ass? Most definitely. One of the more lovable guys I've ever met? Absolutely. But a drunk? Never. Not unless there was something about him that I hadn't seen in the last couple of years since we met.

Second off, as I may have mentioned, Hank Sweeney is black, not that it matters. Except in South Boston it actually does, because the neighborhood was, is, and will probably always be lily-white. Yes, there are minorities in the Town, as the natives—myself included—tend to call it, but they're mostly in the projects and certainly aren't regular patrons of the slew of Broadway's Irish bars. So when Prince Charming said on the phone that Sweeney might well say the wrong thing to the wrong person, he might just mean that Hank could tell someone, "Hello."

Third off, Mulligan's was the former hangout of Toby Harkins, the front when Harkins ran the most feared criminal organization in Boston, a veritable gang of Irish mobsters who ruled the city's drug and rackets trade with what seemed like impunity. These days, I suspect, it's just another bucket-of-blood bar along the main strip through Southie, though maybe old Hank, being the former homicide detective that he is, knows something I don't, which wouldn't be all that unusual.

So I stepped on it, as they say in the movies, hurtling past the Franklin Park Zoo on my left, the golf course where I met Tom Jankle a few days before on my right, through Dorchester, and into South Boston, all in less than ten minutes.

The good news was, I found the place immediately. The expected bad news, and I don't know any other way to say this, so here goes: Mulligan's was a real shithole.

More specifically, it was a windowless brick building. Actually, check that. There was one little sliver of a window covered with bars that made the whole thing look like a maximum security prison, and a more clever man than I could explain why in some metaphoric way, that might very well be the case. The sign above the door looked like it was scrawled by hand. The door itself, made of steel, was covered in the type of graffiti that probably seemed clever to the people who wrote it—"See Jane suck Dick"—but lost its humor in the harsh light of day. All in all, a most uninviting place, which I'm betting wasn't entirely unintentional.

I double-parked, because that's what people in this part of the city do, unless of course they triple-park. I steeled myself for the briefest of moments on the sidewalk, gulped in the clean, crisp, autumn air, then pushed against the door.

It was dark inside, almost black. Actually, hold on. There was really no good way to know. The moment I came through the door, the smoke hit me with such velocity that my first impulse was to slam shut my eyes. The second, which I had to overcome, was to turn right around and escape into the night.

I breathed through my nose to regulate the intake as my eyes adjusted to the assault. I mean, there are Boston Fire Department battalions that wouldn't come into this place without an open radio line to headquarters. The employee lounge at RJR Reynolds's is like a Martha Stewart commercial compared to the environs here. But nonetheless, once I got my bearings, I forged on, all in the name of friendship.

The long bar was on the right of the establishment, and there were booths set off to the left, along with a few cheap Formica tables. The place was, shockingly, crowded, peopled mostly by men with slicked-back hair in slightly soiled tee shirts and women with wide hips and crooked teeth. I think I was probably related to half of them.

I couldn't see Sweeney, which was probably okay, because I really couldn't see anything through all the pollution. So I made my way to the bar and said to the wiry, silver-haired bartender, "I'm Jack Flynn. You called me about Hank."

He looked at me curiously for a long moment, before he said, "Jack, that you?"

"Bobby?" Bobby, as in, Bobby, my father's second cousin, the one who could wriggle his ears and memorized the alphabet backward for the benefit of the many times he was stopped and questioned by the police for drunk driving. I really was related to half the place. I asked, "What the hell are you doing here?"

"Been tending bar here for the last forty years, every Saturday night, whether I want to or not."

Maybe my mother had been right: I really ought to keep in better touch with family. Or maybe not.

Once the smallest of talk was out of the way, we really and truly didn't have anything much to say, so I asked, "So what's the deal with Hank?"

A toothless woman halfway down the bar was screeching for a Bud, so Bobby took leave for a moment, did a quick scan of the rest of the bar, and returned. He nodded his head toward the far corner of the establishment, and said, "He's over there."

I turned, and sure enough, my friend, Hank Sweeney. He was sitting in a corner booth with an empty tumbler in front of him, which didn't seem to matter, because Hank looked stone-cold asleep, and sleep is probably the most benevolent take on the situation.

"How long's he been out for?" I asked.

"Dunno. Twenty minutes or so. He's getting himself in a lot less trouble that way."

I laughed and said, "Hitting on all these young women, is he?"

As I asked this, a raspy-voiced, silver-haired lady of about seventy years old cuffed me in the back of the knee with her metal cane and yelled, "You going to order or are you going to block the bar yakking all night?"

Bobby looked at her with a cross of amusement and anger and said, "Milly, keep your fucking cane to yourself in here. I told you that already. And this guy's my cousin, so get the fuck away."

She looked at me for a long moment, and I could actually see her eyes fight through a state of inebriation to focus. "You're blood, are you? Yeah," she said, sizing me up. "You two look just alike. You could be brothers."

You'd probably have to be there to know just how entirely offensive that statement was.

"The Flynns are a very blessed group," I said, smiling.

She walked away without a reply.

When she was out of earshot, which for her would be about two feet, Bobby leaned over the bar and said to me, "Your friend came in here and demanded that we get Toby Harkins on the phone. Said he had a thing or two to tell him. I explained that Toby's a fugitive, that I had no idea how to reach him, and that he'd best just order a drink and enjoy it in peace like everyone else.

"But he wouldn't take no. Kept asking and asking. Started going around to the tables, threatening people, 'I'm a retired cop. I've got connections. You get me that fucking slimeball Harkins on the horn or I'll run your ass in jail.' All that shit.

"Jack, I know this ain't the Ritz here or anything, but we don't need that shit. You know what I mean?"

I said, "I know what you mean. I know. I'll take care of it and make sure he doesn't come back. Just in case he does, call me again, would you? By the way, how'd you know to call me now? Did he give you my number?"

Bobby waved an arm at me as if I had said something profoundly stupid. "No, he couldn't count to ten, for chrissakes. I went into his cell phone, and yours was the first and only number he had in there, under 'Jack,' so I called it."

Typical Flynn, always thinking. I knocked my fist on the bar in a show of thanks and made my way across the room, through the smoke and the grime and amid the drunken din, toward Hank. I tell you, this whole place could be a lecture hall in the School of Hard Knocks.

I sat across the booth from him and he didn't even stir. Understand, he is a considerable man in every way imaginable, but for now, I'm referring to the physical part of things. His head is enormous, which makes it understandable that his neck, charged with supporting it, is so large. He was splayed against the backrest of the high bench, snoring slightly, his hands twitching every once in a while on the surface of the grimy table. I put my right hand on his left and squeezed it for a moment, and as if he were a battery-operated toy, his eyes came slowly to life.

"The fuck are you doing, Hank? You're going to get yourself killed."

From the look that he gave me—complete and unadulterated confusion—he had no answer to my pointed question. If I had asked where he was, hell, who he was, I don't think he could have answered those either. He stayed quiet for a long while, his eyes fixed on mine, then drifting around the room to get a handle on what was going on. Finally, he said to me in a voice thick with sleep and booze, "Guy's got a right to get himself a drink on a Saturday night."

"He sure does, but ten of them, and at Toby Harkins's bar in Southie?"

Hank gave me a drunken smile and said in that soft voice of his, "Hey, someplace new, someplace different."

I said, "Cut the shit, Hank. Tell me what the hell's going on. Somebody could have busted your skull the way you were wandering around in here, threatening the locals with jail and telling them to put you in touch with Harkins."

"All right, Jack. All right. I got carried away. Give me a break. And a cup of coffee."

Good point. I bet the coffee's great in here, a veritable Starbucks with a liquor license. I made my way back to the bar and Cousin Bobby set me up with a cup of Mulligan's finest for Hank, and a Miller High Life for me. I set the drinks on the table with an odd sense of pride. This, after all, was my hometown.

I said, "So spill."

Hank took a long sip. A Beach Boys song poured from the jukebox, "Help Me Rhonda," one of those tunes you go through life innately hoping that you never hear again, and invariably, you're disappointed.

He replied, "I got drunk. I had an idea. I thought I was invincible. I did something stupid." He paused and met my eyes. "Thanks for bailing me out."

I didn't reply. Instead, we sat in silence. Well, not exactly silence. There was cackling and shouting on the other side of the room as a couple of what I would imagine were regulars were starting to dance. God, please don't have this be a Beach Boys medley.

I said, "Baker died tonight."

Hank's mouth dropped open. He put his coffee mug down. "What?"

I explained about the tumor that had spread from his stomach into his chest, about the pain, the remote odds of survival, the vet telling me that it was the most humane thing to do. I said it all as if I were reciting it, knowing how many times I was going to have to tell people the same sad story. Hell, at that point, I hadn't even called Elizabeth with the news, but that said, Elizabeth hadn't called me now in days.

"I'm so sorry, Jack," he said. "I know what that animal meant to you, and he was a wonderful dog."

By now, old Hank almost seemed sober, though his eyes had wide circles around them and his clothes—a windbreaker over a V-neck sweater over a golf shirt—were disheveled from when he fell asleep sitting up. "Thank you," I said, and then there was more silence as my mind drifted back to Baker lying on that blanket and slowly shutting his eyes for that final time.

He broke it by asking, "You ever do things that you really regret? A decision you made. An action you committed. Or maybe something you didn't do."

He searched out my eyes and his hands fidgeted nervously on the table. I'd never seen him quite like this. As the best homicide detectives are, he's a trained observer, somewhat aloof from all that going on around him, skeptical without being cynical. But here he was, uncharacteristically anxious, drunk, in a place he ought not to have been in so many different ways. I didn't know what to say so I said this: "Sure. We all do."

He looked at me like he wanted something more, specifics maybe. I'll admit, this wasn't really the conversation I had bargained for sitting in Mulligan's bar at nearly ten o'clock on a Saturday night an hour or so after putting down the best dog that will ever trot the earth. I looked around the freak show that was this bar, then back at Hank, and said, "Well, obviously, every moment of every day this week I've regretted rushing that story into print about Toby Harkins, because now and always, Hilary Kane is dead. That what you mean?"

"Kind of," he said, absently nodding. Then he added, "Not your fault, Jack. You did what you had to do. And you got a priceless painting returned."

"And a young woman killed."

More silence. I gulped my beer, draining nearly half the bottle. Hank sipped his coffee.

I asked, "You think the mayor killed Hilary Kane?"

Hank held the cup in both of his hands and talked in that wheezy voice he gets when he's confiding stuff that he wants you to hold true. He said, "If I were still on homicide and I saw those tapes, he'd be my number one suspect. That's why the cops want you to get that stuff into print."

I thought about telling him what Maggie had told me in Paris about her sister finding a computer file in the mayor's apartment that night linking father and son. But I didn't, and I'm not sure I can explain why, mostly because I don't think I know. Instead, I said, "I was trying to reach you earlier today. I needed your help, but I never heard back from you."

"Well, you got me now, here in the flesh."

"And now I'm going to get rid of you. Come on, I'll give you a lift."

As we struggled to our feet in the tight-fitting booth, Hank said, "You ever fear that when you get older someday and you look back over the life you've lived, instead of feeling triumph and pride, you're going to be filled with frustration and regret over how things turned out?"

I paused as I thought about this. Images of Katherine and Baker and Elizabeth and Hilary Kane and Maggie popped in and out of my tired brain. I thought of the empty apartment I was heading home to, the work I faced tomorrow. I swallowed hard and said, "Sometimes, yeah."

"It's not easy," Hank said as he ambled heavily toward the door. Outside, it was cool and crisp and clean, and I gulped in the fresh night air, but the dank smell of smoke and old booze still clung to my hair and my skin and my clothes.

We got into my car, and Hank said again, "It's not easy." And two minutes later, as I maneuvered down Broadway, I heard the soft sounds of him snoring.

Chapter Twenty-six

What I really needed was sleep. What I really wanted was a beer. So when I got home to my waterfront condominium at the end of a day that began in Paris and seemed to last, I don't know, roughly forever, I reached into the refrigerator, past Elizabeth's old tubs of hummus and half-eaten bags of baby carrots, and pulled out the coldest Sam Adams I could find, which was actually the only one left. Hey, look at me everyone; I'm on a lucky roll.

I looked down at Baker's water bowl, still brimming, and his food bowl, filled with uneaten kibble, and shook my head in a sad, slow kind of way. Now was not the time to pack these things away, along with his bed and stuffed toys and the rawhide strips and filthy tennis balls that sat in every corner and beneath every chair in the house. Truth be known, I don't know when that time would be.

I suddenly felt not only exhausted, but utterly aimless. I didn't want to sit on the couch, because that's where I'd always sit with Baker sprawled beside me. I wasn't ready for bed yet, and anyway, bed was where I spent an inordinate amount of time in the company of Elizabeth, and she wasn't of my world anymore either. So I threw on a fleece coat that was hanging in the closet and slid open the door to the deck.

The chill autumn air engulfed me and, at least for the moment, awakened me. It was just four days before that I sat out there with Elizabeth, topless, reading my story in awe, Baker scratching at the door to join us. Four days. Four days that can change a life, end a life, sink a career, ruin a relationship, alter the way you look at everything and everybody. But that reminded me, so I struggled to my feet, ambled inside, grabbed the portable phone and came back onto the deck, sliding the door shut behind me.

I suppose I could have just called Elizabeth's cell phone and been assured of talking to her, but instead I called her new apartment atop Russian Hill in San Francisco. It was midnight, my time, 9:00 P.M. on the quirky coast, and I pictured her sitting in her living room sipping tea watching a rented movie on television, maybe a little bit sad about us, nervous about a future that didn't involve me in a city that was far from anyplace she had ever called home. I was sad, and I wanted to hear her voice. Maybe she wanted to hear mine. Stranger things have happened.

It rang and rang and rang, straight through to her voicemail. Here in Boston, it was her voice on our message telling callers to leave word for either one or both of us. I always liked that part—"both of us." Now, it was her voice giving just her first name, saying leave a message and she'd be sure to call back. I'm sure it was just my lack of sleep, but every little thing made me profoundly sad.

"Hey, it's Jack. Listen, I wanted to tell you this in person, or rather, voice to voice. Things are spinning out of control here, on this story and on everything else. Most important, something terrible happened with Baker tonight. He was acting really sick, and I took him over to Angell, and Lisa Stoles did some X-rays."

My voice caught, and I paused to gulp some salt air and collect myself. "They came back really bad." Another pause, by necessity. "He had a big tumor in his stomach, and all sorts of little ones in his chest—very fast growing, the doctor said. The big one had ruptured and the poor guy could barely lift his head. He was in a lot of pain."

Still another collecting pause as I looked out over the barren black expanse of the harbor on a starless, moonless night. The thought occurred that the machine might cut me off for a time, so I said, "I didn't have a choice. I had to put him down. Baker died in peace with me right beside him. I'm so sorry to tell you like this."

And I hung up.

I took a long pull on the Sam and wondered if things could turn good as quickly and thoroughly as they had turned bad. Probably not, but as Hemingway once wrote, "Isn't it pretty to think so."

My mind wandered, which was good, because anything was better than where it was then. There was a day a couple of years earlier when I was splashing around in this same harbor in the middle of April, chasing a hired gun who I had feared did some harm to Elizabeth. The great Hank Sweeney cannonballed into the water after me, then had to be fished out by the cops a couple of minutes later because he didn't know how to swim. Thinking of the moment, I couldn't help but allow my mouth to form into a half smile.

But what was wrong with him now? Aside from delivering the tapes of the mayor and Hilary Kane, he'd been virtually invisible on this story, and truth be known, I could really use his help. The drunk thing in Southie was the most uncharacteristic stunt I'd ever seen him pull. I'd call him on it in the morning.

Another long pull. I told myself to savor it, because it was the last one. What the hell, maybe I'd go from the beer into the mouthwash.

My eyes were growing heavy. Images of Hilary Kane drifted into my muddled thoughts, then Maggie, followed by the mayor and his son, wherever the hell he was, which may well be my bedroom, the way things were going. Nail this story, I told myself, and get out of the business before it swallowed you whole, dominated your entire life, so I wouldn't wake up one of these days as the typical fifty-five-year-old, twice-divorced mid-level editor in a medium paying job with almost all of life's virtues in the rearview mirror and nothing ahead but more of the painful same. Hang a shingle with Mongillo. Take control. Do some crisis management for companies in public relations peril. Call your own shots.

I thought of my father, of my wife, of a daughter that I never had. Yes, life might be for the living, but why are my thoughts so dominated by the dead?

Sometime thereafter, I heard it. I awoke with a start, my neck stiff from the chair and my skin cold from the ocean breeze. The sound wasn't immediately clear to me. I only knew that it was loud and unusual. My first thought was that Baker was about to start barking and scratching until he got to the origin, not to commit any act of protective savagery, but to see if it was possible that he might get scratched on the head. Then, as I gained cognizance, I realized that the way of my world had changed.

So I sat for a moment to collect thoughts and acquire bearings. That's when I heard it again—the sound of a hard, falling object, bouncing on the floor, maybe breaking, somewhere inside the apartment.

I lifted myself slowly out of the chair and crouched by the glass door, trying to see inside at whatever it was that was causing the commotion. But I saw nothing but black.

Behind me, the wind had picked up. All around me, the night had gone from pleasantly cool to surprisingly cold. My heart was beating so loud that I wondered if I could quiet it down.

I slowly, arduously opened the sliding door, trying not to make a sound. When it was open just wide enough for me to squeeze through, I did, and pulled it shut as slowly and as quietly as I had opened it.

Inside, I remained crouched by the door, listening as intently as I ever had to anything in my life, for the sound of breathing, footsteps, panic, danger—again, anything. I ran through my options, which I quickly assessed as follows: Turn on the lights, or not turn on the lights. With the former, I'd probably learn the identity of the intruder, but he'd be armed, I wasn't, and thus the information would be short-lived, as would I. By not turning on the lights, I was taking away his obvious advantage of gunplay, and using my advantage of geography. I knew the apartment; he didn't.

So I began walking slowly and precisely away from the door, feeling the air with my hands. In a distant corner of the living room, I could see the pale green power light for the CD player in an open antique cabinet that also held the television, which gave me an idea.

Hunched down by the floor, I slowly, breathlessly moved toward the area of the coffee table in the center of the living room. My knee found it before my hands did, but that's all right. I'm young and virile and can take it—I think. I felt around in the dark on the surface of the table until I found the remote control, and held on to it fast as I inched back toward the area of the balcony door.

I heard nothing. Even as my eyes were adjusting to the dark, I saw nothing. Truth is, I didn't even sense anything, but my perceptions, possibly dulled by the cold and sleep, may not have been firing in the sharp way that usually characterizes the pointed life of Jack Flynn.

But things don't crash in the night without cause. Any physicist and detective will agree on that. No, there was something or somebody in here, an invasion that would fit in just perfectly with the way my life has spun out of control these prior several days.

Over by the door, I gripped the remote as if it were a gun. I wish. I put my face right up to it, peering at the tiny abbreviations that described each button. Who could have known that my life would be better off, and possibly longer, if I had spent more time watching TV, and thus memorizing the setup on my universal control.

I set my thumb over what I vaguely thought was the power button. It was the biggest one on there, round while the others were square. I pointed it toward the nineteen-inch RCA that I had bought about fifteen years ago when the Patriots made the Super Bowl and got slaughtered by the Chicago Bears. And I pressed it.

The television came to life, maybe not as fast as I had hoped, but fast enough for results. On the other side of the living room, I caught a flash of motion, and it wasn't just the little dance routine that Britney Spears was doing on behalf of my least favorite soft drink, Pepsi.

Again, another crash as I watched a hulking silhouette jump

over a side table and knock a couple of photographs to the floor—me and Elizabeth, Baker and Elizabeth, my father in his pressmen's apron. I yelled, "Stop, asshole!" which was probably not the smartest thing to do. In the light of the TV, he could easily see me, and if he so desired, put a bullet right through me. The most I could do was change channels, which, while annoying, didn't have the same effect.

He paused for the briefest of moments to get his bearings. His face was covered by a black ski mask. I must say, having a guy in a mask breaking into your house in the dark of the night is something I really didn't need right now, but it was probably inevitable that I had. So for no good reason, and yet for every good reason, I lunged across the room at him.

The wind was hammering against the sliding door. The Coors Light twins were gallivanting across the television screen. My intruder was staring at me from beneath his mask as I leapt over the couch. He had turned to run toward my front door when I dove onto my hardwood floors and brought him down by his ankle. Maybe I should have played football rather than poker in my days back at Wesleyan University.

I braced for what I thought would be the searing pain of a bullet, or the cutting agony of a knife, or maybe the brutality of the butt of a gun slamming into my forehead. Instead, what I felt was a fist, which, while painful, was almost quaint, given the other options. He punched me in the face, catching my left cheek. I burrowed my head against the floor to protect myself and threw my body into his.

I made hard contact. I heard him groan as he fell from a crouch to a sprawl. I climbed on top of him and dug my knees into his stomach and began hammering him about his woolen face with my bare fists. When I reached down to pull his mask off, he somehow found the strength to push me off with his forearms, and as I regained my balance, he connected with a thunderous kick to one of my favorite parts, which, of course, was my groin.

I didn't just see stars, I saw the sun, the Milky Way, the entire galaxy, make it the universe. I heard Frank Sinatra singing "Fly Me to the Moon," and I don't think it was coming from the TV. I fell to the bare floor in breathless agony, reflexively folding into a fetal position, anticipating a withering attack. Instead, in my pounding ears, I heard shuffling, then footsteps, then my front door open and close. And I realized through the heavy haze of pain that I was wonderfully, mercifully, exquisitely alone. After that, all I heard was a commercial on television, a baseball player prattling on about taking Viagra. Terrific. Right now, I'd need that and a crane set to perform.

Eventually, I struggled to my feet. You could have had Cheryl Tiegs and Farrah Fawcett, both in their prime, show up naked in my living room and engage in a sweaty catfight, and all I'd want was a bag of ice. I steadied myself against the wall, contemplating the great fortune of the intruder's departure, and flicked on the switch for the hallway light. From there, I walked into the living room and turned on a table lamp.

That's when I saw it, the reason for the visit, the cause of the rapid departure. This wasn't a hired assassin or even a self-employed burglar. He was a courier, and his package was sitting on my couch. It was a painting, a two-masted boat tossed almost sideways by high waves in dark, churlish seas, with a haunting light on some of the passengers, and other passengers, including what seemed to be a Christ figure, gathered in apparent prayer.

Unless I'm an idiot, and hey, it's a distinct option, I believed this was *Storm on the Sea of Galilee,* by Rembrandt, arguably the most famous painting stolen from the Gardner Museum on that Sunday night in 1990. And here it was, unfurled in all its glory, adhered to a piece of cardboard, sitting in my living room in the exact spot on my couch where my now dead dog and I usually hung out. Beside the painting was a small white envelope, unsealed, and I opened it up and pulled out a plain, white, heavy note card. On it were the words, "This time you really will be hearing from us." It was an apparent play on the last words spoken to the bound guards by the Gardner thieves.

Mother of Christ, if I continued on a roll like this, old Steph-an from the museum would start calling me Jacques and be more than willing to give me a lot more than the time of day.

I sat down on the couch beside the Rembrandt, unsure what you're supposed to do when there's a priceless treasure in your living room. The next flight to Rio was one option, but life was getting in the way of every pleasant possibility. I peered across the room at the clock on the VCR, which told me it was 3:05 A.M. Deadline for Sunday's paper had long since come and gone, not that I would have tried to make it. I had been asleep for more than two hours.

I walked to the front door and locked it. I flicked the security bar on the sliding doors as well. I thought about calling the police, but quickly decided it wasn't a viable option. Peter Martin, bless his lonely soul, was probably sitting right by his phone waiting to hear from anyone with news, but I didn't have the energy to get him involved in the middle of the night. It would mean a visit, a session with his security team, all the accompanying bullshit. All I wanted to do was go to bed, Rembrandt or not.

That's when the phone rang. Apparently, these guys weren't kidding. I really would be hearing from them. The sound echoed through my utterly empty house like cannon fire. I picked it up on the third ring, expecting to get a man's voice that I didn't necessarily know. Instead, what I heard was sobbing.

"Hello?" I said. Sobbing. Pause. Me again, asking, "Who is this?"

Still more sobbing. Impatiently, I said, "Yeah, who's calling?"

The crying quieted, then gave way to the sniffily but forever familiar voice of Elizabeth Riggs. "He's really dead?" It was as much a sad statement as it was a question.

My voice suddenly thickened, and I said, softly, "He really is."

"Jack, I'm so sorry. I loved that dog more than anything in this world, and I know that somehow you loved him even more. I loved what he did to us. I know he's a dog, but he made us more than a couple. He helped create this little family."

Each of her words was driven into my gut in almost the same way that the Rembrandt courier did with his knee. Even more softly, I said, "I know."

"And now we're not together, Jack, and Baker's not around." She began crying again.

In almost a whisper, not knowing what else to say, I replied, "You're right."

"Jack, I'm so sorry, but I've got to go. I'll call you soon, okay, and we'll talk about it more." She hung up the receiver and I clicked off the portable phone and let it fall aimlessly to the couch.

"Well," I said to the painting, "it's just me and you, Rembrandt. Do you have a first name, or were you like Madonna or Tiger and didn't need one?"

I picked the painting up and limped into the bedroom with it tucked under my arm. I looked around the room for a place to hide it, and ended up sliding it under the bed. Good plan, huh? No one would ever think to look for it there. I stripped off my clothes and tumbled onto the comforter. I'd need to be up in a few hours to let the world know about the return of another treasure. I also needed to accuse the mayor of Boston of murder.

Stretched out on the hard mattress, I muttered to myself, "What a way to live a life." Fortunately, before I could think too much about it, I was very much removed from the material world.

Chapter Twenty-seven

Sunday, September 28

Vinny Mongillo was wearing the type of matching black sweatsuit you associate with a Mafia don or a New York gynecologist. He showed up on my doorstep a few minutes after eight on Sunday morning, his face coated in perspiration, and said, "I jumped off the treadmill as soon as you called." I couldn't help but wonder if he planned to sit on the furniture.

He was the first one to arrive from my round of morning alerts. He walked past me, into the living room, and said, "Come on, Jack, don't make me beg. Where is it? Where is it?" He sounded like a schoolgirl on her way to her first 'NSYNC concert.

I led him into my small, hunter green study, where I had the canvas resting flat on my antique desk. When he saw it from a few feet away, he stopped short. He wiped his hands on the thighs of his sweatpants, put them up to his face, and then wiped them anew. In frustration, he said without looking in my direction, "Get me a towel." So I did.

He dried off his face, his hands, his arms, and his neck, as if he were a doctor cleaning up for surgery. Then he inched closer to the painting, one small step at a time, as if he were trying to surprise it. When he got within touching distance, he rested his right hand on the corner of the desk and said, "Mother of a benevolent Christ, I can't believe it."

He kept staring in silence, seemingly entranced, his eyes caressing the painting but never leaving it. Still without looking at me, he said in a hushed, faraway voice, "Did you look at it, Jack? Did you really look at it?"

I didn't answer, mostly because I didn't think he was looking for one.

He said, "Did you see the light? Did you appreciate the way it draws your eyes to these haunting waves, to the fear and the futility of the men on board, so overwhelmed by a force that they'll never be able to understand? Did you see that, Jack?"

Again, I didn't answer. Of course, I had a question of my own: Where'd my Vinny Mongillo go, and who was this guy standing in my study? Of course, I knew the answer to that already. Vinny was just a more complex human being than I had ever allowed myself to believe.

"Did your eyes then drift from the line to the dark? Did they see the Christ figure, sitting in the shadows, Jesus himself, surrounded by passengers who have a serenity that belies the fact that they may very well be on the brink of death? They are being violently tossed about in an open boat on stormy seas, and yet they are calm and collected in the company of Christ, knowing that their faith will carry them on. It's brilliant how your eye shifts from one to the other. Just brilliant."

He stopped and continued to stare. In a slightly different, almost disbelieving tone, he added, "This is Rembrandt's only seascape. Some scholars and art dealers have said it's far from his best work. They say it pales in artistry compared to Vermeer's *The Concert*. Maybe that's true. But look at it, Jack. For chrissakes, look at it. It tells a story. It takes us from one emotional pitch to the next. Fuck the critics."

And finally, he swung around and looked at me. At first, I thought he had fresh sweat rolling down his face, but then I saw the droplets were really tears —tears of joy, tears of appreciation, maybe tears of sorrow that in his own vibrant mind, his life would never be more beautiful than this one exquisite moment when he found himself essentially alone with one of the greatest art treasures the world has ever known.

"Who knows about it, Jack? Who knows you have this here?" He asked this with a voice that seemed to emanate from a different part of his brain.

"You, Martin. Me. The guy who delivered it. The guy who asked the guy to deliver it. So far, that's it."

"Let's kill Martin and take the painting and fly away."

I laughed a low little laugh. He repeated himself, word for word. Now he was starting to scare me.

"We're not going to kill Peter Martin," I said.

"Why not?"

"Because that wouldn't be nice, or legal."

"If we do, this painting is ours. We can be on the next flight to Rio."

"So we'd sell the damned thing and live happily ever after, you and me, on a South American beach? You wouldn't like my bowed legs."

He stared at me in disbelief. "Who said anything about selling it? We'd live together, me and you, and worship this treasure every day of our lives."

At that exact moment, the doorbell sounded, and I didn't so much leave as escape. It was Peter Martin, also dressed in a sweatsuit. I must not be up on the latest in journalism couture. For the record, I was clothed in old jeans and a white polo shirt, untucked.

"You working out?" I asked.

"Curling lessons."

Of course.

When Martin came into the study, he and Mongillo didn't bother greeting each other. Instead, Vinny said, "I can already tell you it's authentic. When this was cut from its frame, investigators found paint chips on the floor of the museum, and if you look here, you can see where it flaked."

We both got closer. Mongillo warned us, "Don't touch." We stood there awkwardly, Martin and I unsure of what to do or say, and Mongillo in silent worship. A few minutes later, I led them back out into the living room and opened up the sliding door to cool everybody down. We all sat on the couch and chairs.

I explained the scuffle in my living room earlier that morning and showed them the note that accompanied the painting.

Martin said, "All right, scrap the plan to go after the mayor. I want both of you on the Rembrandt's return. I'll hire the same company to authenticate it and tell them it's a rush job. We need it by deadline. This may be even bigger than last time. One by one, we're getting these priceless treasures back. I suspect that soon enough, we're going to be hit with a ransom note for the rest of them."

Mongillo nodded in agreement. He was right about a lot, Martin was, as he so often is. It was going to be huge. We'd probably end up as the intermediaries in a ransom bid. We—hell, meaning I—might even be asked by the FBI or the museum to deliver the ransom money. But Martin was wrong in one key area. This was no time to abandon the story of the mayor. Why? Because my gut told me so, and it was time I started listening to myself a little bit more.

"Peter, I have a theory," I said. Well, okay, I really didn't, not a well-thought, coherent one, anyway. But it was coming to me as I spoke, surprisingly clear and endlessly sensible.

"Whoever is returning these paintings to me, they want me off Hilary Kane's murder. They don't want us probing around in that, so they're trying to divert our attention, hoping we get so caught up in the fame and the follows that go along with the Gardner story that time passes us by on the Kane death."

Martin sat staring at me for a long moment. Mongillo got up and walked out to the refrigerator in search of a bite to eat.

Before either could say anything, I added, "It could well be the mayor, directing his kid to start giving paintings back before he gets caught in Kane's murder. That's my operating theory."

"Makes an odd, convoluted kind of sense," Martin finally replied, his brow furrowed. "If true, it certainly worked with me. I want to throw all our firepower onto the paintings, because we know we have it. It's rock solid. The other thing's still a work in progress, and there's nothing definitive about it, intriguing as it might be."

Mongillo returned empty-handed and asked, apropos of nothing, "Where's the pooch?"

Understand, non-dog people—and Mongillo is a card-carrying member of the club—always call dogs pooches—an utterly ridiculous word that means absolutely nothing. They pet dogs with outstretched arms. They think nothing of asking if, say, a golden retriever bites.

"Long story," I said, not wanting to get into it. Mongillo let it drop.

Martin said, "Okay, so we'll keep Mongillo on the mayor while you work the return of Rembrandt. That keeps us going on both fronts, right?"

It did, but I still didn't like it. I wanted the mayor, alone. I wanted him one on one that very day, preferably sitting in his office or in the back of his car or wherever else he'd deign to meet me. He lied to me last we spoke, lied about the last time he had seen or heard from his son, and now I was in a position to call him on it, and I wanted to see the fear on his face, gauge his reaction, determine myself if he had been desperate to pull the trigger on the young and innocent Hilary Kane.

"Flip it," I said. "Mongillo has forgotten more about art than I'll ever know. Give him the Rembrandt"—I looked over and Vinny's eyes lit up at the very notion—"and me the mayor. Maybe we'll wind up with the best Monday front page in the *Record*'s history."

Martin asked, "Do we call the Feds in on this? There doesn't seem to be a lot of doubt that you're going to be asked to mediate a ransom for a return."

I thought about that for a long moment. The breeze, cool and salty, wafted through the open door. The sun outside broke through some high clouds and cast fresh, warm light all across the living room. I said, "Let's hold off. They might leak to the *Traveler.*"

They probably wouldn't. The FBI hates the *Traveler.* But I was flying on instinct, and my instincts told me to keep this all within the paper, even if I didn't understand why.

Martin nodded and stood up. He told Mongillo, "I have security outside, with a van, to transport the painting back to the newsroom. You want to join us?"

"The only time I lose sight of this treasure is when we send it back to the museum," he replied. With that, he picked up the painting like it was a baby, and the two of them, looking like teammates in their matching black sweatsuits in some sort of dysfunctional basketball league, headed out the door.

"Don't lose radio contact," Martin told me.

I nodded.

He said, "It's going to be some day."

Yet again, he was right. It was going to be some day indeed.

Chapter Twenty-eight

The sun had ducked behind a heavy cover of clouds and a chill autumn breeze blew in from the harbor as I stepped from my car and down onto the architectural atrocity that is known as City Hall Plaza.

Whatever urban planner thought that a multi-acre park of unfettered, uninterrupted brick in the heart of downtown Boston would serve as any sort of practical or aesthetic allure should have the plaza named for them, then hung in effigy on it. It is a park only a mason could love, overheated in the summer, a wind-whipped tundra in the winter, void of green, empty of humanity, offering nothing that anyone would regard as a creature comfort. It makes City Hall, located at its heart, seem like an oasis, which is no easy thing to do.

On this day, there were several hundred people gathered on the plaza, almost all of them dressed in their Sunday best. Most were black. Those who weren't were elected or appointed officials trying to show they cared. Boston police had shot an unarmed man the prior week, the fourth police shooting in the last two months, and religious leaders from several predominantly minority neighborhoods had summoned their parishioners downtown in a show of prayerful protest.

Various ministers stepped to the dais praying that the police department would overcome its collective prejudice, that the elected officials would find the courage of compassion, that residents of the neighborhoods would see their way to forgiveness—provided the wrongs were quickly made right.

I stood in the rear, my eyes constantly on the back of Mayor Daniel Harkins, who sat in the first row, his head occasionally bowed, looking both chastened and determined. Afterward, as the crowd dispersed, Harkins appeared before several television cameras saying that all the shootings remained under investigation, that each one was certainly a tragedy, but he was still awaiting the dissemination of evidence and the compilation of reports to learn if any of the shootings were unjustified. Citizens deserve to be free of police violence, he said, but police also have a right to protect themselves while they do an extraordinarily dangerous and often underappreciated job. My legs got shaky just watching him walk a line this fine. Yet another reason why I took a job on the right side of the notebook.

Anyway, Harkins saw me while he was giving his interviews, and afterward, as he walked down a hulking set of concrete stairs that led from the plaza to the back of City Hall, he seemed not the least bit surprised when I caught up with him and asked if he had a moment to spare.

"What now, Jack? You have video of me in flagrante delicto with a member of a barnyard species?" He said this with a devilish smile on his face as he kept descending the steps.

Not wanting to allow him to set the tone, I said stone-faced, "No, sir, but I do have you caught in a lie."

By then, we were at the bottom of the stairs, him a pace in front of me, heading toward his mayoral vehicle—a Ford Expedition that was parked with its engine running in the circular drive of City Hall known as the Horseshoe.

He replied, still walking toward the SUV, "A politician lying? Stop the presses." And then he let out a little laugh.

I said, still flat, "It's about your son. You lied about your son." It almost hurt me to be this entirely humorless, to not engage him tit for tat in a whimsical little dance. But again, I wanted him to play on my terms, not the other way around. It's important in any interview to not just control the questions, but to set the tone in which they are asked and hopefully answered.

He was at the rear door of the Expedition, his fingers on the handle. He turned and looked at me for the first time, the smile gone from his face. He said, "You don't have shit."

"I have you lying."

His hand dropped down to his side. He was wearing a navy blue suit with a dark blue shirt and a cranberry-colored tie. The wind was whipping up from the direction of the harbor, tousling his hair and blowing through his jacket. His face, normally handsome and younger than his years, was ruddy from the hour or so he had just spent in the cold. He looked, in short, slightly disheveled and uncharacteristically worn.

"About what?"

"You want to talk about this right here?"

"It ain't worth going anywhere else for."

At that moment, two elderly women in the company of a forty-something man, all attired in sneakers and windbreakers, shrieked from the sidewalk and came clomping down the driveway.

"Mr. Mayor, Mr. Mayor," the older of the two women yelled, "I love you. I absolutely love you. Could we get our picture taken with you?"

He gave them a wan smile and was about to respond when the second woman handed me a digital camera and said, "Shoot us, sonny." Glad she wasn't saying that to the mayor, because you never know how he'd take it.

Anyway, I've always loved the entitlement of the elderly, so much so that I can't wait to have it someday. The three of them gathered around the mayor and pushed in real tight. I put the camera up to my eye and said, "On the count of three, everyone say fugitive."

The three constituents said just that; Harkins merely glared at me. Truth be known, I didn't think he was going to look all that pleasant in the photograph—a suspicion borne out when the young man pressed a few buttons on the camera, looked at the image, and said with some surprise, "Mayor, you're not smiling."

"Thank you, thank you, but I've got to run," Harkins replied. "Flynn, get in the car."

I got into the passenger-side rear door, Harkins got into the driver's-side rear door, the monstrous SUV sped down the driveway, took a right onto the street, and we were off.

"What do you think I lied about?" Harkins said after a few moments of silence. He said this staring straight ahead, out the front window, as his young driver silently chauffeured us to destinations unknown.

Rather than wait for an answer, Harkins pulled a folded-up sheet of paper from the breast pocket of his suit coat, opened it up, scanned it, and barked to his police detail, "That's it for my official schedule, Les. Take me to the Faulkner Hospital."

"Sir?"

"You heard me. It's in Jamaica Plain. Find it."

Well, if he was going to shoot me, stab me, punch me, or inflict any act of violence whatsoever, a hospital was certainly a preferable destination.

Back at me, he said, "C'mon, what'd I lie about? I want to hear it."

He was in a kind of take-charge, suffer-no-fools, accepting-no-bullshit mode, which for reasons that I wasn't quite sure, I think played into my hand. I didn't want a lot of mind games. I didn't have the patience for the Machiavellian garbage that's so prevalent in any dealing with any politician—the subterfuge, the layers of haze that float above even the simplest truths.

So I said in as flat a tone as I could muster, "I asked you last Wednesday when the last time was that you saw or heard from your son. You said, and I quote, 'Too long to clearly remember. Far too long, and that's the shame of it all.'"

I paused here as the car rolled through the Theater District. The driver stared blankly ahead and the mayor looked at me out of the corner of his increasingly angry eye. Then I added, my voice a little lower, "And that was a lie."

"And why," he asked, his frustration building into a crescendo, "would you say that?"

It was awkward, talking like this in the back of a car, or rather, an SUV. I felt like one of a pair of mob kingpins hashing out territory while trying to avoid the probing ears of federal agents, or Donald and Ivana Trump arguing in the back of their limousine over how to divvy up their New York empire. We were both facing forward, because to face each other made it almost awkwardly intimate— the very act, the shifting of the legs, the movement of the hips.

I turned my face to watch his, and he was, indeed, staring straight ahead. I said, "The night Hilary Kane was in your house, she saw a file on your personal computer. Let's not play games here. You know this."

He sat in silence. The car glided through the Back Bay, up Commonwealth Avenue, through Kenmore Square, past Fenway Park, where all this had started, and onto the Jamaicaway. All along, the entire time, he was silent, as if he hadn't heard what I had said.

Normally in these situations, I refuse to speak. Never step into a gap that the person being questioned is supposed to fill. But finally, I could take no more, and said, "She saw the file about the Gardner thefts. She saw that you knew that Toby was holding on to some of the artwork. She made a printout. Before she died, she told her sister. Her sister told me. My plan is to tell readers."

Still nothing by way of response. By now, we were heading past Jamaica Pond, gliding along the winding four-lane road in light Sunday traffic. Most everyone else had it easy today, God's day, while Mongillo and Martin were back in the newsroom preparing to tell the world about the return of the stolen Rembrandt and Maggie Kane remained in hiding and the mayor next to me fought for his political life.

Again, I stepped hesitantly into the silence, this time saying, "To know about the Gardner pieces would mean that you had to be in contact with your son, because the FBI is saying they didn't provide you with the information. There's some question as to whether they even drew the connection.

"If you're in contact with your son, you've been publicly lying about the extent of your relationship. It also raises legal questions about whether you're aiding and abetting a fugitive. Finally, there are key members of the FBI who are privately suggesting that you might in some way benefit from the heist, from the sale or ransom of the art."

If any one of these allegations was true, and they may very well all have been, it would prove catastrophic to the aspiring career of Boston's incumbent mayor. At the very least, forget the Senate appointment. At most, you're talking resignation, maybe criminal prosecution. That said, if any of them were false, and I put them into print, it would absolutely finish the already nose-diving career of the young and handsome Jack Flynn.

The driver took a right into the parking lot of the Faulkner Hospital and nervously asked, "Which part of the building are you going, sir?"

Harkins spoke for the first time in forever. He said in a much more conciliatory voice, "Just park the truck in whatever space you can find. We'll get out there."

He did, and we did. It was still cloudy, still windy, as Harkins walked across the parking lot toward the hulking brick edifice. I followed a pace or two behind, admittedly curious as to what he was doing, and why. If my good friends down at the Columbia School of Journalism ever teach a specific course in losing control of an interview, they ought to play a videotape for the young charges on exactly what was going on here.

We walked through the large automatic doors that led into the front lobby. At the reception desk, an elderly woman waved excitedly and said, "You're doing a great job, Mayor." He waved back without a smile and we didn't stop. Instead, he strode to a bank of elevators, pressed 3, and we rode up in our perpetual state of silence.

Were we visiting a patient? Was he bringing me to see his fugitive son? Was he going to have me sit with a doctor who would explain that the mayor was mentally incapacitated and it wasn't fair to write a story? What? What?

We walked off the elevator, him the standard step ahead of me, through a set of double doors, and into an empty, rectangular waiting room that was rimmed by institutional, upholstered chairs. It had all the standard accoutrements of the dreary hospital vigil—end tables that held stacks of outdated magazines, plastic greenery, a television set bolted high on a wall that at the moment was turned off.

Harkins stopped in the middle of the room and continued to look to the far end. He was looking in that direction, away from me, when he said in a voice that was somewhere between familiar and far away, "'Til the day I die, I'll never forget it, because it was the happiest moment of my life. I was sitting right over there"—he pointed—"when the doctor came out with the news.

"It had been a complicated pregnancy. This was our first child, and Shelley had miscarried once before. When we got the hospital, she was in a great deal of pain, and the doctors immediately decided to do a C-section. They rushed her into surgery and told me to wait out here, in this very room. I sat in that corner."

He paused. Not once had he looked at me during the start of his soliloquy. He was looking at the walls with the drab institutional art of sailboats on the Charles River, or at the scuffed tile floors. He slowly walked over to one of the chairs and sat down, and I sat a few seats away from him.

"I thought our boy was going to die, the way everyone had been acting. I thought, that's it, the entire pregnancy, all that pent-up joy, it was about to lead to emotional devastation. So I sat in this room for two hours steeling myself, figuring out how Shelley and I would get over it, whether we'd try to have more kids, what it would do to our own marriage, how we could move on with our lives.

"And then the doctor came out and he said, 'Mr. Harkins, it's a boy.' That's it. Easy as that. 'It's a boy.' There were a bunch of people around. It was six o'clock on a Saturday night, visiting hours. And I just broke down and cried."

I thought he was about to do that all over again as he sat in that low-slung chair with the rose-colored cushions, his elbows on his knees and his gaze pointed down at the ground. Then he looked up at me, his head cocked sideways, his face all eyes, and said very softly, "Do you know what I mean, Jack? Do you know what I mean?"

I knew the next question was coming before he began speaking the words. "Do you have kids of your own?"

Well, not exactly. And why not, Jack? Because, Mayor, on that day that you're reliving, you heard the exact words that I was expecting to be told, only it was going to be a girl. And I got the precise news that you had convinced yourself would be yours, only it was even worse. It wasn't only my child who died in the hospital during what was supposed to be the happiest, most unforgettable time of my life; my wife died as well. And in that one moment of that one hellish day, two lives were lost and the lone survivor would never be the same.

So did I know what he meant? Yes, in the abstract, because I've spent too many hours imagining what I lost that day—the bottomless joy and the aching challenges and the everyday heartbreaks that might never be mine, all as I repeatedly warned myself that you can only miss what you once actually had.

But to his specific question, what was I supposed to say? Reveal my thoughts? Recount my most intimate travails? Share my agony? No. Instead, I met his stare and simply said, "Not yet."

He nodded his head, though he understood exactly no part of my answer.

He said, "Well, Jack, when it happens, it changes you forever. They brought me in and had me wash up and when I held Toby for that first time, I never wanted to let go. Never."

He was smiling then, but not a warm smile, more nostalgic, bittersweet. His voice trailed off as his gaze moved downward again. I kept my eyes focused on his, and thought I saw them begin to glisten.

"Still don't." When he said this, his voice was so thick, his tone so hushed, that I had to lean in to listen.

He fell quiet again, and we both sat in absolute silence, the only sound being the occasional rattle of a radiator on the near wall and the distant murmur of what were no doubt nurses talking and laughing at their station. This canyon, I refused to bridge. He had brought me to that visitor's lounge for a reason that he had yet to reveal, so I sat there waiting for him to give me something more.

Finally, he looked across at me again, his face sideways, his ear almost parallel with the floor. His eyes, in fact, were wet, and he said quietly, "Maybe some men could walk away. Maybe you'll be one of those guys. Your kid didn't turn out according to the plan. The newspapers are clawing at you to make sure you've cut all ties. So you do, and you go on with your own career."

Another long pause, as he turned from me to the wall straight ahead, his stare giving way to a vacant gaze. "I never could," he said. "Toby's pretty definitely a thief and probably a drug lord and maybe a killer, but he's still the same human being that I held in my arms in this hospital thirty years ago. It's a cliché, but he is my flesh and blood, my creation. How am I supposed to walk away from that?"

I suppose I should have been writing this stuff down. The three-term mayor of Boston, Daniel Harkins, was admitting to me a long-term lie, at the same time opening up multiple avenues of questions over whether he had aided a fugitive and possibly benefited from his crimes.

I sat those few chairs away blanketing him with my gaze, waiting to see if he wanted to take me further. I committed some of his comments to memory, repeated them over and over in my mind, not wanting to pull out a pen and a pad for fear it would inhibit him.

He looked spent. He actually appeared to have shrunk within the elegant confines of his navy suit. He just kept staring down, the fingers of his two hands entwined in front of him. I was about to speak, to delicately ask him some questions that needed to be answered, when he said, "And now you're going to tell me that by trying to be a father to the worst possible son, by never forgetting that little boy who I held for the first time in this very hospital, that I'm going to lose my political career."

Probably, but I'd argue—though perhaps not here and now— that it wasn't simply fatherhood that would do him in, or even his wayward son, but the lies. It's been said ad nauseum that in politics it's never the crime so much as the cover-up, and this might be another prime example how.

I said, "But the fact you knew about the artwork and didn't take any action is a total abrogation of your public responsibility as a citizen, and more so of your position as mayor. By being passive, you were essentially complicit. That's a reportable story."

He turned now and stared at me. "So you're saying that a father should turn in his son, just call the cops and say, 'Here's where he is. Go arrest him. Let him spend the rest of his life in jail.'"

I thought about that for a long moment, and this time it was me looking at the floor and the mayor looking at me. I didn't know the answer. I think I knew what I'd do, which is maybe pretty much the same thing that Harkins did, which is nothing. Or was it nothing? Because the point here was whether he aided and abetted, whether he, as the FBI intimated, actually played a role in making money off the art.

"Did you know about the Gardner art?" I asked.

"I learned about it within the past couple of months."

"Did you know Toby's location?"

"I learned that in the past couple of months as well."

"Did you kill Hilary Kane?"

"No."

"Did you reach out to Toby, or did he reach out to you?"

"I reached out to him."

"But once you learned where he was, once you came to realize what you had, you thought it was fine to leave your murderous son who's on the FBI's Ten Most Wanted list free with a dozen priceless treasures."

"You're missing the point, Jack. You're missing the entire point. I would never turn him in. I'm constitutionally incapable of doing that—"

"You lied." I said this in a louder voice than I had meant.

"But I was about to do something different, something better. I was on the brink of negotiating the return of the art. And after he gave up the paintings, he was going to surrender."

My eyes opened wide in shock, though probably no wider than my mouth. I sat there staring at him staring at me. There was a buzzing, churning, gnawing silence between us. And then Harkins added, "But then you printed your story on the front page of the *Record,* and the whole deal, the entire thing, went to hell."

Chapter Twenty-nine

In newspaper-speak, we call this a he-said/she-said, the type of story where accusations and counteraccusations are flung and refuted with reckless disregard, always by people who seem a little loose around the lips. The frustrating part is that few of the charges are supported by documents; facts often give way to anger; reality is what the readers want to make it.

In this case, my operating theory remained largely unchanged. Mayor Daniel Harkins got drunk. He invited a young woman in a bar up to his condominium in the Ritz for a visit. Sex, power, and booze are hardly a new combination, yet a perennially fascinating one just the same.

Once in the apartment, she saw something that nobody aside from the mayor was intended to see (and I'm not talking about his Johnson): evidence that Harkins knew about his fugitive son's role in the Gardner Museum heist. She reported it to authorities. She told her sister. She made a printout. And she ran.

A few days later, the mayor killed her. Maybe it was mindless rage. Maybe he feared a public campaign on her part—interviews on the network morning shows, sit-downs with the *Record* and *The New York Times*, appearances on *Nightline,* that would torpedo his chances for being appointed to the Senate seat. Another thought occurred to me as well. Maybe he hadn't read the paper yet that morning. She was murdered early, before eight, and maybe he thought he was killing her before she said a word to anyone about what she saw.

I was playing this through my mind as I sat in a taxicab heading from Jamaica Plain to City Hall, where my car remained parked. The mayor, bless his bared little soul, saw no need to give me a lift back into town, which was probably just as well, because as soon as he stalked out of the hospital waiting room, I used the time alone to furiously scribble every quote I could remember on the note pad that I hadn't wanted him to see.

The story that I had at that point wasn't that the mayor had killed Hilary Kane. No, that would be too clean, and journalism, specifically newspaper reporting, is a dirty, grimy undertaking. But I could—and probably would—write a story saying that Boston Mayor Daniel Harkins had spent time alone in his apartment with a woman who was found murdered less than three days later, according to videotapes obtained by the *Record*. The second graph would read as follows: During the thirty-minute early morning visit, the victim saw a file on Harkins's personal computer that detailed the mayor's awareness of his son's possible involvement in the Gardner Museum heist, according to a family member of the victim.

Then the denial, that Harkins said Sunday that he was trying to broker the return of the dozen masterpieces, and was trying to convince his son, federal fugitive Toby Harkins, to surrender to authorities.

He could deny until the cows came home, until Rembrandt and Vermeer and everyone else hung again on the Gardner's walls, but it would be too late. The compilation of events, from the drunken tryst to the secretly held information to the taint of murder to the obvious pattern of previous lies, they'd kill him politically. He might be able to hold on to office until the next election, but by every possible and practical measure, Daniel Harkins's career would be over. No Senate appointment, no reelection, nothing. He couldn't even get a job as a mayoral driver. He'd probably have to become a lobbyist.

If he really didn't kill Hilary Kane, would this be fair? I don't know. Is it fair that my daughter died at birth and his son lived to take other people's lives? Is it fair Hilary Kane died for doing the right thing? Is it fair that her sister is now living in constant fear?

Still, something bothered me about all this, and yet again, the feeling came from my gut, just as my hesitance did at that first story a week before. Looking into Harkins's incredibly sad eyes at the hospital, there was something innately believable about what he said and the way he said it. I've been around liars every day of every week of every year of my career, and pride myself on my ability to spot them a mile away. Some reporters are great interviewers. Others are poets at the keyboard. My greatest asset, I believe, is an ability to peer into the human soul and discern fact from fiction. Harkins's was a muddle, and it made me uneasy as I thought about the events and the consequences to come.

So what I needed were documents. The only documents to be had were the printouts from his computer. It was time, I came to realize, to acquire them, but the question was, how?

And the answer was, two ways. One, Maggie Kane could rack her brain and figure out where her sister might have hid them. And two, the hopefully sobered-up Hank Sweeney could call on his many contacts at Boston PD to tell me if they were taken during the initial search of Hilary's apartment five days before.

My cell phone chimed. When I picked up, it was the unfailingly straightforward voice of Peter Martin, saying, "Your girl said she's had enough of confinement. She's going to get herself killed."

My girl? Confinement? Sounds like I'm ripe for a grand jury indictment, followed by a splash on the cover of the *Traveler*, "Spiraling Journo Finds Bottom." I asked the first question that popped into my addled mind: "Huh?"

"Maggie Kane. She says she's had enough of the security, the hotel, the hiding. She says she's heading back to work tomorrow and going on with her life."

"Did you point out that her sister's still dead and the killer, despite what police might think, isn't behind bars?"

Martin said, "I did, though maybe not in your inimitable way.

That said, I'm not going to argue too hard about saving $400 a night in hotel bills for her and her bodyguards, and another $1,000 a day in security costs."

Ah, that's my Peter. Rome is burning, and he's worried about the water bill.

He said, "You should also know, the cardinal raced over to Mass General about thirty minutes ago to deliver what the television stations are reporting are the Last Rites to Senator Stiff. He might be dead and gone come tomorrow, and the governor seems to have every intention of appointing a replacement by the time the Senate reconvenes on Tuesday."

As I've said before, there are some days, stories, when the timing could not possibly be more exquisite. Calls are returned early. Documents come available in the middle of the day. Key reporters for the opposing paper are out of town or chasing down false leads. And then there are stories like this one when the timing conjures images of a multiple car crash, with fire shooting into the air and body parts strewn about a blood-soaked stretch of road. If it can go wrong, it will. The rush is on, calls aren't returned, answers are never what you had assumed. But no matter. The paper comes out every single morning whether you have what you need for a good story or not.

Speaking of which, Martin asked, "How'd it go with the mayor?"

"Interesting. Very interesting."

"He spoke? What'd he say?" You could almost hear him get breathy with excitement, as if I were a woman and he asked me what I was wearing.

I told him—though just about the interview, not about my navy blazer and pale blue tie.

At the end of my summation, he said in that unnaturally calm way of his, "So we have it. We can get it into print."

And he was right, for all the reasons I had previously recounted to myself—the video, the timing, the denial, the revelation. It would become a national story the second the morning *Record* hit the doorstep of the Associated Press office and they flung it across the world on their wire.

So why didn't I feel better about this?

I said, "I'm on my way in shortly. Let's talk about it a little bit more when I get there. You should inform Justine that we're about to tie the mayor of Boston to a murder investigation so she doesn't choke on her morning doughnuts."

Martin said, "Will do. And do you realize in the Monday paper, the *Record* will be reporting the return of a priceless Rembrandt and the distinct possibility that the long-time mayor of Boston is or should be a suspect in the slaying of a young city worker?"

The guy was as jubilant as I've ever heard him. I had a role in both these stories, so again, why wasn't I as happy?

When I arrived in my own car, I sat in the driver's seat for a long moment trying to figure out what I needed to do first. In newspapering, the mornings are when you develop ideas. The middle part of the day is the time to gather information. The late afternoon is when you inevitably get your brains beaten out sitting at the computer trying to write what you know into some form of readable prose. Evening is when it's someone else's problem, namely the editors, and later, the copy editors who delight over finding the tiniest mistakes.

I was supposed to be in the gathering mode, but needed to stop my wheels from spinning and head in an affirmative direction. That's when my phone rang. It was Mongillo, telling me in that gloating way of his, "Hey, Fair Hair, remember that big pile of clips that you had sitting on your desk on the Gardner heist?"

"Yeah?"

"You ever read them?"

"What's your point, Vinny?" The answer, he already knew. No, I hadn't read them, partly because I was running all over the world, namely because I didn't give a rat's furry ass about the Gardner theft, truth be known. What I cared about was why Hilary Kane was dead.

"My point is this: I know most of the stuff in the clips already, but one thing jumped out at me as potentially useful. On the third or fourth day of our coverage, the paper makes mention that Boston Police Detective Sergeant Hank Sweeney was one of the primary investigators, serving as a liaison between local and federal authorities. After that, we never mention him again. Why haven't we been debriefing him now?"

A good question. The thought struck me like a bolt how uncharacteristically unhelpful Hank had been over the course of this story.

Before I could respond, Mongillo added, "I just tried him on his cell. No answer."

I said, "I'll find him." And I was off.

Hank Sweeney lives in a high-ceilinged, parlor level, one bedroom apartment on Washington Street in Boston's South End, a neighborhood that used to be on the frontier of danger and is now considered one of the most fashionable addresses in town. From his front door, he was just a few minutes in one direction to Roxbury, which was predominantly black, or in the other direction to Tremont Street, where some of the hottest victualers in Boston lined up along what was known as restaurant row.

"I get my people, I get your people, I get people who I don't even know what they are," he used to tell me. "I love it."

Less than two years before, Hank was living alone in a prefabricated house in a mosquito-infested Florida development situated on what must have been the very edge of hell, if not actually in it. This is what he thought retirement was: aching boredom, overbearing heat, unending loneliness. And then I showed up on his doorstep, innocently enough, looking for a little bit of help on a murder case that had never been solved. He came up to Boston to give me more than everything I'd need, then never went back home. Best as I knew, his bed still sat neatly made in Marshton, just the way he had left it.

Now he was, in the polite vernacular of a decidedly impolite business, a law enforcement consultant. He didn't do the gumshoe work of a private eye. He didn't pack a weapon. He didn't put himself in harm's way, Vinny Mongillo's dinner fork aside. What he did was advise well-heeled clients—and their attorneys—on how they could gain access to critical information and how they might be able to press the right buttons at police headquarters to make things happen in their favor. He did it selectively, and he did it well, and he did it on occasion for me—for free. But now that Mongillo raises the point, not so much on this case.

He had guided me on the argument unfolding between Boston PD and the FBI on Mount Vernon Street that afternoon, and he was the one to deliver the videotapes that incriminated Harkins a few afternoons back. But day in, day out, my good friend Hank Sweeney was not generally to be found.

So I decided to do just that—go find him. I pointed my car in the direction of his apartment and was there in a matter of minutes. I called him from my cell phone outside, but raised no answer on his home phone or his cell phone. I heard the former ringing from the street, but not the latter.

It was a brick townhouse building, four units in all, one on each floor, with big bay windows and a tiny front yard filled with beautiful flowers tended to by the elderly woman downstairs. I walked up the three steps to the door buzzers and rang Hank's. Again, no answer. The more resourceful types would have devised a way to use a credit card to slip through the lock, or shy of that, scale up the side of the house, jimmy up the window and tumble onto his living room floor.

The most resourceful of all would have planned for such an occasion long ago and swapped house keys with Hank. They would have taken that key, plunged it into the keyhole, and walked into the apartment. This, thank you very much, is exactly what I did.

"Hello," I yelled in his entryway. "Hello?"

No answer.

I'll admit, I was slightly uneasy, due to two things. First, Sweeney's a retired cop, meaning he probably still has a gun or two secreted somewhere around his apartment. Second, he might still be on that bender of the night before. Liquor and firearms don't mix, though the NRA and the National Distillery Association would no doubt deny such an outrageous claim.

So I yelled one more time, "Hank? Hank, it's Jack." I pulled the door shut behind me.

I stepped into his living room and saw no signs of life. Fortunately, I saw no signs of death, either. The apartment came furnished, with stuff that looked straight out of the catalogue of Crate and Barrel, right down to the too-perfect knickknacks on the marble mantel and the silver picture frames that Hank had filled with photographs of his late wife. It seemed more like a showroom than someone's home.

The place had an almost unnaturally empty feel to it. It was oddly still. All the windows were shut tight. The heater was off. There was nothing so much as a ticking clock or the occasional sound of running water from one of the apartments above.

I walked toward the back of the apartment and into the kitchen, where a dirty coffee cup sat on the counter, next to a glass with a little water in the bottom and an empty bottle of Excedrin. My good friend Hank probably woke up in a whole world of hurt.

It was brighter back here, and made me feel a little better. There was nothing suspicious thus far gleaned from this unsanctioned tour. I was starting to feel guilty about taking it, but told myself that I was checking on Hank's health and well-being.

From there, I walked into the bedroom, where I stopped short at what I saw. An empty suitcase sat atop his carefully made bed, and some articles of clothing—a couple of shirts, a pair of khaki pants, and a pair of socks—were tossed on the bedspread next to the luggage. A couple of questions rose immediately to mind, the first one being: Who has a bedspread anymore? The second, more important query was: Had Hank just fled town?

This is a guess. This is only a guess. But it appeared that he might have pulled out a large piece of luggage, packed it with clothes, then decided to pare down to something smaller, maybe a carry-on bag. I poked around the bedroom looking for any other signs of his departure, but none came immediately to sight.

So I walked back into the kitchen, picked up the portable phone, and pressed the redial button. An abnormally long series of tones sounded, the phone rang twice, and a recording came on that said, "Welcome to American Airlines. Press 1 for—"

I hung up. Unless you could press 2 for help solving a murder that you think you might have caused, or press 3 to decide whether to savage the mayor's reputation on the front pages of a newspaper for information that doesn't make you feel entirely confident, the recording had very little more to offer. It already told me this: Hank Sweeney, you could bet, was getting out of town.

But why? Where? When?

I stuck my finger into the bottom of the empty coffee cup and the residue still had a hint of warmth. I walked over to the coffeemaker on a nearby counter, a simple Mr. Coffee machine, and pressed my palm gently against the carafe, which was warmer than a little warm. I'm no thermal engineer or whatever they might be called, but my bet is that he had shut this thing off within the last half hour. So I bolted for the front door.

Chapter Thirty

I got to Logan Airport in a new record time, which I reminded myself to call into the newspapers for my appropriate award. I parked, and bolted into Terminal B, where American Airlines is located. I checked the monitors to see what was leaving in the next thirty minutes or so—flights to Chicago, Dallas, Los Angeles, Miami, San Francisco, San Juan, and then I saw it: West Palm Beach, the nearest airport to his old retirement house.

I tried walking through security but was nearly arrested, hog-tied, and strip-searched because I didn't have a ticket. "Looking for a friend," I explained, and was told, in no uncertain terms, to take a flying leap, just not on one of their planes.

So I ran up to the counter, which was gloriously free of people, and told the nice middle-aged woman that I needed a one-way ticket.

"Where?"

Straight to hell. But with no time for any of my asides, I said, "West Palm Beach."

"Everything's full on that flight but first class."

"I'll take it." Peter Martin would think this was absolutely hilarious.

She ticketed me with a jarring amount of efficiency and I was off. My good friends at security weren't exactly thrilled to see me coming through. I had to remove my shoes and my belt, then flap my arms like a falcon. I think they were about to make me recite the first two paragraphs of the Gettysburg Address when their supervisor showed up on the scene and they abruptly let me go.

I was jogging down the concourse, past the food court with the standard Cinnabon and Sbarro shops, when I heard the announcement over the public address system: "This is the pre-boarding call for American Airlines Flight 528 for West Palm Beach, first-class passengers and Advantage Gold, Advantage Platinum and Advantage Executive Platinum are invited to board at this time."

The good news is that I could get on the plane if I wanted. The bad news is, I wasn't going anywhere, even though there was probably never a better time to try to escape this nightmare that had become my life. It occurred to me during my trot that less than a week ago, when Elizabeth was leaving, I probably should have been doing the same thing, running down the concourse, begging her not to leave. The problem was, I really didn't want to stop her and she didn't want to be stopped. So there you go.

As I approached the waiting lounge for the Palm Beach flight, I slowed down to a walk and took a hard look around. A small line had formed at the door, and the several dozen people in the seats were putting away newspapers and magazines, slipping belongings back into their duffel bags, and checking seat assignments on their boarding passes. A quick survey didn't reveal Hank Sweeney, a tough guy to miss.

I walked through the heart of the lounge, up and down the little rows that separated the attached seats, peering, searching, hoping, praying. Still nothing.

The public address announcer said, "We'll start by boarding from the rear of the plane. Anyone sitting in rows 25 and higher—25 and higher."

That's when it occurred to me that I could have this all wrong. Maybe he was flying somewhere else, to Chicago or on vacation to Puerto Rico or maybe out to see a distant cousin on the West Coast. Maybe Sweeney wasn't leaving at all. Maybe he was picking someone up, and was standing back at security waiting. Or maybe he wasn't going or meeting or waiting or avoiding. Maybe this was all a giant mind-fucking, for me, by me.

No time to assess the psychological morass that was allegedly my mind. I started walking briskly farther down the concourse, to check other flights, hopefully to find Sweeney lounging in a chair with his face in the sports section of the morning *Record* wondering how it was that the Red Sox folded up like tin foil for the upteenth season in a row.

And that's when I saw him. He came lumbering out of a men's room with that bearlike gait of his, one side of his body pushing forward, then the other, his head down, his barrel chest out, enormous, not fat. He was heading right for me along the wide, carpeted hallway, a small duffel bag over his shoulder and a magazine—a *Sports Illustrated*, I believe—in his left hand. I stopped and stood in his path, something he wouldn't have noticed because he never looked ahead, not when he was walking, anyway.

When he was on me, he sensed me, stopped short and mumbled, "Excuse me."

"You're not excused."

He looked up, his big brown eyes tired but surprised. "Jesus, son, what the hell are you doing here?"

Always calling me son, ever since I sat with him on his cheap plastic furniture on his overheated patio in Marshton, Florida, a couple of years before, and he helped me about as much as anyone has ever helped me, putting his pension on the line, his reputation, eventually his life.

It's a cliché to say it, but I did anyway: "I was wondering the same thing about you, Hank."

We stood face-to-face in the busy concourse, with businessmen lugging briefcases and tourists with knapsacks and rolling luggage swarming past us in each direction, places to be, people to see, while both Hank and I were inextricably stuck in a moment that neither of us wanted or probably fully understood.

He recovered some from his state of startle, and said in that softer, whiskeyed voice of his, "Ah, just heading down to Marshton to spend a little time at home and do some maintenance on the house. Make sure everything's okay, you know?"

No, I didn't, actually. "Home's here, Hank. Always has been, always will be. You know that, and so do I."

He averted his eyes, looking down, and shuffled his feet like a little boy.

"Rows 10 and higher," the public address announcer said from behind me, the voice echoing through the hall, "10 and higher to West Palm Beach."

"I'm row 16," Hank said, and he let those words hang out there, meaningless and meaningful at the same time.

"Why are you leaving?"

He shuffled his feet some more, like a pitcher waiting for the manager to walk from the dugout to the mound to pull him out of the game. He kept his gaze downward and said, "Son, I'm old. I thought I could make a comeback, in my career, in my life."

He paused, still looking at the old sneakers that he wore on his feet, or maybe at the bluish commercial carpet that adorned the floor.

"But history catches up to you. Time catches up to you. You can't escape the past, even if you don't think the past was really all that bad."

Another pause. The announcement sounded, "All rows. All rows on American Airlines Flight 528 to West Palm Beach."

"So it's time for me to go back to where I belong, sitting in a lounge chair, listening to baseball games on a transistor radio, tending a garden. Maybe I'll take up golf."

He paused again. His face got tight around his jaw. His voice, already uncharacteristically narrow, grew almost reedy. He added, "Son, it's time for me to go."

This wasn't much of an answer, so I asked again, "Why are you leaving?"

This time, he looked me square in the eye and said without hesitation, "To preserve my dignity. To not lose the respect of people I like. To save myself and every other thing that I worked for."

I sighed heavily. A plane must have just pulled in from some distant place, because a fresh torrent of people were making their way past us on their way to baggage claim.

"This is the final boarding call for Flight 528 to West Palm Beach. All seats, all rows."

He stood still, and so did I. I told him, "I need your help, Hank. I think I caused a woman to die."

"It wasn't your fault, son."

"You know that?"

"I know it wasn't your fault." His voice grew softer, more familiar. As I've said, I'd only met Hank two years before, less even, but had the sense that I'd known him forever. He was dead serious in some endeavors, like solving murder cases, slightly comic in most others, one of these guys who knew that life was something of an unfolding gag, got the jokes, and wasn't afraid to laugh at all the appropriate lines. There were times when you wanted to hug him rather than shake his hand, he was that kind of guy, times when you could just sit with him in the front seat of a car on a stakeout that would probably lead to nowhere and talk about nothing for two hours, and somehow, some way, the time would seem to fly.

People who I've known for just a couple of years are people who I would never describe as friends. They're acquaintances, maybe on the waiting list for friendship, if time bears our relationship out. My friends are people who have been around for the longer part of forever. Except Hank. He was a friend from the moment I first knocked on his screen door.

"Hank, tell me why you're leaving."

He readjusted the shoulder strap of his bag. He shook his head, slowly and sadly. "You'll know in due time," he said, staring down again.

"I need to know now."

"I've got to go, son. I've really got to go."

"Guy walks into a bar, Hank. It's the first line of a joke, unless it's you walking into Toby Harkins's old place in Southie. Why'd you do that?"

"I've got to go."

And he began walking, slowly, around me. I turned and kept pace.

"Hank, don't do this."

He looked at me as he walked and said, "Son, I'll tell you this. Be very, very careful about who you trust, in life, but especially on this story."

With that, he started walking faster. I looked ahead and saw that the door to the jetway was still open, a young man in one of those inevitably unflattering polyester uniforms standing in front of it. He glanced at his watch, the young man did, took a last look around the empty lounge, and began to shut the door. Hank yelled out, "One more."

He headed toward the door. I thought about following him right through it, right down the plank and onto the plane, but then I'd be stuck in Florida while my life in Boston was coming apart at the seams. Actually, tell me what's wrong with that scenario again?

So I stopped. Hank called over his shoulder, "Be very careful." He handed the attendant his boarding pass and ambled through the door without ever looking back. I stood watching in a sad state of shock, watching as the young man flicked the door shut, watching as a foot appeared and the door bounced backward a little bit, watching as the figure of Hank reemerged. He told the persnickety little airline worker that he was sorry, he needed ten seconds, and he'd be right back.

He walked over to where I was standing and handed me a manila folder. "Here," he said. "You'll make better use of this than I did." Then he turned and went back through the door.

I stood watching as he walked through the door and down the ramp. Hank Sweeney, friend and confidant, was inexplicably gone.

Chapter Thirty-one

I was reviewing a roll of the dead and the departed as I walked back up the concourse, past security, and down the escalators toward the parking garage. First and foremost was Baker, whose death weighed on my heart as heavy as one of those water-logged sticks he would drag from the Charles River. Elizabeth Riggs: gone. Hank Sweeney: gone. Vinny Mongillo: leaving. Peter Martin: no place else to go, which was good, so I'd have him for a while. I knew all too well that my world could be lonely. I had never realized it could actually be barren.

But what happened to Hank, my trusted friend? Why on God's good earth did he feel the need to suddenly, cryptically escape? I thought back to him giving me the blow-by-blow analysis of the showdown between the Boston cops and the Feds in the front seat of my car. I thought of him delivering the videotapes from police headquarters that implicated the mayor. I suspect the folder he had just handed me might provide some valuable clues to the mystery of who killed Hilary Kane, so for that reason, I refrained from opening it in public and waited until I got into my car.

This was my mood as I headed through the garage. If they awarded a gold glove for catching bad breaks, I think I'd be a clear winner, which is how I knew that the apelike person in the ill-fitting black suit standing near my car was almost certainly waiting for me. He probably drew the assignment because I had a pair of one syllable names.

So instead of stopping, I walked on by, as the song goes. He looked at me funny, just standing there in the roadway smoking a cigarette from the side of his mouth as if he strived to be a cliché. I walked around the circle, concealed the folder in the back of my pants, and walked back toward my car. This, I knew, would be an absolute load of utterly joyous fun.

I walked silently past him, so close I could smell the Slim Jim on his breath, to the driver's-side door and unlocked it. "Mr. Flynn?" he asked.

"Mister has an R in it," I replied. A little Boston accent humor. Very little, apparently, because his forehead scrunched up in what I imagine was deep thought. "Huh?" he asked.

"You're full of questions."

I was obviously in no mood to accept anyone's bullshit, despite the fact that everyone around seemed to think I was the ultimate receptacle, a veritable human Dumpster for all of life's garbage.

Ape-man recovered somewhat, and said, "Somebody wants to speak to you."

Well, I've got to admit, that's always good news in the reporting business, usually anyway, but it didn't seem such a surefire thing here. I replied, "Who might that be?"

I didn't have the time or the patience for another one of these get-in-the-backseat-of-a-dark-sedan-and-we'll-drive-you-to-where-you-need-to-be things. I wanted to get into my car and see what the hell it was that Hank Sweeney had given me. I had to get back to the newsroom and sit with Peter Martin and Vinny Mongillo and decide if we were going to take down the mayor on evidence that I thought was slightly south of solid. And if so, I would be directed to write the story, by deadline, and deadlines hadn't been so good to me of late.

"He'll tell you that."

"I'm not going anywhere but in my car."

He moved a step closer and said, "You don't have to go anywhere. He'll talk to you on the phone." And with that, he pulled out one of those exceptionally little cell phones. When he punched out a number and put it up to his ear, the thing looked ridiculous set against his fat, whiskered face.

My car door was still open. The keys were in my hand. Sweeney's folder was still shoved down the back of my pants. The occasional vehicle circled the lot in search of a space.

He handed me the phone.

I said, "Bob's Shoe Repair Shop, where you'll never get callous service."

There was silence on the other end of the line, until a man's hesitant voice said, "Is this Jack Flynn?" I tell you, these guys were far too easy.

"In the voice and flesh. What do you want?" I said this abruptly, impatiently, with not a whit of fakery. I was feeling abrupt and impatient.

The man on the phone said, "Hold the line, please."

With that, there was a series of clicks and tones, as if a call were getting patched through to some faraway place using technology that I would never in a million years be able to understand. After a few seconds, another man's voice came on the line, clear as a bell, all fresh and easy.

"Jack, that you?"

He talked as if he were steering his BMW along a windy country road on a Saturday afternoon on his way home from shooting a 78 at his private country club, this guy did, happy-go-lucky, loosey-goosey, entirely relaxed.

"It is. What can I do for you."

"Jack, this is Toby Harkins calling. Listen, thanks an awful lot for taking a moment to chat. I appreciate that very much."

I have sat in the Oval Office with presidents. I have dined with senators, quarreled with governors, reported from every one of our United States, traveled to six continents, all on the wings of a simple phrase: I'm a reporter for *The Boston Record*. But never, ever, in a career that suddenly seems prematurely long, have I been on the horn with the FBI's most-wanted fugitive, a guy whose mug shot adorns the post offices in the biggest metropolises and the tiniest farming towns, arguably the most pursued criminal in the world.

So I said, "Toby, you never call, you never write. I'm really pissed off at you."

He laughed—politely so, in almost a hail-fellow-well-met kind of way. I had never met Toby Harkins, never before talked to him, never even seen him, pictures aside. His reputation was that of someone who could turn on his charisma the way a beautiful woman can selectively, suddenly tantalize you with her good looks. He ruled, they say, with two parts fear and one part charm, captivating those he couldn't make cower. And I could hear all the evidence of that in my few seconds on the phone with him so far.

"Hey, Jack"—always using my name, like we're old friends—"I've got a little business proposition for you."

He paused here, and I asked, "Is this one of those things I'm not going to be able to refuse?"

He laughed again, but not as much as before. I suspect that on my third attempt, funny as it would no doubt be, he wouldn't be laughing at all, and the messenger monkey beside me would probably slug me in the head.

"You can do anything you want with it, but I hope you see it as in your best interest to accept it," he said, still light, familiar, but with a subtext.

I didn't reply—no need—so he added, "I hear there's some interest in me back in Boston."

He laughed a little. I didn't.

He said, "I've got a story to tell," he said. "I want to tell it to you. I want you to print it verbatim, your questions, my answers, like one of those Q and As that newspapers sometimes run. I've been keeping up with the papers, you know. I've read your stuff on me being a suspect in the Gardner heist."

Now mind you, a couple of thoughts were occurring to me during this bizarre moment, the most prominent of which was, how did I know this was really Toby Harkins on the other end of the line? So I asked, "How do I know this is really Toby Harkins?" I mean, that's what I do, I'm a reporter; reporters ask questions.

He replied, "Right now, you go on faith, then you agree to meet face-to-face; when you do, you'll see it's me."

A car pulled up to where we were standing and the driver, an elderly balding man with what looked like his wife beside him, motored down his window and asked, "Are you gentlemen leaving?"

"Get the fuck out of here before I break your fucking face." That was Ape-man, who didn't quite seem ready for prime time yet.

Harkins said, "If you follow my conditions, if you meet with me, if you run my quotes as I say them, in their entirety, and if you hold off writing about my father until you and I get together, then I'll make arrangements to have returned to you all the remaining artwork stolen from the Gardner Museum. It's a pretty good position for you to be in. You get an exclusive story from the country's most wanted fugitive, and you get credit for steering priceless paintings and drawings back to their rightful place."

He made a good point, well articulated, clearly thought through. Problem is, I didn't like someone, anyone, telling me how to do my job, what I could write, and more important, what I couldn't. So I said, "Sounds interesting, but I think what you want is an ad, not a story. I can switch you over to the main line. When you get the recording, just press 2 for the advertising department."

Of course, I couldn't switch him over, and of course, I didn't want to lose this exclusive. It would be my best chance to find out why Hilary Kane had died, and at whose hand. It was secondary, but I also didn't want to forfeit the chance to bring all the stolen art back to the Gardner's walls. But I didn't want to seem like a pushover, an easy target.

Harkins said, "You don't get it then, Jack." This Jack thing was just starting to bug me, but I let it ride for now. "I have a hell of a story for you. You're going to want to print my quotes as I say them, like when you guys run transcripts of speeches by the president or the governor."

"Toby, you ain't the president or the governor. You're a killer who's running for your life, and now you're asking me to help you out."

I have no idea why I was saying what I was saying. It was one of those times when your mouth gets ahead of your brain and fails to display any sort of restraint. There was a long pause on the other end of the line, before he finally said, aggravated now, "Jack, I guarantee it will be one of the biggest stories you'll ever write. You get the art back. You get me in an exclusive. You'll get the truth about my father's involvement."

A long pause, as I pretended to think things through. The only hitch was the deal with the mayor. Could this be a coordinated family attempt to get the story held just long enough so he could get his Senate appointment?

I said, "I can't guarantee yet that I'm going to hold the story on your old man, but you'll know by tomorrow if it runs or doesn't run. If we get together, when?"

His voice was tight. He wasn't used to people challenging him, casually refusing orders, telling him that his fate rested with somebody else. He said, obviously trying to control his anger, "Within the next twenty-four hours. My people will be in touch with you. We'll do it at a secret, secure location, for obvious reasons. You'll be thoroughly searched for any sort of transponder or locating device. If you're carrying one, you'll be killed. If you're followed, you'll be killed. If you alert authorities, you'll be killed."

"I'm sensing a theme here."

"If you do everything right, you'll be a hero."

He hung up. The familiarity, the jocularity, was done and gone. He didn't even say good-bye. I handed the phone back to the building-size man beside me, who, likewise, turned and walked away without a parting word.

"I wonder if they make that suit in your size," I called out to him. I mean, the buttons on the damned jacket were so strained they were dangerous.

He just kept walking, never turning around. I got into my car, the most exhilarated I'd been since Hilary Kane's death. The return of the artwork, yeah, that would be good, but far better than that was the educated hunch of mine that Toby Harkins would have something damned interesting to say.

Chapter Thirty-two

It wasn't until I got to my desk in the newsroom of *The Boston Record* that I placed the manila folder before me and slowly, nervously, opened it up. The room around me was coming to life, with copy editors trickling through the door for their evening shift and the volume on the City Desk televisions turned loud as unnecessarily frantic announcers teased the top stories on the upcoming six o'clock news.

I looked over toward Vinny Mongillo, but he wasn't there, and Peter Martin failed to herald my arrival as he's prone to do. In the distance, I saw them gathered in the glass-walled conference room. Martin had a remote control in his hand and was clicking it at one of the televisions as if he was the first and only person to ever use such a device. Mongillo had his fist buried deep in a bag of what looked to be Fritos. The last time I saw someone eating Fritos, it was my colleague Steve Havlicek, who has since died. I tell you, people were fleeing my life like it was a rancid swamp.

I stared down at the first page of a printout. It was a Word file, thank you Bill Gates, a simple sheet with the words, "Toby Has," at the top, in boldface, underneath which was a list of eight pieces of art which had been taken from the Gardner. Two of them had already been delivered to me, *The Concert* and the *Storm*. Below that, also in boldface, were the words, "Toby Can Get," followed by two other pieces. Finally, in boldface, was the description, "Already sold," with two more works listed underneath.

I turned the page and there was what appeared to be a new, separate printout, this one containing a list of bank names and account numbers, wiring numbers, bank deposit box locations and specific branches, along with multiple men's names that immediately struck me as aliases for one Toby Harkins. Some of the bank locations were in London, others in Ireland. At the bottom was the word, in all capital letters, "CURRENT." That was followed by an address in Dublin. Below that was the word "more," in parenthesis, but when I turned the page, there were no others.

I sat in a bewildered silence for a long moment as the news blared at the City Desk—something about Senator Stiff Harrison—and editors consulted with their weekend reporters and Barbara at the message center repeatedly announced, "Call for Vinny Mongillo."

Assuming Hilary Kane had turned over to whatever authorities she visited all that she retrieved from Daniel Harkins's printer, then Toby Harkins's involvement in the Gardner theft was the smallest trifle that they had. Far more important was the rock-solid evidence of a connection between the sitting mayor and the fugitive son, and more important than that, they had apparently up-to-date information on the location of America's most-wanted fugitive.

I played this out in my mind. It was understandable, perhaps, that they didn't want to leak his location, because by doing so, they might simply be scaring him away, pushing him to flee farther into the unknown. That said, I didn't get the leak from Special Agent Tom Jankle until probably two full days after the FBI had received the printouts from Hilary Kane. Wouldn't that have already given the Bureau enough time to capture its suspect?

And wouldn't the FBI also recognize that if the mayor was involved, which he obviously was, that he would have immediately alerted his son about the information floating around in the public realm? If his son was in the process of escaping anew, wouldn't it be better to blanket the public with information about where he'd just been, in hopes of new clues as to where he might be heading?

Or was it something else entirely? In almost any criminal case involving nearly any public disclosure, law enforcement almost always conceals at least one pivotal detail. Earlier in my career, I covered a series of killings in the old Massachusetts mill towns of Lawrence and Lowell. Women were found dead with their ring fingers severed but left at the scene. The police released this detail, but left out another key fact: that the killer placed an identical band upon every severed finger—rings which, ultimately, led to his capture. Later, I asked the chief detective on the case, Why? Why not fully disclose? He told me that they always leave something out for two reasons: to know if future killings are committed by the chief suspect, or by copycats; and to be able to weed out the surprising number of serial confessors who have nothing to do with the crimes.

So now what? My stomach was in knots. My head hurt. I missed my dog, my wife, my ex-girlfriend, my friend Hank. As much as anything, I missed the confidence of knowing that almost anything I did with a computer keyboard would somehow, in some way, turn out right. At that moment, I had no such confidence at all. Just ask Hilary Kane, which you can't, and therein lies my main point.

I closed the manila folder and brought it into the conference room, where Martin, Justine Steele, and Mongillo were enraptured by the nightly news. I looked at the screen and saw a television reporter with a nasally voice that was destined to leave her forever on the weekend shift say, "And now, Luke, we'll cut live inside to Senator Harrison's press spokesman, Giles Hunt."

The scene immediately cut to the fat-faced Giles at a podium with the Massachusetts General Hospital insignia on it. He was looking down, reading over some notes, and then he suddenly looked up into the cameras and said solemnly, "I have a very brief announcement, and then I'll make the hospital's chief physician available for any medical questions. At 5:12 P.M. today, Senator

Herman Harrison passed away here in his hospital room, surrounded by his wife and children. He died in peace. As many of you know, doctors had stopped administering a chemotherapy regimen last week when it became apparent that the drugs were no longer staving off a cancer that had spread to most of his vital organs. Over the past twenty-four hours, the senator was lucid, but in a great deal of pain. During that time, he made a telephone call to the governor asking that she immediately name a successor upon his death, rather than extend the typical courtesy of not appointing someone for several days. There are key votes on Capitol Hill this week, and Senator Harrison wants the interests of Massachusetts and of America fully represented. The senator's wife, Evelyn, has indicated that she is not interested in serving out the remainder of his term, nor are any of his children.

"On a personal note, it's a very sad day for us all. The staff is feeling a deep sense of personal loss for a man that many of us have worked with for over a quarter century in public service. We also feel for the family, and yes, for the public, for the loss of such a great public servant.

"Now I'd be willing to entertain any questions for myself or for Dr. Bucik."

Martin muted the sound and turned to me with a mix of excitement and relief. My eyes stayed riveted on the television, not on Giles or Dr. Bucik or anything to do with Stiff Harrison, who really was stiff now, but on the reporter asking the first question, a woman named Elizabeth Riggs.

She was standing in the second or third row with a carry-on bag over her shoulder, obviously just off a morning flight from the West Coast. *The New York Times,* no doubt, assumed she was familiar with the political geography of Massachusetts, and quickly dispatched her to cover this unfolding saga. I don't specifically remember receiving a call from her about a return home, but I'd focus more on that later.

Martin, sitting down, said, "The *Storm on the Sea of Galilee* story is done. The painting is with the scientists, who say that initial tests show it's authentic. Beyond that, you've just seen what happened on the tube. We have Amy Contras"—a very competent State House reporter—"on the story of Harrison's death and the governor's likely next step. This makes the Mayor Harkins story that much more urgent. Tomorrow morning, the governor will likely appoint him to fill the Senate seat. We need that story in the paper."

He sat there looking at me, as did Justine on the other side of the table. I took a seat next to Mongillo, who continued to crunch away on the Fritos, though he took a second to hold out the open end of the bag toward me. As any adult would have done, I declined.

I slid the manila envelope across the table toward Martin and Steele and said, "This will probably interest you." Always better to be understated with editors, I find. That way, you only excite, never disappoint, when they see the real goods. Overpromising is the worst thing you can do in the news business, and probably in life as well.

"These are the two files that I believe Hilary Kane pulled from Harkins's home computer a couple of nights before she died. The first file, that's the genesis for our leak, the story linking Toby to the Gardner thefts. But the second file, far more fertile, was never mentioned to me, and hasn't seen the light of publicity."

I fell quiet. Mongillo walked around the table and read silently over their shoulders. Barbara kept beckoning him, and he continued to ignore her.

A few minutes later, Martin looked at me. He was either scared or jubilant, I'm not sure which. Maybe both. Mongillo kept reading and crunching, and when he was done, gave one of those long, low whistles. "Fair Hair's got himself the goods," he said softly.

Martin said, "So we have him dead to rights. We've got him." He clenched his fists into little balls on the table as he spoke as if he were about to punch at the air.

I replied, "It would seem that way, yeah, but for a couple of problems. First, we have no proof that these printouts are authentic. They were given to me by way of guidance. They're nothing official. They're not stamped with any sort of police evidence marking. So I'd be loath to quote directly from them."

Martin asked, "Who gave these to you?"

I grimaced to myself and replied, "If we use them, I'll tell you. But give me a little bit of time before I do."

Martin unfurled his fingers and put them up to his puffy face. He said, "But you could use them as the basis of questions for Harkins, no?"

I nodded. "Certainly, though I haven't yet. They were just put into my hand within the half hour, after I left the mayor."

Martin asked, "What did Harkins say when you talked to him earlier?"

I chuckled a little bit, though I'm not entirely sure why, then I told them how he confessed to having contact with his son, about his belief that he could get Toby to surrender, and about how all hope was abandoned the morning my story ran.

Mongillo looked away in an exaggerated sort of way and said, "That was a high-impact story all right." I stared at him for a moment, until I realized that trying to intimidate Vinny Mongillo was like trying to get a politician to shut up.

Martin asked, "What did he say about the Kane killing?"

"Denied any role. Didn't say anything else."

There was silence all around the table. I should note that with most controversial stories, it's almost always the reporter who is pushing it hardest and the editors serving as the brakemen, and the higher the editor, the harder they're pulling the lever to stop the runaway train. Ultimately, it's their responsibility, and they don't want to go down in an infamous history as having cost the paper its reputation, not to mention millions of dollars in a libel suit.

But I could already see it on Martin's face. He wanted this story in print, sooner rather than later, and because we publish once each day, the next day's paper would probably be just soon enough. And I could already feel it in my gut. My uncomfortable preference was to hold on to this thing for another cycle and see how the situation shook out.

"We've still got it," Martin finally said. He said this while look-ing not at me, but at Justine, who would have to give her blessing to the final decision. "His interview alone, his admission that he was in contact with his son, is one hell of a significant story. These computer records are nice if you can get a Fed or someone over at PD to confirm them, but you know what: Who really needs them?"

I didn't reply for a long time, for what might be described in a pulp novel as a pregnant pause. When I did, I said, "There's some-thing else."

Justine said with a sardonic smile, "There's always something else on this story." I nodded at her.

I said, "I got a visit after sitting with the mayor. A henchman in a really bad suit, bad haircut, bad teeth, bad accent, bad every-thing, cornered me in a parking garage and said I needed to talk to someone. He dialed up a number on his cell phone, handed it to me, and on the other end is a guy who says he's Toby Harkins."

You could see the looks all around the table. Justine's jaw actu-ally dropped. Martin's expression went from excited to outright exhilarated. Vinny stopped crunching in midmotion, something I've never seen him do before.

"So Toby and I are chitchatting, and he says he'd like to get together. He's got a story to tell, and if I'm willing to hear him out, he'll return the remaining works that were stolen from the Gardner Museum, to us."

I fell silent and looked from one to the other. They were all frozen in time and space and emotion, as if someone had just flashed the temperature down a thousand degrees and this would be how posterity remembered us all, with amazed but perfectly ridiculous looks on our faces.

Martin broke out of the spell first, as could be predicted, and said, "So if you're willing to take an exclusive story from America's most wanted fugitive and splash it on the front page of *The Boston Record,* he's going to reward you with the return of the treasures in the costliest art heist in history?"

I nodded. As I was doing that, Mongillo, apropos of nothing, said in an uncharacteristically mesmerized way, "A clean news break, then all those priceless treasures."

"There's a catch," I said, and Justine nodded, as if she alone, and perhaps she was right, understood that there's always a catch. I explained to them that he insisted on a Q and A to accompany the story, and more importantly, that we had to hold off on any story about his father until after Toby and I met.

Suddenly, the dreamy, exhilarated looks dissolved into confusion and, in Martin's case, anguish. I added for emphasis, "If we go with the Dan Harkins story for morning, we lose the potential Toby Harkins story for Tuesday."

And then the world, or the world as it existed in the conference room of the *Record,* fell silent. You could hear a Frito drop, which I think I actually did.

From there, we played it all out, the four of us did, played every possible angle—whether the caller was real or a mayoral-engineered fraud (probably real, given that we'd already had two masterpieces returned); whether Toby Harkins would really abandon the plan if we ran with a story about his father (probably would, given that he's used to getting his way on every front); whether the Toby story would be better than the mayoral story (probably, but one would inform the other, still giving us both). Competition wasn't a huge issue on this front, mostly because the *Traveler* wasn't getting the leaks, the paintings, or the calls that we were. Of course, that could change in a minute if we ran with the Dan Harkins story and Toby shopped his exclusive around.

Peter Martin looked at me and said, "Okay, Jack, your reporting, your mayoral interview, your life on the line in a tête-à-tête with Toby. What's your call?"

It occurred to me how ironic it would all be if because I had rushed that first story into print a week ago, now I dug my heels in on something far more solid, and we ended up losing it all. Still, I felt something in my gut, though that could have been an ulcer or a hernia. But what I think I felt was a gnawing sense to slow down, get more information, trade up, be careful. Of course, all of this belies what we typically do at a newspaper, but I was learning that sometimes you have to be different in this business to succeed.

Be certain of this, we could decimate the career of Mayor Daniel Harkins within the next twelve hours. I mean, it would be over, stripped of any of its past success, hung to dry on the pole of devastating publicity, another great pelt in the famous collection of Jack Flynn. But it didn't feel right this time.

I said, "I think we wait."

No one disagreed. Justine nodded her head, almost imperceptibly. Vinny crunched anew, but only momentarily. Martin said, "So here's what's probably going to happen. Tomorrow, the governor will appoint Harkins as the interim senator from Massachusetts. She'll give him an appointment letter to carry to Washington. I would predict that he'll spend the rest of the day in Boston to take care of his affairs, probably resign, clean out his office, and then on Tuesday morning, fly to Washington for the start of the Senate session. At that point, he must present an appointment letter to the clerk of the Senate, and then get officially sworn in, most likely by the vice president."

He paused, probably to allow us to appreciate his vast knowledge of all things Washington and political, and we did, we did. But if I ever have that kind of detailed knowledge of the minutiae of federal government, shoot me in the head, please.

Martin added, "My point is, we still have a second shot at this, Tuesday morning. Before Harkins is given the oath on Capitol Hill, his appointment can probably still be delayed or derailed, if not by the governor, then by senators who don't want him as part of their body. So if your friend"—he looked pointedly at me— "Toby doesn't come through sometime tomorrow, then we say fuck it and jam the mayoral story into print on Tuesday."

Yet again, Martin had brought order to chaos, boiled down a complicated scenario into its most logical elements, and formulated an endlessly practical plan.

All of this meant that at some point in the next twenty-four hours, another gorilla in a bad suit would show up at my doorstep or be waiting in my car or sitting in my favorite restaurant, waiting to escort me to a place that no reporter has ever been—in the company of Toby Harkins. I probably should have been a little anxious about this upcoming reality. I'd be smart to be anxious about it. But all I felt was a renewed sense of opportunity that I hadn't experienced since I heard the first vague radio reporters of Hilary Kane's death.

Vinny and I stood up in unison to get back into the newsroom, when Martin said, "One more thing. Vinny. I need you in Dublin by morning to check out this address that was pulled off the mayor's computer file. Maybe you'll run into Toby himself, but as important, find out if the FBI or Scotland Yard have been by."

With that, Martin picked up the phone on the side table and punched out a number. He told whoever it was on the other end that he needed a reporter on a plane to Dublin that night. "Good, good," he said, then he mouthed to Vinny, "You can still make the 8:30 flight."

Back into the phone, he asked, "How much?" Silence, then, "No, I think there's a misunderstanding. I just want a seat on the flight. I don't want to buy the whole fricking plane."

And with that, we left the conference room en masse to face a future that had already arrived.

I leaned on Vinny Mongillo's desk and said, "Sorry you got dragged into this last-minute trip. It's the second time you've had to rush overseas in a week. I bet you're not going to miss that part of the business."

He had taken the half-eaten bag of Fritos, crinkled up the top, and flung it into the trash. His desk phone was ringing. His cell phone was chiming some sort of marching song. His hair was matted down against his forehead, and his forearms were folded over his chest. He had already filed a page-one story for the next morning's paper on the return of the Rembrandt that he so loved.

He pursed his lips and looked down with those big brown eyes of his and said, "Yeah, it's just awful, racing to the airport, touching down tomorrow in another world, challenging authority, nailing the mayor or whoever we're about to get, maybe getting all the art returned."

He fell into silence, and I said nothing in return. He added, more softly, "This may be it for me. My last story. At least I'm going out with a bang."

I nodded. I don't know why this choked me up, but it did. Actually, of course, I know why it choked me up. Vinny Mongillo, the purest, most relentless information gathering machine I have ever met, was put on this earth to be a newspaper reporter, and he was right, this might really be it. I tried to picture the day that my phone would ring at work with Vinny on the other line pitching a story about a client who was paying him $10,000 a month to call in all his chits and connections in the biz. I couldn't. I wouldn't.

He said, "I'm worried about you on this one, Fair Hair. Your mood's been off. Your nicely structured little world is coming apart. You're blaming yourself for something that probably wasn't your fault. So don't let all this prod you into doing something stupid with Toby or the mayor."

I nodded in acknowledgment, looking away all the while.

"I want to bring this story all the way back around," I said. "I want to find out what the hell I did wrong. And I want to find out who the fuck killed Hilary Kane."

Vinny replied, "I'll be on the ground in Dublin for less than a few hours. If all goes well, I'm on a flight tomorrow afternoon back to Boston. I don't want you muddling through this thing alone in that uncoordinated way of yours."

And here, he smiled, that big, white, toothy smile of his that I'd seen a million times before and always thought I'd see a million times again, but maybe not anymore. I don't know. Maybe I'd just go into business with him.

"You're going to give Martin a conniption if you don't haul ass for the airport," I said.

"Exactly what I'm trying to do," he said, still smiling.

He stood up and gathered a couple of notebooks and some pens together and pulled his passport out of his top desk drawer.

Then he silently turned and wrapped his enormous arms around my shoulders and pulled me close to his very large, distinctly perfumed body.

"Be careful," he said, his lips almost uncomfortably close to my ear, but that was okay, this time anyway.

"You more than me," I said. And then he, like Elizabeth, like Hank, like everybody else, turned and walked away.

Chapter Thirty-three

Any $50-an-hour hooker or million-dollar-a-year real estate agent knows there's one true thing about business. It's all about location, location, location, and sitting in the *Record* newsroom as darkness descended upon a September Sunday night, I knew this wasn't where I would best attract the anticipated solicitations of a Mister Toby Harkins.

I mean, to get to me at my desk, Toby and his henchmen would have to somehow subvert the *Record*'s newly constituted security plan. Toby could mess with the Gardner guards, with the Boston police, with the FBI, with Scotland Yard, but don't, under any circumstances, get on the wrong side of Edgar Sullivan.

So I made a couple of quick calls, the first one being to the private cell phone of Tom Jankle, special agent with the FBI. I had questions. He had answers. The issue was, would he give them to me. Would he tell me why he held back on me last Monday night, why he leaked what he did and didn't leak what he didn't? Would he tell me whether the FBI had nearly captured Toby Harkins in Dublin, whether they were gin clear on the involvement of the father with the son? These are the things I wanted to know, needed to know, before I met Harkins at a place of his obvious choosing.

"Yeah?" he answered.

Phone manners had gone the way of the Celtics dynasty and the $6 bleacher seat at Fenway Park. These days, it costs twenty bucks just to park at the game, another ten-spot for a hot dog and a beer, $65 for a decent seat and four bucks for a bag of peanuts, all so an overpaid bunch of prima donna choke artists can blow every homestretch to the dreaded Yankees. Maybe next year.

Not that this has anything to do with the price of Spam in Kuwait. So I said sharply into the phone, "Jack Flynn here."

A hesitation. "Hello there, Jack Flynn."

"How are you, Agent Jankle?"

"I'm well. Very well. What are you doing dedicating yourself to the public's right to know on this fine autumn night?"

I could have beat around the bush, even if I've never quite understood the phrase or the action it supposedly represents. What kind of bush?

So I said, "I'm trying to find out—check that, I will find out, with or without your help—why you withheld so much information from me in your office last Monday night. You had a goldmine from Hilary Kane. You gave me some pyrite."

Forgive the tough-guy talk, but I had had enough of the confusion, the obfuscation, the hazy motives, the two-bank setups. Like I said, I had questions, I wanted answers—just some straight-up, no frills information.

There was silence on the other end of the line, silence that persisted for so long that I asked, in no conciliatory way, "You there?"

He cleared his throat rather than provided a verbal answer. Eventually, he said, "Yeah, but I'm trying to figure out what I can tell you and what I can't."

"Agent Jankle," I said, sharp, my words like metal rods, "Hilary Kane is dead. Maggie Kane, as you well know, almost joined her in the benevolent beyond. I've been punched and kicked and stuck in a hospital in Rome, which is someplace that no civilized person should ever have to be. I've had a man break into my apartment in the middle of the night."

I paused here for dramatic effect, or maybe that's melodramatic effect. Then I added, "And you started me on all this. I was having a perfectly merry time sitting with my girlfriend in some damned fine seats at Fenway Park watching the Red Sox when you kicked my life on its side. It's not a matter of what you can or can't tell me, what you want or don't want to tell me. Sir, we're at the point here and now when there are things that you *need* to tell me—immediately."

Again, silence, though as I looked around the sparsely populated newsroom, the few reporters and editors present were now unapologetically staring at my end of this unfolding conversation. All we needed was a guy coming around selling Cracker Jack and the whole thing would have been complete—Jack Flynn, circus freak, come see him while he's hot.

Still silence on the other end of the line, silence for so long that I finally said, quietly, "Do you get my point?"

"Jack," Jankle said, "I want to help. I've wanted to help you from the very beginning. I'm just trying to figure out the best way to do that right now, for your sake and for mine."

His voice drifted off into another void, though a moment later, he added, "How about you meet me at nine P.M., Yawkey Way, outside of Fenway Park, Gate A."

"Make it worth my while," I said.

"I will. I will."

I hung up with some flair, if only to let everyone know they could go back to whatever it was they were doing. Then, proceeding on some sort of roll, I picked up the phone and punched out the first nine digits of Elizabeth Riggs's cell phone number before letting my finger rest over the tenth button, the zero. Again, I had questions, she had answers. Why didn't you call? Where were you staying? Why not at home? I looked at the clock on the nearby wall and saw it was 7:00, the throes of her deadline, so instead of pressing down, I placed the receiver carefully back in the cradle. I convinced myself that these inquiries would be better to pose in person, though when that might be was anyone's guess.

So I gathered up a couple of legal pads for the upcoming festivities and headed into the night, a place where anything could happen, and as it turned out, anything would.

I'm not a stalker, but I play one on TV. This is what I was thinking when I found myself in the lobby of the Boston Harbor Hotel amid a little detour on my way home from work. I had an epiphany, or maybe it was just a guess. Regardless, it occurred to me that Elizabeth, having missed the water views she so loved from the place we once shared, probably checked into this very hotel and requested a harborfront room.

I picked up a house phone that was resting on an antique desk and asked the operator to be connected to a Ms. Elizabeth Riggs. There was a long moment of angst, on my part, anyway, before the woman on the other end said in an indistinguishable accent, "Certainly." Then the phone began ringing.

My palms were sweating like that time back in high school when I asked my deepest, sincerest teenage crush to the prom, and she said—well, nevermind what she said. These things aren't important now, or at least that's what my psychiatrist would tell me if I could find the courage to enlist one. On the third ring, the most familiar voice in the world said, "Hello, this is Elizabeth."

I hesitated, though not necessarily on purpose. My voice caught for a small fraction of a fast second, or maybe it was my brain. Either way, I said, "Hello, this is Jack."

Get it? I was mimicking her. I don't know if she did. Hell, I don't know if I did.

Then it was her turn to hesitate, just long enough for me to say, "Flynn. F-L-Y-N-N. We used to live in the same condominium, sleep together every night, and have very good sex, at least by my modest standards."

She said, surprised but not necessarily amused, "Jack. How—how—are you? Where are you?"

"I'm great, and I'm in your lobby."

"Jesus, you could track down a black widow in a coal mine." She said this with a laugh, though I'm not quite sure that, while true, she thought it all that funny.

We had spoken the night before, or, technically, earlier that very day, but it still seemed like forever ago, and if I remember right, she concluded the conversation in a fit of tears saying that she'd speak to me soon. So I guess she was right, even if she didn't necessarily mean to be.

I said, "I thought I'd just say hi." I was shuffling my feet on the thick lobby carpet. I could feel my cheeks burn from embarrassment, or nervousness, or some other not-so-random emotion that I wasn't accustomed to. The words on both sides were delivered like wet noodles, and I instantly regretted walking into this hotel and placing this call.

I added, "So I've said it. I'll leave you alone now. You're probably on deadline."

I hesitated, and so did she, until she replied, "No, Jack, why don't you come up for a moment."

A moment.

She gave me her room number, and I was off.

Heading upstairs, I recalled the first time that I kissed her. It was in an elevator at a roadside motel in Portland, Maine, both of us covering a terribly depressing story about children burned to death in a day care center fire, and somehow, amid the endless misery of that awful day, finding each other in the hotel bar, and in that find, discovering years of happiness that should have gone on forever. But shouldn't I have known that they never would?

I knocked on her door just once, softly, and she opened it immediately, expectantly. She was dressed in what she used to call her "uniform," a pair of perfectly fitting boot-cut jeans, faded, and a tee shirt with her long sleeves pushed up beyond her elbows.

Her hair was slightly messy, no doubt from playing with it as she tends to do on deadline. Her face, especially her eyes, looked tired, and I knew it was because she gets exhausted flying on airplanes, regardless of the time of day. She said, looking me square in the face, "Come in," and I did. But the most noticeable, most important thing about the entrance was our failure to kiss.

We walked into the room with big, wide windows looking out across the blackness of Boston Harbor. She sat on the bed, me on an upholstered chair with a matching ottoman before it. Her laptop was open on the desk, beside a pot of coffee and a single cup. To break the ice, she said to me, "You beat me to the punch. I was going to call you tomorrow."

"Well, I saw you on the news, asking a question, and I figured I'd just say hello in case we both got tied up with other things."

"I'm glad you did."

"Yeah, so am I."

If I'd ever been involved in a more tortured, more awkward exchange, then my mind must have blanked it out completely and fortunately. This was like watching a fifty-car interstate highway pileup on a snowy night, only without any of the fascinating gore. We were talking about the fact we were talking, as if we were either eighty years old or had never previously met.

So I said, "I definitely shouldn't have stopped by, unannounced. I'm just sad about Baker and aggravated over Hilary Kane and generally at wit's end about life." I paused and added, "And I miss you."

She looked down now, as if the rug posed some new and fascinating aesthetic challenges, and replied, "I'm really sad about Baker too. I really am." When she looked back at me, her eyes were wet.

Note her failure to say the simple, soothing words, "I miss you too."

We both sat in silence looking anywhere but at each other. Then I stared at her face and said, "We fucked things up pretty well, didn't we?" I paused and added, "I fucked things up pretty well."

"We did, Jack, you and I. You have issues, and I didn't deal with them very well. Other women would have, and will."

My stomach felt at once empty and heavy. My head was starting to hurt. My eyes burned. This was a conversation I didn't want to have, the last chapter in a book I didn't want to read.

So rather than continue, I slowly, sadly, nodded my head, my lips pursed and my gaze down. I got up in a labored kind of way. I stepped toward her sitting on the edge of her king-size bed, leaned down, and kissed that same soft cheek that used to be pressed against my head in slumber every single glorious and inglorious night. And then I walked out of the room in silence, not fast, not slow, just forlorn. She did nothing to stop me. Maybe it really was good that I came here, but for the life of me, I couldn't figure out how or why.

Chapter Thirty-four

This just wasn't my day—or maybe my week, or more probably, my month, much as I usually love the autumn, what with the foliage and the crisp air and the constant sense that important things are about to happen. As I turned the key in my apartment door, it pushed open before the lock clicked, meaning 1, I had forgotten to lock the door, which is impossible, because it locks automatically, a fact that used to drive Elizabeth crazy when she took the garbage out and found herself stranded in the hall, or 2, someone was in my apartment, or 3, someone had come and gone.

Two and three could have gone either way in terms of desirability and preference. Would I rather be ransacked or attacked? Or were Toby's heroes waiting inside to whisk me away to destinations unknown for my face-to-face with their boss? Or had someone dropped off more artwork for me? The way things were going, I could walk in on the *Mona Lisa,* and wouldn't that be news to all Vinny's friends at the Louvre?

Options raced through my mind. Do I walk away and call the police? Probably not, considering that their presence could ruin any chance of meeting Toby Harkins. Do I holler into my own apartment? Didn't seem right, and the reply could be a simple gunshot, which might not be so simple if it were aimed in the direction of my head. So I pushed the door open and slowly stepped inside the darkened front foyer. A sliver of light hit a nearby wall, meaning a lamp in the living room was illuminated. It's important to note that I used to leave lights on for Baker. Hell, I'd even leave the stereo playing sometimes, usually with Frank Sinatra or the occasional Ella Fitzgerald. But today, I had fingered the light switch, then walked out filled with sad thoughts.

I crept slowly through the small foyer toward the living room, one tiny baby step at a time. My heart was pounding. My head was spinning from the glimpse of sleep I had the night before.

Step. Wait. Step. Wait. Step. Wait. I was moving my feet along the tile floor, searching the walls for shadows, my ears straining for even the hint of a sound. But I saw nothing, heard nothing, smelled nothing.

I was just inches from the corner that would give way to the living room. If I poked my head around, maybe I'd get shot or maybe I'd be quickly captured or maybe I'd see another priceless masterpiece sitting there on my couch as I did the night before. I seemed to have lost all privacy in this life; my apartment was like a bus depot, the way people were coming and going, and the hallowed ground that used to be my newspaper career was a veritable minefield of danger and mistakes.

So what the hell, I gripped the wall and peered slowly around the corner, my eyes nervously scanning the room. And that's when I saw it, just as I suspected, another priceless masterpiece sitting right there on the couch. Only this was no Rembrandt or Vermeer, but rather a Kane—Maggie Kane, her short blonde hair tousled and her eyes dipping slowly into a state of shallow sleep.

I was relieved. She was beautiful. It was, all things considered, a nice combination.

I stepped around the corner, cleared my throat, and said, "Please, make yourself comfortable."

Her eyes fluttered open and when she saw me, realized me, her face broke into a wide, warm smile. "I am," she said, not getting up, not really moving at all.

I leaned against the doorway looking at her looking at me for a long, quiet moment, giving her a chance to regain her bearings and allowing me to breathe a quiet sigh of relief.

I said, "I'm glad to see you don't let things like locks and laws get in your way."

She smiled anew and asked, "Are you going to call the cops on me? You left a key right on the ledge over your door, you know."

I had, actually, or more accurately, it was Elizabeth who used to keep one there for all those aforementioned times when she would lock herself out. I walked slowly into the living room, uncharacteristically conscious of my movements, and sat heavily in the upholstered chair facing Maggie Kane.

She said, laughing now, "Tough day at work, honey?"

"They're all tough these days," I replied, straight-faced, not sharing any of the frivolity.

We locked gazes for another long, quiet moment. She finally took a swig from a bottle of water that I assumed she had pulled from my refrigerator. "What the hell are you doing here?" I asked.

"Where else am I supposed to be?"

Good question, until I really mulled it. When I did, I replied, "With some security guards, at a hotel?"

"Sick of them, sick of the hotel. You guys had me in some dump out at the airport. I was going crazy."

She shook her head and stared off into space. I walked into the kitchen, opened the refrigerator, and realized I was fresh out of Sam Adams, which was just as well, considering my upcoming meeting with Jankle and whoever else. So instead I grabbed a Coke.

Back in the living room, I leaned back in a chair and said, "This hasn't been a good stretch for either of us, has it?"

She shook her head, looking at me, looking away. She didn't say anything, and after a moment, she took a long chug of water. It was mostly dark in the room, but for the one low lamp. I said, "And I'm really sorry about it. About all of it."

Again, she shook her head. She said, still staring off, "What's the worst loss you've ever had?"

Life was all about loss, lately, or even longer than lately—loss of wife, loss of daughter, loss of feelings, loss of control, loss of the confidence to know that when I did my job, I was doing right and I was doing well.

But I didn't much want to talk about it, not then, not with her. She was coming to grips with her own immense loss, caused by yours truly, and I knew that she'd rather talk than listen. So I said, "That's a tough question. What about you?"

She looked down at her water and then off again into the dark and finally at me. As we locked gazes, the room suddenly struck me as particularly empty, given the lack of Baker who, if he were around, would no doubt be trying to entertain our female guest in some fashion, maybe with a tennis ball, or perhaps just sitting beside her demanding an ear massage.

She said, "I lost my son," and then paused. The words, just four of them, spoken plainly and directly, hit me like gunfire, though I should probably be careful about such analogies these days. Or is that a metaphor? Either way, I was somewhere beyond stunned, for a variety of reasons. I had pictured Maggie Kane living the relatively carefree life of an attractive, single, early thirty-something woman. Of course, she'd have the typical neuroses that some such women have, the fears, the hang-ups, all that and maybe more. But I had believed that life had come relatively easy to her, and now this one declarative sentence flung open doors and windows into spaces that I never imagined could possibly exist.

"I made a mistake when I was young that turned out not to be a mistake at all. I got pregnant. I had the baby. He was the most precious thing in my entire life."

She smiled as she said this, a wan smile, but a smile just the same. She seemed to have climbed into her own familiar world of soothing memories. I stayed quiet, mostly because there was nothing that I could possibly say.

She said, "The father's name was Brad." She paused. At this point, I could have told her just how much I hated the name Brad. Not as much as I disdain Eric, but almost. Still, I thought it best to keep quiet.

"He wanted to be involved, even though he wasn't very mature. I wanted Jay to know his father, so I'd share him as much as I could. Well, one evening, around suppertime, Jay was over at Brad's apartment. I was supposed to get him back that night. I hadn't seen him in two days. Brad calls and asks if he can keep him another night.

"I said, 'No, I miss my boy.' Brad gets argumentative. He starts in about how he's going to take me to court about getting better visitation rights, about how if he can't see his kid more, he's going to pay less support. All this stuff. I told him, 'Go ahead. Do it. Just get my kid back here within the hour.'"

She paused again to collect her thoughts. She put her hands up to her cheeks and rubbed her own face as she stared off at the carpet with big, blank eyes. Then she looked at me and said in a lower, huskier voice, "An hour passed, and no Brad. He's not answering his cell phone or his home phone. An hour after that, my doorbell rings and I figure it's finally him. When I open it up, there's a policeman there, a state trooper. I don't know why, but I always remember these incredibly shiny boots. He asks if I'm Maggie Kane. Then he asks if he could come in.

"I'm petrified, trying to keep everything under control. Before I know it, we're sitting in my living room and he tells me that Brad had a head-on collision with an eighteen-wheeler. Brad had drifted into oncoming traffic. Jay was in a car seat in the back. Both were killed instantly. I lost the most important thing that I'll ever have in my life."

She looked away again, her chin pointed up and strong as she gazed toward the blackened expanse beyond the sliding doors. She wasn't crying, and I kind of knew how she felt. She had already shed all the tears she had over her boy's death, and there were none left to fall.

I asked, "When was this?" I spoke low and soft, trying to be curious but mostly soothing.

"Five years ago last week."

I felt a lump in my throat. As she was running for her life, contending with the slaying of her sister, she was also mourning anew during the anniversary of her son's death.

Before I could say anything else or ask anything more, she said,

"Jay wouldn't have been on the road if I hadn't been such a bitch to his father. All he wanted to do was keep his own son for another night."

Her head remained bowed, but still no tears.

"That's not your fault," I said, firm and fast. And I believed that. If you followed her logic, then I got my wife pregnant, and she died during childbirth, so I actually killed her. And I didn't believe that, at least I didn't used to. These days, who knows.

She nodded, her face still down. "I know," she replied. "At least in my saner moments, I know. But I don't know if it makes it any better. It doesn't make the loss any less immense. It doesn't make my sadness any less overwhelming."

After a long moment, she looked back up at me and said, "So that's my biggest loss." She gave me a sad, tired smile, then asked, "What's yours?"

In my mind, I saw a gallery of loss—from Katherine to my unnamed daughter to Baker to my father to my recent girlfriend to Vinny Mongillo. I expected a call at any moment from Peter Martin saying he was taking a job at the goddamned *New York Times* or *The Washington Post*.

I listened for a moment to the stern September breeze slapping at the balcony door and an antique mantel clock ticking toward my meeting with Jankle and the general din of a restless silence. Then I said, "My wife died during childbirth." And I proceeded to tell her the whole story, about the pains during the delivery, about the frantic command to leave the room, the look on Katherine's face, the frightening hour in the waiting room, the doctor summoning me into a conference room, pulling the sheet from my wife's face and kissing her damp, cool forehead good-bye.

And then I told her how it had all affected me, and as I was telling her, I seemed to be telling myself. I couldn't have a normal relationship. I couldn't commit myself for reasons that I couldn't quite understand, even to someone who I knew I had once loved. That said, I told her about my recent visit with Elizabeth, about the general angst of it all, about my fears that this many years later, I should be moving on, and wasn't.

As I talked, Maggie had her feet on my couch, her knees tucked under her chin, her arms wrapped around her shins. When I was done, she unfolded herself and stood up and walked over to where I was leaning forward in my chair. And she kissed me, on the forehead, her hand on my temple. I felt moisture from her eyes as she allowed her face to linger against mine. She was crying, or maybe weeping, not over her loss, but over mine.

She stepped back and looked at me and said, "I had no idea."

I said, staring back into her eyes, "I had no idea about yours."

She walked back to the couch and reached into her leather bag groping around for God only knew what. She pulled out a cell phone, held it in front of her and said, "It's everywhere, the loss is. This is Hilary's phone. I found it this morning and the very sight of it almost sent me over the edge."

My eyes immediately flashed from sad to shocked. It's as if I heard drums sounding in the room, saw rockets blaze by. The air even seemed to change temperature.

Trying to remain calm, trying not to cause alarm, I asked, "Why do you have your sister's phone?"

"When she was at my place the day before she died, she forgot it." She smiled and added, "That's just her. She was always leaving keys, gloves, her purse, anything that wasn't attached to her body."

"May I see it?"

She leaned forward and handed it across the coffee table to me. I looked carefully at the darkened face of the Motorola flip phone. I pressed the power button, wondering if it had the juice to turn on. Immediately, lights lit up. Words and numbers flashed across the small screen. Then everything settled back into the typical symbols and figures and the phone fell dark again.

I was transfixed, almost embarrassingly so. When I realized this, I looked at Maggie and said, "Do you mind if I just play with this for a moment and see if there's anything worthwhile?"

She shrugged and said, "Go ahead."

I knew beyond any doubt that the police and the FBI had already culled through her home, office, and cellular telephone records trying to discover who she called in the hours and days before she was killed. I also knew that as a reporter, I had no shot at these records. The phone itself, though, was an entirely different animal, or in this case, opportunity.

I played with some buttons until I finally got the phone to list the last ten incoming calls. I scanned through them quickly. Some had names assigned to them, others were just numbers, still others said Restricted, meaning the caller wasn't identified, not to Hilary when she answered, not to me now.

I pressed a few more buttons and the last ten outgoing calls appeared on the screen in the same general pattern—some with names, like "Maggie" and "Laura," and others with just numbers. One of those numbers struck me as vaguely familiar, but for the life of me I couldn't pinpoint why.

I got up and grabbed a legal pad out of the kitchen and wrote all the names and numbers down. Then I came back into the living room and asked Maggie if I could hold on to the phone for safe-keeping. She agreed.

I quickly banged out a call to Vinny's cell phone, figuring, since his flight took off in a matter of minutes, that he'd be impossible to reach. He picked up on the first ring with his typically curt, "Mongillo."

"I need a favor."

"I need a drink. Peter Martin has me in a middle seat in fucking coach. These fucking chairs were built for runway models, not for real people with real appetites."

I didn't touch that one. Instead, I told him I had a few telephone numbers that I needed identities assigned to.

"Give 'em to me. Make it quick before they make me turn off the phone.

I read him the unidentified numbers in question. He hung up without so much as a good-bye or a good luck.

I checked the clock and realized it was twenty minutes until my rendezvous with Tom Jankle.

"Where are you staying tonight?" I asked Maggie.

She had been sitting on the couch watching me, and she shrugged, as if it didn't matter, as if she didn't care.

"Not a big planner, are you?" As soon as I spoke the words, I regretted them.

She met my gaze and replied, "I haven't really had the chance to be since my sister was killed." She said this matter-of-factly, not accusatorily, God bless her.

I nodded. "I've got to go out for a while. I'm going to lock you in. Put the deadbolt in place, and plan on spending the night here. If you're in bed when I get back, I'll grab the couch."

She started to say something, then stopped, smiled, and said softly, "Thank you, Jack."

And like that, I was gone, wary not of what I didn't know but of what I did.

Chapter Thirty-five

I stood outside Gate A of Fenway Park on an increasingly breezy late September night looking up and down the darkened street for my destiny, which would come in the form of a rather peculiar FBI agent by the name of Tom Jankle.

This exact spot, on this precise night, could have been ground zero of Boston's longest hopes and most heartfelt dreams. The Major League baseball playoffs began on this day, and a couple of hundred miles to the south, the Yankees were playing a team that didn't really matter, and the various members of the Red Sox were watching it all on national TV. And here I was, standing outside the ballyard watching yesterday's litter float past in the unfriendly breeze. The desolate scene was a metaphor for my life. Or again, maybe that's an analogy. As Peter Martin might say, who gives a flying frick.

Nine o'clock, the designated hour, eventually gave way to 9:30, and the only people I saw were the occasional testosterone-charged gaggle of college fraternity members making their way toward Landsdowne Street for another night of beer guzzling at the area's clubs. No sign of Jankle, and thus, no sign of hope. It was all beginning to remind me of that endless wait outside the Louvre two days before—two days that felt like a month. At least that concluded reasonably well, even if a perfectly gorgeous woman openly laughed at my nudity.

So there I stood, the wind blowing harder, the air growing colder, my nerves ever more frazzled, when a navy blue van slowly turned left onto Yawkey Way, lumbered past me on the opposite side of the street, then banged a U-turn and pulled up to the curb. When the side panel door slid open, I flinched, half expecting—or maybe more than half expecting—that I was about to be gunned down with or without cause right outside of Fenway Park.

Instead, I heard the easy voice of Special Agent Tom Jankle casually say, "You look cold out there."

"You would too if you'd been made to wait for more than half an hour."

He stepped out of the van with a smile, his bushy mustache twitching in the streetlight, as if he were always chewing on something that didn't actually exist. His hair had that boyish Pete Rose freshly washed gloss to it, silvery black and slightly mussed. He walked past me without shaking my hand and said, "Sorry about the time, but I was getting a whole slew of stuff for you. You're going to thank me in a moment."

He was carrying one of those strange metal briefcases that you always see as the last objects on airport baggage carousels, as if they exist only reluctantly and no one actually owns them. In the other hand, he was jangling a small key ring. "Follow me," he said.

We walked past the metal garage-style grates that were pulled shut over the yawning entrances, to a narrow steel door with no sign, just a simple discolored knob. Jankle thrust a key into the hole, gazed warily up and down the street, then pulled the door quickly open. He held it for me, then yanked it shut behind us.

We stood in the dark together until he pulled a penlight from his pocket and flashed it around. I could see the hazy outlines of a beer stand against a far wall—Coors/Coors Light, $4.75, a shameless rip-off—and beside it, a snack bar with shelves for bags of popcorn and peanuts. On the concrete ground before us were piles of orange cones and pallets of boxes. The whole place was vacant and raw, permeated by a sense of defeat. We were here because the Red Sox lost. I was here because I had in some way lost.

Jesus mother of Christ, I really had to get a grip.

"Stay close," Jankle told me. He walked slowly through the labyrinth of obstacles and said to me without turning around, "Be better if we were here to watch the first game of the play-offs, no?"

No shit. Be better if Hilary Kane were still alive. Be better if he'd never sent his thugs to get me last Monday night. Be better if a lot of things were different, but most of them probably weren't worth bringing up there and then. So we walked in silence down a ramp toward the main concourse, then up another ramp toward a block of pale light, though light might be the wrong word. What was up ahead was just somewhat less dark. Maybe that, too, could be a metaphor.

As we ascended the ramp, I could feel the air growing cooler and a little less stale. The smell of old beer gave way to the freshness of an autumn night. And suddenly we emerged into the open air, into the stands, specifically the box seats between home plate and third base. The park was blanketed by a moon-splashed dark, eerily quiet, strangely still. The breeze was halted by the outer walls, lending an odd sense of serenity to the environs within.

"Nice night for a game," Jankle said, giving me that typical half smile of his, as if he could find amusement in virtually any situation at any time.

I didn't know if he was talking about baseball, or the games he was about to try playing with me. We soon would see. By way of explanation of our location, he said, "I've been a big fan for a long time, so the owners let me come and go."

I didn't respond. I wondered if that meant on game nights as well. I wondered how his superiors might regard such an, ahem, perk. Truth is, I was pissed off. This was the guy who thrust me into a situation where I cost a young woman her life, and he was sitting here acting somewhere far beyond cavalier about the whole thing, as if, perhaps, she had died in the name of some worthy cause. Maybe that's what he believed. Maybe that's what he fucking believed.

"Let's sit down and relax," he said. And we did, the former though not the latter, parking ourselves in the red field boxes with a seat in between us. He held the metal case in his lap, inserted a key and opened it. Then, while looking inside it rather than at me, he said, "So you now know there was more to the story than what I gave you."

As he talked, he pulled out a microcassette recorder, removed a small tape from a plain manila envelope, and stuck it into the slot. He readied the tape, then put it down on the seat between us. He shut the metal case and put it on the ground beside him. Then he looked at me flush for the first time since we'd entered the park and said, "I leaked you some good information. It paid off for you. You got some paintings recovered, which I didn't even foresee."

"It also got Hilary Kane killed," I said.

He looked down, nodding. "I didn't foresee that, either," he said.

"How could you not?"

He didn't immediately answer. At first, I stared at him trying to gauge his mood and motivations, but he betrayed little of the former and none of the latter. I got the sense with this guy that his highs weren't all that high and his lows never dipped all that low, that life was lived in the safety and security of a sanguine middle ground. Not a bad way to live, actually.

He took a deep breath, looked back at me, and said, "Out of some frustration, I brought you onto the periphery of the story. This is all on background, by the way. You can use it, just not attributable to me. Call me a ranking investigative official."

Great. Last time we set ground rules like this, Hilary Kane was dead within eight hours. What poor soul was out there waiting to meet their maker because I'm a lunatic at the keyboard?

"Understood?"

I nodded.

He repeated himself: "Understood?"

"Yes."

He chewed and twitched and did all that other stuff he does. Some might think it's endearing, but for reasons I can't fully artic-ulate, his mannerisms were starting to bug me.

He said, "We've had Danny Harkins under court-sanctioned electronic surveillance for the last six months, based on the belief that he is complicit with his son in some of the crimes, and that he knows where his son is located now. That surveillance essentially involves wiretaps on his cellular telephone, his work lines at City Hall, and his home telephone at his Ritz-Carlton condominium.

"We've been frustrated, or at least I have. We know through secondary informants that he's had elaborate contact with his son, but he's somehow concealed it from us. Then this deal happened with Hilary Kane. She saw what we've been trying to see. We didn't know if he knew what she knew.

"So I was trying to smoke him out, as the saying goes. I wanted him to realize that she saw something in his apartment, something that would make him panic, get on the telephone, make some calls that he wouldn't have otherwise made, act in ways that aren't characteristic."

He paused here, looked at me, and added, "And then we'd make our case. And in the process, we might even nail the nation's number one most wanted fugitive."

We both sat in silence. I gazed down at the park, at the tarpaulin covering the infield glistening in the moonlight. I imagined what it would be like to sit in these seats at a game on that very night, maybe with Hilary Kane. She'd be wearing a baseball cap, cheering loudly, scarfing down popcorn, asking questions.

Actually, I don't know where that thought came from. Just kind of popped into my addled mind.

I turned to Jankle and said, "You panicked him all right, didn't you?"

He gave me a rueful nod. "That we did. And now we have this delicate matter of proving our case while somehow trying to continue to use him to apprehend his son. You understand, this ain't easy."

"Hilary would tell you just how hard it is, if she could be here to do it. Short of that, I bet her sister would let you know."

He nodded again, looking down, as if conceding my successful jab. "It was a miscalculation," he said. "We saw the mayor as a thief, but not a murderer."

More silence. Then he reached down and picked up the micro-cassette and said, "So here's a peace offering. You can take notes off this, but I can't let you take the recording with you."

I looked at him blankly, and he added, "It's a recorded conversation between Dan and Toby Harkins, August eighteenth. It will be self-explanatory."

He unceremoniously hit the Play button, and silence ensued. I don't know why, but I thought of Rosemary Woods, President Nixon's secretary, erasing a critical tape for eighteen of the most repugnant minutes of silence that any right-minded American might ever hear. Finally, I heard a voice say, simply and abruptly, "Yeah?"

It sounded like the younger, more felonious Harkins had just answered the phone.

"It's your old man."

"Hey, old man."

"Listen, you have the paintings all rounded up?"

"Everything's under control."

"You have all of them?"

"Yeah, except for two. I sold them for cash. We're going to need it."

"And the plan is still in place?"

"Everything's like we talked about. I just need to think it through a little more and line up all my ducks."

"It is, Toby. It is. All right, I'll be in touch."

And with that, the line went dead.

Jankle shut off the recorder and asked me, "You want to hear it again?" I did, and the second time through, I took careful notes, a veritable transcript of the short conversation. When the tape was finished, he carefully placed the recorder back in the metal case and said, "So they had a plan, father and son. We know this much. We know that the father knew the location of the son. We obviously know they were in direct contact. Unfortunately, we haven't been able to eavesdrop on their conversations since."

I asked, "What if the plan was to surrender?"

Jankle pursed his lips and sucked in his cheeks as he considered what I had just said.

"Doesn't gel with anything else that we have," he replied. "And if they were surrendering, why sell two priceless stolen treasures? Basically, Dan Harkins, the mayor of Boston, is already complicit in that. He also knew where a fugitive was hiding, a murderer, and instead of turning him in, he helped him stay on the lam."

I nodded. Everywhere I looked, everything I heard, seemed only to add to the ambiguity of it all. Or did it?

I played the taped conversation over in my mind. I ran through the crystal clear images of the videotape of Harkins and Hilary walking through the lobby, and of Hilary nervously leaving half an hour later.

There's no question, this tape, reported in the *Record*, would devastate Dan Harkins's career, his future, his life, as would the existence of the videotape. I pretty much had him dead to rights, so to speak, with a federal law enforcement source saying he had been under electronic surveillance for the past six months. So why wasn't I rushing to print with this? Could it be that in the wake of my massive fuckup with the previous story, that my journalistic trigger finger was freezing, and that I wasn't doing my job? It had never happened to me before, this reportorial impotence, and I didn't like the feeling one bit.

I asked, "What else?"

Jankle, his head down, looked at me sidelong. You could hide a family of Koreans in his mustache, it was so thick. He said, "Well, we didn't see it coming, but somehow that leak got us some of the paintings back. We're pretty damned happy about that. I feel like I owe you, which is why I'm giving you this. And if it makes you feel better, and I hope it does, we will go after Hilary Kane's killer with a vengeance, and maybe even find a way to prosecute in federal rather than state court."

That did make me feel better, because I had the lingering sense that no one gave a damn about her amid the ass-covering and accusations.

He added, cryptically, "We're not so sure Boston PD is taking any of this very seriously."

He was looking at me expectantly, though I wasn't sure why. So I asked the obvious, which is often what we do in the sometimes majestic and occasionally mundane business of reporting the news. "What do you mean?"

Jankle replied, "We have a suspicion that maybe the locals, some detectives, tipped off the mayor that he was under surveillance, and that's why we haven't been able to grab him on tape. Truth is, we always had suspicions in this case that there was too close a relationship between Boston PD and Toby Harkins, and that he might even have been tipped when his indictment came down, which is how he knew to flee."

Lights went on, not in the park, but in my head. Pieces began flying into place, fitting together. Hank Sweeney flashed in my mind, that morose look on his face as he walked through the jetway door bound for anywhere but Boston, escaping a past that I was now starting to understand. It was coming clear that he had helped Toby way back when, and now he couldn't bring himself to tell me.

I looked at the face of my cell phone, which told me it was 9:55 P.M. I was terribly sad for Hank but rejuvenated by the revelations on the story. I had about two hours to the drop-dead deadline of the final edition. I suddenly felt the driving need to get something in print.

I asked, "You're reachable on your cell if I need you in the next couple of hours?"

"At your service," Jankle replied.

With that, I got up and walked along the aisle and down the ramp of the darkened park. It was the bottom of the ninth, tie game, my turn at bat. Sorry about the cliché, but hey, how often am I the star performer at Fenway Park?

Chapter Thirty-six

I always know I'm hyped on a story when I'm constantly writing and rewriting the lede on the keyboard of my brain, and that's exactly what I was doing as I pushed through the steel door and out onto Yawkey Way on my way to take down the sitting mayor of one of America's great cities.

Yes, he had denied any involvement in Hilary Kane's death and his son's illegal flight, and yes, he was convincing in that denial. I would include that prominently in my story, and allow the readers—smart people, mostly—to make up their own minds. Daniel Harkins's version would be set against a veritable treasure chest of information—that he had a sexual tryst with a murder victim three nights before she died, that the victim had seen potentially criminal material on his personal computer, that he had an irrefutable tie to his fugitive son, and that he had been the target of a federal investigation for at least the past six months.

As I played this out, I became a little bit embarrassed and aggravated that I had taken so long to jump into print with the story, but those feelings were overcome by the kind of intense emotional drive that takes over amid all such blockbuster stories. I was, to say the least, jazzed.

On Yawkey Way, I saw the navy blue van still idling at the curb.

The breeze still blew in from the east. Traffic was light. People were nowhere to be seen.

I headed toward Kenmore Square, to flag a cab that would take me to the *Record*. On the way, I belted out the number to my voicemail, and there was Vinny Mongillo, still on the ground at Logan, telling me that the number I had given him was to the Boston office of the FBI. Ding ding ding. Hilary Kane had talked to Tom Jankle before she died. Why is it that every step forward in this damned story is followed by a step back, and that every revelation only prompts more questions.

Then I called Peter Martin's office, and despite the fact it was ten o'clock on a Sunday night, he, of course, picked up the phone on the first ring.

I said, "We've got the FBI saying they've had the mayor under investigation for six months for ties to his son, and they've allowed me to hear a recording of an incriminating telephone conversation between the two. We can't afford to hold back anymore."

He asked a few of his typically pointed, always-on-the-mark questions. He was a true newsman, even if he looked more like an actuary. At the end of the brief conversation, he said, "All right. I'm going to go tear up the front page. I'll let Justine know. You have about ninety minutes to make this work."

And that was that.

Though not quite. The week before, my story got in the way of a good life, specifically Hilary Kane's, which came to a fast and ferocious end in the parking garage beneath the Boston Common. Out on Brookline Avenue, on my way to type up one of the most explosive tales of my career, life got in the way of a good story. Here's how:

I walked past the Cask 'n' Flagon, a bucket of blood overlooking the backside of the famed left-field wall, also known as the Green Monster. I walked up and over the Massachusetts Turnpike bridge. I was heading down toward the square, to something resembling civilization, when a man, a veritable animal, a mananimal, stepped out of a barren side street directly in my path.

I mean, this guy was big, and ugly. Think Joey Buttafucco, then imagine his bulkier, less sophisticated older brother. The guy looked like he drank water out of a trough and ate food from a metal bucket.

"We meet again," he said in a guttural voice, almost as if it were a great effort for him to form words in that tiny power plant of a brain. He said this as his face was about two feet from mine—so close that I could smell the garlic and onions that weren't just on his breath, but probably still caught in his crooked teeth.

"I don't think we've ever met before now," I said to him, slightly startled, literally stopped in my tracks.

Then, without announcement or ceremony, he pulled his right arm back, and the whole image instantaneously, though belatedly, became strikingly familiar—and I do mean strikingly. He was the man who I had met in the street outside the Gardner Museum the prior Wednesday, the one whose sucker punch left me napping in the gutter.

In fact, "gutter" was the exact word I was thinking when his fist again connected with my stomach and I crumpled into a heap of unbridled—though not unexpected—pain. I fell to my knees on the cool sidewalk and dry-heaved in the general direction of the pavement, all while the mananimal stood over me asking in his garbled syntax, "You remember me now?" And of course, as if following a script, he laughed.

His problem, and arguably mine too, was that I was still filled with the adrenaline that accompanies any major story. The pain quickly melted into my reservoir of determination, and as he leaned toward me about to deliver another adolescent taunt, I climbed to my feet, looked him in the eye and delivered a thunderous blow to the bridge of his nose.

He gave a surprisingly shallow little yelp for a man whose voicebox was probably the size of a carton of Marlboros. He staggered back, fighting to retain his balance, blood spurting from his nostrils. At the precise moment he turned backward to break his fall, he came in direct contact with a brick wall. Next thing you know, he was sprawled out on the ground.

I checked my pockets to make sure I still had my notes. Then I set out down the street. Problem was, I didn't get more than two steps before an octopus like arm reached around my neck and tightened over my Adam's apple.

Immediately, I squirmed around and shot elbows into what felt like canvas bags filled with sand, which I think was my assailant's chest. I kicked backward with my legs but failed to connect.

A voice, clean and firm, said to me, "Make one more move and I'll blow your brains all over my new shirt. And then I'll get really angry."

As he spoke, I felt a cold metal object press against my right temple, a very strong signal that it was time to give in. A split second later, a sport utility vehicle glided to the curb. The rear door was thrust open from within. I was thrust inside from without. The man who had me by the neck yelled over to the mananimal, "Get the fuck in the front seat, and don't bleed on the leather."

With everybody settled inside, we immediately pulled out. The guy to my right, the gunman, seemed to be the ringleader. I sensed this because when I said, "Listen, guys, this is very kind of you, but you can just drop me off at a cabstand," he grabbed my face, pulled it toward his, and hissed, "If you say one more word, I'll blow your fucking pea brain right out the back of your stupid fucking head."

For a guy who makes his living with words, meaning me, this didn't create an easy situation.

A moment later, the ringleader reached into a small shoulder bag on the floor and pulled out what looked like a wool hat. I looked out the window as the SUV glided through Kenmore Square. The ape in the front seat had a cloth of some sort shoved up into both his nostrils. The driver wore a baseball cap and glasses and never turned around. The guy to my left didn't utter a word.

"Put this on your head," the ringleader said. He handed me the black thing and I put it on. He then violently reached up and pulled the edges down well below my eyes, all the way to my chin.

"I can't breathe," I said. And as the last word came out, I felt a fist connect reasonably hard with my right cheek. My first impulse was to punch back. My second impulse, my survivor's instinct, was to sit still and not do or say anything else.

Everyone around me sat in stone silence. The radio was off. The heavily tinted windows were tight as a drum. The vehicle stopped at a light or two, then sped off. I felt us go left, then straight, then veer slowly to the right as we accelerated, and sensed that we were on Storrow Drive, heading toward downtown Boston.

Funny thing is, my stomach hurt, my cheek was swelling, my brain ached, but I still couldn't stop writing the story of the mayor over and over again in my head, refining the lede, elaborating on it, restructuring the next few paragraphs and the order of the critical information involved. Question was, would I get to write it?

Sitting there, other questions came to mind, first and foremost: Who were they? Where were they taking me? And of course, that simplest and most important question: Why?

I hoped that they were the henchmen who would lead me to Toby Harkins, though at this point in the game, anything goes. The thought crossed my wool-covered mind that they could work for Mayor Harkins. They might have seen me meeting with Jankle. They might have been planning to kill me before I had the chance to write my devastating story.

The car kept speeding along without stopping, meaning we were, in fact, on a highway, not on city streets. My escorts rode in absolute and utter silence, professionals all. I wanted to ask if anyone would mind listening to NPR, but felt it best to continue to keep my big mouth firmly shut.

After about ten minutes, I felt us turn and descend a little. They say that when one of your senses is blocked, your others come alive in ways you could never possibly imagine. That, I was learning, was an old wives' tale at best, bullshit at worst, because sitting in the back of this SUV between two guys whose high school nicknames could both have been Himalaya, I didn't have the hint of a clue.

And then, after a turn right followed by a quick turn left, the car stopped. The doors were flung open. The ringleader grabbed my arm and yanked me outside. He held me in front of him with both his hands on each of my shoulders and pushed me along.

"Make one wrong move, and I'd love the chance to break your skinny fucking spine," he said. As I digested that thought, he added, "You'll be in a wheelchair for the rest of your stupid life communicating by blinking your fucking eyes."

"Step up," he said sharply. I felt around with my foot and found a stair. I hesitantly climbed it, then another, and another. When I got about four steps up, someone on the front end pulled hard at my wrist and the guy behind me pushed on my back. I stumbled through some sort of opening and as I was off balance, the person in front pushed me down hard into a chair. Nobody said a word.

A moment later, I heard the voice of the ringleader say, "Let's go."

I felt him lean into me as he said, "Same rules. You say a word, I'll punch your face. You say a sentence, I'll break your neck."

At that rate, I assumed a paragraph would get me killed, so I stayed church quiet.

I heard a door shut hard somewhere to my right and in front. I heard an engine start. I assumed we were on some sort of small airplane, flying off to destinations unknown, though I could be fairly certain it wasn't going to be anyplace I'd particularly want to be. I wanted to tell them that I didn't bring a change of underwear, but again, wisdom and its accompanying silence prevailed.

A new voice called out from the front of the plane, "We're set for departure."

I heard the sounds of buckling around me, though no one bothered with mine. What the hell. I didn't know how many of the morons from the car were actually on the plane with us, but I suspected I'd find out.

As I readied myself for the plane to begin rolling, the oddest sensation occurred instead. Rather than taxi, we lifted straight up in the air. We weren't on an airplane at all, but a helicopter.

I've always wanted to take one of those chopper tours of Boston, seeing my hometown in all its grandeur from high above—the nooks, the crannies, the parks and the treetops, the relationships between streets and neighborhoods and rivers and harbors that you can never possibly appreciate when you're literally in the thick of things. But I suppressed my desire to pull off my woolen mask, lest I encourage an immediate physical relationship with the ringleader's fist or the pavement below.

We kept rising and rising, the whirl of the propeller overhead overriding what would have been a stifling silence. We leveled off at God-knows-what altitude, and then thrust forward for a place that I didn't yet know.

It was like that for nearly twenty minutes, the helicopter swiping through the night air, occasionally bumping and grinding, dipping and rising and turning. Normally I might find myself getting airsick in these situations, but my body was on such high alert that I don't think it had the capacity to feel much of anything at all.

Without fanfare, the copter finally slowed and hovered for a long moment, then began to descend, not straight down, but at a forward angle, gradually slipping toward the ground, lower and lower and lower. And then came a significant jolt, rocking the helicopter from one side to the other. Seconds later, the door flew open. I immediately smelled salt air, even through the hood. I heard what I suspect were the stairs thrust into place. Someone grabbed my arm. Evidently, the shared experience of the chopper ride didn't lend itself to any sort of fraternity, because whoever it was threw me forward like a rag doll. I braced my arms out in front of me to try to cushion my fall. As I did, someone else grabbed me, squeezed my arms painfully hard and said, "Walk down the stairs. Now. Step. Step. Step." I did what I was told until I found myself on the soft, cool ground. And I mean, on the ground.

When I got to the bottom, I heard the familiar voice of the ringleader say, "I've got 'em." At the same time, I felt an arm come hard underneath mine and swing me violently around. I staggered and kept falling until I was rolling on the damp, muddy earth. I heard laughter, then I felt a shoe connect hard with my chin, and for the briefest of moments, aside from a ringing in my head, I felt nothing at all.

"Get the fuck up," the ringleader said. I assumed he was talking to me. He repeated himself, less pleasantly the second time than the first, even if that didn't seem possible. "Get the fuck up."

I pawed at the dark expanse with my hands, reaching, groping, for anything that would help me in my struggle to stand. But there was nothing there, so when I got on my two feet, I staggered again, and one more time felt an arm swing under mine and fling me, and this time I went crashing into a hard, round surface, which I could only surmise was the solid trunk of an old tree.

While I was lying on the ground in a light fog, I heard another voice, strong but distant, yell, "Hey, cut the shit." And I thought to myself, here we go again.

Then I heard the ringleader, my tormentor, say, "I'm just showing him who's in control."

The first voice, closer now, replied, "Keep your fucking hands off him."

"Fuck off. He broke TJ's nose."

And then came the sound of fist into flesh. I grimaced, assuming it must be mine—the flesh, not the fist—but felt nothing other than relief. I heard it again, and again, along with a string of profanity, and a couple of other voices yelling out "Hey." One guy said, "Let them go."

I lifted the wool up over my eyes for the briefest of moments and saw two seriously enormous men rolling on the ground about ten yards away beating the living bejesus out of each other, punching and clawing and flailing and kicking. Two other men stood near them, unsure what to do.

I gazed around. I felt salty wind on my face, as if we were next to the ocean. We appeared to be on the edge of a thick grove of towering pine trees. It was dark, moonless, and right there and then, I knew if I slipped into the trees I could have easily escaped my captors, possibly made it to a main road, and flagged down a car to take me to safety. It was, by every measure, the instinctual thing to do. Probably the wise thing as well.

I lay on the ground, my mind running faster than my legs ever could, figuring, processing, playing the angles and the ramifications and the scenarios that would make up a very important future. One of the men in the fistfight screamed. The two onlookers jumped into the fray, and I was even freer than before to bolt into the night.

But something stopped me, and that something was news. Yes, if I ran, I might still make it to a phone to call in the Dan Harkins story, but there was too good a chance that these guys who had ferried me to this distant point had done so in the name of Toby Harkins, and despite the physical abuse, I wasn't willing to walk away from the distinct chance that I was about to come face-to-face with America's most wanted fugitive.

So I stood up. I pulled the wool back over my eyes, so to speak. And I waited. Maybe I'm an assholic moron. Maybe I was about to be killed. But I couldn't bring myself to run from even the slightest potential of information this good.

Five minutes later, the fight receded into a kind of "Fuck you," "No, fuck you," volley. I eventually felt a hand grab my elbow, and heard the voice of the new man say, "Come with me. Don't try anything funny."

We walked for about three minutes, across what felt like a grass and dirt path covered with leaves and twigs that crunched underfoot. The crickets continued to chirp. The air was filled with the scent of fresh pine. I was filled more with curiosity at that point than fear.

He tugged at my arm to stop. He said, "So far, so good, so don't do anything stupid now. I just need to pat you down." And he did, pulling the cell phone out of my pocket and not returning it. "You're clear," he said, as I heard him push open a door. "Step down." I felt around with my foot and descended one stair. A door shut behind me.

"Do you have to use the head?" he asked me.

God, yes. I nodded, still unsure if I was allowed to speak. He led me by the arm, shoved me gently through a doorway, told me, "You can take your cover off in the bathroom. Put it back on when you come out." And he shut the door behind me.

I pulled off the cover to see that I was in a tiny, spartan, windowless bathroom, with just a toilet and an old sink, the kind where the drain plug dangles on a chain from a dank faucet. The walls were cinder block. There was no mirror, no towels, no soap, nothing that I could fashion in any way into a weapon, not that I'd have even the slightest idea how, or, for that matter, the desire to do it. I felt around my face for blood, and saw none on my hands. I did my thing, I put my hat back on, and I walked out.

My escort was waiting at the door. He led me across a hard floor, straight, then left, then right. He sat me down on a coarse cloth chair and said, "You're being watched. If you try to leave, you'll be immediately killed, so my advice to you is not to do anything stupid. As soon as you hear the door shut, pull off your hood if you like. We'll take care of you shortly."

Take care of you shortly.

I wasn't 100 percent sure I liked the sound of that. I wasn't even 25 percent sure. Regardless, the door shut, I yanked off my hood, and drank in my environs.

I was in a small, windowless room in some sort of bunker, with cement floors, walls and ceilings. It looked like it was decorated by the same people who designed Alcatraz. There were just three chairs in the room, all of which looked like they were purchased at a yard sale, facing each other, beneath an overhead light. The walls were unadorned. There was no rug. Rustic would be a compliment. Minimalist describes a style; this was just plain old and bare.

I sat and I sat and I sat. I had no watch. My cell phone was someplace other than with me. I could picture poor Peter Martin calling it every two minutes and screaming at some confused thug, "What do you mean, he's a hostage. We're on deadline. Let him fricking go!"

Finally, the door opened, and standing before me was the elusive, reclusive Toby Harkin, America's most wanted, right there, right then, in the flesh.

Chapter Thirty-seven

My friends at the *Traveler* had dubbed him the Casanova Convict. They'd written that he could either charm or harm, depending on his mood, and I could sense that, actually see that, from the exact moment when Toby Harkins walked into the room.

He was something of a pretty man, with refined features on an unblemished face. His thick black hair was slicked back, Wall Street style. His eyes were a blaze of blue, which some might say weren't unlike mine. His hand, when he offered it to shake, was surprisingly soft, especially considering where it had been and what it had done. Not to worry, I'm still every inch a heterosexual, but I couldn't help but be momentarily taken when a man whom I had only known in pictures had suddenly, in the flesh, entered my life.

"You look like you've fallen," he said, seeming sincerely concerned as his eyes drifted from my face to my soiled clothes. He added, "I hope my guys were professional with you."

Yeah, professional killers. Professional assholes. "They got me here alive," I replied, and he didn't press me for more details.

Regarding Toby Harkins again, he was slighter than I might have expected, thin, wiry. He wore a pair of olive-colored cargo pants and a tight blue-striped polo shirt that was stretched across his shoulders and arms. He looked like he could have been heading out for a weekend on Cape Cod, which made me wonder if that's in fact where we were.

"Thanks for coming, Jack," he said.

There's that Jack thing again, just like on the phone. I replied, "You're welcome, Toby. Of course, I wasn't offered a whole lot of choice." The exchange was a bit of déjà vu, taking me back to the first conversation I had ever had with Jankle six nights before, after his own lackeys had escorted me to his downtown office.

Harkins smiled. I didn't. It was important for me to keep in mind that I wasn't sitting here with any ordinary source, but a ruthless killer who had embarked on a reign of terror in the Boston underworld unlike anything that the city had ever known. Legend has it that he always shot his victims in the forehead so that he could see the look in their eyes the moment they realized they were about to die. I wondered if he'd want to see that look from me before this night was out, but if he did, he wouldn't get the story that he seemed to want even more.

I said, "So there's a point to all this, I assume."

He looked at me for a long moment, caught slightly off guard by the idea that someone was questioning him, rushing him along, an anomaly in a world in which he always retained complete control—his flight from justice aside.

"There is," he said, leaning back. "But slow down. First off, thanks for holding off on printing that story about my old man. You did the right thing, and I'll explain why in a moment. But know that I appreciate it."

"I held back," I interjected, "because we didn't have all our facts lined up, not because of any request from you."

He seemed not to care about that, and said only, "Regardless, the right thing got done, which is too rarely the case, Jack." And he smiled again, though at what, I wasn't sure.

He asked, "You got both paintings?"

"Received the second one, the Rembrandt, on Saturday night. We'll be reporting its authenticity in tomorrow morning's paper."

I hesitated, then asked, "Have you been following our coverage every day?"

Truth is, I didn't give a rat's furry ass whether he read my paper every day. The question was merely an unsubtle attempt to find out if he had been in hiding in the Boston area, and thus able to acquire the paper. He responded, smiling again, "I do, Jack. I do. Online."

Ah, another online reader, taking for free what others paid for. The Internet was going to be the death of newspapers, I tell you, but that's not really the point here.

"And if you hold up your end of the agreement, you'll get all the others back as soon as the article appears in print," he said.

It's probably worth noting here that we had no agreement, Toby and I. What we had was a single phone call that preceded this face-to-face meeting in which no ground rules, no accommodations, no deals had been set or met. I saw no need to raise the point, and instead said dismissively, "Let's see where this takes us."

He sighed deeply, his thin chest rising and falling as he exhaled.

"Jack," he said, and believe me, this Jack thing was getting old. "Jack, this is big. My story is important. I don't think I'm going to survive much longer, but you might be my only hope."

In many ways, politicians and high-level crooks—who are, as I've said, often one and the same—share a lot in common, and one of the most prominent traits is this: They think that the entire world revolves around them, that people care, that everyone wants to help. I guess it comes from having fearful underlings catering to your every whim every hour of the day.

I wanted to explain to him in elaborate detail just how little I cared, but at the same time, I wanted to hear what it was that he had to say. So I nodded and said, "Tell me what you've got."

He seemed satisfied with that response. He leaned forward in his chair, his elbows on his knees, and said, "The FBI wants me dead."

Stop the presses. I mean, whoo-fucking-eee. That's what he grabbed me off the streets of Boston and flew me on board a helicopter to the middle of nowhere in the dark of an angst-ridden night to tell me, that the FBI, the investigators who've been trying to track him down for years now, want him dead?

"And your point is?"

He furrowed his otherwise smooth brow and bit his bottom lip in thought as he looked sternly across at me.

"I mean, they really want me dead. If they find me, they're going to kill me."

I considered this for a long moment as I studied the fear in his eyes and the anxiety that flashed across his face. It sounded like the typical lament of a criminal who had spent a career confounding some of the best-trained law enforcement officers in these United States, and now was living to regret it. His head was filled with grandiose conspiracy theories. The rustle of trees in the autumn breeze was, in his mind, the movement of government snipers in the nearby brush. The passing plane overhead was a spy drone capturing his every move.

When I was about to respond, I heard a distant shout coming from outside the slightly opened door, a faraway voice that in any other place, in any other setting, would have been caught in the filter of the mind, but there and then, proceeded through to the realm of greater meaning. There was no good reason to hear shouting in these faraway woods. I knew that, and I didn't have to be a psychology major at Harvard to know that Toby Harkins knew it as well. If the look on his face didn't tell me, then it was the revolver that he pulled out of the back of his pants.

He eyed me suspiciously and asked, "Were you followed?"

"Followed?" I asked, incredulously. "Your guys beat the shit out of me and put me on a helicopter. You think I have spy satellites tracking me?"

"Take off your shirt," he said. He was serious. The last time another human being asked me to remove my shirt this seriously, it was Elizabeth. We were drunk out of our gourds after a dinner party with some friends. We had just walked into the foyer of our apartment, but now is probably not the time to explain where it all went from there.

I peeled my shirt off—both for Elizabeth back then and Toby now. He walked around me, though not to admire my lats and pecs. He was checking for wires.

"All right," he said, businesslike now. No more of that "Jack" stuff, at least for the time being. I put my shirt back on, and outside, there was another shout. Then there was a knock on the door to our room. It opened, and a young man, twenty-five-ish or so, with close-cropped hair, walked in and said to Harkins, "Hank Sweeney's outside. Says he wants to see you."

Think about that for a minute. *Hank Sweeney's outside.* My good friend, Hank Sweeney, in the flesh, proving Jankle correct in his assertion that there were Boston PD detectives who had gotten too close to Toby Harkins and his crime syndicate, and Hank Sweeney, my Hank Sweeney, was foremost among them.

"Hank fucking Sweeney?" Harkins asked, with a cross of incredulity and anger. He looked down in thought, then said, "Send him the fuck in."

A moment later, Sweeney came walking through the door. Last I saw of him, he was walking through a door in the other direction, specifically heading down the jetway toward his flight for West Palm Beach and his ramshackle retirement home in Florida. I had assumed then that I'd never see him again, though I wasn't quite sure why. Now I knew.

He nodded at me, almost imperceptibly so. If he was embarrassed, he didn't show it. Instead, he said to Harkins, "Time's up, Toby. Honor the agreement with your father and turn yourself in, or we're going to do it for you."

Toby stared at Hank. Hank stared at Toby. I regarded them both, completely unsure of what to make of this situation.

After a long moment, Toby said, "Detective Sweeney, I would strongly urge you to shut the fuck up and get the hell out. You're all bought and paid for. You're no good to anyone anymore."

I saw Hank's jaw tighten and his fists clench. He said in a voice that was marked by none of his typically easygoing raspiness, "You made a deal with your old man to surrender, Toby. And I'm here to enforce it."

Harkins let out a laugh, mocking in its tone. "You're going to enforce it, detective? You're really going to enforce it?"

With that, Harkins pointed his gun at Hank and said, "If I give myself up, the FBI will kill me instantly, just like I'm going to kill you right now."

I stood up from my seat. Maybe Hank's corrupt, but he wasn't going to die on my watch. Harkins whirled toward me with the gun and said, "Down, Jack. This doesn't involve you."

Before I could reply, Hank said, "Toby, if you shoot me dead, you're dead too. Jankle knows that if he doesn't hear from me in fifteen minutes, they're coming here to get you. Either way, you're done. It's just a matter of how you want to do it."

Harkins looked momentarily confused, boxed in by circumstances that seemed increasingly beyond his control. In the silence, he turned to me and said, "So I hope this proves it to you. My old man was telling you the truth. He's been trying to get me to surrender to authorities, to come back to Boston and face the charges. He says that's a better way to live out my life than always looking over my shoulder, forever being on the run."

He smiled to himself, dimples forming on his unshorn cheeks. "I'm not so sure he's right," he added. "But I'll give him credit. He's a hell of a persuasive guy."

Harkins then turned to Hank and said, "You're a piece of garbage, Hank. A corrupted piece of trash. Don't you dare try to tell me the right thing to do."

He added, "But because you're rotten to the core, I've got a million dollars for you if you get me out of here alive and free. No banks, no checks, just cash in a suitcase. Your kind of deal, Hank, and better than a life in prison after I rat you out."

He looked at Hank and so did I. Hank stood staring at him, his eyes as dark as his skin, his arms tense, his legs ramrod straight.

Before he could answer, an answer I really would have liked to have heard, there were more shouts from outside, followed by the sound of gunfire—a report that began sharp and hard and then dissipated into the night air like a cloud of steam.

Toby stared Hank down. Another shot rang out. "You fucking asshole, Hank. You're going down with me."

Someone yelled in the distance, and inside the bunker, a man on the other side of the door screamed, "Feds on the island! Feds on the island!"

That was followed by commotion—the hard sounds of footsteps, a door being flung open, a heavy object knocked to the ground. Outside, still far-off, I heard what sounded to be machine-gun fire, yells of warning, screams of agony, bedlam.

In this one room, Toby bolted toward the wall nearest the entry door and flicked out the overhead light. I mean, Ray Charles didn't spend as much time groping in the dark as I had over the last few hours.

Instinctively, I fell to the floor, on all fours, and crawled in the direction of the door, but about two-thirds of the way there, I ran smack into the form of Toby Harkins. I knew it was him because he whispered into my ear, "Come with me or I'll fucking kill you." As proof, he applied the barrel of his gun to the back of my neck. It's lucky I don't have a dermatological aversion to metal these days.

So there we were, Toby and I, crawling across the grimy floor of an ancient bunker in God knows where while Hank Sweeney waged an internal battle between good and evil and federal agents and organized hoods engaged in a massive firefight on the edge of the property. If I stay in this ridiculous business of news and words, I think I'll become the restaurant critic, though watch, I'll take the job and die of food poisoning within two months.

We crawled outside the room. We then crawled out the open front door, up the landing, and down one step to the ground. He stood up, hunched, and signaled for me to do the same. Then we bolted for a grove of soaring pines to the right side of the structure. Once there, he crouched onto the ground, and forced my shoulder down so I was doing the same. The barrel of his gun was never pointed anywhere but my face.

And there we sat, behind a tree trunk, catching our breath. The air was cool, the ground moist, the night dark. I'm trying to think of some other clichés, but none come immediately to mind. Still, they're all true.

In the near distance, the sporadic blasts of machine-gun fire continued, and when I trained my eyes somewhere other than the gun that was aimed at me, I could see shards of red penetrate the black.

Toby regained composure and whispered to me, "Jack, if you try anything stupid, you won't be the first guy I've killed."

And probably not the last, either, the way this night was going. I replied, "Understood. Now tell me what you mean by the FBI is trying to kill you."

"They want me dead because of what I know," he said, low and hoarse, nervous.

I was about to ask the obvious follow-up question, when a voice magnified by a megahorn called out, "Federal agents with a warrant. Drop all your weapons, turn on all lights, and proceed into the clearing."

It was familiar, that voice, though maybe it's because it sounded like every other magnified police voice I've ever heard on TV. Still, I believed it was Tom Jankle. I'll admit with a slight amount of shame that I was feeling slightly torn. Yes, Jankle would make an arrest, and I'd still be at the forefront of a fantastic story, but then I'd never properly hear what it was that Toby Harkins wanted to say.

So I asked the question, in something just north of a whisper, "What do you know?"

His eyes peered out across the expanse, looking, wondering, calculating. That's when a spotlight that had been probing through the trees paused on us. Someone yelled something indecipherable, and gunfire tore through the air.

Toby dove for the base of a nearby boulder, and so did I. We were shoulder to shoulder, pushing against each other for cover behind the rock, with the sound of bullets tearing at leaves, exploding against the wood of nearby trees, blazing past us through the night air.

After a few seconds of gunfire, silence, followed by Jankle's voice on the bullhorn again saying, "We have your location. We have you cornered. We're coming in behind you. Come out, immediately, with your hands well over your head."

"I'm going," I whispered to Toby.

"One step and you're dead," he said. And he held his gun

against my neck, pressing my face against the boulder. Forgive the obvious, but someday, somewhere, a kid is going to ask his father what the phrase "Between a rock and a hard place" means, and my name is going to come up.

"Come out, immediately. We have thirty armed federal agents. We have killed or captured all of your accomplices. Surrender or face the consequences."

These are not the normal decisions of everyday newspaper reporters, this do-I-want-to-be-shot-in-the-head-while-I-hide-or-in-the-back-when-I-bolt thing.

Do I get the soup or the pasta? Do I take the train to work or drive? Do I go to the gym or head straight home? What I wouldn't give to be sitting in the University Club bar with Hank and Vinny at this very moment ordering hamburgers and swilling cold beer, and not giving half a damn that it's all going on my tab. Lou, another round of drinks for all my friends, please.

"Get the fuck out here!"

That was still Jankle, or his soundalike, growing impatient, and obviously profane. I looked at Toby in the dark. We were so close together that I could feel his breath on my skin. We were so close together that I could hear one of our hearts beating, and I wasn't sure whether it was his or mine.

I nodded to him, as in, now what? He stared back at me, but I couldn't read the expression, didn't know what it meant, had no idea where he was going to take this. I was only sure of one true thing: in his mind, he had nothing to lose. He already thought the Feds, for an as still yet unexplained reason, wanted to kill him. All of which put me very far into harm's way.

Harkins grazed his hand along the gravelly ground and picked up a sizable rock. I braced myself, wondering if he was about to slam it into my head. Instead, he scouted a distant spot on the other side of the clearing and fired the stone in that direction. I mean, come on. That's the oldest trick in the book—"Look over there," and they all really do, like something that Sgt. O'Rourke might have tried on *F Troop*.

But sure enough, the rock plunked against something hard, and immediately, there were multiple bursts of gunfire in that exact direction, the roar filling the air and spreading out amid the black sky and the trees. Toby yanked at my arm, virtually lifting me up off the ground, and the two of us scampered from the edge of the grove of trees to deep within it, running furiously among the sturdy trunks, pounding across the uneven ground, pushing farther and farther into the dark depths.

I'm going to make a confession here. As we ran, his grip loosened, naturally so. His trigger hand was no longer pointed directly at me, because to have done so would have slowed us down considerably. At any point, I believe I could have given his arm something of a karate chop and disappeared into the trees on my own, circled back, and escaped. Risky? Yes. He might have regained composure. He very well may have caught a long look at me before I vanished. He could have shot me. But more likely, not.

And yet I stayed. I stayed because of my curiosity. I stayed out of a sense of duty, not to Toby Harkins or to the FBI or even Hilary Kane, though certainly her more than anyone else. No, I stayed out of duty to the *Record*'s readers, the good people of Boston, who might never have a better chance to know where the nation's most wanted fugitive was and what had become his fate. I stayed because I wanted to know, and needed, in turn, to inform.

And a good thing, too, because as we pounded through the forest, our arms in front of our eyes to push back dangling branches, our gaze glued ahead to avoid the thicket of trees, we suddenly found ourselves face-to-face with the law.

Tom Jankle stepped out from behind a tree on the edge of a new clearing. He flicked on a high-powered spotlight and shone it in our eyes. He said, calmly and collectedly, "Freeze and drop your guns or I blow your fucking brains out."

Toby screeched to a halt. His arm tightened around mine. We were about ten yards away from Jankle, who could see us from behind the light that he was holding far better than we could see him.

Harkins held fast to his gun. He yelled back, "I have a hostage."

First thing I thought was, *Jesus Christ, he's got a hostage.* And then it occurred to me in an increasingly uncharacteristic moment of clarity: I was the hostage.

And with that, I went from between that rock and a hard place to quite literally staring down the barrel of my own demise.

Chapter Thirty-eight

I got to thinking, standing there on the edge of that dark forest with Toby Harkins's sinewy arm wrapped around my neck and his gun pointed at my head, and Tom Jankle standing but ten yards away, his gun pointed in the general direction of my head, that there wasn't a whole lot of good that was about to come out of this situation.

Suppose, for example, that Harkins shot and killed Jankle. I was the only witness to that act, and I would surely be next on his hit list, and since Toby goes through bullets like Hugh Hefner goes through Viagra, that would probably mark me as an immediate victim. And suppose Toby was right, that the FBI wanted him dead, and that Jankle shot him right there, right then. Again, I would be the only witness, and Jankle might well kill me on the spot, then blame the whole thing on a confused shoot-out obscured by the dark.

I felt little streams of sweat running down my back, chilly in the autumn air. Cool perspiration formed along my forehead. I stood there silently, a little bit frightened, but oddly, far more fascinated, about how this standoff would end. We grow up in this reporting business believing we are always detached, and over the years, having seen colleagues killed and corrupted, I've learned otherwise. But even here, with a pair of guns aimed in my general vicinity, I had a naïve, if diminishing air of invincibility.

So I stood and I watched and I wondered.

"Toby, we go back way too far, you and me, to have any bullshit happen now. Put the gun down, and let's figure out what we're going to do about this."

That was Jankle, only adding to the confusion of a complex situation, at least as far as I was concerned, though maybe not in Toby's mind. Let's review how many nuggets of interest were contained in that two-sentence declaration. *We go back way too far,* and *Let's figure out what we're going to do about this.* Well, okay, just two, but pretty significant ones.

Maybe it's just me, but that doesn't strike me as the normal way in which a federal agent would address the nation's number one most wanted fugitive in a standoff where there's a relatively innocent life on the line, meaning mine. How far back do they go, and why? Why would he work together to "figure out what we're going to do about this?" One more question: What the flying fuck was going on here?

Of course, other questions nagged as well, such as, would a bullet from Toby's semiautomatic handgun kill me immediately, or would I writhe on the ground first like a freshly caught fish on a cutting table? Is Jankle a good shot, or might he take me out by mistake while trying to shoot at Toby? Can I call my mommy, or would these two disapprove?

Toby replied, "Put the gun down and let me slip away into the woods and you'll get credit for tracking me down before I somehow got out alive."

There was silence between them, silence as if Jankle was considering this exact scenario, which made absolutely no sense to me, but seemed to have some plausibility for the two of them.

Jankle said, "And what do we do with him?"

He nodded at me as he said it. I took on the feeling of an unnecessary appendage, or like someone's inbred, untrained terrier, an incessant nuisance, really stupid, something beyond dispensable.

"You don't let him out alive."

I cleared my throat, though it was my head that was the truly clogged part of my body. *You don't let him out alive.* I was suddenly part of a deal, a bargaining chip, a negotiating point, that which was tossed back and forth in the ruminations of an awkward moment. Decisions could be made that were right or wrong, and regrets might come to haunt them later, but never me, for I'd be dead.

Jankle stared back at Harkins. At least, I think he was staring, but in the light, in my current frame of mind, these things were tough to tell. He said, "Shoot him right now and I'll let you go."

Harkins tightened his grip on the gun and pushed it harder against my temple. I could actually feel the tension in his hand, the tiny movement of the cold barrel against my skin. There was a long second, a gruesome second, when there was virtually no doubt in my brain that Toby Harkins was about to pull the trigger. I wondered if heaven had a grassy field where I could throw a tennis ball for Baker.

I felt the need to say something. My head, my life, my responsibility. There was no one else in this crowd who was ready to speak up for me.

"Toby," I said, starting slowly, "the second you pull that trigger, Jankle's going to shoot you dead right here. And it's going to look like self-defense, because you would already have killed me."

That seemed to register some, at least in terms of the tension in his hand. This was like one of those ridiculous dials that focus group members turn during presidential debates to express agreement or disagreement with a candidate. Say the right thing, Toby loosens his grip ever so slightly. Say the exact right thing and maybe he lowers the gun. Say the wrong thing and I'm dead.

I stood there, sweating even more, wondering about Jankle's play, about their past, about my future, about whether I'd see the light of another glorious day.

Toby called across to Jankle, "Answer that. How do I know?"

"What are your other options?"

Jankle added, "Kill him or I'll kill you both right now. He's a worthless hostage. I'd rather see him dead."

I kind of cleared my throat again, but had no idea what, if anything, I could or would say. If Jankle was trying to help me, he was certainly pursuing a perverted means. For his part, Toby neither tightened nor loosened his grip, though I could all but hear his mind whirring as he tried to calculate the conclusion of every possible scenario. Believe me, I was doing the same thing, but I wasn't the one with any decision-making capacity at the moment.

Harkins said to Jankle, "You told me I'd be free for the rest of my life. That was your guarantee. I have that first meeting, that time we got together on the seawall, I have it on tape."

"So do I," Jankle fired back. "And I never told you that, at least not in the context of you reaching out to the fucking press." He sounded angrier here, Jankle did, and he said, "What the fuck were you thinking, you little piece of slime."

"Fuck you," Toby yelled back, and I could feel the tension in his hand, in his whole arm, all over again.

This is not what anyone needed, this heavy dose of anger added to an already overwrought situation. Normally I'd be utterly fascinated by this dialogue, and truth be known, I was. But the big problem still remained that I couldn't conjure a single scenario that ended with me walking away alive.

"I made you," Toby said to Jankle. His voice was beyond strained, pocked by fright and frustration. I actually thought it was about to crack, and maybe him with it, which probably wouldn't be all that good for me.

He continued, "I made you rich. I gave you more information than you could ever use. I made you a star agent. I gave you money and status and anything else that you ever wanted and needed, and you're telling me that you're going to kill me now?"

Jankle stood statuesque in the quiet dark. I could hear crickets chirping and leaves rustling and the sound of Harkins breathing, but nothing else.

Jankle, after a long moment, said, "Toby. I gave you freedom. I protected you. I flipped state cops and held back Boston PD detectives who were gunning for you. I let you run the city, unfettered. And when the indictments came down, I warned you to get out of town."

At this point, both these clowns could have shot me in the head and I'm not sure I would have flinched or felt it. I was so caught up in the unfolding drama that I was losing touch with the reality of my impending death, drawn closer by every statement, every sentence, every word that was uttered in the dark. The two of them were acting like I was dead already, which was not, best that I could tell, a particularly good sign.

Still, the revelations were extraordinary. Basically, what they were saying was that Toby Harkins was a fully protected federal informant who ran a murderous crime syndicate with the full authorization of the federal government. The Feds also convinced the likes of Boston PD—meaning Hank Sweeney and probably others—to stand down on any arrest or investigation. In return, the FBI got what sounded like a boatload of information about other organized crime figures in Boston, and Jankle had achieved extraordinary celebrity by putting them behind bars. Being a reporter, I wanted to ask questions, most notably, which one of you gentleman killed Hilary Kane? But I sensed this wasn't the exact right time to do it.

"So I'd say we're even," Jankle said, his voice marinated in contempt. "Wouldn't you?"

Silence. Jankle said in a louder, more taunting voice, "So tell me, Toby, why'd you want to meet with a reporter?"

"I wanted to unload the paintings."

Shouting now, Jankle said, "You wanted to confess that you were a federal informant, you dumb fuck. You were looking to rat on me in hopes of cutting some sort of deal."

"Not true." Harkins was outright panicked. His eyes were wide, his voice was shaky, and so was the hand that held the gun that remained pressed against my head. "You wanted me dead. You were trying to kill me."

Jankle was incredulous. "Trying to kill you? Trying to fucking kill you? I tried protecting you. I leaked word that the fucking broad with the mayor stumbled across the files that said where you were. I did that so you'd know what to do with her before she started yammering to the wrong people."

Harkins replied, "I didn't kill her."

"No shit. I decided you'd fuck it all up, that you were out of practice, that you're getting fat and lazy on the run. So I decided to do it myself."

I could sense Harkins's arm nearly go limp as he processed that which he was just told. I, too, was floored. Tom Jankle, my source, was also Hilary's killer, because he didn't trust that the scenario that he had intricately mapped out would be properly carried out. I became so angry I wanted to grab Harkins's gun and shoot Jankle dead right there amid the tall pines of an unknowing night.

"You're saying my father didn't kill her?"

"He doesn't have the balls. I fucking did it—for you."

"You did it for yourself," Harkins said, softer now. "You should have told me. I unloaded those two paintings to throw this asshole off the trail." He was, I believe, referring to me. Friends, allies, are tough to find these days.

These revelations were followed by a protracted silence, not broken until Harkins said, "And now you're telling me that if I kill him"—he shook the gun against my skin as he said this—"you'll let me walk away?"

"I will."

I felt Harkins become so taut that the barrel of the gun was chattering against the side of my head, as if it were shivering. He was getting ready to kill me. In a world in which I knew too little else, this I understood as fact.

I didn't think. I didn't process. I didn't foresee, calculate, devise, or anything else. What I did instead was slam my body directly into Toby Harkins, at once pushing him, then driving my shoulders hard into his ribs and stomach like a sophomore freak on the Oklahoma University offensive line. I felt a gush of breath rush out of him. I toppled over him as he fell. And then I heard the nearby sound of a gunshot—his, followed by another one a little farther away.

Lying on the cold ground, I immediately, frantically, felt my chest, my head, my limbs, for the sensation of warm blood. Nothing. I looked at Harkins, sprawled out beside me. He was dazed, but apparently uninjured. The gun was no longer in either of his hands, but I couldn't see it on the dark ground. I slammed my fist into his nose, not out of vengeance, but to keep him on the ground.

I felt around for the gun, but still no sign, so I crawled slowly toward the base of a tree. The light that had been trained on us a moment ago was now lying on the ground, pointing arbitrarily toward an inconsequential patch of woods. I wondered if Jankle had dropped it and fled. I was wondering this, as a matter of fact, when I heard muffled voices followed by the sickening thud of bone hitting flesh.

I moved cautiously in the direction of the abandoned light. When I was but a few feet away, off to the side, I saw Jankle in silhouette on his knees, his hands wrapped around a wounded thigh. About three feet away was the massive form of Hank Sweeney, gripping a gun that was trained directly on Jankle.

I heard Jankle seethe, "I saved your fucking ass years ago, saved your fucking life, and this is what you do to pay me back."

Sweeney said, "You gave me no damned choice."

He paused and added, "And you give me no choice now."

I heard a clicking sound, as if Sweeney was getting ready to fire again. I don't think he or Jankle knew I was there within earshot and eyeshot, not to mention gunshot. So I called out, "Hank, he's not worth it."

Hank looked over at me, as if shaken from a reverie. "Jack," he said, "you're all right?"

"I'm fine."

"Where's Harkins?"

"Unconscious."

"I shot Jankle in the leg. I thought he had killed you."

"Put the gun down, Hank."

Jankle said, "Shoot him, Sweeney. You can't kill me, and I'm not going down without taking you with me."

I saw Jankle's weapon on the ground between us, out of his

reach. I regarded Hank for a long moment. He spent a lifetime putting away the city's most heinous criminals, always with what I believed to be an unwavering sense of wrong from right. But something, somewhere, had gone terribly awry, and the look on his face in the dark of this unfathomable night said he didn't know how to get back on the right side of life.

I kept walking. Hank kept pointing. Jankle remained on the ground with a foul look on his face.

"Hank, hand me the gun," I said.

Now it was his arm that was quivering. Sweat was rolling down his shiny face. The expression in his eyes told me he was about to shoot, and if he did, that would mean that he either had to kill me next, or know that he would be splashed across the front page of the next day's *Record* as the retired Boston homicide detective who gunned down a once-respected federal agent. There's more than bad publicity in that; there's the death penalty.

"Hand me the damned gun, Hank. Do the right thing. He's not worth it. You are."

Finally, he looked at me, the gun still pointed at Jankle's head. Then he dropped his arm in one gradual motion, took the gun in his other hand, and turned it over to me, handle first. As he did this, Jankle skidded along the ground toward his own firearm. Hank took two strides toward him and kicked him so hard in the face that his jaw would forever be coming out of the top of his head. Agent Tom Jankle, to say the least, was out cold.

Hank said to me softly, his voice raspy again, "I'm one of those cops that Jankle flipped. It's a shame I've lived with ever since."

Standing just a few feet from a man I would consider one of my closest friends, I said, "What did you mean, that he gave you no choice?"

"I thought I had Harkins cold in the Gardner theft. Jankle came to me and said if I pursued it, that I should be very worried about the health of my wife and my son."

He paused here, looking down through the dark. "So I didn't say anything. Next thing you know, I get a promotion. The whole thing kind of goes away. My wife and boy are fine. I put it in the back of my mind, but not really. You're never entirely done with it. I'm supposed to enforce the law, not break it."

And I'm supposed to write stories, not cause them, pursue the truth, not obscure it. But that's what had happened on the complicated road to reason.

"You just saved my life. If you can forget about it, so can I," I said.

He smiled and replied, "Let's both give it a try."

I nodded at Jankle's form sprawled out across a collection of broken branches and puffy weeds. "He alive?" I asked.

Sweeney crouched down and put his finger under Jankle's nose. "Yep."

We walked across the clearing, into the shallow woods, to where Toby Harkins lay. But in what I thought was the space, there was only tamped down weeds. I ran and grabbed the lamp and flashed it around, but saw nothing.

"He's gone," Hank said.

"Brace yourself," I said quietly. Then I hollered, "We need some help back here."

Flashlights shone through the woods. Men yelled back. I called out, "Toby Harkins has escaped. Look for Harkins."

I turned to Hank and asked, "Where are we, anyway?"

"At the truth," he said, nodding knowingly, draping his arm over my shoulder.

Indeed, we were. It took a long time getting there, but it was a damned nice place to be.

Chapter Thirty-nine

Friday, October 3

It was one of those remarkable autumn days when summer takes a curtain call amid the brightly colored leaves and the chilly nights, as if the entire season has stepped back out of the dugout and waved to the crowd in the way that Ted Williams and Carl Yastrzemski never did or would.

We were sitting at an outdoor café along Boston's Newbury Street, Vinny and me—or is that Vinny and I? I never know these things. Anyway, it was the two of us. He had a fresh fruit plate in front of him covered with yogurt, along with a low-fat bran muffin, no butter, as well as a can of V-8 that he had brought in himself.

"You allowed to do that?" I asked. "I mean, isn't there someone, somewhere, who cracks down on bringing your own vegetable juice into restaurants?"

"Fuck you."

He had lost five pounds in five days, he said, meaning at this rate, next year this time, he wouldn't actually exist. Not a bad thought, considering the argument he was waging with me.

He was sitting there extolling the virtues of placing his name first in the title of the crisis management consulting firm that we were about to open. He was telling me that the name Mongillo had become synonymous among the ruling elite and the rank and file of Boston with hard work, with extraordinary contacts, with easy access all along the corridors of power. I was making a stroking motion with my right hand, when he interrupted and said, "I mean it, Jack. You've got to start thinking like a business-man now, about making money, and you know and I know that we'll make more money if my name goes first."

I didn't particularly care; I just didn't want to be seen as a pushover in our first-ever business meeting. "All right," I said. "You get your name first if I get to pick our slogan."

"What do you have?" He asked this skeptically with a mouth full of cantaloupe.

"Your downfall is our windfall."

He speared a large hunk of pineapple with his fork and ate it without expression.

"This is serious shit," he said, after chewing for a moment. "This ain't the goddamned newsroom anymore, where we get paid whether we put in a good day's worth of work or not, and in your case, usually not. Come on, Fair Hair, get with the program."

It was tough to take him seriously as the next Jack Welch or Lou Gerstner, sitting there in a flannel button-down with a dab of purple-colored yogurt on his upper lip.

He said, "I've already gotten calls from the head of the phone company wanting to hire us at ten large a month. Remember they got into that brouhaha for shutting off service to a battered-women's shelter because the place was a month late paying their bill—and it ended up, the phone company had lost the check?

"And I got another call from a former congressman who will remain momentarily nameless who would like to be governor. He wants us to address the potential publicity around an incident involving him, a prostitute, a Bijon Frise, and a park ranger. That's another seven-and-a-half large a month."

I said, "I got a call from my old friend Harry Putnam asking me if I've gone nuts."

I gave in on the naming rights, then ordered dessert—a ginger-bread sundae—just to drive him crazy.

When it arrived, I said, "I hate when they drench the damned thing in this delicious hot fudge sauce, so the ice cream melts too fast." He looked like he was ready to punch me harder than Toby Harkins's people ever did.

So I changed the subject.

"How close are we on a lease?"

He explained that he had negotiated a deal for space on the twenty-ninth floor of a downtown high-rise that would give us each identically sized offices with views across the harbor to Logan Airport. We would have a shared secretary, additional space for cubicles for any new hires, and with the lease came membership to a top-floor dining club.

"All we have to do is sign on the dotted line and show up at work," he said.

We both sat in a long state of silence, watching the passersby, seeing nothing at all. I thought of myself reporting to a high-rise office building every day, wearing a suit and tie, maybe carrying a briefcase, sitting with my feet up on a minimalist glass-top desk, phone cradled to my ear, gazing out at the boats bobbing in the water. And what would I be saying on the phone? Hire my company? Run our side of the story? Would I be telling reporters, people just like me, that they have their facts all wrong, even when I know, when they know, they don't?

Hello, adulthood.

I asked, "You going to miss the newsroom?"

Mongillo almost seemed startled by my voice, or maybe it was the question. I don't know. He picked up a red grape with his fingers and popped it into his mouth. "Like what? One deadline sneaking up after another? The cell phone ringing twenty-four hours every damned day? The constant pressure to produce? The what-have-you-done-for-me-lately attitude that Martin gives off?"

I replied, "Yeah, that."

He looked down and said, "I don't know, will you?"

I thought for a moment. Actually, what I was doing was scraping the remnants of chocolate sauce from the plate and spooning it into my mouth, but I can do two things at once—what is it that they call it downtown, multitasking? Oh yeah.

"Yeah, I will."

I thought of the adrenaline rush of nailing a story cold, the omnipotent feeling of badgering some politician who you know had done something wrong, the fascinating paths toward elusive truths. Maybe I was just tired. Maybe I was romanticizing things. But I suddenly had an empty feeling in a place that should have been filled with anticipation.

Now's as good a time as any to point out that I had hammered the Toby Harkins/Tom Jankle story home. Ends up, that bunker was in Boston Harbor, on Great Brewster Island, almost nine miles offshore. On a clear day, I could probably see it from the balcony of my condominium, not that I ever looked. I slipped out of the woods with Hank that night, as the FBI agents, wink-wink, searched the cliffsides for Harkins. I bet they were searching real hard. At the bottom of one rocky cliff, I asked Hank if we were swimming for safety. "You can," he replied. "But I'm going to ride in my boat." And with that, we climbed into the rented outboard he had come in on.

Buzzing along the black skin of the harbor, the chill sea mist flying in our faces, the glittering skyline beckoning from the shore, I felt not just reinvigorated, but enlivened. I had survived, and I decided there and then, so would Hank.

It was 3:00 A.M. when I hit the newsroom, so I didn't write that night. Martin was, of course, waiting by my desk, pacing, still furious that we'd blown deadline on the story that we'd initially planned, even though I had called him from a pay phone on the way down to give him the reason why. When I elaborated in greater detail in his office, I thought he might climb on my lap and try to neck. We decided I shouldn't leave the newsroom for fear that some cop or agent somewhere might try to arrest me for leaving the scene of a crime, or worse, so I stretched out on a couch in the conference room and grabbed a few hours' rest.

The story itself was a thing of beauty. It led with the revelation that Toby Harkins, the nation's most-wanted fugitive, was a long-time FBI informant, essentially receiving federal protection even as he committed murder and ran what we like to call in newspaper-speak, "a far-reaching criminal enterprise." I quickly got into FBI Special Agent Tom Jankle's murder of Hilary Kane, his confession and such. I recounted the gunpoint conversation between Jankle and Harkins amid the old military bunkers on Great Brewster Island, where yours truly was the bull's-eye that was inexplicably never hit. I pointedly included Jankle's line that he had tipped Harkins off to the impending indictment that led to the flight from justice. And I detailed Dan Harkins's involvement, his awareness of his son's whereabouts and his attempts to convince Toby to turn himself in. My bet was and is, it doesn't matter that he was trying to do good. The mayor will be thrown out with the dirty bathwater.

Of Hank Sweeney, I left him out—mostly. He stood over my shoulder as I wrote, giving me a legion of key details about the extent to which the FBI went to protect its prized informant for all those years. Hank agreed to be named in print, probably as some sort of penance for long-ago mistakes. But no need. I quoted him as an unnamed retired law enforcement official intimate with the details of the case. Let a judge or a congressional committee try to get it out of me.

Speaking of which, Jankle was charged by Boston police for Hilary Kane's murder the following morning after a court-authorized search of his house turned up a gun that had gone missing from an FBI evidence locker two years before—and had recently been discharged. Ballistics experts matched it to the Kane crime scene.

And I've been invited to appear before the House Government Affairs Committee, which is investigating the FBI's role in all this. I politely declined, and they politely presented me with a subpoena. That's supposed to happen next week.

What else? Baker, I miss him every hour of every day, the only living thing in my life that got all the jokes and didn't mind hearing them again and again. Elizabeth? She left town without ever saying good-bye, not that I blame her. She wanted something that was no longer mine to give, or maybe it was just too soon. To her credit, she hung around long after any logical person would have left and gave me more than just about anyone had given me before.

Peter Martin, on the other hand, watched me write that day from a safe distance, like a zookeeper might regard a particularly ornery lion feasting on the corpse of some ravaged prey, maybe a zebra. After I sent the stories in, after he carefully edited and reedited every word, he came out into the newsroom and offered to have my baby. I think he might have been serious. Sometime, over a beer, I'm going to explain to him about birds and bees and the physiological limitations of the mortal man.

And then there's Vinny, sitting here with me finishing the rest of his fruit plate.

"I will, too," he said, his big brown eyes as sad as I've ever seen them, except for that time at Amrhein's over in South Boston that he watched a waitress accidentally drop his prime rib special—the last cut left of the night—on the floor.

We looked at each other, quiet. The world, literally, was passing us by, well-dressed locals with places to be and people to see, all striding purposefully along the sun-dappled sidewalk.

"You want to forget the whole damned thing?" I asked.

He nodded, his face breaking out into a broad grin. "Yeah, I do," he said.

And with that, I felt like the weight of the adult world was instantly lifted from my broad shoulders, like my life was again instilled with a sense of natural purpose. There were politicians to chase and truths to uncover and stories to write, all to be published in the beautifully packaged pages of *The Boston Record*, the finest newspaper I have ever known.

Vinny reached over and, for a second, I thought he was going to lick my dessert plate. Instead, he wrapped his massive arms around my shoulders and hugged me. I smelled pepperoni. I felt perspiration. It was all like a wonderful dream.

He reached into his computer case and pulled out a sheaf of papers, which he promptly, ceremoniously, ripped in half in front of me.

"The lease?" I asked.

"Take-out menus," he answered. "I'll stay a reporter, but I'm not going to let it kill me."

That's when I saw him. At first, I just saw a flash of light gold. But then my eyes came to focus on the fuzziest, most perfect little creature that I'd seen since, well, since I'd sent Baker off to that dog park in the sky the week before. He was maybe ten weeks old, all brown eyes and blonde fur, a blocky little golden retriever puppy who sauntered up to the wrought-iron gate that separated the restaurant patio from the world around it. It's as if he had been scouting me out for days.

I jumped out of my chair and scooped him up in my arms, a miniature golden bear who pressed the top of his head against the bottom of my chin.

"He's gorgeous, isn't he?"

And with that, my reverie was broken. I looked out onto the sidewalk to see the equally beautiful personage of Maggie Kane, her skirt as short and casual as that mop of blonde hair. I hadn't seen her in a week, hadn't seen her since I went back to my apartment that Monday night after writing the stories. She waited there for me to tell her what happened, and I did, the two of us sitting on my couch, her wearing one of my blue oxford cloth shirts, her legs tucked under her body, both her hands wrapped around a cup of hot tea. After I recounted the prior night's events, we talked more about the son she barely had and the daughter I never did, about life and about loss and the way the former gracelessly, inevitably, leads to the latter. Come midnight, she asked if she could spend the night again, and she did, in my bed, while I remained out on the couch, always polite, maybe too much so.

In the morning, she kissed me on the cheek as she was leaving. I wasn't sure what to say to someone who had shared what we had shared over the past week, who had lost something similar to what I had lost. So I said nothing more than good-bye.

I stared into the puppy's eyes. "He's incredible," I said. Then dawn broke over Marblehead; the thought occurred that the dog was a gift for me.

But was I ready? Was it too fast? Was it respectful enough of what I had with Baker?

I looked at her and she at me. "I was tired of looking backward," she said, a huge smile filling every perfect inch of her face.

She put her hand on the bridge of the puppy's square nose and added, "And he's here to help me look ahead, to move on."

I nodded, a little jealous and a little relieved.

She said, "Come walk with us."

I put the puppy down, turned to Vinny, and said, "Meet you back at the newsroom. Can you pick up the check?"

He looked somewhere between panicked and perturbed, but nodded.

I climbed over the metal gate and stood for a second on the sidewalk gazing silently at this beautiful creature—the woman now, not the dog. And we began walking, the three of us, away from the past, through the moment, and toward a future that we didn't yet know.

My mind scanned back over the day, over the past couple of weeks, over a lifetime in which so much good seemed to end so bad. At the first intersection, I brushed the back of my fingers against the side of her face—something I had wanted to do for what felt like forever. She took my hand in hers and didn't let go.

Acknowledgments

I'm fortunate, blessed even, to have spent my adult life coming and going from a newsroom, especially in cities as vibrant as Boston and Washington, and more especially for a newspaper as thoughtful and compelling as *The Boston Globe*. To that end, I owe many good people my thanks on this project, whether they realize it or not. I've learned and borrowed significantly from the exhaustive work that the *Globe*'s Steve Kurkjian invested into the Gardner Museum theft, and have been aided by his wise counsel. Likewise, the late Elizabeth Neuffer, who died too young, too tragically, in Iraq, wrote one of the most enduring and extensive stories on the theft, which helped me immensely. And I was also was enlightened by the fascinating stories written by Tom Mashberg for the *Boston Herald*.

I'd also like to thank a former federal investigator and a current one, both of whom prefer the cloak of anonymity, but were generous with their time and insights. Thanks as well to Pam Bendock, a trusted veterinarian and good friend, who guided me through some touchy aspects of the text. And much gratitude to friend and former colleague Mitch Zuckoff for his keen eye.

I could never properly thank the wonderful people of International Creative Management for starting me on this novel writing venture and then propelling me along the way. Specifically, Richard Abate has been invaluable—in his ability to make deals, provide sage counsel, and offer constant encouragement. There is no better agent. Thanks as well to his ever efficient and always calm assistant, Kate Lee, for overseeing all the details and being immeasurably kind.

At Atria Books, I have been granted the firsthand benefit of Emily Bestler's legendary skills—both with words and with those who write them. She nipped and tucked and pushed and prodded and made this a far better book for her efforts. Sarah Branham, an associate editor, ably oversaw every aspect of publication, and I appreciate her work immensely. A special debt to Laura Mullen, a real pro, who gets the word out to the people who matter. And as always, as ever, thanks to George Lucas, my first editor and my friend. He taught me more about writing books than I ever realized I could learn.

Thanks as well to the great people of the *Globe,* who have entrusted me with jobs better than I would have ever dared dream, whether it be roving the country as a national reporter or covering the White House or, as now, writing a twice-a-week column. Michael Larkin hired me and edits me now; I have no idea how to thank a guy for all he's done. Heartfelt thanks as well to editor Marty Baron, a newsman to the core—thoughtful, and demanding.

And to family and friends, the people I've known forever who offer the deepest and most important encouragement, I can say only this: Thank you.